DARK DESCENT INTO DESIRE

J. J. SOREL

BOOKS BY J. J. SOREL

THORNHILL TRILOGY
Entrance
Enlighten
Enfold

THE IMPORTANCE OF BEING WILD
THE IMPORTANCE OF BEING BELLA
TAKE MY HEART
BEAUTIFUL BUT STRANGE
Flooded
Flirted
Flourished

DARK DESCENT INTO DESIRE

DARK DESCENT INTO DESIRE

A Gothic Romance

By

J. J. Sorel

Copyright © March 2020 J. J. Sorel

www.jjsorel.com

ISBN 9798638851774

Due to a high steam level, this book is for ADULTS ONLY.
All the characters are consenting adults.
ALL RIGHTS RESERVED
No part of this book may be reproduced or transmitted in any form, including electronic or mechanical, without written permission from the publisher, except in the case of brief quotations embodied in reviews or articles. This is a work of fiction. Names, characters, businesses, events and incidents are pure product of the author's imagination. Any resemblance to actual persons, living or dead, or an actual event is purely coincidental and does not assume any responsibility for author or third-party websites or content therein.

Cover by MOI and www.wolfsparrowcovers.com
Line Edit by Sarah Carleton from Red Adept Editing.

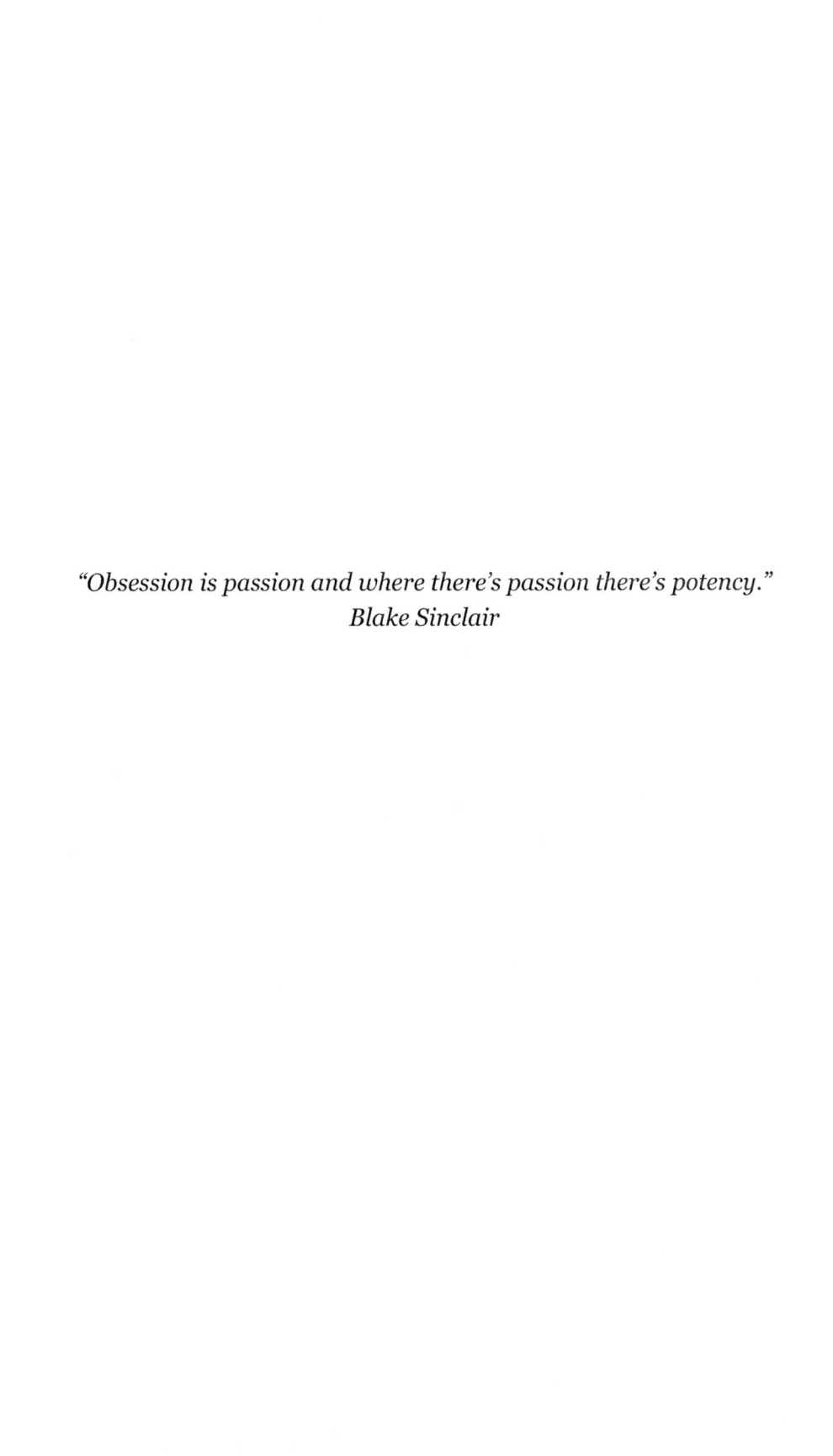

"Obsession is passion and where there's passion there's potency."
Blake Sinclair

ONE

BLAKE

I TURNED MY ATTENTION away from the window and noticed James, with his signature bouncy strut, heading toward me.

We made for an odd pairing, but then, people connected to those who offered something they lacked. In James's case, he was easygoing and extroverted, which was the opposite of me.

He flopped down onto the leather armchair by my side. "Sorry I'm late. A big night." His eyebrows lifted, and a playful glint explained clearly what he'd been up to.

"Let me guess. A flat-chested blonde teetering on spindly heels that ended up around your ears in some seedy restroom?"

James laughed. "You're as dry as that Scotch swishing in your glass. Speaking of which..." He turned toward the waiter and lifted his chin.

We met regularly at our club—a club for gentlemen, in the old sense of the word, and not one of those sleazy joints where men lurked about watching scantily clad girls hanging upside down on poles or gyrating over some desperado's hungry crotch.

I'd been frequenting that members-only club since leaving Cambridge, which was where I'd met James. Coming from a peerage that went back to the Tudors, he'd invited me onto the club's books.

Being exclusive, the club fitted me like a glove by protecting me from the glare of cameras and gossip. When a *Times* article catapulted me into the limelight, journalists dying to ask me about my bedroom habits had hounded me. Apparently, according to the magazines, I was one of London's most eligible bachelors.

Eligible for what? A happy life?

Our club offered a private environment to enjoy a quiet drink. Generally, I'd meet with James and share a few Scotches while listening to stories of a wild night he'd had cavorting with one or two attractive girls.

I lived a short walk away from the club in a two-story mansion James referred to as my *Mary Poppins* house.

After draining half his glass, James sighed. "Ah... that's better. Nothing like the first drink of the day to get the heart pumping."

I smiled. "So, what have you been up to?"

"I have discovered this new little club." His eyebrow arched.

"Let me guess. Dark, sticky, and tacky?"

He laughed at my sardonic tone. "All of that, but with class."

"Okay... so the eighteen-year-olds come from money?"

He sniffed. "Wealth alone doesn't always deliver class. Look at you. You epitomize sophistication."

I sat up. "I'm filthy rich, James."

"But its new wealth, isn't it?"

James was right. My beginnings were anything but classy. I liked to think of myself as a man of taste who'd cultivated an interest for the finer things. *Why be rich otherwise?*

"Do continue," I said, steering James back to his story.

"A friend dragged me to this new little hidden gem in Soho."

"Trendy, I suppose," I said.

He shook his head. "Nothing like the typical club scene at all."

"Oh... a sex club?"

"Of sorts." He sat back. "Let's put it this way. There was not one limp dick in the house."

"Mm... that sounds really sordid. Go on."

"It's a club where girls sell their virginity."

"That's gaining popularity. I received an invite to a viewing from an agency. I don't even know how they got my name."

He held his chin. "Mm... let me guess. That little something called *Forbes* top one hundred. And that sweet article about you being the man to hump."

"Huh." I sniffed. "That fucking *Times* article. I'd prefer to keep my wealth private." I jiggled the ice in my glass.

"You're a girl magnet, Blake. Tall, dark, and handsome. If I weren't into girls, even I'd screw you."

I chuckled at his ridiculous suggestion. We were both hot-blooded heterosexual men. Period.

The waiter arrived and lowered our drinks onto the table between us. I nodded with gratitude.

"Now, back to girls selling their virginity," said James. "Have you ever slept with a virgin?"

"I don't sleep with young girls." I lowered my brow. "And I don't sleep with women in general. I only fuck them."

He lifted his hands in defense. "Hey... steady. They're not *that* young." Sitting back, James shook the ice in his glass. "What about that happily-ever-after scenario? Don't you want one of those?"

"I don't believe in those. I've yet to witness a happy marriage. It's a life sentence where two individuals trap each other out of fear of loneliness only they end up lonely anyway."

He grimaced. "You make it sound so fucking grim. Don't you think it's nice, the idea of a baby bouncing on one's knee and a hot little wife baking a cake in a skimpy maid's outfit?"

I laughed. "How inappropriate and nineteenth century."

"What? The skimpy maid's outfit?" he asked.

"No. The cake baking."

He laughed. "Well, I couldn't bake anything to save myself."

"Then you'd better pray that we don't descend into a dystopian nightmare and lose our cooks."

"It's hot the idea of coming home to a sexy wife baking a cake."

I shrugged. "Why not? I just don't believe in the concept of happy families and that a happy life requires a happy wife." I sipped my Scotch pensively. What I hadn't told James was how my life had begun. No one knew about that. All that existed was a short-on-detail Disney version I'd rolled out just for the record. "Tell me all about your night. This subject of marriage is making me drink faster."

James laughed at my dryness. "That's what you do." He pointed. "You get off on my little adventures. A form of voyeurism."

I grinned. "Oh, I'm a voyeur, all right. I'll own up to that quite freely."

James laughed. "Aren't we all?"

I summoned memories of Rebecca, the voluptuous maid from Raven Abbey, bent over the kitchen table, the cook's big dick ramming hard into her, and her squeals of delight. Or maybe it was pain. I could never tell, but she kept allowing him in, so to speak. At the age of thirteen, I would sneak a peek through a crack in the door. That was the beginning to my dark descent.

"Tell me about this club." I stretched out my legs.

"It's hidden down an alleyway. One can't get in without two things."

"Those being...?"

"An invite and proof of wealth ... oh—three things. They need a blood test."

"A blood test?" I asked.

"That's if you want to fuck without a condom."

"You fuck them there?"

"Pretty much." James looked at me. "Oh, come on, Blake. Don't go all righteous on me. It's sex. And these girls are willing and, you know..."

"Desperate? They're poor, and they need money, right?"

He sipped his drink. "At least it's only once, given that virginity can only be sold once."

"Did you end up buying one?" I cringed at how that sounded. The thought of a young innocent commodifying her virginity was morally difficult to grapple with. But James was a friend, and apart from his predilection for eighteen-year-old virgins, his heart was in the right place. I also had to remind myself that it was consensual and they weren't underage.

"Not yet."

"What does that mean exactly?"

"The one I like is asking for one hundred thousand pounds. I'm used to picking up girls at clubs for as little as a weekend of wining and dining and a night or two at a luxury hotel. Even a week on the Riviera for those special girls"—he raised an eyebrow— "doesn't cost that much."

"But, James, you're rich."

"One hundred thousand, though? For one night?" He held out his hands.

"Depends on how much you want it."

"To be honest, I haven't been able to get her out of my mind. She's beautiful." He drew a curvy line in the air.

"She's voluptuous?"

"No, she's nearly flat chested. But she's got a cute round ass, and her little pink..."

I interjected, "You saw her pussy?"

"They parade each girl."

"And they pose with their legs apart?"

He nodded, biting his lip. "Didn't I tell you it was sordid?"

"But you didn't buy a girl?"

"I paid a thousand to get in. Everyone does. That goes to the girls that don't get a buyer, apparently."

"Oh, well, I guess that's kind of fair." My eyebrows gathered tightly as I contemplated the intimate details. My dick jerked a little, which added a streak of guilt to my fascination. My innate decency hated the idea of women forced to subject themselves to such debauchery.

"Are you in?" asked James.

I turned my head sharply to look at him. "In? By that, you mean, do I want to visit this den of iniquity?"

James laughed loudly. "You sound like my grandfather."

I smiled. "It sounds a little depraved... but I suppose I could do with a little eye fucking."

"Ah... that's more like it. And who knows? You might find the girl of your dreams."

I thought about that. I hadn't fucked in a while. It always left me a little cold afterward. Not that I didn't feel desire. My dick never remained inert for long. For me, sex was never about love. I didn't believe such an exulted state existed. How could I? I'd never experienced it.

"Once you've tasted virgin pussy, it's hard not to want to go back for more," James said, snapping me out of my thoughts.

I sat forward. "Tell me... why are virgins so coveted?"

"Tightness, my friend. A sweet, perfect exotic flower that only blooms once." He paused to reflect. "You know, there's something profoundly powerful knowing you're her first."

I nodded slowly, intrigued and, I had to admit, a little hot under the collar.

TWO

PENELOPE

THE CRACKS AROUND THE door frame of the only home I'd ever known had widened since my last visit a few days earlier. That forty-year-old flat was crumbling and forgotten, just like those who lived in that council estate, which was a kind of parallel universe where drowsy souls drifted about a foggy urban wilderness.

The stale stench of cigarettes nauseated me as always, and no matter how much I aired the place out, that acrid smell clung stubbornly to the walls.

I turned on the lamp and found my mother asleep on the couch. Paraphernalia scattered about on the coffee table gave her ugly habit away. She hadn't even tried to hide it. It used to be in the bathroom, where she'd leave a spoon or a belt lying about, but she no longer cared. One thing I'd learned about heroin addiction—that prick of a needle didn't just dull pain but one's conscience too.

Her arm drooped by her side, a red bruise in the crook of it as evidence.

Resting my finger on her neck, I felt for a pulse. An aching gap followed. As always, my heart froze despite the fact that I'd seen her parked somewhere between life and death for as long as I could remember.

One never got used to this kind of thing. As a twenty-three-year-old, I felt helpless and eaten by grief.

She stirred, and the breath that was stuck in my throat finally escaped.

"Who's that?" she asked. If a zombie could talk, it would sound like my mother on junk—slurry and vague.

"It's me. Penny." Fury pumped through me. "Fuck! Not again. You promised."

I'd lost count of how many times she'd promised to kick that filthy habit, which she'd had all my life even though she swore she'd been clean while I grew in her belly. I'd never know if that was true. My mother had made an art form of lying.

All I had to go by were my high marks at school and my unwavering focus. Maybe she'd told the truth for once. Either that, or I was lucky for possessing a curious mind, a good eye for drawing, and the tenacity to become someone other than Penny from the estate.

"Is Frank here?" I asked, referring to her on-off boyfriend, who'd kept us going over the five years that he'd been around.

I should have been grateful, but he hung out with the bad crowd— a crowd I couldn't avoid, given that I lived in one of London's oldest, scummiest estates. It was a breeding ground for drug traffickers, and was frequented by men in expensive suits, lowlifes in saggy joggers, and girls who sold everything they had to offer for drugs.

My mother's droopy eyelids lifted ever so slightly, enough for me to read that he'd been there and that she'd filled her veins with her "forgetting potion," as she called it.

As I considered my mother's brutal history, a profound pang of sadness diluted my angry frustration at finding her like that again.

"You spent the money, didn't you?" I headed to the fridge, which was empty except for a half carton of milk and a six-pack of beer.

"How are you darling?" she asked. "I haven't seen you in days."

"I've been at Shelly's. You know I use his studio."

"Oh, your friend the homosexual. I don't like you hanging out with those weirdos."

"Huh?" I put my fists on my hips. "And I suppose your drug-addicted mates are less weird?" I picked up the syringe carefully. "At least Shelly doesn't take drugs."

"Don't talk so loudly," she slurred. Ravaged by drugs, my mother's beauty had faded. Her red hair, a tangled mess, hadn't seen a brush for days.

"Go to bed, then. Here." I bent down to give her my shoulder. For someone who didn't eat much, her body was heavy.

"I'm sorry, kitten. My darling Penny. I'm sorry."

The only one advantage of living in such a tiny flat was that I didn't have to carry her far. I took her weight and, in twenty or so little shuffles, made it to her disheveled bed.

I helped her down onto it and covered her with a blanket.

"I suppose you haven't had anything to eat for a while?" I asked.

"I'm not hungry, lovey. Let me sleep. We'll talk in the morning."

I let out a deep, frustrated breath and left her alone.

I went to the kitchen and opened the cupboard door, which fell off its hinges and onto my foot. I cried out in pain. It wasn't the first time. That flat was a crumbling mess, much like my mother and my life. If it wasn't for Sheldon, I would have either starved or had to sell my body or something radical like that. There were no jobs to speak of except in aged care, and I was too worn-out caring for my mom.

Sheldon was a friend from art college, where we both studied fine arts. I'd received a scholarship, which covered my fees, while art supplies gobbled up my tiny student allowance. I painted at his studio, and on weekends, I stayed at his Soho apartment. Like the brother I'd never had, Sheldon was kind and supportive.

A knock came to the door. Opening it, I discovered Lilly, my best friend, full of bubbly energy. We'd grown up together on the estate and were neighbors. She lived alone with her brother, Brent. After their parents died in a car accident when Lilly was ten, Brent, who was five years older, had taken on the parental role.

"Hey, Lil." I stepped away to let her in.

"How are you?" Her eyes wandered over the room. I hadn't had a chance to tidy up the mess my mother had left. With anyone else, I would have shriveled from shame, but Lil knew my mother.

"Like shit," I replied with a long sigh.

"Have you had anything to eat?"

I shook my head. "No. There's nothing in the cupboards. Mom used the money I left for drugs."

Her lips drew a tight line. "Come on. I just got paid. Let's get a burger where that cute guy works."

I smiled. "Why not. I'll pay you back one of these days."

Lil took my hand and squeezed it. "Just remember me when you're selling your art for millions."

Her optimism always put a smile on my face. "I got a call today from a gallery. They've accepted my paintings for a group show."

"That's really cool. Are you showing the *Mad Witch* series?"

"Yep. I sent some photos, and they gave it a nod." I grabbed my coat and bag. "I'll just quickly check on Mom."

She returned an understanding nod.

I poked my head into my mother's bedroom, and satisfied she was still breathing, I rejoined Lil at the door. "She's asleep."

Lilly shook her head. "It's kind of weird. Why spend so much on a drug only to sleep?"

"Tell me about it. I suggested she take sleeping tablets instead. It's the lesser of two evils. And it would be a hell of a lot cheaper."

I walked with her along the cracked concrete path, which was a makeshift playground for kids and where drug deals took place.

"Hey, girls," said Jimmy, looking pleased with himself after making a sale.

"Hey," said Lilly.

"You want to grab a pint? I'm buying."

"No, thanks," I said. "It's food we need, not alcohol."

His gaze lingered. Jimmy had always had a thing for me, but I wasn't interested. He was harmless, though.

"Another time," I said.

He kicked a stone around with his feet. "You always say that."

I shrugged and continued on, dodging a homemade motorized bike as it

scooted past us with one kid balancing precariously on the handlebars.

LILLY PICKED A FRY OUT of a carton and munched on it. "Yesterday, one of my regulars came in to have her nails done. I noticed her designer heels. She's from the estate and works as a salesgirl. I had to ask if she'd found herself a rich boyfriend. She answered, 'Something even better.' And then, lowering her voice, she told me she'd sold her virginity for fifty thousand pounds."

I raised my eyebrows. "Shit. Her too?"

"Yeah. It's becoming quite popular, isn't it? When I asked her if it was an agency, she told me it happened at a club. One of the girls that night was offered half a million pounds."

I whistled. "I wonder what she had to do for that."

"I'd let them do anal for that," she said with a smirk. "According to Annie—that's my client—she stayed the night. He fucked her twice and made her blow him. And by the morning, she had fifty thousand in her account."

"Did he at least wear a condom?"

"I didn't ask." Lilly took another fry. "We're both virgins. Unless you're keeping something from me."

I shook my head. "No way. I haven't had a chance to sleep with anyone. I've been too busy with art college and being a fucking mother to my mother... and the boy that I wanted likes boys."

"Ah, Sheldon. How is he?"

"He's looking after me. If it wasn't for Sheldon, I wouldn't be able to go to art school. He even pays for my supplies sometimes."

"Aren't his parents loaded?"

"They are. And he reminds me that he'd prefer to pay for me than have me drop out. He even suggested I move in with him."

"Into his four-bedroom Soho house? Shit, Penny, that would be amazing. Why don't you?"

"If it wasn't for Mom and her helplessness, I would. At least, I'm at Sheldon's on weekends."

"Is he seeing anyone?"

"There's a guy he really likes, a cop who's ashamed of being gay and is driving poor Shelly crazy."

"I'm thinking of doing it," said Lilly, her sudden change of subject jolting me back to that sticky subject of our innocence.

I studied her. "Selling yourself, you mean? That's prostitution."

"Yeah. For one night. And then I can set up my own salon." Her face lit up with excitement. I understood Lilly's ambition for a better life only too well, because I also harbored the same desire.

"One night?" I visualized some ugly foul-smelling man running his hands over me and grimaced. "I'm not sure I could do that."

"Even for five hundred thousand pounds?" Lilly asked.

"But your client received fifty thousand, you just said."

"Yeah. But hey, she's nothing on you. You're stunning. And with those big tits and that shapely ass—God, Penny."

"I'm chubby."

"No, you're not. You're curvy. I'd kill to have your body."

I stared at Lilly. With her lovely thick blond hair, gorgeous blue eyes, and svelte body, she was beautiful. "You could raise the same amount, Lil. You really could. But this is horrible. I shouldn't be encouraging you."

"I'm going to do it. Will you at least come with me for moral support?" she asked.

"Where is it?"

"A club in Soho."

"You had to apply?" I asked, sitting forward.

"I went in and paraded." She bit her lip. "That was after I'd sent a photo and a doctor's report."

"Are you fucking kidding me? That's taking it a bit too far."

"Hello, pap smears. And it was a female doctor. At least I know I haven't got some virus or STDs."

My head pushed back. "An STD from a vibrator? Or your fingers?"

She giggled. "The clients need to know what they're paying for, I guess."

"So did this client of yours describe the guy?"

"Yep." Lilly's mouth turned down. "Predictably, he was old and flabby."

"Yuck."

"Yeah. But one night, and then I can set up my own business and leave this shithole."

"But this is your home. I'd miss you."

She smiled sadly and touched my hand. "Don't worry, we'll always be besties."

I couldn't imagine my life without Lilly. I wasn't sure where I would have been without her. All those cozy sessions, drinking cups of tea and eating our homemade scones while watching telly together—normal activities that most folk probably took for granted meant the world to me. I'd never had that growing up. My mother didn't do normal. She just did drugs, loud music, alcohol, and before Frank, one man after another sitting on our cigarette-burned couch. I'd leave the flat and stay with Lilly.

And now Lilly was proposing to do what most women in our impoverished circle did—sell herself. I despaired that I had no alternative suggestion for her.

"Will you come with me?" she asked.

I nodded hesitantly. "I suppose. What exactly do you have to do?"

"I have to parade in the nude and make sure I'm hairless."

"Bald?"

My shocked tone made her laugh. "No, you nutjob. No pubes."

Grimacing, I shook my head. "You have to wax. Ouch."

"I already do my legs, anyway." Her mood darkened. "There's one thing you must promise."

"What's that?"

"That you don't tell Brent."

Lilly's brother, Brent worked as a bouncer at the local casino. He was out all night, so at least he wouldn't be around to ask questions.

"Of course. I'm not that daft."

"He'd blow the joint up."

That wasn't an exaggeration. Brent could be rather explosive.

"Okay. I'll come along," I said. It was the least I could do for my best friend, even if the concept sickened me.

Lilly squeezed my hand. "That would be super."

The little tremor in her voice wasn't lost on me. I tilted my head and studied her.

"What?" she asked.

"Are you sure about this? I mean, there are other ways. How about if we set up a rescue-me account or something like that?"

Lilly pulled a face. "Huh? As if anyone will donate to someone starting up her own salon."

"You never know." I sighed. Lilly was right. It was dog-eat-dog out there. Too many people like us were in need. "That's it. Enough of my weird art that only people like us like. I'm going to create a series of monochrome Rothko-inspired pieces so that I can make enough money to get us a little flat somewhere out of this shithole."

"But I love your paintings. They're so beautiful and weird. They're like fairy tales on acid."

I laughed. "I was born in the wrong time, I think. Too many hours spent at the Tate, gawking at the Pre-Raphaelites."

"As always, I have no idea what the fuck you're talking about, but it sounds posh and clever, and it's you, babes. It's you. You need to be yourself. You'll sell. I believe in you."

A lump formed in my throat. I took a deep breath. It was not the time or place for tears in that bright, greasy hamburger joint. "Thanks, Lil. Your support really keeps me going. You, Brent, and Shelly. Without you guys, I'd be a mess."

"You're the strongest person I know—other than Brent, that is," said Lilly, nodding decisively. "If anyone can change their life, you can."

"But you can too. I wish you'd think this through. You're a very sensitive girl."

"I've thought of nothing else. It's only one night, and then I'll be free to be my own boss." She sucked on her straw. "I've toughened. And I'm sick of working my ass off for crumbs. Most of the clients who come in always ask for me. I'm good at what I do, and I should be earning more."

"You should, and you will," I asserted. "Together, we're going to do brilliantly."

We looked at each other and giggled.

THREE

BLAKE

PASSING MEADOWS AND PASTURES, I rolled down my car window. The smell of grass and dirt flooded me with memories of my childhood, though not of the warm, fuzzy, nostalgic kind.

While some children had playgrounds, beaches, and gardens, I'd had the rugged moors, where, swept along by the relentless winds, I often played in caves. Some nights I could even still hear that soaring gale as though it roared through my soul.

As I eased on my accelerator, I headed up the driveway to my destination. Situated in the Cotswolds, Grace Hall was a much sought-after retirement home.

My attention went out to the fields, where some slumbered while others, clutching frames, crept along the paths—each step almost a miracle.

I parked my car in the visitors' car park. Nearby, a pair of nurses with cigarettes in their hands looked up and gawked at my attractive car, a pale-blue Aston Martin that radiated that James Bond allure. I drove it because of my weakness for elegant cars, not because of some boyish fantasy of getting about in a designer suit while saving the world single-handedly.

I stepped out of the car and headed toward the stairs to the entrance of the stately honey-stoned Georgian mansion.

"Good morning, Mr. Sinclair," the receptionist said as I stepped into the foyer.

I nodded a greeting and headed up the grand staircase, passing a large open space that had once been a grand ballroom and was now a common room with a drowsy atmosphere.

Not too far down a long hallway, I came to a familiar door. I knocked and entered and found Milly, as usual, off with the fairies, staring at views of rolling hills and sky.

She turned, and her face lit up. "Blake. My boy."

At the age of ninety, Milly's body had given up on her, but her mind was as sharp as ever.

"How are you, today?" I asked, kissing her on the cheek.

"I'm feeling great. I had a good sleep." Studying me in her typical fashion, Milly seemed to see right through me. "What about you, Blake? You're looking tired, and you've lost weight."

My mouth tipped up at one end. I'd been visiting for five years, and each time she expressed the same concern. "I've actually put on weight."

"Have you met a nice girl yet? You're so handsome." She smiled.

Milly had been a maid at Raven Abbey, a gothic castle, complete with dark corridors, a haunted turret, and hidden chambers. Even the dead overstayed their welcome there. As a young, impressionable boy who'd already had his fair share of darkness, I learned to sleep with one eye open after my mother and I moved into the servants' quarters, where Milly also lived.

"Have you heard anything of that monster, Dylan?" she asked in a broad Yorkshire accent.

My body stiffened at the sound of my childhood enemy. "Nope."

"He's an evil so-and-so. And why didn't his father press charges? Dylan would still be locked up, which is where he should be, and not loose in London somewhere."

"Sir William wanted to avoid a scandal." Lame as that reasoning was, I understood my late mother's former employer's unwillingness to besmirch the family name after his son Dylan had made two attempts on his life.

"Dylan was always such a spiteful lad. Even as a five-year-old, his cold eyes showed malice. My poor Harry suffered. As did you, dear boy. I'm worried he might come for you. He was livid when he lost his inheritance to you." She pointed. "Rightfully, I might add. If you hadn't saved Sir William..." Touching her heart, she shook her head dramatically. "Goodness knows where any of us would've ended up."

"I can look after myself." I sat back and took a deep breath.

She took my hand and stroked it. "Look at what you've become. You're so tall and handsome you should be in the movies."

I sniffed.

"At least before I die, please promise me you'll find yourself a good woman."

Her faded hazel eyes shone with concern.

"One day I will." Although I had no intention of ever marrying, I always reassured Milly that I would.

Her frown faded into a smile. "A round of five hundred?"

In addition to our history, we shared a love of cards.

During the day, I made a killing buying up estates from the children of wealth who couldn't afford death duties and inheritance taxes. And after hours, I played cards.

Milly had taught me well. She loved a flutter and had won my undivided respect for her ability to remain blank faced even when holding a royal flush.

I removed my wallet and emptied some notes onto the table.

"Where are the coins?" Milly asked, looking disappointedly at the crisp ten-pound notes I'd brought along for our card game.

"I thought we'd splash out a little today."

She frowned. "Nothing beats the rattle of coins, though."

I chuckled. "I suppose so. These days, Milly, they're rare."

She pointed to the drawer by her bed. "The cards are in there."

I opened the drawer and, next to the cards, saw something I'd never seen there before—a journal.

"Have you started writing?" I asked, removing the pack of cards.

"I have. And don't you go poking around in there."

Her feisty tone brought back memories of Milly and her bossy ways. I had to grin, despite a growing thirst for that book.

I'd spent years observing furtive glances between Milly and my late mother. One day, I hoped to understand why my mother, who'd mysteriously disappeared, had taken her secrets with her.

The following day, I was in my London office. I'd been on one phone call after another, tussling with the council over the development of one of my recently acquired estates. I shut the folder and stretched my arms. Turning away from the postcard view of Westminster, I looked through the wall of windows to a neighboring building.

My inner voyeur stirred.

She was on her knees. While seated, he positioned himself close to her face. Taking out his cock, he shoved it into her mouth. They liked it rough and met on a Wednesday or Friday. They were hard to miss, given that they performed in front of the window.

I unzipped my trousers and sat far away from the window to avoid becoming someone's performance piece.

As I watched the woman playing with her tits, the phone buzzed. I wiped my hands before returning the call.

"There you are," said James. "I've been trying to call all day."

"I've been dealing with heritage layers and a pair of squabbling siblings."

He laughed. "That sounds entertaining."

"More torturous than anything. There's nothing like the smell of cash to incite hatred within a family."

"I've seen it all too often. I suppose you're buying the family jewels."

"It's a pretty estate. In Norwich. An old Georgian Hall. They've fallen into debt. She wants to sell, he wants to keep it, and so it goes, on and on. If I had a soft voice and patience, I could become a counselor in this business."

James laughed. "I could never see you being that, you old cynic."

"Hey… steady on. I'm what thirty going on fifty."

"Yes, the body of a stud and the mind of a pipe-sucking mad uncle."

"Mad? Me? Never." I grinned.

"Tonight. Remember? We're off to the Cherry Orchard."

I sat up. That was unexpected. "The play by Chekhov?"

He laughed. "That was my response. An artful and rather apt subterfuge for a place dealing in virgins."

"Disrespectful to the master playwright, in my book."

"Stop sucking on that pipe, uncle."

I chuckled. "So, it's tonight." I mulled over it. "Why not. I'm always open to something different. Is it discreet?"

"Very. Meet at Siciliano's. Eight o'clock?"

"See you there."

FOUR

PENELOPE

THE CHERRY ORCHARD HAD A high-class retro feel. Embossed velvet wallpaper and gold framed armchairs hinted at luxury and taste.

Lilly kept reminding me it was a business arrangement—a one-time transaction. I would have preferred to sell a kidney rather than my virginity, but then, desperate times required desperate measures.

"This is nice," said Lilly, whose vocal quaver wasn't lost on me.

"Lil"—I took her trembling hand—"you don't have to do this. We can find another way."

"I'm going through with it. You're here to encourage me, not put me off."

I sighed. "Okay. Whatever you say."

As we waited for someone to show us through, two men walked in. They were tall, very well dressed, surprisingly gorgeous, and hardly the type I expected to see. They could have had their share of girls, free of charge.

The tall, dark, and handsome one oozed sophistication. I found it hard not to stare. His pants hung elegantly from his waist, and his crisp white shirt revealed enough of a buff physique to make any girl drool. There was something remote in his dark-blue eyes that intrigued and intimidated me at the same time. And that was just from one glance.

His eyes found mine and remained. My cheeks fired up. That was new. I'd never blushed from a man's stare before.

He towered over me, so I had to lift my face. As he continued to gaze at me with those deep-blue eyes, my legs weakened. I had to lean against Lilly, who was having her own moment gaping at the hot stranger's friend.

I lost all sense of place and time, staring at the gorgeous man, who held his sensuous mouth in a tight line while a streak of aquamarine smoldered beneath those enviably long lashes. Although mesmerized, I forced myself to turn away.

Even with my back to him, I could still feel his eyes burning into me. I stole another glance. That unshifting stare seemed a little inappropriate, especially when his burning gaze wandered down my body.

Was he surveying the merchandise? The thought of that sickened me. I looked away. Any man at a place like this would have to be rotten.

A woman came to meet us. Dressed in slacks and a pink cotton shirt, she looked more like a suburban housewife than anything else.

She crooked her finger. "Come with me, ladies."

Just before stepping through the red velvet drapes, I turned for one final look at the man. Like deep-blue magnets, his eyes drew me in again. Although those chiseled features spelled "*heartbreaker*," the fire of attraction raged within.

The room we entered reminded me of a dressing room in a theater. Girls leaned into a mirror, applying makeup and chatting. Some didn't even look sixteen.

"They're underage," I whispered to Lilly.

She was off in a world of her own.

"Lil."

"Did you see those guys?" she asked.

I nodded.

"He was gorgeous," she said.

"The tall, handsome one?" I asked, realizing that was a vague question, considering that both men were tall.

"The one with the wavy light-brown hair."

"I was too busy staring at Mr. Dark and Sophisticated to notice."

She squeezed my hand and giggled. It was the lightest she'd been all night. I supposed seeing sexy men gave Lilly cause for hope.

I looked around the room. There must have been about forty girls in there. I noticed some whose bodies hadn't even developed. Dressed in string bikinis that covered very little, they appeared jittery and bit their nails while their friends whispered words of encouragement.

The woman in charge entered and gave them what sounded like a pep talk. I heard her say, "Think about the cash," to a really young girl, who she pushed out to join the others as she lined them up for their little parade.

She looked over at Lilly, beckoning her to hurry along.

"Shit. They're really young. They're underage," I whispered to Lilly.

The woman in charge turned and looked at me. Wearing an icy expression, she approached me. "Can I have a word?" she asked.

Sensing that I was about to be kicked out, I touched Lil's hand. She drew a tight smile and nodded reassuringly. There was nothing I could do. Poverty was a powerful decider. Morality came off second best when debt and hunger loomed large. And virginity was a powerful commodity.

"You'll change into your bikinis. And no more whispering or gossiping, okay?"

"I'm not here to sell myself. I'm here to give my friend moral support."

"Then I'll have to ask you to leave." She followed me out to the reception area. "We're here to facilitate life-changing opportunities for those who have the courage to take control of their lives."

"You make it sound like one of those self-help seminars."

"This is all about self-help. I don't know of too many girls who enjoyed their first fuck or ended up marrying the guy. At least this way, their lives change for the better. Now, please leave. Unless…" Her eyes ran up and down my body. "You're very beautiful, even without makeup. If you're still intact, you could easily raise half a million."

I crossed my arms as her eyes hovered over my chest. "No, thank you. I'll do it the old-fashioned way."

She laughed. "And marry wealth, you mean? Good luck. They're all in there, buying their thrill before settling down with rich girls. Money attaches itself to money."

I shrugged. I couldn't be bothered telling her that my ambition didn't extend to marrying wealth.

"Remember, if you change your mind..." Her tone softened. "Why don't you go have a drink and think about it? Think of what you could do with all that cash."

I sighed. It was tempting, especially with that handsome stud whose eyes had fucked me already. I sensed he might be in the market for me. But it felt wrong. Sleazy. Besides, by his mere presence in that establishment, he'd already become a creep.

Taking sheepish steps, I made my way back to a civilized world where things happened naturally.

I ran into a couple doing a drug deal and a young girl squabbling with her boyfriend and reminded myself that life wasn't that black and white.

FIVE

BLAKE

I ONLY STAYED BECAUSE OF HER.

As each girl gyrated her ass and offered to show me what awaited should I wish to pay, my thoughts revolved around the dark-haired beauty whose bewitching eyes had collided with mine. I'd noticed her mouth-watering curves too. Curves had a way of alerting my cock. Even buried in loose unattractive clothes, she was a flower I would have loved to sniff and pluck.

James was lost in his own little erotic paradigm. The girl who had caught his interest paraded before us in a pink bikini, after which he insisted on a private showing, costing him five thousand pounds, where one could touch but not fuck.

My cock remained limp. The girls were too young and skinny. A smart mouth could do more for me than some young girl needing cash in return for her pussy and sanity. And I'm sure it would fuck their heads up. How could it not?

Although that place wasn't my thing, I waited for the dark-headed flower to make an appearance.

When she didn't, I felt a tinge of disappointment, despite respecting her for not parading.

Blending with a cocktail of cheap perfumes, the pungency of male desire thickened the air. Most of the clients were middle-aged men who breathed heavily. Some even stuck their hands down their trousers. It was really fucking gross.

I told myself that James had to up his game. The guy was a chick magnet. *Why would he need to be here?*

Just as I was leaving, I spied someone I'd hoped never to see again. He was gesticulating at a creepy guy with a scar down his cheek, the type of person one expected to meet in such an establishment. Fancy silk wallpaper or scum-stained walls—sleaze always smelled the same.

Having spotted me, Dylan Fox gave a penetrating stare that chilled my bones.

When the woman running the show whispered something in his ear, I sensed he was part of management. His body language suggested he was in charge, and knowing Dylan Fox, he wouldn't settle for anything but domination. Even as a conniving child, he'd stopped at nothing in his need to rule.

I left, determined to do some digging because I could have sworn that some of those girls were underage. Ammunition to bring down my enemy had just landed on my lap.

THE FOLLOWING DAY, I roared down the M1 and took the turn for Northampton. Running late for my appointment, I hadn't slept, which wasn't unusual—I had chronic insomnia. At least this time, that dark-haired beauty had entered my thoughts, instead of the cast of evil faces that normally plagued me.

I drove into the gardens of a Georgian estate that I planned to buy. Poplars lined the road, and a feast of colorful blooms filled the vast grounds. It was as though I'd stepped into a parallel universe, in that those old estates trapped time. That was what made them so desirable to visitors and why transforming them into resorts had swollen my bank balance.

Pulling up at the car park, I noticed three people standing at the pillared entrance, waiting for me. As someone who believed in punctuality, I hated being late.

Stepping out of the car, I grabbed my jacket and put it on.

"Please accept my apologies," I said on my approach. "The traffic was bad leaving London."

The realtor smiled sweetly. Her eyes twinkling, she stretched out her hand. "I'm Melissa Campbell. I work for Jonathon Sharpe."

I took her hand and nodded. "Pleased to meet you." I shifted my focus to the pair selling their family home and offered my hand to the girl first. "Blake Sinclair."

She nodded and smiled.

Melissa said, "This is Jane Joyce, and her brother Michael."

I took the brother's hand and shook it, while he stared at my car, googly-eyed.

"That's a beauty. It's the exact Bond model, isn't it?"

Reluctant to get into a discussion about the engine, of which I had scant knowledge, I nodded and directed my attention to the building.

"Should we go in and take a look?" I asked.

Melissa was busy gaping at me with wide-eyed expectation, while Michael seemed gripped with want as his hands ran over the body of my car as if it were a woman's shapely thigh.

His sister, Jane, looked as though she'd burst into tears at any moment. I'd seen it before—kids of wealth whose parents had left more bills than assets. After being spoon-fed all their lives, they'd been thrust into frugality.

As we walked about the checkered floor, I looked up, bathed in the illumination of color from the stained glass window. Sitting proudly at the top of the landing, that feature alone overwhelmed my senses.

"It's fully heated," said Melissa. "And it comes with all the furnishings."

"You're not planning on gutting it, are you?" asked Jane.

"If I were to buy it, that would be my right," I replied. "But judging by its condition, I can't imagine that will be necessary." I turned to Melissa. "You have all the structural reports for me, I trust?"

"I'll email those to you," she said, her eyes remaining on my face.

We walked into the grand ballroom surrounded by windows that looked out onto the extensive grounds. The light was perfect. I visualized a restaurant and a bar. The model was perfect for my standard resort. The price was a bit higher than usual, but I felt sorry for the pair.

After I'd made them an offer and left them to discuss it among themselves, I stepped out onto the ground and called James. He'd left a message earlier.

"Ah, there you are," said James.

"I scrambled out early. I had a morning appointment in Northampton."

"Are you back tonight?"

"I'm driving back after a coffee and some lunch."

"There's an exhibition later on. I thought you might be interested." He sounded flat.

"What's wrong?"

"I'm kind of lost. We'll talk later?"

"Sure. I should be back by late afternoon. I'll call you, and we can meet for a drink beforehand if you like."

"Look forward to it. Catch you then," he said.

I hoped he'd obtained the blond girl's phone number so that I could find out more about her friend.

I wasn't normally in the habit of chasing girls. Sex was something that arrived at my behest, in that I bought it. No strings attached. No quibbling over not staying the night or inviting her into my home. I could enjoy dirty, guilt-free sex. But this girl was different. I couldn't recall this kind of lingering obsession for a girl before, considering I hadn't even spoken to her. *Very odd.*

SIX

PENELOPE

THE IMAGES LEAPT OFF the canvas. Gifted when it came to drafting, Sheldon painted three-dimensional shapes with enviable skill.

"I love this one," I said.

Sheldon held his chin. "Mm... I did that one in one night. After Roger broke my heart, I painted like a demon. I seem to create my best work when I'm sad."

"Isn't that what it's all about?" I sighed, thinking of how my colors intensified the more my life spiraled downward.

"I guess so." He sipped wine almost mournfully.

We were both slumped in chairs, waiting for the public to arrive. The lighting was brighter than I would have liked, but the curator had insisted on it, and when it came to showing art, Marius had an edge over his competitors. He also didn't charge as much commission as they did and took risks with student art. Sometimes he even lost money with avant-garde shows that mainly attracted impoverished folk looking for an interesting scene and free wine.

"Is Drew coming?" I asked.

"He promised me he would." Sheldon lacked his typical ebullience.

"Please tell me he's not in the closet," I said. Sheldon had this horrible habit of falling for guys in denial, who only hooked up with him to satisfy their sexual needs.

"No... he's a bona fide queen."

I giggled despite his glum face. "Hey. What's up?"

"I saw Roger the other day. He was with a girl. My fucking heart snapped." His mouth tightened, and his hazel eyes misted over.

I took his hand. "Darling, he's a cop."

"So?"

We'd had this conversation before. Sheldon had been seeing Roger, a policeman, on and off for a year, and it was meant to be casual. I'd witnessed his unease after I answered the door at Sheldon's one night and found Roger there, staring at his feet. I offered to leave, but being selfless and aware of my predicament at home, Sheldon had insisted I stay.

Marius sauntered into the room, explaining to a pair of waiters which wine to serve and instructing them to avoid the stragglers. I looked at Sheldon and rolled my eyes. I was always going to exhibitions for the free booze and snacks.

"At least Drew's true to himself," I said. "That way, you can have a proper relationship."

"But Drew's transitioning. I like my men to be men."

I thought of Roger, who was the last guy one would have thought was gay. He had a rugged, almost savage kind of masculinity that Sheldon pined for.

"You're only twenty-five. I'm sure you'll meet a brutishly handsome man one day."

"I wish." His eyes returned to their natural sparkle. Sheldon and I were always discussing men—shirtless, of course—and art. "Come on," he said, rising and offering me his arm. "Let's ponce around with our noses in the air, pretending we're art critics or experts so that we can listen to opinions."

My mouth twisted. "Mm... I'm not sure I want to hear. And we're owed some bad karma," I said, referring to the many times we'd attended exhibitions and thrown our critical banter about like know-it-alls—something I regretted now that I'd matured.

"Let them bitch, for all I care. As far as I'm concerned, your *Mad Witch* series is fucking wild and beautiful, just like you are." He hugged me and stroked my hair. I loved Sheldon.

"And your pieces are amazing."

"A bit controversial," he said. "I can't imagine the highbrows going for them."

"Hey, it's finally dawned on me." I pointed at the large canvas. "This is a modern take on the half-man, half-woman freakshow act."

He clasped his hands. "Yes. That's why I painted them. You know how much I love freakish things. After Dismaland, Banksy's bemusement park, I was never the same again."

I studied the image of two twisted figures dancing—a bearded man in a ball gown and a girl with a high bun, chandelier earrings, an oversized man's jacket, and a moustache. "It's brilliant, Shelly. You should be proud."

He smiled.

The doors opened, and suddenly, a crowd spilled in. Predictably, the art-students and hipster arty types had arrived first.

My cell pinged. Peering down at the screen, I saw Lilly's smiling face. "Hey, I hope you're on your way," I said.

Lilly had me worried. Ever since that night, she'd been hitting it hard. I knew that selling herself wouldn't end well, despite the two hundred thousand pounds sitting in her account. When I visited her, she could hardly move off the couch. She was in so much pain that I offered to take her to the doctor. The hot young guy had been outbid by a creep who'd been so brutal and fucked her so hard, including anally, that the next morning, she was unable to walk.

"I don't think I can make it," she said.

"What are you doing now that's so important?"

"I'm just here having a drink."

"Are you still in pain?" I asked.

"I'm a little better."

Standing in the corner of the gallery, away from the din, I was about to answer her when I noticed two tall men enter. Wearing sports jackets and jeans that fitted in a way that only expensive jeans could, they screamed of wealth.

Capable of smelling money a mile off, Marius ran straight to them.

I studied them a little closer, noticing that they were hot, particularly the dark-haired man, whose jacket, by the way it was molded to his big shoulders, looked sewn on.

My breath hitched. "Holy crap."

"What?" asked Lilly.

"You're not going to believe this, but guess who's just walked through the door?"

"Who?"

"Those guys from the other night. Remember, the one who you liked and his tall dark-haired friend?"

Mr. Dark and Mysterious found my eyes and held on. I gripped my cell, and my breath stuttered. How could a gaze from a good-looking stranger do that to me?

"Really?" Lilly's voice brightened.

"Jump into a cab, and get here now. The dark gorgeous one keeps looking at me. I'm nearly losing the plot. I need you here. Please."

When she didn't respond, I asked, "Are you there?"

"All right." She exhaled. "Text me the details."

"I gave them to you earlier. Remember that leaflet?"

"I don't know where it is. I was a bit drunk at the time. I've already had a few tonight."

"Then get here before the next drink. Don't worry about a thing. I'll hold your hand. You'll open your salon. I'll help."

"Thanks." She sniffled. "It's Brent's night off, and he's asking questions."

"You can't tell him. He'll go crazy."

"How am I going to explain the money?"

"You won it on a scratchy," I suggested. "It's buzzing here. You'll enjoy yourself."

"I should get out. At least that way, Brent won't see me moping about. See you soon, babes," she said, sounding jollier than before, much to my relief.

I closed the call, and Sheldon joined me with two glasses of champagne. "Here, lovey."

"Thanks." My eyes headed over to the handsome stranger who kept looking at me and making my heart race.

"Have you seen those tall hunks?" asked Sheldon.

"Sure have," I said, forcing myself to look away.

"They're a bit too good-looking for me. But great bodies, especially Mr. Tall, Dark, and Hetero."

I laughed and let Sheldon take my arm. We ambled about with our noses in the air, playing our silly but fun game.

From the corner of my eye, I noticed the sexy stranger staring. I even sensed his attention when I wasn't looking. When I turned, his eyes were on mine, leaving a smoldering afterburn.

We stood behind a group of people studying my paintings.

"That's so wild... I love it. But I don't think I could live with it," one of the women said.

Sheldon squeezed my hand in support. He gave me a quick glance and shook his head as though to say, *"Don't listen to them."* He turned his attention to the door. "Oh, he came."

"Who?"

"Drew. And he's wearing Louboutins. Hell."

"It's all the rage, Shelly. Guys are dying to experience the crippling pain of fashion. It's no longer a chick thing." I grinned.

"I suppose," he conceded, sounding flat.

"You're just pining for your butch cop."

"I am. Oh God. Here he comes—or should say, here it comes. I'm not allowed to refer to him as a *he*."

"Then refer to Drew as a she," I said.

His mouth tipped down at one side. "Mm... I suppose we can be friends. Drew's so nice and supportive. I just wish she wasn't so into me."

I squeezed Sheldon's hand, as Drew joined us.

Sheldon's new lover's face was masculine in that angular-jawline way, even though his voice was soft and his wrist dangled. "Hello. Nice to meet you." He kissed me on the cheek before hugging Sheldon. "This looks amazing." He gestured to the art.

I stood there by their side and listened to Drew ooh and aah over the art while helping myself to cheese and wine.

Thirty minutes later, Lilly walked through the door.

The gallery space, the size of an average shop, had filled to capacity. I couldn't believe the turn out. Although I'd promised my triptych to Shelly earlier, given that he'd paid for the paints, I couldn't get that woman's passing comment out of my mind. Sadly, criticism lingered longer than compliments.

I headed over to Lilly and hugged her. "Hey, that was quick."

"I got a cab straightaway." Her eyes moved around the room and then lit up. I turned and saw that the sexy stranger's friend had noticed her. He looked surprised.

"I need a drink," she said.

I took her by the hand. "Come on, I'll get you one."

SEVEN

BLAKE

MAGIC. IT WAS PURE magic seeing her there.
Although her outfit looked very Oxfam, she wore it well. The fitted skirt revealed her swaying hips, and a loose red shirt did little to hide the fullness of her breasts. Her long, dark, plaited hair revealed a swan neck that made my tongue salivate. I watched how her breasts moved ever so slightly with her breath. Despite the fact that she boasted curves that would keep a man up at night, I found it hard to leave her eyes.

I sensed that, having recognized me, she tried to ignore me, despite her furtive glances.

Why is she here? Perhaps she was a friend of the artist. She stood close to a guy whose body language didn't seem like that of a boyfriend.

"She's here! The girl who's been turning me upside down all week. I'm going to speak to her," said James. "I feel like I know her." He raised a brow.

I hadn't seen James that distracted over a girl before, and that was saying something, because along with cars, fine wine, and art, women were James's obsession.

Marius, the gallery owner, joined us. "Ah… Mr. Sinclair. So glad you made it." He shook my hand. "Most of the oils are by Sheldon Sprite, a final-year student at LCCA, except for that enchanting triptych"—he pointed to three panels depicting women in long robes and flowing hair, floating among skyscrapers—"which is by a fellow student, that pretty little thing over there." He cocked his head subtly at the girl who had my blood running hot.

"Tell me about her," I said.

"She's a third-year student. Her work's pretty out there—not in that Tracey Emin way. There's only one Tracey." He chuckled as though it was our personal joke.

Joining in, James said, "There sure is only one Tracey. One wouldn't quite know where to place that soiled bed installation she's famous for."

"Art's not just about ornament. It's a public statement—an individual's take on life," I said. "The audacity of the work is its appeal, although I prefer Banksy. He makes bold public statements with the skill of a craftsman."

Marius hung onto every syllable I uttered. I could have described the color of a turd, and he still would have nodded obsequiously. As an avid collector of modern art—most of which hung on the walls of the estates I'd converted—I'd added to his bank balance

"Introduce me," I said, cocking my head at the beautiful girl.

"Follow me," he said.

Marius joined the girl who'd raised my temperature. "There's someone here who'd like to be introduced." He gestured toward me. "This is Blake Sinclair." He regarded me. "This is Penelope Green, the creator of that fascinating trio of paintings." He pointed to the art.

"Pleased to meet you. I'm intrigued by your art," I said. Extracting my eyes from her beautiful face, I regarded her painting. When I noticed her considerable skill as an artist, she won my immediate respect.

"Thanks," she said, shifting from one leg to another.

"Well, then, leave you to it." Marius looked at me. "If you have any questions... or are interested in..."

"I want to buy them," I said.

Penelope looked at me as though I'd admitted to killing someone. I shook my head. "Is that a problem, Ms. Green?"

"Call me Penny, please." Her face relaxed a little, although her voice seemed tense.

"Have you got another buyer?" I asked.

Marius responded with a decisive "No."

Sensing that my offer had startled her, I stepped back, giving her space. "Excuse me for a moment."

I left Marius alone with Penelope. Artists were known to be precious about their work, and she had every right to feel that way. Her talent was on fine display—brilliant in a way I hadn't experienced at student shows before.

Talent was an aphrodisiac, as the saying went. However, with Penelope Green, the aphrodisiac wasn't so much her considerable talent but her natural beauty. That was rare in my circle, where beauty was as manicured as everyone's nails.

Spying the waiter, I headed over and grabbed a glass of champagne. I took a sip and winced. Although it tasted awful, I needed something to ease the sexual tension. I stole another glance at Penelope, who looked over at me and then quickly away again.

I'd lost James. He'd cornered the girl of his dreams and was chatting away, making her giggle.

EIGHT

PENELOPE

I FOUND SHELDON DEEP in conversation with Drew. I tapped him on the shoulder and gave him an apologetic smile. "Can I have a quick word?"

Sheldon followed me to a quiet corner, where a passing waiter happened to be. I pounced on him, nearly making him lose his balance—such was my need for a drink. I passed a glass to Sheldon and then took two for me.

"Shit, you're hitting it hard, babe," he said. "Has it something to do with the blue-eyed sex god in that Italian designer jacket?"

I had to laugh. When it came to clothes, Sheldon seemed to have a psychic ability at reading labels. "Uh-huh." I gulped down some champagne. "I'm sorry to lure you away like this."

He shook his head. "Why aren't you hanging out with him? Have you seen those shoulders? He's looking right now. He's interested. And he's dripping in money."

"He's also a sleaze."

His head pushed back. "He doesn't look like a sleaze. And so what if he is? He's a fucking sexy sleaze."

"Remember I told you about that virgin auction house?"

He nodded. "I sure do."

"He was there."

"Oh. Really? He was buying?" Sheldon's surprised glower made me chuckle.

I did wonder why a hot man like Blake Sinclair would need to buy sex. I could imagine plenty of virgins throwing themselves at him just for dinner and a sniff of that expensive cologne, which lingered flirtatiously, playing havoc with my senses.

"Well... let's put it this way he was stepping in as I was leaving."

"And so? People buy sex all the time."

"I hate the idea of anyone I'm with buying sex."

"You're jumping the gun, aren't you? You haven't even unbuttoned that silk shirt that would pay my monthly art-supply bill." He looked over my shoulder.

"What?"

"The way he keeps checking you out suggests you could at least run your hands down it. Mm... all the way."

My tummy tightened, and a little fiery sensation traveled through me. "I want more than that. I want a boyfriend, not a one-night stand, even if he is gorgeous."

"You're an idealist, lovey."

What Sheldon said made sense. And in any case, I had no right to judge Blake Sinclair. I didn't even know him. But that burning gaze of his kept undressing me in a way that my body craved.

"He wants to buy my three panels. I thought I'd better speak to you first, because I promised them to you."

"That's sweet of you, but if he's offering your price, you should take it."

I was about to respond when Marius joined us. We both turned our attention to him.

"Penelope, Blake Sinclair's offering a hundred thousand pounds." Although he tried to remain cool, his words bubbled over with excitement.

My mouth dropped opened. I looked at Sheldon, who was equally shocked.

"Holy crap. Take it," Sheldon insisted. "Don't worry about me. I'm sure you can create something that will be just as good."

Marius nodded in agreement. "Blake needs an answer. He also requested that you meet with him. He's interested in getting to know you and your art. Privately." His eyebrow lift spoke volumes.

Is it just art he wishes to buy?

I gaped at Marius as though he'd asked me to perform a lewd act in front of a crowd.

What does that amount of cash even look like? The thought of a studio, where I could live and paint, shook me back to reality. "Um… sure."

Marius released a tight chuckle. "For a moment there, I thought you were going to refuse. You gave out a cold vibe, Penelope. I mean, if you want to survive in the art business, you have to smile when meeting a wealthy client. And Blake Sinclair's in the *Forbes* top one hundred."

Sheldon whistled. "That rich." He stared at me as if to say, "What are you waiting for?"

I kissed Sheldon on the cheek.

Marius waited impatiently, his attention switching from me to Blake, who looked serious and disinterested, ignoring the attention his powerful, handsome presence attracted.

"Lead the way," I said.

Blake Sinclair had his back to us, which made it easier for me. I could barely stand, let alone walk with his blue eyes smoldering all over me.

My heart pumped fast. *What can I say? "You're a sleazy, virgin-buying creep, but I'll take your money anyway?"*

He turned, and his beautiful face softened at seeing me. I let out a deep breath in a bid to relax my throat. By my side, Marius was all smiles. I thought he was going to kiss me. Blake Sinclair's generous offer would deliver the hardworking curator a nice chunk of commission.

Taking his cue from my new benefactor, Marius left us alone.

My fingernails dug into my damp palm. I couldn't look at him, because my eyes wanted to drown in those aquamarine eyes that kept changing from light to dark. Although he wore unaffected confidence as well as he wore his Italian jacket, I sensed a complex man.

"You'll sell?" His deep voice resonated through my ribs.

I nodded. "I'd be crazy not to."

He studied me for a moment, and his lips tipped up at one end, which was about as cheery as I'd seen him so far. "You're reluctant to sell?"

I shook my head. "It's not that."

He waited for more, but I'd lost my ability to think. He gave me space, which I appreciated.

After I'd failed to elaborate, he asked, "How about if we leave here? Have you had dinner?"

"You're asking me out?" I hated how shrill my voice sounded.

"It's a bit noisy in here. And the champagne is a little off. I'd love a real drink, and I'm fascinated by your work. Your talent. That's all. Nothing too serious." He tilted his head and smiled for the first time.

A dimple in his cheek weakened my resolve, even though a voice within reminded me that he bought desperate girls for sex.

I glanced over my shoulder, looking for Lilly, and found her leaning up against a wall, wearing an unshifting smile and engrossed in whatever her Prince Charming uttered.

Taking a deep breath, I nodded. "Okay. I could eat something. I've been busy all day and haven't had much time." I bit my lip. "Um... should we say something to Marius?"

He lifted his large hand. A sapphire ring stole my breath. The blue stone accented his eyes, and I fell into a trance. As a painter obsessed in color, I tried not to drool over its beauty.

He smiled gently. I couldn't believe he was the same man. His face had changed completely. I wasn't sure which I preferred—the brooding, inscrutable version or the charming, sensitive one. *Both.*

"I'll quickly have a word with Marius. Don't go anywhere," he said.

"I won't." My smile quivered.

For some reason, I thought about my dull underwear. Why that came into my fraught mind, I couldn't tell. Maybe it was because after he passed me his scent lingered and traveled into my nostrils and all the way down to my crotch, which throbbed against my very unsexy cotton panties.

I watched him move through the crowd. Now that he wasn't so close and robbing me of air, my senses returned. Firstly, I had to tell Lilly. Considering her tipsy state, I needed to know that she was okay, even if I would have preferred a quiet exit.

I looked over at Sheldon, who was chatting to an older couple, pointing up at his work.

I waited until Blake returned, and as he walked toward me, my legs weakened, and my heart sped up again. I didn't know how the hell I could eat, especially with his eyes plowing into mine and those sensual lips, which his tongue had a habit of brushing, ravaging my faculties.

Wearing a faint, almost uncertain smile, he returned to my side.

"I need to see that my friend Lilly is okay. Do you mind waiting?" I asked.

"Of course not."

I paused. "Can your friend be trusted?"

His brow gathered as he studied me. "If you're asking if he'll try to seduce your friend, then he probably will."

"She's a bit fragile, that's all. What I meant to ask is…"

"Is he a womanizer?" He tilted his head.

I nodded.

"James likes his girls. He's not really the marrying kind, by his own admission." He stared at me. "Didn't I see you both the other night?"

"Huh?" Fire pumped through me, waking me out of my schoolgirl crush. "Are you implying that I visited that place?" I paused for a moment to collect my words. "I saw you too. You were there. Exploiting desperate girls, I might add."

"What are you talking about?" He frowned.

"Just that you attended that sleazy place."

"Now, look, Penelope. I was there only because James asked me along for support."

"But you looked?"

His head pushed back. "I didn't. And why are we discussing this?"

"Because Lilly had a bad time."

"Oh... I'm sorry to hear that." He paused. "In all honesty, I'm not surprised. It's that kind of place."

"And you should know, right?"

"Excuse me?" His eyes darkened to a deep shade of anger. He lifted his cleft chin. "And what about you?"

"I left just as you were entering."

"Why are you suddenly judging me?" he asked.

"I suppose it's your prerogative to exploit desperation. I'm sure you've never experienced hunger and mounting bills and a life that offers no way out."

"That's where you're *very* wrong, Penelope. Be careful. Don't be fooled by appearances." His low, grave voice sank deep into my gut.

"I might be young, but I'm not a fool." I turned my back on him and stormed off, like an idiot.

Fueled by anger, more at myself than Blake, I got to the other side of the room.

Fifteen minutes earlier, I'd been staring at the promise of a new life, and now here I was—the same Penelope Green, living in a stinky estate with a mother who could barely open her eyes.

I noticed Blake leave. *Shit*. I'd blown it. I kicked myself.

NINE

BLAKE

THE HEAVY CANDLESTICK TREMBLED in my hand, and my throat constricted. I couldn't yell. He looked at me with those pathetic, pleading eyes as if only I possessed the power to release him from the devil's grip. Those were his words. His hand squeezed my ass as though his life depended on it. I'd seen what he was capable of. Although he overpowered me, he being a man and I only a boy, just as he touched me, I stood on my toes and slammed the golden candlestick over his bald head. A crack appeared, and blood spurted out, dripping down over those creepy black eyes and decrepit cheeks.

Crashing metal echoed off the marble floor. The vibration traveled up my calves. His cold hand gripped my foot, and I kicked it away. He'd touched me one time too many.

Repelled by his cries for help, I ran breathless into the wood without stopping until I arrived at the moors. The howling wind pushed me along. I wished I could fly like the ravens that hovered over that somber gray place.

I entered my cave, a dark, foreboding place that was less frightening than the depraved beasts that I hid from.

But my soul wasn't free. The rocky walls distorted, forming faces of demons, just like those sneering monsters on the chapel facade. A silent scream clenched my jaw. Trapped by evil smiles and cruel eyes, I couldn't escape. Even the roaring howl of the wind couldn't drown out that choir of dissonant shrieks.

A knock startled me awake. I jolted upright. It took a moment to orient myself.

A large opulent bedroom in accents of teal and burgundy slowly came into focus. It was my bedroom in Mayfair and not hell.

I lifted my exhausted body off the damp sheet. Shivering, I clutched my arms.

"Is everything okay?" a voice called from the hallway.

"Yes, Pierce," I returned.

A comforting warble from a robin reminded me that it was daytime and that I'd just had a nightmare.

I took a deep breath and walked around, enabling the flow of blood to my tense muscles.

Opening the drapes, I looked over at Grosvenor Square bathed in morning sun. People ran or walked their dogs while children bounded about, innocent and full of life.

I headed over to the phone and cleared my voice. "Good morning, Maria. Just some coffee and juice."

"You're not hungry?" she asked in her Italian accent.

"No. I've got to be somewhere soon." That wasn't quite true, but at least it would stop her fussing about me not eating breakfast.

"Oh… I've made brioche. Fresh."

Maria was always insistent. I did like having someone who cared. And her food was scrumptious.

"Sure, thanks."

"Subito, signore."

My new acquisitions hung on the wall. The triptych had arrived the day before, replacing a pair of Ingres nudes I'd paid a small fortune for—more than the hundred thousand pounds I'd paid for Penelope Green's art.

In each painting, the same woman appeared, wearing a long, flowing red gown that was vibrant against the gray city of distorted rectangular buildings. A man with his back turned watched before a gothic window as a woman flew through the city. This story was told over three panels. The art was masterfully created.

I searched for a hint of the girl who had invaded my mind. She'd misunderstood me. *How will I convince her that I'm not in the habit of buying virgins?*

A knock at my door made me jump. Those paintings had a strange hypnotic power over me. Only a truly gifted artist could attempt surrealism. And for me, Penelope Green's talent grew each time I visited her work.

"Come in," I said.

Maria carried a tray filled with food. I had to smile. "Maria, that doesn't look like a brioche."

She waved her hand. "Only a little toast. Just in case." She smiled, but as she studied my face, I knew I was in for some interrogation.

"Are you okay, *Signore* Blake?"

"I'm great. Now, put it down there, and off you go." I used my kindest tone.

Just as she was leaving, Maria looked up at my new acquisitions. "Oh... they're new." She studied them. "They're so interesting. *Gotica*."

"Gothic, you mean?" I asked.

"Mm... the artist has a fine hand and eye. It's like the man's in a church looking out at the beautiful girl, his object of desire, who is lost in a distorted machine-like city that she's trying to escape."

I nodded slowly. "I picked them up at a student show."

"The artist will probably do great things."

I felt buoyed by her prediction, as though Maria had spoken about someone close to me. "If I ever see her again, I'll relay your compliment."

She scrutinized me with her typical intensity. "You like this girl. She's very pretty."

"How can you tell?"

She pointed at the painted figure. "Does she look like her?"

I conjured up Penelope's beautiful face and nodded. "There is a resemblance."

"And you didn't get her number?"

"You know me. I don't like questions."

She twirled her hand dismissively. "Ask her out. You're too handsome. The girls would fall at your feet if only you would act more..." She lifted her chin up and pushed out her chest, giving her impression of cockiness.

"Thanks for the lesson in the art of seduction," I responded dryly. She smiled with a wink before leaving.

Although I couldn't imagine that being a cocky bastard would win over Penelope Green, I needed to do something to convince her that I wasn't a cad. Maybe flowers and a note of apology.

Flowers, yes. Apology? I had nothing to apologize for. She was the one who'd jumped to conclusions, although Penelope's feistiness sent blood gushing to my groin as I recalled her pretty eyes firing up.

My cell vibrated. The name Peter Barnes, a private detective I'd recently hired, came up.

"Blake." His gravelly voice was so loud that I held the phone away from my ear.

"What can you tell me?" I asked.

"Only that the Cherry Orchard's registered to a conglomerate that is not that easy to pin down. But I did find one lead."

"That is...?"

"A name that's connected to a leading figure from an Eastern European gang."

I rubbed my head. "Right."

"I've got a few leads. I'll do some poking around, and perhaps we can meet at the end of the week. I'd prefer to do things away from the phone," he said.

"Sure."

TEN

PENELOPE

THE MODEL FOR OUR life drawing class had that kind of muscular body that sent Sheldon into a meltdown.

Cupping the side of his mouth, he whispered, "He's gorgeous."

I had to smile. The model did have that Adonis appeal. And him being naked as the day he was born wasn't exactly making things any easier for poor Sheldon. I only hoped the model's shriveled member wouldn't rise for the occasion.

A break was called. We'd been drawing all morning. Life drawing was my favorite subject, although I preferred female models. They were easier to draw. All those masculine sinews put me in awe of the Italian masters, particularly Michelangelo, and their ability to depict the male figure.

As I headed for the coffee machine, a bunch of roses and a pair of legs headed my way, and this time, it wasn't my surreal take on the mundane.

Angie, the administrator, noticed me passing. "Ah... there you are, Penny." She handed me a bunch of roses of every color known to that genus.

After I regained my senses, having buried my nose in the intoxicating bunch of fragrant flowers, I asked, "Are they really for me?"

She smiled. "An admirer."

Over my shoulder, I heard Sheldon remark, "A rich admirer, I'd say."

"Lucky you," she said, passing me an envelope.

The card nearly fell from my hand. I looked up at Sheldon, who took it from my hand and sniffed it. "Mm… it's perfumed." He held his chin. "Now, who could these be from?"

My legs, by this stage, were nearly buckling from the weight of the blooms coupled with shock and all other kinds of indescribable emotions.

Sheldon took the bunch from my arms. "Here, let me help you. Shit, there must be at least sixty roses."

Shaking my head in disbelief, I uttered, "Holy crap."

He remained there with the roses in his arms. "Well, come on. Aren't you going to see who they're from?"

I sat down and opened the envelope. The card read: *Can we start again? Dinner? Your paintings look lovely in my home. Thank you. Blake Sinclair.*

I kept reading it over and over as if I'd missed some small detail. It was handwritten, and I ran my fingers over the card, feeling the pen markings, like a psychic with a piece of jewelry.

"It's from him, isn't it?" asked Sheldon, placing the flowers down on the seat next to me.

I nodded. In a trance, I passed him the card.

"You must go. I mean he's absolutely fucking gorgeous."

"I know. He's almost too gorgeous."

Sheldon tilted his head in sympathy. "Don't be scared. I'm sure he'll be a gentleman. Unless, you know…" He growled. "You don't want him to be."

I laughed.

Blake hadn't left my thoughts, even though I tried to quash this sudden obsession, because Sheldon was right—Blake Sinclair terrified me. I hated the thought of him learning about my life at the estate, and my drug-addicted mother. Swamped by guilt, I hated how shallow that made me. But what would a man of his class, used to the finer things in life, do with someone like me?

I imagined he was after my body, and after he was done with me, he'd probably move onto the next flower to pluck. Maybe it was a sport. I'd read about rich men and their kinky ways. Perhaps he had a thing for impoverished art students.

"Can you imagine him dropping me off at my home, with the walking dead, and drug dealers lingering about?"

Sheldon's mouth turned down in sympathy. "Oh, Penny... just enjoy it. And anyhow, tell him you're living with me in Soho. It's partly true."

"I feel like an idiot, pointing my finger at him for something that wasn't even my business."

Sheldon nodded. "You did overreact. It's fear. I can understand it. But he's seriously yummy. I mean, the guy's hot, and I bet he works out."

I had to agree with all of that. "So, should I reply? He's printed his number on the card."

"I would've been on the phone and in his bed by now." He giggled.

"That's the point. I'm expected to sleep with him, aren't I?"

"Penny, you're going to have fuck some time. Baby, you're twenty-three, for God's sake." His head pushed back. "And to be honest, I'd kill to have my virginity taken by someone like Blake Sinclair."

"Hmm... I suppose."

After I left Sheldon, instead of returning to class, I headed outside and found a quiet spot on a bench canopied by a sycamore.

I kept looking down at the card with his number. After five minutes and endless deep breaths, I tapped his number. My hand shook as I gripped the phone.

It went to voicemail, and his husky voice traveled deep into my core.

I waited for the beep and then stammered, "Um... this is Penelope Green. Thanks for the roses. I... just called to thank you." I closed the call, overcome by self-loathing at how stupid I sounded.

The phone vibrated in my hand, and I took the call without looking to see who it was.

"Penelope." His deep voice traveled all the way to my nipples.

"Yes."

"It's Blake. I just missed your call."

"Oh... um... I just called." I took a deep breath. I couldn't believe how imbecilic I'd become. "I received the flowers. They're beautiful. There's lots of them." I giggled nervously.

"Good. Fragrant, I trust."

"Very much. They made me dizzy. The scent, I mean."

"Good. I mean not so good feeling faint. But roses have that affecting charm about them. I love smelling a rose in full bloom."

I hadn't expected that.

"Penelope?"

"Call me Penny, please," I said.

"Penny... would you like to have dinner? Or a drink?"

"Sure. That would be nice."

"So, dinner, drink, or both?"

"Dinner sounds good." My voice sounded weak and quavering. In order to still my racing heart, I reminded myself that I wasn't talking to the leader of a nation or a king or anything. This was a normal person.

Well... maybe not so normal. Hell.

"Great. Say, seven tonight?"

"That sounds good."

"Wonderful. I look forward to it. Text me your address."

"Oh... you're going to pick me up?" I clenched my jaw.

"Would you prefer to meet me somewhere?"

"That might be better," I said cautiously.

"How about if we meet at a bar in Piccadilly?"

"Yes. Good. Just text me the details, and I'll see you there at seven."

"Will do. I look forward to seeing you. Your paintings look great."

"Oh, you've hung them?" I kept forgetting that he'd bought my work, and that I'd become a wealthy artist. It still didn't feel real to me.

"In my bedroom," he said with that clit-tickling voice that could have recited the telephone book, and I'd probably still burst a vein.

I paused. Why did my paintings being hung in his bedroom sound so intimate? They were inanimate objects after all. But then, to me, that triptych held a power. "Oh... that's a very personal space."

"It is. And they're right at home. They change with the light. In the morning they greet me with a smile. In the afternoon, they're a little more introspective, and by nightfall, they become figures of supreme mystery."

My heart skipped a beat. "Yes. Light and shadow change paintings. I love that you've seen that, because that's such an important way to experience art. I wish I could be more eloquent."

"You're sufficiently eloquent, Penelope. The sophistication of that work speaks for itself."

"Thank you. That's very complimentary. I... I never quite know what I'm going to paint. My approach is 'stream of consciousness.'"

"That's why it works. Art, for me, is about magic," he said.

"You sound very knowledgeable. And I'm a little obsessed."

"Obsession is passion, and where there's passion, there's potency."

A shiver of warmth touched my soul. "That's so true."

"I'll text you the address, then." His deep voice roused me from the dream of hearing him speak. It was a form of verbal foreplay.

As a storm of desire raged through me, I had this feeling that I might never be the same again.

THE SKIRT HUGGED MY hips more than I would have liked. I kept tugging at the clingy fabric. At least I'd chosen a knee-length version and not the mini that Sheldon had suggested.

Shopping was an exhausting process of elimination. In the end, I opted for a tight-fitting skirt with a tulip-shaped flounce and a silk shirt that I couldn't stop stroking. The whole outfit cost me more than my monthly allowance. But I couldn't meet with a man like Blake Sinclair in my Oxfam hand-me-downs. Despite priding myself on my secondhand chic, a date with Blake was hardly the time to show off my individuality at bargain-basement prices.

I looked at myself for the umpteenth time in the reflection of a window I passed. The green shirt suited my dark hair as Sheldon had enthusiastically declared, and the black skirt, although fitted, made my ass look smaller—a feat in itself, given my size 14 ass.

Crossing my arms, I shivered. Although it was summer, the early evening air had a bite. I felt my nipples spike against the back of my hand—one of the problems with wearing silk, I'd discovered—and rubbed them discreetly, crossing my arms to hide them. Even my sexy lace bra was new. That purchase came after Sheldon dragged me into a lingerie store. The way he gushed over the skimpy ensembles made me laugh. He loved the female form from an artist's perspective, and unlike me, he regarded my curves with envy. I'd always wanted to look like Lilly—blond, blue-eyed, and slim.

I finally arrived at the lane where the bar was situated. Victorian lamps painted a subdued warm ambience over the cobbled paths. Each of the intimate bars that lined the alleyway was lamplit, making for a discreet meeting place.

Taking a deep breath, I stood at the doorway. Being ten minutes early, I lingered indecisively, wondering whether I should go for a walk, when I saw him through the window. Even with his back to me, I knew it was him. I almost chickened out. Fear had taken its grip. *Or is that anticipation?* Butterflies had invaded my belly the moment I heard his voice on the phone.

Blake Sinclair must have sensed me at the door, because he turned and his eyes found mine. My heart raced. I could barely walk to his table. Vivaldi's *Four Seasons* played in the background. I recognized it because one of my lecturers often played it.

His eyes spellbound me. I attempted a quivery smile and crossed my arms to hide my hardened nipples, which seemed to have a mind of their own.

"Hi," I said. "I'm a little early."

"As am I. I always like to arrive early or at least on time." His eyes lingered, waiting for a response, as though he'd given me an insight into a habit he didn't normally share.

Before I had a chance to stop him, he rose from his chair and held out a chair for me.

Dressed in a white linen shirt over loose-fitting beige slacks, his casual look was effortlessly sophisticated.

"What can I get you?" he asked.

"A G&T, I suppose."

He beckoned a waitress, and she was by our side in a flash. Something told me that Blake Sinclair could make anyone jump to action.

After he ordered, his attention returned to me. "I trust you found it okay?"

"Yes. I took the tube."

"From college or from home?"

I gulped. *And now for the gritty details of my life.* "I was in Soho."

"That's where you live?"

I nodded. I had to extract my eyes from his hypnotic stare. I looked down at my hands and then slowly looked up at him again. He was so handsome that each time I visited his face I learned something new about it. With that tanned, smooth skin, he looked around thirty, but his vibe seemed like that of someone older, adding to his sex appeal. I'd always had a thing for older men.

"You seem to have a lot going on in your head, if you don't mind me saying," he said.

"How would you know that?" I asked, feeling naked all of a sudden.

"I'm not sure why. But you seem very familiar to me, Penelope."

"Please call me Penny."

"Penelope suits you. May I call you that?"

I had to admit my name sounded sensual issuing from those fleshy lips.

"Do you live alone in Soho?" he asked, running his finger along the rim of his glass.

"Um... no. It's Sheldon's house. He's been kind enough to let me live there. I also use his studio, which is up the road."

"Sheldon Sprite. I know his family."

"Oh, you've met them?" My voice was unintentionally high-pitched.

"Just at a few gatherings. I don't know them well. I'm familiar with Sheldon's work."

"He's an amazing artist."

"As are you, Penelope."

The waitress arrived with my drink, and not too soon either. My hand trembled as I lifted it. I wished I could be cool, calm, and collected, fluttering my hand about, just like the other women in the bar.

I gulped down my G&T like it was water.

"We ended on a bad note the other night." He studied me. "I'm not the big bad wolf you might think I am. I didn't remain at the Cherry Orchard. I'd like you to know that."

"I believe you." I took another big sip.

Blake must have noticed my hand trembling. "Am I making you nervous?"

I nodded. "I'm not very confident around men I don't know well. Especially men like you."

"Men like me? There are others?" he asked with a subtle grin, which he wore well.

"No. You just give off an air of sophistication that makes me feel inferior."

His eyebrows drew in. "You see me as arrogant?"

"Not exactly." I played with my glass. "Although, I suppose you could come across as that to some."

"You're not the first to accuse me of that." He cast a tight smile. "I don't suffer fools, and I'm choosy when it comes to company. I'm probably more like you than you think."

I jerked my head back. "How would you know that?"

"Your art. There's something in it that speaks to my soul."

I caught a glint of softness in his eyes, making me wonder if in fact he was sensitive and wore that air of superiority as a shield.

"You're moving in the realms of mysticism, Mr. Sinclair."

"I like those realms, Ms. Green," he retorted, with a flicker of a smile that weakened my knees.

"If you didn't resemble a male model, I'd say you possess creative spirit."

"Can't I be both?" His lips moved up at one side, revealing a dimple.

"Beautiful people can be a little vain." Thanks to the gin, I'd finally relaxed.

"Are you vain?" His eyes plowed in so deep that it was impossible to hide.

I shook my head. "I have nothing to be vain about."

"That's not true. You're very beautiful, and you're extremely talented. You're in a league of your own. You have plenty to be vain about."

"I don't see myself like that. I am overweight. And my technique's somewhat underdeveloped."

"I disagree with all of that. Technique's important, but one doesn't want to become a slave to it."

I opened my mouth in surprise. "My lecturer said something to that effect."

"I think I read it somewhere," he said, taking a sip of his drink.

I shifted subtly in my chair, hoping I wouldn't leave a damp mark because I was melting from his steamy gaze.

"Are you hungry?" he asked.

"Um... for success?"

His lips curved. "I meant to ask whether you wished to eat."

I appreciated that he hadn't made fun of my naivety.

"Oh. Sorry."

He shook his head. "No need. Be yourself, Penelope."

That wasn't easy around him, especially with that deep husk caressing my name as though he were making love to it.

"I'm not hungry. But I probably should eat," I said.

"Good. I've made a reservation at the Ritz." He looked down at my empty glass. "Shall we go?"

I rose, hoping that the heat coming out of my vagina wasn't obvious.

He towered over me and placed his hand gently on the middle of my back as we exited the bar.

The night air was refreshing and welcoming. I took a deep breath and tried to walk steadily, even though my high heels, being new, gave me grief as they dug into my ankles. We arrived at a shiny black Bentley, where a very tall man awaited us. He greeted me with a nod and opened the door for me.

I slid in, and my skirt, sticking to the leather, rode up, revealing my chubby thighs. I lifted my body and wiggled the skirt down.

Blake gave me a subtle smile.

ELEVEN

BLAKE

NORMALLY, CHEAP PERFUME made me recoil. But radiating off Penelope's milky skin, it was an aphrodisiac. Her ill-fitting silk shirt did little to hide those curves and those tantalizingly erect nipples, which had me salivating from the moment she entered the bar. In an effort to hide my rising member, I adjusted my position.

Sitting so close to her had made me ravenous. That was new for me. I didn't usually feel this way around pretty women. It took more than an attractive face and beautiful curves for me to have that reaction. But knowing that Penelope was pure added that extra allure. I'd never had the desire to fuck a virgin before, but Penelope had become an obsession.

Penelope looked out the window like a child at Disneyland.

"It looks different at night with the lights," I said, admiring the impressive sky-piercing spires of Westminster, flooded in soft light that revealed crevices and everchanging shadows adding to its architectural mystique.

"It is." She turned to face me. "Do you always get around in this big car?"

"When I go out at night, I like to have a driver. I also have my own car that I enjoy driving on long trips. I like speed." I grinned. "That's one of my bad habits—driving too fast."

"One?" She grinned.

I shrugged. "We're all entitled to a few, aren't we? We wouldn't be human otherwise."

"You've got me curious now."

"The clean version—I'm not into coke, just the odd cigar here and there, and I like single malt."

"The dirty version?" Her dark eyes twinkled with mischief.

I mirrored her cheeky grin. "Penelope, we've only just met."

Her gaze lingered as though she was trying to understand something complicated. "I've never been in a car like this."

"I hope it's not too old-fashioned for you."

"No. It's a novelty, I suppose. And I do like the leather seats." Her hands slid over the upholstery sensuously. I imagined it being my skin, and blood gushed down to my groin.

"Are we going to be there soon?" she asked.

I turned to study her. "Are you still nervous?"

She nodded with a tight smile. "I've never done anything like this before."

"Just be yourself. I'd like to know the real Penelope Green—the artist who paints like a master."

"A master?" Her brow creased.

"I've seen a lot of art. Yours is a rare talent."

Her big dark eyes massaged something deep inside of me. She might have been young, but the longer I looked, the more an old soul shone through.

"Why are you looking at me like that?" she asked.

"Because you've got a witchy face. If I'm not careful you'll enchant me."

"Witchy? Enchant? Oh my God, Blake. You sound as though you've stepped out of a gothic novel."

I sniffed. "I have a thing for the past. I mean not so much my own." *Oops, too much information.*

"How so?"

I shrugged and forced a fleeting smile.

She stared at me for a moment and then looked away.

We pulled up at the curb as well-dressed folk climbed up the stairs to the theater across from the restaurant.

Patrick opened the door for Penelope, and I helped her out.

I took her by the arm gently, and we stepped into the busy restaurant and the maître d', who knew me, showed us to my regular table by the window. One of my quirks—or perhaps it was a phobia—was that having people too close to me constricted my breathing.

I held out the chair for Penelope, and again, she frowned. Waiting until she was comfortable, I asked, "You're not used to men opening doors and pulling out chairs for you?"

She shook her head. "No. It's never happened. It feels strange, as though I'm incapacitated in some way."

"It's meant to be chivalrous. A gentlemanly gesture. But hey, I'll refrain if that makes you feel better."

"No. I kind of like it. It's just a little dated. But then, everything about you seems old-fashioned."

"I'll take that as a criticism."

"You shouldn't. I'm not into guys who air punch or get around in packs, yelling at football games. I'm kind of fascinated with the past too."

I nodded. "You're a romantic, then. That's clear enough from your art."

"I'll take that as a compliment," she said, looking from me to the waiter who'd just arrived.

I took the wine menu and went straight to my favorite choice. I was a man of habit. Being that way saved time and offered a predictably satisfying experience. "Would you like red or white wine?" I asked.

She shrugged. "I like both."

"The fish is excellent here, and with that, white would be the choice. Would you like to look at the menu?"

Penelope shook her head. "No need. I like fish. Just whatever you're having."

Good. She wasn't fussy. I liked that. It gave me control.

"We'll go for the seafood cocktail for entrée. The salmon for the main course. Vegetables. And the Gustave Lorentz Pinot Gris."

The waiter nodded. "Very well, sir."

"This is such an amazing place," she said, looking up at the ceiling, which boasted a fresco of dancing nymphs in diaphanous robes.

"I like it here. The lighting's subdued, which suits me. A lot of restaurants tend to go for bright lights."

She nodded. "I hate bright lights."

We smiled in that way people do when discovering they have something in common.

TWELVE

PENELOPE

"OH LOOK, THE MOON'S reflecting off the window." I pointed at the antiquarian bookshop's bay window.

"The moon always brings poetry to a night," he said, staring up at the sky.

My body melted again. *Who is this guy?* He had a soft, artistic side to his nature that surprised me. Even when walking, he switched from doing a supercilious strut to ambling elegantly close by my side.

He turned to face me. The big shiny black car waited for us. Although I was tipsy, I wasn't sure what to expect. After such a delicious dinner and the best wine I'd ever tasted, I'd finally relaxed. Blake had even laughed a little. His handsome face, which looked gorgeous no matter what mood he was in, lightened, and he almost let me in. But there was also something guarded about him.

Looking the part of rich tycoon in a fitted blue sports jacket, he regarded me. "What would you like to do now?"

I shrugged. "Have you got any ideas?"

"We could go for a spin around the Tate. Or we could go back to my house, where I could try to seduce you. Or…"

"Or?" I asked, my face burning from his audacious suggestion.

Am I ready to go to bed with him so quickly? I couldn't deny it—Blake Sinclair had woven a spell.

"I can almost see the thoughts ticking away in that beautiful head of yours."

"The Tate sounds good," I said, disappointing the wild cat within.

He nodded neutrally with no hint of disappointment. Unlike me. I wanted Blake to express his urgent need to ravish me. I liked knowing he was hungry for me after I'd been staring at his mouth all night, wondering how his lips would feel against mine.

I looked up at Blake. "Can I change my mind?"

He opened his big hands. "As long as you grace me with your company, I'm happy for us to just walk if you like."

"Okay." I looked at the Thames with the moon's reflection rippling away. "It's a beautiful night, and after that dessert"—I touched my belly—"I probably should exercise a little."

"You're still young, and you're not overweight, Penelope."

He stopped and looked at me. Under the lamplight, his blue eyes had gone dark, almost black.

"I'm not that young."

"You're twenty-three."

"Yes. How do you know that?"

"I know a lot about you," he said matter-of-factly.

"Now you're creeping me out. You've had me investigated?"

He shook his head. "It's on public record. You're an artist. You sell art."

"Oh… really? I've only ever sold a few works."

"It's still registered. Date of birth and the like."

"What, even my address?" I didn't hide my alarm.

"Not that. But hey, I'm not the big bad wolf." He smiled, and those dimples made me want to slap and kiss him at the same time.

"So you've said," I replied dryly.

His grin faded into a serious expression. "You still seem a little uptight toward me. Is it because of the Cherry Orchard?"

"Not really. You're just a little intimidating."

He took my hand and stared deep into my eyes. "Your beauty intimidates me too."

Now it was my turn to frown. "How?"

"You're innocent. You're like a fragile flower. I want to keep drawing it in, but in order to retain its beauty, a flower shouldn't be plucked."

"But it eventually withers."

"I can't imagine you ever withering." He drew me close.

I breathed him in, and his masculine scent, infused with subtle cologne, made me melt into his embrace. I looked up, and before my next breath, his head lowered to mine. My lips parted in anticipation.

He ran his tongue along his cushiony lips, and then they touched mine.

My brain shut down, giving my body total say.

His mouth, soft and moist, gently caressed mine. He tasted of wine and honey. His arms held me tight, and I floated on a cloud. His tongue touched my mouth. I allowed him in, and he entered, his tongue twining around mine.

Pulsing with desire, I pressed against his strong frame, and then I woke out of my aroused haze and gently pulled away.

He brushed a strand of hair from my face, and the burning need in his eyes matched my body's. "You're going to destroy me."

I searched for lightness in his tone, but his face remained serious. A shiver ran through me. "Why would you say that?"

"Because I'm weak around you. I've thought of little else since meeting you. Maybe your art has bewitched me."

"There are no spells embedded in my work."

"Of course, there aren't... but you have power over me." He pulled away to look at me under the street lamp.

"You make it sound painful," I said, trying to understand him because his expression was so intense.

Am I really tormenting him? He was tormenting me with those gorgeous blue eyes that I kept falling into.

"I'm not an easy person to be around," he said.

"In what way?"

I felt as though we'd entered a place only lovers and people who'd known each other longer than one night visited.

"Penelope, I don't sleep with women."

I made a face at him. "Huh? But that kiss..." My eyes widened. "You're gay?"

He smiled. "No. I'm not gay. I would have thought that was pretty obvious."

I nodded slowly, recalling his big erection pressing against me.

"What I meant to say was that I fuck women, but I don't sleep with them."

"Okay. Um... right. I see." I couldn't think straight. "Is there a reason?"

"Isn't there always a reason for our peculiarities?"

Our eyes locked. Taking a deep breath—this was the most intense encounter I'd ever experienced with a man—I ran my tongue over my lips, which he must have read as an invitation.

He took me into his arms again. His hot mouth ate at mine. Raw and hungry—that was how he came at me. Penetrating my mouth, his tongue ravished me. I imagined his cock doing that to me, and my vagina throbbed with painful arousal.

But would I come out in one piece?

"Penelope, if we keep doing this, I might get arrested for indecency because I want to touch you."

I wanted his hands all over me, too, and his large cock rubbing against me had turned me into a steamy mess.

"I've never been with a man before, Blake."

He studied me, and a gentle smile softened his regular-featured face, except for a slight bump on the bridge of his nose, which made him even more beautiful.

"We can take this slowly. I do understand." His hand rested on the curve of my waist, tantalizingly close to my breast. "Let's have a G&T somewhere quiet, shall we?"

I could barely walk, which had little to do with the two glasses of wine I'd already consumed. "So, does that mean I'm not going back to your house?"

He stopped walking and looked at me. "Would you like to come back to my house?"

"Yes," I replied, falling into his gaze again.

Blake led me to the sleek black limousine, and opening the door for me, he helped me in. Chivalry had a sudden glamorous appeal, especially in the hands of a sexy man.

BLAKE FITTED HIS STUNNING environment perfectly. Now that he'd removed his blazer, I drank in his strong physique.

But why doesn't he sleep with women?

I looked at him in the hope of understanding him. But instead, his mesmerizing eyes distracted me.

My heart pumped madly as he lowered himself close and took my hand. The electricity from his touch rushed through me. I brushed my mouth with my tongue and fell into his arms. His mouth touched mine, and as our hot moist mouths fused, a spark ignited and grew into a blaze.

His hand slid over my blouse. Aching for his fingers, my nipples tightened. I'd never felt this kind of burning desire before. My body was on fire.

As his fingers stroked my cleavage along the ridge of my bra, his moan vibrated down my throat. Our lips seemed unable to stay apart for long.

"I'm burning for you," he rasped.

Unbuttoning my shirt, he almost ripped it open. All the while, his eyes held mine, turning me into a blubbering mess.

I wouldn't have been able to move if I'd tried. I wanted him to ravage me and cause pain, pleasure, and everything in between—the whole spectrum of passion. I sensed there was more than just that one simple release that only my fingers had ever managed.

My shirt slunk off, revealing my new silky camisole. His eyes darkened with lust as he smothered my breasts with his hands. The straps dropped, and his fingers slid over my nipples, making them throb. He lifted my arms and removed my camisole and then unclasped my bra. My heavy breasts fell into his hands.

"My God, you're beautiful." He sounded tormented.

Sucking my nipple, he let out a staggered breath. The sensation of his teeth teasing my flesh sent a lightning bolt between my legs. He lifted my skirt, and I parted my legs to release the ache.

The heat of his body burned through me. It was passion like I could never have imagined. Sliding over my thighs, his fingers stroked my throbbing sex through my lace panties, which were virtually stuck to me.

His breath hitched. "I want to devour you."

He hooked a finger under my panties. A pulsating ache, too much to bear took possession. His finger rotated over my clit gently.

"You're so wet." His voice was soft and caressing, like his finger.

After he helped me wiggle out of my panties, he buried his head between my legs.

When the tip of his tongue landed on my clit, I flinched from sensitivity. As he licked, I clenched and released at the same time, succumbing to waves of spasms. His subtle groans were muffled by my pussy. He seemed to be as hot and bothered as I was.

His hands gripped my ass as I trembled through an orgasm. He drank everything that poured out of me.

The orgasm grew and grew. An agonized moan left my lips. He continued to devour me, tormenting and teasing me as I clawed into his shoulders. It was a time-stretching climb to the fall. When his tongue fucked me, entering a place that only my fingers had ever explored, I shuddered and gasped, drowning in a cascade of stars.

He wiped his lips with the back of his hand. "You're extremely tight."

"Is that a problem?" I murmured, relaxing my toes.

He caressed my breasts again and kissed me. I could taste myself, which instead of repelling me made my senses ping with a force so primal I gyrated my pelvis as though to tease him in—encouragement that he didn't need, going by his jagged breathing.

I wanted to see him naked and feel his hard cock and for him to take me over that forbidden edge.

For all I knew, Blake was a charmer who fucked unsuspecting young girls. A wolf in sheep's clothing. *A sexy fucking wolf, at that.*

He sat back and watched me. His gaze inflamed me as a cocktail of saliva and cum slithered down my thigh.

"I want to be inside you. To feel you," he said, his voice tense as though hijacked by urgency.

"I'm on the pill." I smiled meekly. "It's made me put on weight, I'm afraid."

"You're perfect. Your curves are fucking sexy." I liked hearing that, although I knew it already by the lust in his hooded eyes.

"I've had a blood test," he said.

He took me into his arms again, and I melted. How could I not? The heat radiating off him drew me in with talismanic force. It was as though my body had become one mass of trembling, sticky flesh.

"I'd like to..." I murmured softly. "It's just that..."

He gave me a moment, but I remained tongue-tied.

"You were saying?"

"I guess I can't stop thinking about what you said earlier—that you don't sleep with women, that you only fuck them..." I took a breath. "Am

I to be a one-night stand?" I untangled myself from his arms, so that I could think straight.

"I probably couldn't stop at one time with you." He paused. "I can't promise that it will develop into anything. I will, however, give you everything your heart desires in the time that we share. All I ask is that you don't talk to anyone about this or expect me to be a normal boyfriend. I don't do normal. And..."

"And what?"

"You don't fuck other men."

A shocked laugh tickled my throat. "I'm hardly going to start whoring myself just because I've given myself so easily to you."

He remained silent.

Does he agree that I'll be giving myself easily?

I wondered if I would be consumed by need and emotion.

I buttoned up my shirt without my bra, I picked up my smalls, and placed them in my bag.

"Are you leaving?" His brow lowered.

When I stood, my legs wobbled as I wriggled back into my skirt.

He took my hand. "I'd do anything for you to stay, Penelope."

"I don't want you to buy me."

Blake took me by the hand and remained quiet. "I don't know what else to say. Your taste has already become an addiction."

"It's just sex, then?"

He nodded. "It is. But you're smart. I need brains to get hard." His mouth tipped up at one end. "Sorry if that's coarse."

The mention of his hard cock made my pussy pulsate again. I almost heard it groan, *"Let him fuck you."*

We remained locked in each other's gaze, his hand in mine, and then I fell into his big arms again.

THIRTEEN

BLAKE

SEEING HER ON THE BED, those big beautiful eyes following me as I removed my clothes, affected me more than I could have imagined. My heart hadn't stopped pounding since my hands had smoothed over her curves. I'd fucked a lot of women in my life, but this was something else. Her flavor was indescribable and addictive.

I removed my briefs, and her eyes widened.

I lowered myself onto the bed—a place that no woman had ever been in. Not even close. I'd always opted for hotel rooms.

My fingers were addicted to her silky skin, and those sexy contours. "You're so soft."

A sigh exited her parted lips, capturing the very essence of sensuality. I palmed her nipples, and my lips lowered for another taste. Her full breasts brushed against my cheek. I imagined rubbing my dick against them.

I touched her clit, which was inflamed. Her pelvis rose toward me. Like every inch of my flesh, my cock ached, springing up like steel against my navel.

I entered her with my finger. "How is that?" I asked barely able to think, let alone speak.

"It's nice." Her breathy tone rippled through me.

She had the flexibility of a dancer, and her juicy pink opening made my blood run hot. The need to fuck her hard and deep made my head spin. I was drunk on lust.

My focus shifted from her heavy-lidded expression to her dripping pink cunt. I lowered myself, shifting my weight onto my arms.

Her hands ran up and down my bicep. "You're very strong. You've got bigger muscles than I imagined." Her sweet voice made my spirit sing.

"I work out a little. Can't say I'm a fan." I enjoyed how her hands felt on my body—a powerful motivation to return to weights just to please beautiful Penelope.

Soft as silk, her inner thigh puckered from my touch. The head of my dick entered, and she trembled. "Are you okay?" I asked.

"Yes."

"Do you want me to enter you?" I was going to say "fuck you," but it seemed profane. How unlike me to think that. Another first.

She took my cock into her little hand and stroked it.

"Direct it in," I stammered.

"You're really big."

"That's something I can't do anything about that." I hissed behind my teeth as she pulled at it as though going on a journey of discovery. "If you keep doing that, I'll come."

She smiled up at me, and that was just as arousing, with those pink cheeks and ruby lips.

I knew then and there I wouldn't come out of this in one piece.

Seeing my cock in her delicate hand nearly tipped me over the edge. She placed it at the entrance of her wet cunt and pushed her pelvis forward. I had to remind myself to breathe. Her hot, sticky muscles squeezed so tightly I groaned.

"It's not going to fit," she said.

"We'll take it slowly," I whispered.

"You sound like you're in pain."

"I'm painfully aroused," I replied.

As I pushed in a little deeper, her wince made me stop. "Are you okay? Do you wish me to stop?"

God, I hope not.

"I'm good. I'd like to you continue."

I started to think of anything but her beautiful soft, chocolate eyes or those big firm natural tits. I entered gradually. There was a fight ahead. Guarding innocence, her hymen pushed against the head of my dick. Trying to repel me.

Fat fucking chance of that happening.

I had to push a little harder.

When she shuddered and exhaled a moan, I stopped.

"It hurts a little."

"Do you want me to continue?" I asked.

She nodded.

I entered a little deeper, and her legs opened wider to accommodate me. I finally made it through and withdrew. She seemed a little more relaxed, so that each time I penetrated, our rhythm increased.

I took to her mouth with the same hunger as my cock took to her cunt, and the deeper I fucked her the stronger she moaned.

"Are you okay?" I asked.

"Uh-huh." She clasped my ass and pushed me in deeper. A rush of blood engulfed me, followed by a climax like I'd never experienced. My lack of staying power was a first, too, as I normally fucked long and hard.

Panting, I dropped to her side and held her close. When my breath returned, I said, "I came too quickly. I've never experienced that before."

She studied me as if I'd revealed a big secret.

I stroked her cheek. "Are you okay?"

"It hurt initially, but it felt nice too."

"Thank you." I smiled. She went to move but I kept her still. I needed to feel her body against mine, and something as basic as her heartbeat in rhythm with mine felt good.

"Should I go?"

I stroked her hair. "No, please stay."

"But..." I placed my finger on her lips.

Another first.

The ghosts would have to stay away. I knew they were close and that I would have to protect her from them, but for now, my body ached for hers. And I'd only just whet my appetite.

FOURTEEN

PENELOPE

I WOKE AGAINST HIS warm body and felt his hard dick twitching against my ass. His soft breath caressed my ear while his lips rested on my neck.

"Good morning," he said.

The room was dark, with only a streak of light sneaking through the velvet drapes. Since it was Sunday, I didn't have to hurry, which was nice because I was ready for more lovemaking. Although a little sore, my pussy swelled as Blake rubbed himself against me.

I turned around, and our mouths met. As I drifted off into pure lust, savoring his warm, pillowy lips, I wondered why Blake had broken his golden rule and slept with me.

I fell into his strong arms, and we devoured each other's lips. His hands smothered my breasts, my nipples erect and crying for his mouth as he licked and provoked them with his teeth. I parted my legs as my clit pulsated, thirsting for his touch.

"You're beautiful," he said.

Although I'd lost count of how many times he'd said that, my spirit soared.

He placed his head between my legs. Imagining that I might be a little on the nose, I tensed. Blake held me close. If anything, his cock hardened. When his tongue touched my sensitive clit, I exhaled a deep breath and surrendered.

He licked me so exquisitely it almost hurt. Determined to make me see stars, his tonguing was relentless until my legs tensed, and a powerful release flooded me.

I laid my head against his hard chest as I regained my senses.

I touched his velvety hard penis, acquainting myself with it. Just feeling it made me throb with need.

Blake gently touched my hand. "I'm really sensitive at the moment." His deep drawl traveled straight to my core. "I need to be inside you."

Aching for him, I parted my thighs.

As he entered, the stretch burned, sending shuddering heat through me—nothing but delicious pain. I arched my back and pushed him in as far as possible. The friction from his ravaging cock made my toes curl. Drowned in a golden flood of pure bliss, I gripped his ass.

His lips ate mine, our tongues tangled, and his hands fondled my breasts while he ravished me. The friction was too much to bear, threatening to overwhelm me.

"I need you to come," he rasped.

Rocking my pelvis, I released my clenching muscles, and a rainbow of color rained down on me.

His head fell back, and he groaned. Trembling in my arms, he seemed in agony. Such was the intensity of his release that I felt the veins of his cock pulsate, as he shot deep inside of me.

After it was all over, we held each other, and our panting slowly eased.

"Oh my God," was all I could say.

Blake remained speechless. Enough had been said. His lips couldn't stop devouring me. His fingers couldn't stay away. He smelled of me, and I was certain I smelled of him.

We had a shower together, and we became steamier than the hot water gushing over us. Blake stood behind me and pressed himself against me. His dick, which was rarely limp, sprang against my ass, and as he slid it between my thighs, I encouraged him from behind. His strong body holding me, grasping my tits, and the dirty little whispers coming from that normally cultivated tongue set off an even wilder orgasm.

After I dressed, I sat in his lounge room. Drunk on Blake, I hadn't noticed anything but his eyes and body the night before.

"It looks like an antique shop. There's so much to see," I said, lounging back on the leather sofa.

"You don't feel comfortable?" he asked, pacing about looking for something.

He seemed a little agitated suddenly. His sudden mood shift jolted me back to earth.

"On the contrary. It's really gorgeous in here. Did you decorate it yourself?" I touched a figurine of a dancer.

"When I see something I like, I buy it. With time, the collection grows."

"That sounds organic. I prefer it that way. It gives one an insight into a person, visiting their home."

He remained quiet and sipped his coffee.

I studied the red walls crowded with art, all quality pieces that had I not been hazy with emotion, I would have studied them closer.

Despite his quiet manner, I persisted with the light talk. "You've got amazing taste in art. Do you have an advisor?" I'd just let this man fuck me mindlessly, and I had a right to know something about him.

Don't I?

"No. I know what I like." His eyes plowed into me as though we were talking about human attraction. That intense gaze was the same as when his cock was inside of me, making me gulp.

"You seem to place a lot of importance on beauty, don't you?"

"It's everything, isn't it?" His lips curled ever so slightly on one side. A smile would have cracked his face.

"Beauty is everything if one can afford it," I returned, soberly.

"Fair point." He finished his coffee and set the cup down on an antique table. "Life's too short to be surrounded by ugliness."

"But it's in the eye of the beholder. Some people find old industrial landscapes beautiful and detest the classics. They find them too staid and old-fashioned."

"Great art is never dated. That said, we all have strange little desires that don't always match common taste."

I strolled around the room to study the art a little closer, even though my emotions raced. I wanted him to remind me how addicted he was to my body. His sudden distance felt icy and jarring.

"What did you mean the other night when you implied that your life hadn't always been easy?" I asked.

FIFTEEN

BLAKE

PENELOPE HAD DONE something to me. Even the way she ate her muffin, made my cock hard. We'd fucked all night and morning. Now it was time to part ways. I didn't do small talk the morning after. If anything, I needed space. That was how it should've been. But my head and body were at war.

After gulping down my second cup of coffee, I took a deep breath. My past wasn't a subject I wished to explore. It was dead and buried, even if my overactive subconscious disagreed.

"I started off poor, and then, in a stroke of luck, I became rich."

"Where were you born? That's if you don't mind me asking."

I leaned against the marble-columned fireplace. "I'm from Yorkshire. I grew up close to the moors."

Her face lit up. "Oh my... I'd love to visit the moors. I did one year of English lit and read *Wuthering Heights*. That book really had an impact on me. Are the moors as ruggedly beautiful as described in that book?"

"They are grim and alluring at the same time. The wind soars, and the storms can be deadly. It's filled with bogs that, if one doesn't watch one's step, can swallow a person up." I paused for a response, but Penelope seemed to hang off every word I uttered. "I also read that book. The author captured it well. Raven Abbey, an estate where I grew up, was not far from the Brontës' home."

"Oh, that's so romantic." Her enthusiasm bit contagiously. A tinge of nostalgia flushed through me.

"From the comfort of an armchair, nature in all its ruggedness radiates a powerful appeal. However, nature can also be unmerciful and cruel."

"That's bleak."

"*Bleak* aptly describes my childhood home."

"You don't miss it, then?"

I shook my head decisively. "I like the city."

"I've never been out of the city. I crave nature. The woods and the stories. The folklore."

"That doesn't surprise me," I replied coolly.

She looked at me and frowned. "Why do I get this feeling I'm holding you up?"

"I've got a busy day ahead." Although I kept it cool, I still indulged myself by watching her natural sway of the hips as she walked to her bag. My body burned for her again.

"I'll get Patrick to drive you home."

"No need. I can ride the tube," she said abrasively.

I admired her strength. No teary tirades but a tough wall of reserve that I recognized in myself.

I sensed that we had a few things in common. Sexually, we were tigers. Unlike the nymphomaniacal way women selling themselves behaved in bed, Penelope's natural sensuality had taken me somewhere I'd never been before. The man I pretended to be struggled because I couldn't stop thinking about her taste, her curves, her scent, and the way she felt with my cock buried deep inside of her.

After calling Patrick, I said, "He's on his way."

I held my distance because with one whiff of Penelope, I would have ripped off that silk shirt and devoured her again. Instead I maintained that reserved persona I'd mastered over the years.

She remained silent, and her tension cut into me. I wanted her to leave so that I could regain my composure. I'd made it a rule never to go beyond one night. But with Penelope, there had to be more.

But will I come out in one piece?

I walked her to the door, and seeing Patrick waiting by the car, I kissed her on the cheek.

"Bye, then," she said coldly and rushed off with her head bowed while I stood there and watched.

Her scent remained with me as I returned to the empty room, which suddenly had transformed into a room devoid of Penelope.

Fuck. Fuck. Fuck.

I picked up a pillow and smothered my face and cried out. This was not meant to happen. I missed her already.

SIXTEEN

PENELOPE

I SAT IN THAT BENTLEY, which radiated the smell of leather. Confusion suddenly swept through me, and a small panic attack followed. I didn't want Patrick to know where I lived.

We ended up heading to Soho on the pretext that I lived there, which was half-true. I sent a quick text to Sheldon to warn him.

As I sat in the Bentley, Blake's scent seemed to emanate from my pores. My vagina throbbed. We'd fucked three times that morning.

But then it all went weirdly flat. From high to low in an instant.

There Blake stood, detached. He didn't even look at me. He planted a kiss on my cheek and then almost pushed me out the door. My heart had shriveled into a tight ball. I wondered if I'd ever see him again.

Patrick pulled up at Sheldon's double-story home. Although it irked me to be so false, pride still flushed through me.

I let myself in and found Sheldon frying bacon and eggs.

"Babes." Sheldon's happy face contrasted sharply to my sagging spirit.

"Hey. I hope you don't mind me coming in like this."

"*Mia casa, tua casa.*" He giggled.

I hugged him, and without warning, tears erupted.

"Oh, Penny, what's happened?" He looked worried. "Let me guess… Blake Sinclair."

Falling onto the stool at the island, I nodded.

He poured me a cup of coffee and passed it to me. "I suppose you didn't spend the night talking?"

Shaking my head, I smiled sadly, and a tear splashed on my cheek. "Although we did talk a lot. He's so worldly." I shook my head. "Oh my God."

"He's all man?"

I nodded with a long sigh. "Yeah. Irresistibly so."

"You got together?" His mouth stretched into a tight smile. "Only if you want to talk about it."

"I did. And I do want to talk about it." I shook my head.

"That good?" He tilted his head.

"It was amazing. I experienced sensations I would never have thought possible."

"Multiples?" He raised an eyebrow.

"You're not kidding. And he was so…" I held my hands apart.

"Oh God." His brows gathered. "He's got a big dick too. Yum."

Yum, all right. The thought of it made my palate drip in the same way a chocolate cake would.

Sheldon buttered some toast. "Why are you sad then?"

"He was so cold this morning. He virtually pushed me out the door, as though he was scared somebody would find me there."

"Does he live alone?" he asked, placing fried egg, bacon and tomatoes onto a plate.

"He's got staff. But they weren't around. He also admitted to me that he didn't sleep with women. Only fucked them."

Sheldon looked up at me wide-eyed. "He said that? Shit, that's kind of sexy in a mysterious way. And now you're wondering if it was just a one-night stand, I suppose."

I nodded. "It didn't feel that way this morning when we were in bed." I looked up at Sheldon and smiled coyly. As close as we were, I wasn't ready to describe how frighteningly pleasurable having Blake Sinclair inside of me felt.

"Maybe he's just awkward the next day. No alcohol to free the tongue. It's not unusual after the first night."

"Oh." My heart sang. That might explain it. Maybe I was being needy too soon. "I love having you to talk to, Shelly. I didn't think of it like that." I dipped toast into the egg yolk, and my spirit returned. "Mm... this is so yummy. Thanks, Shelly."

"Sex always boosts my appetite, and not just for cock." His eyebrow arched, and I giggled.

"Speaking of which, you're looking rather chipper today," I said.

"Guess who paid me a midnight visit."

"Mm... in uniform?"

He nodded. "Deliciously so. And he seemed at ease for once. He'd had a few drinks. It was amazing."

"Then perhaps he's starting to relax about his sexuality."

Sheldon shrugged. "One night of wild passionate love with someone I feel hot about is better than one month of being with someone because of some irrational fear of being lonely."

"You'll never need be lonely with me around, Shels," I said, touching his hand.

"You're a sweetie. I'm so glad you're here." He smiled. "Come on. Eat up. And then let's go shopping and have some fun."

I smiled. I thought of the hundred thousand pounds sitting in my account. "I should really house hunt."

"No, you shouldn't. Live here. It's my house. My rich parents gave it to me. Rent-free. That way, you can develop your career."

I sighed. "I'm worried about my mother."

"Rehab?" he asked.

"I've tried. She insists that she's okay."

"Maybe she just likes doing drugs," he said.

I couldn't argue with that sad surmise. "A form of medication, I suspect. I'm not sure what happened to her. I don't even know my father. For all I know, she could've been raped."

Sheldon winced. "You're talented. Beautiful. A heart that's pure."

"Thanks." I smiled sadly. "I do wonder who my dad was. But thinking about the men my mom brought home over the years, I can't imagine he was anyone to make me proud."

"At least she kept you safe."

"She sent me next door to Lilly's." I recalled the numerous times, even as a three-year-old, I'd been cared for by our neighbors. Now it was my turn to look after Lilly.

That was what we did—we looked after each other.

SHOPPING HAD BEEN EXHAUSTING, so I rode a cab for once. He dropped me off at the front of the estate. In the distance, I spied the regulars loitering about in the shadows, among them Jimmy O'Hearn, who I'd grown up with.

Having stopped at the supermarket, I lugged heavy bags of groceries. The grounds at that hour were filled with all manner of comings and goings. People from all walks of life came to buy pills, weed, and heavier stuff. Everything was for sale there.

With a cigarette hanging out of his mouth, Jimmy was attractive in that heavily tattooed bad-boy way. "Hey, come into some cash?" He pointed at my shopping bags.

"I sold some art."

Some drugged-out guy he'd been chatting with stood close and put his arm around me. "I've got some nice sniff."

I shrugged out of his clasp and looked at Jimmy.

"Hey, leave her alone. She's family." Jimmy looked at me with a smirk. "A bit of snob, though."

After I stuck a finger up at Jimmy, the pimply guy reacted. He didn't get the joke. "You're too good for us, are you?"

Jimmy pushed him back. "Lay off her!"

I wore a tight, grateful smile.

He smirked back, which was Jimmy's way of showing some heart. Guys like Jimmy didn't smile. Like most people at the estate, he'd had his share of misery. I'd helped care for his mother, who had cancer, when I was sixteen. With only Jimmy and his younger sister there, I brought over soup or leftovers and helped care for her. After that, whenever Lilly and I came home late, he'd make sure nobody tried to hit on us.

I turned and saw Jimmy holding out his hand. "Here, let me take those for you."

Passing one of my heavier grocery bags, I said, "Thanks. You don't have to."

Ignoring me, he took all my bags. His blue eyes shimmered with warmth. He'd always been keen on me.

"Sorry about Ewen. He's not that bad. He's just a little crazy in the head, like most of the idiots around here."

"I'm used to it, Jimmy," I said.

We trudged up the stairs to the second level, stepping over empty cans and fast-food cartons along the way. The neighbor's rubbish had been picked at by birds and spilled out everywhere, leaving a stench in its wake. It was a world away from the opulence I'd just experienced at Blake's home.

I stood at the door. "Thanks. I appreciate it."

He remained there, looking awkward. "Hey, congrats on selling your art." He nodded, and I could see he wanted to say more, but he was a little shy around me.

"I'm glad you're okay. I was wondering how you were."

"Ah… you know me. I can look after myself."

"You're looking strong," I said.

"I've been working out a bit." His mouth lifted at one end.

"I better go in."

Jimmy knew about my mother's drug habit. "Can I help?" he asked.

I touched his arm. "If I need that, I'll ask. Thanks." I hugged him, and his frame tightened before softening a little.

SEVENTEEN

BLAKE

EVERY SUNDAY, I VISITED Milly, who I considered family even though we weren't blood related. When she became an invalid, I moved her from Yorkshire to my home in Mayfair, and despite the round-the-clock care, she still pined for the country.

Milly became my surrogate mother after I lost my own mother to Sir William, her boss. I sensed there was something between them, but that remained a mystery.

I fell into thinking about Penelope again. Her taste lingered on my lips, and just the thought of being inside of her made my cock hard.

Lost for words, I retreated into myself. Normally after fucking, I'd part with a woman. There was no morning after, so to speak. Ever. Penelope was a first. I'd even fallen asleep holding her, which wasn't part of my plan. I woke to find her soft warmth pressed against me. I'd suddenly discovered what holding someone really felt like. Good. Really good. I'd never longed for that experience until Penelope.

Extricating myself from her body while she slept had been torture, but I had to. I might have harmed her. Reluctantly, I crept off to an adjoining guest room and ended up staring at the ornate ceiling. I couldn't sleep. I just kept feeling her breasts against my chest and hearing her sighs when I fucked her the second time. Her wild spasms had clenched my dick, setting off a mind-blowing orgasm the like of which I'd never experienced before. Penelope's responsiveness left me breathless. By morning, I'd become greedy.

At dawn, I snuck back into the bed.

She fitted into me naturally as though our bodies were made to be one. And then she turned toward me, her beautiful face smiling shyly. I devoured her rosebud lips imagining how they'd feel wrapped around my cock. As I fucked her from behind, I climaxed so violently that Pierce might have mistaken my tormented groans for one of my nightmares.

When I tried calling her, I got her voicemail. I didn't leave a message, because I hated leaving messages unless it was business. I tried once more, but she didn't pick up.

Remembering how Penelope's phone had played up after she'd tried to call her friend when we were driving back to Mayfair, I called Patrick.

He picked up straight away. "Blake."

"I need you to do something for me."

"Sure."

"Buy a cell phone, set it up with a sim card, and deliver it to Penelope. You've got the address where I left her this morning."

"I'm onto it."

"Thanks. And Patrick, let me know when she receives it, and text me the number."

"Will do."

I SLIPPED THROUGH THE RECEPTION area, ran up the stairs, and knocked on Milly's door.

"Come in."

I walked in and found her at the window with a blanket over her knees. Her warm smile always made my day. I went to her, and bending down, I kissed her on the cheek, taking away her signature lavender fragrance.

"Hello, Blake. I almost didn't think you'd make it."

"I got a little delayed. Sorry." I smiled tightly.

"Oh, you haven't anything to apologize for, my boy. It's a miracle that you come so regularly. I'm humbled by your devotion." She smiled.

"I'd always let you know if I wasn't coming." I placed the bag of goodies at her table. "Just some chocolates and magazines."

"Oh, you spoil me." She studied me. "Something's different. Tell me— have you met a woman?"

I contorted my face. "Huh? What gives you that impression?"

"There. You have. You'd normally jump in quickly and deny it. When one's been around as long as me, it's easy to read the signs."

I took a deep breath. There was no hiding anything from Milly.

I sat down to join her at the window seat. In the distance, a large flock of birds formed a V shape and, as always, filled me with wonder.

"What's her name?"

"Penelope," I responded resignedly.

"She must be pretty."

"She's more than pretty. She's beautiful. An artist."

She rubbed her hands together. "That's so romantic. I prefer that to learning that she's from a rich family. They're not to be trusted, those types."

I smiled at her hushed tones.

Her eyes narrowed. She studied me further, like a doctor would, only Milly was checking for the pulse of my soul. "You look a little sad, though."

"Am I that transparent?" I couldn't hide my annoyance, which was more at myself for wearing my heart on my sleeve than at Milly.

"There. You just admitted it." She looked at me with the concerned expression of a mother. "You can't remain a bachelor forever, love."

I moved my head around to release the sudden tension in my neck. "I'm only thirty." I took a deep breath. "And I've got some issues."

"Are you still suffering from those nightmares, my love?" Even though it wasn't my favorite subject, her gentle voice soothed me.

Milly knew about my affliction. She'd experienced it at Raven Abbey. Although it was a large building, my cries had echoed. And the walls had ears.

I nodded slowly.

"A good woman will understand. I'd like to see a picture of her," she said. "Better still, why don't you bring her here?"

"And have you pick her brain and frighten the poor girl?" I grinned at the thought of Milly meeting Penelope, even though I sensed that Milly would like her. Penelope was no fake—a little nervy, but she was genuine.

And there it was again, my body reacting at the thought of her curves and those playful dark eyes. A silent sigh made it all the way to my dick, making my jeans tight. That had been happening all morning. I had to shift about and quickly think of anything but Penelope's full breasts and her sweet clit creaming my tongue.

"Five hundred?" I asked, hoping that a card game would offer me respite from the erotic replay on loop.

"Yes. Of course." Milly's hazel eyes brightened. "Now, this time, don't let me win. I've got a drawer full of ten-pound notes. Be a darling and pull them out. I keep giving them away."

"You must be popular."

"Let's just say that my secret nightly visit with Mr. Gin has suddenly been boosted somewhat."

I shook my head. I should have admonished her, but at ninety, one could allow for a few unhealthy habits. And Milly made a sport of poking her tongue at death.

"As long as you're not still smoking," I said as Milly pointed at the cards in my hand. "Remember what the doctor said."

"It's only three a day. And hell, I feel as strong as an ox. Just, these have failed me, that's all." She tapped her legs.

I LEFT MILLY AND was heading toward my car when my phone pinged. The pang of anticipation faded when I saw that it wasn't Penelope calling. "Patrick."

"I delivered the phone. I just texted the number to you. Only, she wasn't there. The guy that answered the door told me she'd gone home."

"Really?" I asked. "Isn't that where you dropped her this morning? Did she happen to mention that she was staying with a friend?"

"Nope. I dropped her off at the Soho address."

"Okay. Thanks."

I sat back and thought this through. *Why tell me she lives in Soho?* I called her number, but it still went to voicemail. Taking a deep breath, I said, "Penelope, it's Blake. Call me…" I paused. "When you can." I wanted to say "ASAP," but that would have sounded a tad desperate.

EIGHTEEN

PENELOPE

I WAS HOVERING IN THE corridor at college, waiting for a lecture that was about to commence, when Sheldon passed me a package delivered to his home.

Mystified, I opened it and discovered a cellphone with a message from Blake to call him.

I stared up at Sheldon. "It's from Blake."

"That's fancy-schmancy." He studied the phone. "Holy crap, Penny, it's the latest. Top range."

"Mine's broken." The new phone trembled in my hands.

After that cool departure, I'd tried to convince myself that Blake was off the menu—that he'd only used my body. And although I loved every second of it, except for those few moments of pain, I was pissed off at him. If ever I'd needed an embrace and a few sweet whispery words, it had been at that door.

"He must really be into you. He sent his hot driver. Oh wow... how Hollywood."

A smile stole my grimace. "What should I do?"

"Call him, you crazy girl. He's gorgeous."

"But he's so hard to read."

"You don't want to see him again because he's enigmatic? I couldn't think of anything sexier myself."

That set a pulse aching through me. Of course I wanted to see him again, and despite my body screaming for it, my cautious heart had the upper hand.

"Call him." Sheldon nodded. "It's not always up to the guy to do the chasing."

"I don't want to chase anyone."

"Hello... he just gifted you with a one-thousand-pound phone. You're one tough cookie. If that were me, I would've dropped out and become his slave by now."

I laughed. "That's so ridiculous."

"Love makes us do and say crazy shit. That's what makes it so much fun." He kissed me and sashayed off.

If only the situation were so light. I thought of Blake's intensity.

Looking down at the phone as though it were a rare jewel, I drifted into my lecture. As I sat down, the phone pinged.

The lecturer looked over in my direction with daggers in his eyes. The golden rule was that phones be turned off or we'd be expelled from the lecture. I apologized and tucked it away in my bag.

As it was, I didn't pay attention to a word the lecturer uttered.

One hour later, I was shuffling out of class and walking down the hallway with my eyes at my feet when a voice from behind called my name. I turned, and Blake, illuminated by light pouring through a window, stood before me like an apparition.

"I left you a message," he said.

While hordes passed us in the corridor, my heart raced so rapidly I nearly fainted.

"Um... I was in a lecture." His cologne floated up my nose and brought back the feeling of Blake's strong naked body in my arms.

Wearing a loose linen shirt and fitted dark-blue pants, Blake epitomized class. His dark hair was combed back, and his blue eyes were like deep wells that I wanted to splash around in.

"Have you got a moment?" he asked, looking around as a streak of students scurried along.

My legs felt boneless. "Let's just go outside," I suggested, finally finding my voice.

We walked in silence as I led him to an empty bench under my favorite tree.

I waited until we'd sat before saying, "Thanks for the phone."

"Oh, so you do have it?"

"Shelly brought it in this morning."

His gaze lingered. "Why did you say you lived there?"

A part of me bristled at his bossy tone, but then my heart fluttered. He must have cared.

I felt him even though our bodies weren't touching. The electricity between us made the air between us spark.

"I stayed with my mother last night. I flit from one place to another."

He nodded thoughtfully and took my hand, which went from damp and cool to hot and tingly. "I wanted to see you again last night."

"Oh really?" I asked, puzzled. "But at the door, yesterday morning, you were so cold and distant."

"I'm not great in the mornings. And look, I've never seen a woman to the door before at that hour. In broad daylight."

"Really?" I studied him, looking for more, and fell into his large mesmerizing eyes. I felt like Alice going through the looking glass, but instead of bumping into a cast of weirdos, I tumbled into a land of dark, red-hot erotica.

He took my hand. "I've got a meeting to go to. Dinner. Tonight?"

I thought of Lilly. "I'd love to, only I promised a friend I'd be there for her. She's not well at the moment."

"Is that Lilly?"

"Did your friend tell you about her horrible experience?"

He shook his head. "What about after? We could meet."

"I'm staying there through the night. I haven't seen her for a couple of days, and she needs me. We're like sisters."

He nodded. "I understand. Tomorrow night, then?" He caressed my hand. The softness of his touch flooded me with memories of his fingers on my body.

"I'd like that." I smiled, rising from the bench.

He led me behind the tree, where he took me into his arms and kissed me passionately. His ravishing tongue parted my lips and entered, as though it was his dick inside of me.

As his body pressed hard against mine, I felt his erection against my thigh.

The intensity of his desire swept me away. After we unlatched arms reluctantly, an ache swelled between my legs, and my hardened nipples stretched my blouse. His eyes settled on them while his tongue brushed his reddened lips.

Pushing back a stray strand of hair from his perfect forehead, he said, "Penelope, I want to fuck you so badly it hurts."

Voices woke us from our carnal haze, even though his gaze continued to smolder.

He was so gorgeous I wanted to hate him.

"Call me," he said. "Or at least, leave your phone on so I can call you later." He sounded stern, almost bossy.

Having gone to putty, I could handle him acting like an alpha, as long as he made me feel desired. "I will."

Blake paused. "Are you going home now?"

Stirring out of my dream, I took a moment to nod.

He observed me biting into a nail. "Is that a bad idea or something?"

"Um... no.... I mean, I'm good."

His brow lowered. "One day you'll have to tell me where you live."

I smiled meekly.

He kissed the back of my hand and strode off as though he owned the world.

The words "one day" kept repeating themselves in my mind. That meant the future. *Doesn't it?*

A STRANGE FEELING THAT someone was following had me looking over my shoulder. Although I saw nobody, I sprinted over the cracked pavement back to my home. A dread of being at that squalid place sucked my spirit into a black hole.

Jimmy clasped a can of beer while gesticulating and blustering away to a bunch of guys in saggy gym wear.

Cocking his head, he called me over. "Hey Penny."

"Hey. What's up?"

"Some big Russian prick came sniffing around earlier."

"What's this got to do with me?" I asked, growing concerned.

"He wanted to know where Lilly was."

I went cold. Maybe that was why I'd sensed someone following me. They must have known Lilly and I were connected.

"You didn't tell him anything, did you?"

"No fucking way. I told him I'd never heard of her. He smelled of trouble. A big motherfucker."

I let out a jagged breath.

"What's it all about, Penny?" he asked.

"I'm not sure. He's probably fallen for her."

His eyes narrowed as he studied me close, as a detective would. "Well, at least she's got Brent to protect her, because that guy seemed pretty fucking eager to find her."

I touched his arm. "Thanks for the heads-up."

NINETEEN

BLAKE

THE SOMBER PUB MADE one forget it was daytime. My leather shoes squelched along on sticky carpet, and I spotted him straight away. Paunchy with a ruddy complexion, he was the type of man who finished a pint within three gulps.

He stared up at me with bloodshot eyes. Smelling of cigarettes, he nodded a greeting. "You look different in the flesh."

Whether that was a compliment or not, I couldn't say. I supposed he was referring to those poorly written articles, which I detested. But my choice was either to give the odd interview or submit to endless pursuits by some unwashed paparazzo.

"Can I get you another?"

"A pint of stout," he said with a strong Scottish accent.

After the barman placed our drinks on the damp runner, I turned to Barnes. "Do you mind if we sit by a window?"

He studied me. "Sure. I had the feeling you wanted this to be discreet."

I looked over at the tinted window. One could look out but not be seen. *My kind of window.*

Once we'd settled, I said, "Tell me what you've got."

He puffed out a slow breath. "Fox is in thick with an Eastern European gang of smugglers. He's filthy. Only…"

"What?"

"He's got a few powerful men eating out of his palm."

"How's that?" I asked.

"Men with a taste for young girls who'll do anything to keep the cover on that ring. There are drugs involved. But Fox is more into the prostitution side of the business. Specifically, virgins. And the younger they, are the more valuable."

"I bet." I thought about James and his predilection for young women. He drew a line at eighteen, he'd insisted. For all his weaknesses—and he had a few—his moral compass sat somewhere close to mine. He wouldn't have been a friend otherwise.

So why do I feel a sudden pang in my gut?

The thought of anyone having sex with underage girls, and children in general, disgusted me in such a visceral way that it made me want to vomit. And the mere implication of James's involvement in that scene left a bad taste in my mouth.

"How did you manage to find out?"

"I've got my contacts. And your generosity made it easier to get information." He smirked. "Around that scene, money talks louder than anything."

"Who are the obstacles?"

"There's a politician and a couple of cops." Barnes drained his glass, and wiped his mouth with the back of his hand. "There's one girl who managed to escape. She'll need a new identity and cash to set her up somewhere else."

I nodded. "And she'll testify?"

"I think so. That's if they don't get to her before that."

Shaking my head, I said, "That sounds pretty grubby. How old is she?"

"She's seventeen. They kidnapped her from a village in Serbia when she was fourteen. They've had her trapped in a brothel, fucking her brains out, for three years. A week ago, she escaped."

"Where's she hiding?"

"She's at a shelter. The main problem is that the shelter doesn't have the staff. They would need round-the-clock bodyguards."

"That's something I can arrange."

He nodded. "That's a start." He paused. "What are you hoping for?"

"Bring down Dylan Fox. He's a dirty grub."

"To make room for the next dirty grub to rise, you mean?"

I stared him in the eyes. "It's personal."

He studied me. "Okay." He removed a scribbled note from his pocket. "Here's all you need to know. Her name's Tatiana, and there's the shelter's address. You can liaise directly with them. They'll introduce you. Set up a couple of heavies to protect her until the hearing, and hope for the best."

"You don't sound too optimistic?"

"I've seen this shit before. It will take a gutsy—or maybe I should say *foolish*—person to attempt to break these rings. I've seen journalists fall. These brutes corrupt juries. If it were me, I would try to find another Achilles heel. You may blow fifty thousand, or even worse, it could be you that they come after. Make sure your cupboards are clean."

I left a hundred-pound note for the tab.

His face brightened. "Thanks. If there's anything else…"

"I'll let you know," I said.

My tread was slow and heavy as I mulled over the detective's chilling advice. My cupboards were far from clean.

TWENTY

PENELOPE

BLAKE TOUCHED MY HAND under the table. Despite that heated session behind the tree, I sensed he wasn't into public displays of affection. Bubbling under the surface of that cool and restrained expression, I sensed a deep and complex man riddled with contradictions. I knew he was like that not from what he said, given he kept that to a minimum, but by his body language and his eyes, which softened when he stared at me and smoldered when he touched me but then would go remote when he thought I wasn't looking.

"Can I get you another drink?" he asked.

It was the same intimate darkly lit bar as before. We even sat at the same table, tucked away in a quiet corner by a window. Blake needed to sit by a particular window. When I asked why, he shrugged it off as though it were a natural human inclination.

He'd offered to have Patrick pick me up. Being at the estate, I suggested we meet instead. A tense pause followed. I wasn't ready to reveal that part of my life to him. I'd become paranoid that when Blake discovered my background, he'd run away from me.

As his hand settled on my knee, my body tingled.

"What would you like to eat?" he asked.

You.

I bit my lip. "I really don't mind. I'm not that hungry."

"Mayfair, then?"

Although anticipation gushed through me, I nodded as coolly as possible.

I followed him to the shiny Bentley parked on the curb, where Patrick stood in wait.

"Hey, Patrick." I smiled.

He returned a smile. "Nice to see you, Penelope."

This time, I waited for him to open the door and indulged in the novelty of being treated like royalty.

Once we were seated in the car, Blake moved up close and, taking me into his arms, crushed me with affection. His warm lips pecked at my neck. My heart pounded, and just one breath of his scent brought back memories of him inside of me.

We pulled apart and stared into each other's eyes. His eyes had darkened almost to a shade of black. He'd worn that same look when entering me—fragile and lost to the sensation, just like me.

"Have you had anything to eat? I could get Maria to prepare one of her delicious pasta dishes."

"Although that sounds nice, I'm not that hungry at the moment."

He turned to look at me and caressed my arm. "I'm hungry."

I was about to say I didn't mind eating, but something told me he meant something else.

"For you," he added. "I've thought of nothing else. Two nights is too long to wait." He paused and looked at me. "About the other morning..."

I took a deep breath. "I didn't understand it, to be honest. You virtually pushed me out the door."

He wore an apologetic smile. "I'm new to this."

"And so am I." I frowned. "You've never had a woman in your life?"

"I've been with women, of course. But none have stayed over."

A hot thirty-year-old man not having a girlfriend ever? How can that be? The alarm bells should have sounded. Instead, as the heat of his soft palm on my thigh teased, making my legs clamp, it felt like I'd won a prize. At least there wouldn't be a bevy of exes banging down his door.

"But that's kind of peculiar."

He turned to look at me.

My nipples hardened as his gaze started at my eyes and wandered down to my breasts, which were a little pouty due to the fitted blouse. Sheldon had been right about that—sexy clothes made one feel hot.

"This is nice. A little revealing," he said, stroking the fabric of my blouse.

I tilted my head with a questioning frown. "You don't like clothes that show a little flesh? I just thought, given your..."

He brushed my nipples with the back of his hand. "My addiction to your body, you mean?" He undid two buttons of my shirt to the edge of my lacy red bra.

"I like red on you. I'd love to feel you in silk." His voice had a seductive rasp that traveled down to my swollen pussy. He reached into his inner pocket and brought out an envelope. "Here."

"What's this?" I asked, my voice tightening as his finger continued to flutter over my cleavage, puckering the skin and making my nipples ache for his lips.

"Open it. It's a credit card." He adjusted his position and I caught a glimpse of his bulge, sending my hormones into a frenzy.

I shook my head in disbelief.

"There's no limit. Spend it as you want."

"Huh?"

He leaned in and kissed me. "I want you to have beautiful things. I want you to be happy."

"I am happy." I looked down at the card. "This is a little too much, especially after you deposited all that money into my account for my paintings."

He whispered into my ear, "Just let me fuck you. That's all I ask."

I bit into my cheek. "Like a prostitute?"

"A prostitute would never stay at my home, Penelope. Or spend so much time with me or…"

"Or what?"

He squeezed my hand and looked into my eyes. "Let's not do this. Suffice it to say, that wasn't my intention. That's not how I see you."

We arrived at his two-story home, which overlooked a park, in a tree-lined street with expensive cars. On the pavement, there was not a scrap of rubbish in sight.

The credit card remained in my hand. Blake had thrown me a curve ball and he knew it. Responding to my sudden distance, Blake, who seemed to take his cues from me, reverted to introspection.

Patrick opened my door, and I slid out.

Blake opened his arm. "Come."

I moved close, and he placed his arm around my waist gently.

Blake removed his jacket and placed it on a coatrack at the entrance.

"Can I get you a G&T?" he asked, with the formality of a stranger.

"Um… sure."

He pointed at the sofa. "Please make yourself comfortable."

I sat and placed the credit card on the table. When he came back with our drinks in hand, his eyes landed on the card responsible for placing a wedge between us.

Passing me the glass, he said, "Would it make you happier if I took that card away?"

Taking a deep breath, I crossed my legs. "I would prefer not to have it. While I appreciate your generosity, it makes this feel like a professional arrangement."

He sat down close and turned to look at me. "That's not what this is to me. I'm swimming in uncharted waters. I've never had a woman give that part of herself to me. It has affected me in a way that words cannot describe."

I set my glass down and looked for signs of something other than intensity. He brushed his fleshy lips with his tongue, which was like a magnet for mine.

Our lips met. The kiss bordered on being violent. Such was our mutual attraction and passionate desire.

TWENTY-ONE

BLAKE

THE THINGS I WANTED TO do to her required a bed and not the sofa. As I directed her to the bedroom, the promise of feeling her again made my blood run hot.

Penelope's tetchy response to the credit card surprised me, even if, on a deeper level, it made me respect her. Perhaps in many ways I *was* buying her.

For someone who needed control in his life, I was terrified by the fact that Penelope had the upper hand. I'd become unrecognizable, emotionally speaking.

"Slowly," I said, watching her unbutton her blouse. I took a deep breath. My natural voyeur's instinct enjoyed every teasing moment, no matter how much my dick ached to be inside of her.

The skimpy red bra just covered her nipples, and my breathing just got heavier after she let her skirt slink to the ground. She remained before me in a tiny thong. I wanted her to turn and bend over. That would come later, I thought.

I unzipped my trousers and joined her on the bed. Her pose against the silky teal antique spread with her long dark hair splaying made an exquisite image, one I would have paid a fortune to own.

My heart pounded as I parted her warm, soft thighs. Her panties nearly stuck to my fingers.

Caressing her pussy gently as she writhed on the bed, I removed her panties. I wanted her to open her legs and for her to touch her pretty cunt. But dirty little sweet acts were for later. For now, my tongue hankered for a taste.

I unclasped her bra, and her breasts fell into my mouth, her nipples poking my tongue. Stroking my cock, she seemed tentative, unlike professionals, who would have made a meal of it with their plump lips. Jittery and uncertain, that soft little hand moving up and down my veiny shaft, made me creamier than any experienced woman ever could have.

"You've got beautiful breasts," I said, looking at her erect nipples wet from my saliva.

"I could be slimmer."

"You're perfect."

I slithered my finger in between her sticky folds. I hissed behind my teeth at how tight and wet she was. I moved my finger slowly, and Penelope's back arched.

I lowered my face between her legs, and her scent alone made my cock ache. I licked gently, swallowing her juices. Cunnilingus was something I rarely did, but with Penelope, I couldn't get enough of her taste. I craved her clit like I did a cherry in season.

She trembled through a release, and my tongue filled with her cream as my fingers entered, her muscles spasming tightly around it.

"I need to fuck you badly," I said.

I undid my shirt so that our skin touched, and noticed her eyes on my dick while she brushed her tongue over her lips.

I kissed her and entered her deeply, as she flinched in my arms.

"Okay?" I asked, my heart racing and sending a gush of blood into my pelvis.

"Yes." Her breathy response drove me in hard.

Her nails dug into my arms, adding that special sensation of pain. Like a rainbow in a gray sky, pleasure and pain sat well with me.

Taking my weight onto my arms, I breathed in her female scent, which turned my senses inside out.

She was hot and creamy. Her breasts danced against my chest provocatively, and I lost all control. With just a few thrusts, the intensity of the friction erupted into a volcanic release like something I'd never experienced before.

I groaned like a beast in heat and then submitted to a warm shower of sparkling stars.

We fell into each other's arms.

When my breath calmed, I said, "I came too quickly."

"I like how you feel," she said softly, laying her head on my chest as I stroked her silky hair.

It was a nice place to be, calming almost. Different. I hadn't shared that type of naked affection before.

"What are you doing to me?"

She pulled away from me. "What *am* I doing to you?"

I pulled her back into my arms and continued to caress her. "You've gotten under my skin."

"Is that good or bad?" she asked, removing herself from my hold.

I sat up and brushed back my hair. "Good... I think."

Penelope started to say something and stopped herself.

"Enough about me. Tell me... how is it you've never slept with a man?"

"In the art scene, the guys are either gay or annoyingly cocky." She paused to look at me, and a little smile touched her rosebud lips. "I just haven't met anyone I've liked."

I nodded pensively. "That's unusual for a twenty-three-year-old."

She sat up. "How much information have you gathered on me again?"

"Penelope, when you're someone like me, it's important to know who you're allowing into your life."

"Am I in your life? I mean, we only met ten days ago."

I chose my words carefully. "I'd like to explore with you."

"Like traveling, you mean?" Her milky-smooth forehead creased, which brought a smile to my face.

I stroked her arm. "Mm... that too."

"Then what did you mean?"

Penelope didn't like riddles, I'd discovered, which presented another challenge, given that I'd spent my whole life tangled in them. "With us. Sexually."

Her head turned sharply. "You're not into threesomes? Because that's not me."

"I'm not into threesomes, Penelope." I grew serious. "I want you for myself."

"You mean exclusive? Does that mean that you won't go out with other women?"

"I won't need to fuck around. And I expect you not to either."

"Huh?" Her face had gone a feisty shade of pink, which made my dick rise again. "That sounds a little bossy."

"I don't like sharing." I tilted my head.

Her face smoothed, and a little smile touched her pouty lips. "I don't mind sharing food or money... but... not you."

I relaxed into her arms, reminding myself again that this was just an infatuation. *But then, how can one lie with a beautiful woman like Penelope and not become addicted?*

I wondered if it was my money that had attracted her. *What would I seem like without it?* The mirror only ever revealed the actor to me—a man of the world with expensive tastes. Occasionally, on bad days, I caught a glimpse of that wild child from the moors.

Although that unwashed boy still inhabited my soul, I'd spent years cultivating this new me, ridding myself of my northern accent by adopting a posh accent. Sometimes I even heard Sir William's deep timbre exiting my lips.

When it came to sophistication, I'd learned from the best.

TWENTY-TWO

PENELOPE

HAVING NEVER TASTED anything so delicious, I savored the mouthwatering pasta, my tummy receiving it with hungry approval.

While Maria arranged before us plates of the yummiest Italian food I'd ever tasted, I continued to process her initial wide-eyed surprise at meeting me.

When Blake left the room to take a call, she whispered that I was the first woman he'd ever invited into his home during her eight years there.

"Really?" I asked.

Wearing an apron tied around her waist, she placed her hands on her hips. "He's a great man. Generous. He saved me you know."

Blake returned, and she looked up at him with a smile and then continued to move about the kitchen.

She stood at a coffee machine similar to the ones found in cafés. "Coffee?"

He shook his head and looked at me.

"I'm good," I answered. "This pasta's incredible."

Blake regarded Maria warmly. "So, what were you two whispering about?"

I looked up at Maria. Because of the way she'd stopped short when Blake returned, I wasn't sure how to respond.

"I was just telling Penelope that she's the first woman you've ever brought into the kitchen."

Blake sat at the table and poured wine into my glass. He held up the bottle toward Maria. She shook her head, and he continued pouring himself a glass.

He looked at me. "I don't normally entertain."

I smiled tightly at that abridged response.

"When did you move to England?" I asked Maria, who sipped coffee from a tiny cup.

"Nine years ago. I came here for a holiday with my husband, who I escaped from because he always hit me." She looked over at Blake, before continuing, "*Signore* Blake saved me. He gave me a beautiful job, and I have a beautiful life because of him." She came over and kissed him on the cheek.

Blake tapped her hand affectionately, giving me an insight into their closeness. It warmed me to see that, because in the little time I'd spent with Blake, I sensed he was a loner, although not in a sad way. I imagined he had enough power and charm to attract a crowd.

"Maria, please. I think Penelope's heard enough."

She looked at me. "I hope to see you again, *bella*." I was about to remind her of my name, when she added, "If there's anything, just let me know. I'm off to watch *Fast and Furious*." She laughed. "I like big sexy muscle men saving the world. Don't you?"

I giggled. "If I were in trouble, I suppose they'd come in handy."

Blake squeezed my hand and looked at me with a glint of humor in his eyes.

"*Ciao*," said Maria.

"She's great," I said to Blake. "Only she called me 'Bella.'"

"That's 'beautiful' in Italian." His eyes smiled, and he looked the most relaxed I'd ever seen him.

Maybe having me around his domestic life had lifted that shroud he clutched onto. Or perhaps I read too much into it.

Blake leaned back and sipped his wine, watching me polish off the best pasta I'd ever had in my life. I looked up, and he smiled at me. It was so nice. He even looked boyish and sweet. I wanted to squeeze his cheek.

"What?" I smiled back.

He leaned over and brushed my cheek. "You've got a little sauce on your face. I like that you enjoy eating."

"It's hard not to. Maria's an amazing cook. Is this how you eat all the time?"

"Sometimes. Depends." He sat back with wine in hand, again making his answers short on details, like where he liked to eat or what his favorite food was. "Maria has made me healthier. She uses a lot of vegetables and herbs that she's grows here in the back garden."

"Oh really? That's so cool." I studied him. "I'd love to see that sometime. I haven't really seen the whole of this house. It's always night time."

He remained quiet.

I continued anyway. "Did you have a similar home in Yorkshire?"

He shook his head. "No. It was a huge Gothic estate. My mother worked there as a maid, and we lived in the servants' quarters."

"That must have been so interesting. Was it like a castle?"

He nodded.

"Did you have any siblings?"

He shook his head.

"Are your parents still alive?"

Blake moved his head from side to side to stretch his neck, something I'd noticed him doing whenever questions were asked. "No."

I left it there. Too many questions. I was letting a man I hardly knew fuck my brains out and treat me like a princess. For a twenty-three-year-old brought up around the stench of poverty, that in itself should have sufficed. But Blake felt real to me. There was something fragile in that tough exterior that made me want to know him. *All in good time.*

IT TOOK ME A MOMENT to remember where I was. It was so quiet. Smooth silk sheets reminded me that those seemingly endless orgasms had lulled me into sleep. The last thing I recalled was clawing Blake's muscular biceps while he devoured my pussy as he would a delicious treat, and then tormented me with slow, achingly pleasurable thrusts, deep and hard, leaving me breathless.

The raw, bone-melting passion left my tongue hanging out, proverbially speaking. I'd fallen into his arms, and out of his lips, which were carnal one minute and soft the next, had come the words "Thank you." I'd thought that strange but sweet anyhow.

I stared up at the dark etched ceiling with its indistinct swirly patterns. Perhaps Blake had gone to the bathroom, I thought.

Tick tock—the clock marked time as though accenting silence. Wide-awake, I reached over to the lamp at the side of the bed and switched it on. The old French clock with its turning wheels, making time tangible, revealed that it was four o'clock.

I felt abandoned and, despite ample covers, cold. I craved the feeling of Blake's warm body. I wanted to see what he looked like asleep and find out whether he was still beautiful when those perfect eyes were hidden and not smoldering all over mine.

Accustomed to ear-piercing sounds of cars revving, drunks singing, or angry murmurings clinging to the dark of night, I thirsted for noise. And while a bird chirping in the morning might have lifted my spirits, the messy sounds of the city comforted me. They reminded me that I wasn't alone, which was how I felt in that room—isolated, as though that house sat solitary in the world.

I looked up at my paintings. The story had an eerie resemblance to mine. The maiden was adrift in a chaotic city as impenetrable and dangerous as any forest.

Rising out of the bed, I covered my arms. On the armchair, I saw a robe. I tiptoed to it and draped it over my shoulders, smothering myself in its luxurious warmth. Blake's scent emanated from it, and that throb of longing was reignited.

I opened a door and found a walk-in closet. I turned on the light, and my eyes widened. It resembled a men's clothing store. The rack held a long line of jackets in a multitude of textures and colors. I stroked them. Silk ties and shirts of every color—bar outlandish reds or purples, which would never have been Blake—were lined up in racks. Everything neat and in order, placed with precision. I thought of my messy drawers and cupboards. I had a terrible habit of not folding my clothes.

I crept out of the bedroom and noticed doors everywhere. I could almost imagine skeletons in the cupboards or sheeted ghosts whirling past.

Foreign environments brought out the detective in me. I liked to absorb small details which was nothing but curiosity driven by an artistic impulse.

As I turned a knob ever so quietly, the door's squeaky hinges threatened to give me away, so I snuck in without opening it any wider.

Moonlight streamed through the window onto a desk. It was obviously a study—the smell alone told me that. Switching on the green-shaded reading lamp, I soon discovered a room with wall-to-wall shelves filled with books.

The room's warm appeal had me enthralled. I stroked the surfaces and stopped at the leather-topped desk. A leather chair had been positioned by the window, where I imagined Blake looking out in contemplation.

My focus wandered back to the desk, where photos captured my interest. I leaned over to look closer and recognized myself.

Shit.

There were several shots of me asleep. Not naked or salacious in any way, but with my eyes closed and my mouth agape.

I whispered, "What the fuck?"

My hair was spread all over the pillow as I slept, oblivious to the world. I'd never seen photos of myself asleep, and once I got over the horror of my drooling mouth opened wide enough to have swallowed an owl, I became fascinated. I could almost glean a smile. So that was what an afterglow from multiple orgasms looked like.

That romantic moment didn't last because a chill resurfaced. *Twisted and weird* was the only way to describe a man who took snapshots of the woman he'd just fucked while she slept.

Lost in my own world, I jumped when a deep voice intruded on my silence.

"What are you doing here?"

I turned and saw Blake, stark naked with the moonlight bathing his masculine frame. I snapped a mental photo of male perfection. Michelangelo, or more appropriately, given the dark shadows that bathed that mass of muscle, Caravaggio would have rolled in his grave, itching to paint Blake. I know I would have loved to. That idea played out in my subconscious while my body melted at the sight of him. But then I caught the dark anger in his eyes, and my spirit shriveled into a tight ball.

"Um... I came looking for you." He must have noticed my trembling legs, for his face softened a little.

TWENTY-THREE

BLAKE

HER FACE CRUMPLED WITH FEAR. I drew her away from the table, where those photos that I'd taken in a moment of madness lay.

"I knew that was a bad idea," I said quietly.

"What?" she asked, her feisty tone making me flinch.

"Having you stay."

Penelope looked at me as though I'd killed her cat.

"I meant to say..." I adjusted my weight. "I couldn't help myself. You looked so beautiful."

"It's just a little creepy." She moved to the door. "I think I should go."

I followed her back to my bedroom, where she proceeded to remove my robe. I liked seeing her in it and wished I could rewind that last scene so that my hands could slip in and smooth over her warmth. That was inappropriate, considering the sudden tension, but my dick turned to steel as her eyes fired daggers into mine.

"Why would you photograph me like that? Are there others of me in the nude with my legs apart?"

I wish.

I would have paid thousands for photos of her post orgasm, her lips parted, those gorgeous brown eyes shining with guilty desire, with her legs apart and her pretty pussy creamy just after I'd fucked her.

I took a deep breath. "You looked so beautiful asleep that I wanted to capture it. And no, I don't have pornographic shots." I arched an eyebrow. "You would've known. I would have asked for your consent."

She scrambled about, picking up her bra and the torn panties, which I'd ripped off earlier.

"Penelope, it's still dark. Go back to bed. We'll talk about this later."

"Where were you?" she persisted, sitting on the bed.

If only she knew how she twisted me inside out. Seeing her naked robbed me of words. She must have noticed how my dick sat upright against my navel.

"I slept in the other room."

"But why? I don't bite," she said. A tiny smile tried to push its way through.

"You do a little." I grinned.

She rolled her eyes. "Why won't you sleep with me? It feels weird."

"I don't do relationships, Penelope. And I need to sleep alone."

"Then what are we doing?"

"We're fucking." I pushed my hair back almost violently. "I also like talking to you."

"You mentioned you didn't want to share me. Isn't that a relationship?"

"It could be seen as that." I sat down on the bed and took her into my arms.

She let me hold her, and I buried my face in her soft neck.

"Come to bed," I whispered.

She lay down.

Heated from her angry outburst, her lips burned on my mouth, and her body melted into mine.

I turned her around and rubbed my dick against her cool round ass, my finger lubricated by her drenched arousal. I could barely breathe. It was as though I'd discovered her for the first time again. My hand trembled—such was my hunger for her. I entered her with my fingers, and her tight muscles contracted. I needed to be inside her or else I'd come on the spot. I'd never been this hot for a woman before.

I pushed the head of my cock into her pussy, my heart in my mouth. I was no longer in control.

Her firm peach-shaped ass pushed up against my balls. She wanted this as much as I did. Burying her head in the pillow, she muffled her cries. Her butt dancing back and forth encouraged me to continue.

It was way too intense. I felt a pleasure I'd never experienced before.

Blood charged through me. Penelope's orgasm contracted tightly against my dick, tipping me over the edge. A deep groan grew in my chest. I'd never been that vocal during sex. The primal force was so extreme my heart almost leapt out of my ribcage.

I turned her around so that I could see her. With that perfect rosy complexion she looked stunning, especially after sex—another photo I would have loved.

We lay in each other's arms. This time, I remained there. The risk was great, but I couldn't leave her.

I woke at nine o'clock. Although it was Sunday, being a light sleeper, I normally didn't sleep in that late. The bed was empty, which should have seemed normal. But a few hours earlier, I recalled, Penelope cuddled up to me. I sat up and looked about for her clothes. She was gone. A horrible thought gripped at me. *Did I do something in my sleep?*

I wanted her there to share breakfast. I enjoyed seeing her smiling face and chatting about art and finding out more about her.

My call went to voicemail. Frustration brewed. I fought back the urge to toss the phone against the wall.

I texted: *Where are you? Why did you leave?*

The robe that she'd worn was on the chair, and just as I draped it over my shoulders, the phone pinged.

Her text read: *I'm on the tube. I had to leave. This is a bad idea.*

My finger hovered over the letters. I couldn't think of what to say. *We spent two nights together, and now she's running? Am I that fucked up?*

As it was Sunday, I needed to visit Milly.

I picked up the phone. "Morning, Pierce. Just coffee and some juice. Thanks."

I sat on the edge of my bed, which I rarely did, since I moved fast in the mornings. Staring down at my hands, I needed myself back. At least I knew that person—dark, removed, and a sexual deviant who got off on watching a stranger having his cock sucked by his secretary.

A quiet knock at the door roused me. "Come in."

Pierce brought in a tray and set it down on the table by the window.

"Thanks."

"Will that be all?"

"Yes. I won't be around today. Have the night off."

"Very good, sir."

My phone buzzed. I picked it up straightaway, hoping to hear her sweet voice.

"Patrick."

"We have a problem. That girl, Tatiana, that you asked me to keep an eye on."

"Right?"

"She left the shelter last night and didn't return."

"What happened to the guards that were meant to be watching over her?"

"Can't say. They're not around to ask."

"Okay."

I closed the call, scrolled down my list, and pressed on Peter Barnes's number.

I pictured Fox's sinister grin. Seeing him at the Cherry Orchard had made our history resurface. He'd always vowed to get revenge for losing his inheritance to me.

What game is he playing?

Knowing what he was capable of, I had to get to Fox. Either that or leave the country, and that wasn't going to happen.

TWENTY-FOUR

PENELOPE

"WHAT DID HE SAY?" I asked about the Russian man who'd arrived at Lilly's doorstep.

"He wants me to be his girlfriend." She shook her head. "He's so ugly and fucking savage. How did he find me?"

My phone pinged.

"Get that if you like," said Lilly.

It was Blake again. It read, *"Can we meet?"*

Short and sweet, as usual, no *"I'm missing you"* or *"Let's try to see where this goes."*

I let out a sigh.

"Let me guess. Tall, dark, and filthy?" Lilly cocked her head. "Speaking of which—although he's not dark—Blake mentioned you, but just in passing, because he's not the gossipy type. Far from it." I rolled my eyes at how abridged Blake's conversations could be. "According to him, James keeps asking after you."

"Really?" Her face lit up.

"He's gorgeous, and he's into you."

"And end up miserable just like you are right now?"

I knitted my fingers. "I can't just be his sex thing."

"But you stayed at his house. From what you've described, that's not normal for him. If he was using you, he'd arrange to meet you in a hotel. Or a dirty weekend away." She smiled. "That sounds kind of hot."

It did. "Only we'd have to get suites with single beds."

Her forehead creased. "Huh?"

"He can't sleep with me, although he did for an hour or so the other morning."

"Then, he's trying."

"He nearly squeezed the life out of me."

"That's sweet," she said.

"I mean really tight, to the point where I couldn't breathe."

"Holy shit. What's happening to us? We're surrounded by fucking psychos."

I had to laugh at that.

"Tell me about James, then," she said.

"That's all I know."

"But has Blake told you whether he's a player."

"Lilly, you met him at a place where men buy virgins."

"Blake was there, too," Lilly said.

"Yes... but he insists he left."

She shrugged.

"And I'm finished with him." My voice trembled as I fought back tears.

"Why?"

"Because he doesn't do relationships. I want to get out before my heart breaks. I've seen what being a booty call has done to Shelly. It's broken him."

She nodded thoughtfully. "Should I call the police?"

That jolted me. "I'm not sure." I thought of Blake. He would know what to do. *Any excuse to call him*, my heart insisted. "Leave it up to me. I'll think of something. Now, girlfriend, you're getting off that fucking couch, and we're going shopping. And then we'll check out listings for shops on the net. You're going to open that salon."

Lilly lifted her slim frame up. I couldn't believe how frail she looked.

"First, we're going to OD on calories. Greasy french fries, a hamburger, followed by a big muddy chocolate cake, washed down with a few glasses of wine."

"That sounds like fun," Lilly replied, allowing me to lead her into the bathroom.

"Have a shower, and I'll get some clothes ready. Okay?"

She smiled, returning to her former bubbly self, which was a relief, because I needed her positivity.

After I'd arranged her clothes, I pressed on Blake's number, and chose not to text. I craved his voice.

"Penelope." He picked up within a breath.

His deep sexy voice brought back the memory of his touch, and in a flash, I became mindless. "I..."

"Can we meet?" he asked.

"Um... this is about Lilly."

"Then we should meet. It's best to be discreet."

I gripped my phone. "Okay."

"When can we meet?"

The urgency in his tone touched me deeply. "I'm having lunch with Lilly, and then we're shopping. Perhaps later?"

"How's six o'clock? Can I get Patrick to pick you up?"

"No. I'll meet you at Piccadilly. At the same bar."

"I look forward to it. And, Penelope..."

"Yes," I said.

"It's nice to hear your voice."

"Okay, then. Um... till then." I waited. *Can he hear my heart pounding?* "Are you still there?"

"Yes. I like hearing your breath."

I bit my lip hard to override the ache in my core, which was deep and smoldering like Blake.

"See you then." I ended the call and sat on the bed waiting for my heart to steady.

WE VIRTUALLY SKIPPED ALONG. Shopping had revived Lilly. For me, it wasn't just the pretty silk dress I spent a week's food money on, but the thought of seeing Blake later that day.

"Let's have a coffee." Lilly led me into a trendy café.

We sat up at the bench by the window and made our orders.

"This has been so much fun." Lilly touched my hand. "Thanks."

"I'm just happy that you're feeling better."

"I am. But…" Lilly played with a coaster. "What am I going to do about Alex, the Russian?"

"You can stay with me if you like."

"And Brent? What do I tell him?"

"Let me talk to Blake."

"I thought you were about to leave him." Clearing space for the waiter to set down our order, she smiled at him.

"I am." I stared down at my fingers.

"Why? I mean, he's filthy rich, gorgeous, and into you."

"Why won't you go out with James?" I asked, tilting my head.

Wearing a guilty smile, she bit her lip.

"You have?"

Nodding, she poured two sachets of sugar into her cup.

"You didn't tell me," I said.

"I haven't seen you in two days. We went out last night."

"Then why did I find you looking so glum?"

"Because of that fucking savage Alex. It's freaking me out."

I touched her hand. "Don't worry, we'll figure this out." Shifting the focus back to romance, I asked, "So did you and James…?"

"Fuck?" she asked.

I nodded.

"No. He wanted me to go back to his house. But I caught a cab home instead."

"Why?"

"Because I feel really fucked-up about my body. And I'm still healing down there." She cocked her head toward her groin.

"Shit. It's been over a week, Lil."

"There's no damage, as such. I'm scared. It was so fucking painful."

"It's not when you're aroused." My face heated at that admission.

"Mm... I have to admit I did get a bit throbby when James kissed me and played with my breasts."

"There... you see? You're going to come good." I wiggled my eyebrows at that double entendre.

She giggled. Sipping her coffee, Lilly looked up at me. "Apart from him not wanting a relationship, what's the issue with Blake? I mean, can't you just see what happens?"

"I'm scared I'll get hurt." I paused for a sip of coffee. "I also found images he took of me."

Lilly leaned forward. "Sexy ones?"

I shook my head. "No. I was asleep. He took photos of my face while I slept."

She tipped her head back with her mouth wide open and tongue hanging out.

I laughed. "Almost that bad. I mean, who looks good asleep?"

"Babies." Lilly grimaced. "God, that's kind of weird. But hey, so? I mean, that's hardly a good reason to bail."

I bit my fingernail. "That's not really why I ran. It's more what happened in bed that worried me. And he's so hard to read. He's full of contradictions. One minute he tells me he doesn't do relationships, and then he gives me a credit card with no limit."

"Holy fuck. Take it, Penny. You're young." Her face lit up. "Hey, we could go to Ibiza for a month. Imagine all the fun we could have? I could give that scumbag Alex the slip. Hey... what the heck? I'll pay. I can afford it. Let's do it. I could use a tan."

Although Lilly's exuberance had a contagious bite, the thought of Ibiza pulsating in endless techno, sickeningly sweet alcohol, and randy, pimply guys quickly lost its appeal.

"Maybe." I looked at her seriously. "You don't think what Blake did was strange?"

She shrugged. "It's hardly porn. Maybe he likes the way you look when you sleep."

"He said that." I sighed. "I miss him."

"How long's it been? One minute?"

I laughed. "I've known him for ten days. Shit. It feels longer. He's really intense."

"James isn't. He's kind of geeky in a sexy, rich way."

"I hope you go out with him again."

"He called this morning to see how I was." She studied me earnestly. "Do you think I should call him?"

"Yeah. You bet," I said.

"He'll want to fuck. He's pretty hot to trot."

"Are you into him? Are you attracted? Does he make you...?"

"Creamy?" Lilly said. A slow smile formed, and she nodded.

"Then that's your answer."

"Look at us. Woo-hoo. Hot, rich guys chasing us."

We looked at each other and giggled.

"So do you think I'm being too harsh on Blake?"

"I do. And hell, take that credit card, Penny."

"So we should just keep sleeping separately while I allow him to fuck me senselessly and leave it at that, then?"

She shrugged. "Sounds pretty good to me. You're only twenty-three. Surely you don't want to marry the guy."

Lilly made sense. I just needed to protect my heart, because around Blake, I no longer recognized myself as that strong, determined woman I'd spent my life honing.

TWENTY-FIVE

BLAKE

PENELOPE WAS ALREADY FIFTEEN minutes late. Being one of my pet peeves, her tardiness was something I needed to overlook, along with a few other quirks. We were already on shaky ground, and she had the upper hand. That was never meant to happen.

Just a taste. That was all it took. I'd felt her soft curves on my fingers, and now I was obsessed.

My phone pinged with a text: *Sorry. The tube's broken down. I'm jumping in a cab now. Penny.*

I tapped: *Where are you? We can come and get you?*

She replied: *No need, I'm five mins away. See you soon.*

Five minutes later, she entered the bar, her cheeks rosy from having rushed, and her hair out and a little tangled. My dick jerked. Dressed in a fitted green dress that showed off her sexy body, Penelope had every man's attention. I felt possessive and hated the idea of men's eyes all over her.

As she moved, her breasts bounced slightly. I thought of them falling into my mouth when we fucked. I had to take a deep breath to still the rush of testosterone.

"Hey. Sorry. The damn tube. Again." She fell into the chair.

I looked at the waiter, who came straight over. "What would you like?"

"A G&T, please," she said, looking up at the waiter.

"The same for you, sir?" he asked, staring down at my glass.

I nodded.

After he left us, I asked, "Why didn't you let Patrick pick you up? I'd prefer it."

She studied me. Her dark eyes had that hint of fire that made my heart skip a beat. In bed, with my cock buried deep, it made me want to devour her. But in the light of day, her indomitable spirit had me watching my words. Another first.

"Would you just?" She held my gaze.

I took her hand and stroked her palm gently. Her eyes softened. "Penelope, I wish you hadn't run out the other morning."

The waiter arrived with our drinks. She looked up and thanked him. She waited for him to depart and responded, "I had to."

"Was it the photos?"

"Not exactly." She took a sip. "When you weren't in the bed with me, I felt alone and a little frightened."

"Frightened? That doesn't sound like you."

"I know." She bit her lip.

"You're self-assured. I like that about you. You just don't like be told what to do."

"No, I don't. And you do seem a little bossy."

I grinned. "I have this pathological need for order."

"OCD, you mean?"

"I'm not a fan of labels." I adjusted my position. "But I suppose that might describe me a little."

"I know people have their quirks," said Penelope. "And I kind of like the fact that you're a little bossy. Otherwise, you'd be too perfect, and that's not much fun."

"Does that mean you'll let me take you to dinner?"

She looked down at her drink. "Why won't you sleep with me?"

Here came the therapy session, whether I liked it or not. If it meant tasting her again, I had to remove the straitjacket or at least undo one of the ties. "I'm a somnambulist."

Her head tilted. Frowning, she said, "You sleep walk?"

"Not in that"—I stretched my arms out — "kind of way." I smiled at my attempt at making light of a difficult subject. "I thrash about in bed."

"Nightmares, you mean?"

I nodded. "I can get physical. Hence the somnambulist label. I've had hypnotherapy. All kinds of therapies."

"You're frightened you'll hurt me?" she asked.

"Pretty much." My spine stiffened. I should have ended it there, but as I fell into her dark eyes, I couldn't move.

Her brow contracted. "Have you slept with someone before?"

"It's a long story." I gulped back my drink.

"I've got time." She stared me straight in the face, challenging me. Her dark eyes penetrated so deeply into me that it was no longer my cock that burned.

"If I tell you, will you let me touch you again?" I asked.

She nodded.

"Even if you don't like what you hear?"

"I'm tough."

"You are. Tougher than I could've imagined," I said softly.

"What does that mean?"

Her defensive tone told me I'd have to remain quiet about having her followed, especially now that I knew about that filthy estate.

"Just that you're a woman of strong convictions, and you don't suffer fools."

"Tell me what happened to you, Blake." She set down her glass.

"Another?" I asked.

She nodded, and I beckoned the waiter over.

I squared my shoulders. "When I first moved to London about ten years ago, I met a woman. She was ten years older and married." I paused to choose my words carefully. "Anyway, she was the first woman I'd slept with."

"Really? At twenty? You were a virgin before that?"

I rubbed my neck. *Far from it.* "No. I'd been with other girls, just not slept with them as such."

She looked up and thanked the waiter as he set down the drinks.

I waited a moment before continuing. "The next morning, she was bruised." I gulped back some liquor and looked Penelope straight in the eye. "I hit her in my sleep."

"Oh." Her searching gaze made me want to run.

"If you want to walk out now, I'd understand, even though"—I stroked her hand—"I'd love you to stay."

Reminded just how damaged I was, I drank solemnly, expecting her to walk out.

"Are you on medication?" she asked.

I shook my head. "I've tried sleeping tablets. But I'm prepared to seek help again."

Her silence added to the tension in my neck. "Look, Penelope... I'm not mad or mentally deranged. It's just nightmares that..." My mind yelled, *"Leave now!"* but my heart kept me pinned to that seat. Her eyes shone with sympathy. Apart from Milly, I hadn't experienced that before.

"We've all got our peculiarities, I suppose." She spoke as though trying to convince herself of something.

"Penelope, I'm going to start therapy again."

She nodded slowly, her eyes falling into mine.

Though I was dying to know why she lived in that slum, I figured one of us being cross-examined was enough for the moment.

"What happened to her?" she asked.

"I gave her money. That enabled her to seek a divorce. She hated her husband, who, ironically—according to her—beat her so badly that what I did was nothing in comparison."

"She wanted to continue seeing you?"

I brushed the side of my mouth with my thumb. "Yes. But I put an end to it. We were very different."

"You fell asleep the other morning," she said.

"How was that? I am curious?"

She bit into a nail, making my back stiffen. "You held me tightly." She paused. "I mean really tightly. You don't remember that?"

I shook my head. "Hell." I took a deep breath. "Did I hurt you?"

A decisive shake of her head did little to quell my self-loathing. I couldn't believe I'd fallen asleep. That was never meant to happen.

"Then you understand why?" I touched her hand.

She lifted her lids and looked at me seriously. "Why are you like this?"

"How?"

"Messed up."

Opening out my hands, I said, "I'm not sure."

"You must know."

Oh, Penelope, if only you knew. You would run a fucking mile.

"What now?" I asked.

"Like, right now?" she asked, sitting up, a hint of a smile radiating some much-needed warmth and respite.

"Dinner?"

Her smile grew. "Why not? And hey, I suppose we've only just met, and perhaps with time, I might be able to help. That's if you want to talk."

"Does that mean you'll come back to my place?" I asked, trying to keep my tone cool, despite the flush of warmth showering over me.

AS WE LEFT THE RESTAURANT, I took her hand. She looked up at me and a sweet shy smile touched her lips. Although we were over the kind of formality new lovers exercised, there was still an element of that between us.

Opening up to Penelope had liberated me to some extent. I felt lighter as we rode back to Mayfair. Holding her hand, I asked, "Would you like to come to Bath on the weekend? I need to visit an estate I'm about to acquire."

Her head did a sharp turn. "Really? You want to spend a weekend with me?"

"I'd like that." I took her into my arms and kissed her cheek.

TWENTY-SIX

PENELOPE

BLAKE REMOVED HIS JACKET and came toward me, brushing his lips with his tongue. I melted into the armchair. All night his eyes had been in ravaging mode.

In the car, he'd unclasped my bra and smothered my breasts with his hands, his heavy breath in my ear. I wanted his eyes all over my body and doing things to me that I'd never thought of before.

Our lovemaking had become raw and needy. Maybe Blake wanted to ensure that my body could take it, knowing that I was relatively inexperienced. It could take it all right. Multiple sheet-ripping orgasms had made me insatiable.

His bulge caught my eye as he walked toward me. I shifted in my seat to unstick my panties, which had almost dissolved onto the cushion of the brocade sofa.

He crooked his finger. "Come over here."

I walked toward him, and he gestured. "Remove your dress."

He sat back and unzipped his pants.

I giggled nervously. "You want me to strip?"

"Let me watch you."

I bit my lip. I'd let this man do things to me I couldn't have ever imagined. However, the thought of him seeing me naked with the light on made me tense.

My tummy protruded, and no matter how much I tried to suck it back, it remained stubbornly full. My ass was big, and my tits were bigger than I would have liked. I imagined them becoming woeful pendulums once I aged.

I just couldn't process the idea of being ogled by a debonair, stunning six-foot-two man, whose muscular body was like that of a Greek god.

My eyes remained on his face while my green dress pooled at my feet.

He lowered his pants. His dick pushed hard against his briefs. He removed them, and his cock sprang out. My sex ached, and my mouth watered. I'd never sucked a man's dick before, but as he remained seated, with his cock hard and red-blue from arousal, that was exactly what I craved.

"Remove your bra." His tone had an authoritative bite that normally would have made me stick up my middle finger in defiance. But my body was in command, and I complied.

Driven by dark desire, Blake didn't hide his attraction for my body. His raspy sigh at seeing my breasts naked made me feel beautiful.

"Fondle yourself," he said.

I palmed my nipples and jiggled my breasts, which made me giggle.

"Remove your panties," he continued.

I slipped out of them.

"Lie on the bed."

I lowered myself onto the bed.

"Open your legs. Let me see your cunt."

A swelling ache swept through me. Lying down, I spread my legs.

"Touch yourself."

He stroked his cock as I played with my clit, which was so inflamed and sensitive I flinched.

"Can you see how big my cock is? It's because of you. You're a hot woman, and you have a beautiful cunt."

His voice had that deep, impaling drawl to it.

"Fuck yourself with your finger."

I'd masturbated alone and although I'd orgasmed, it was never as intense as having Blake's sultry gaze burning into me.

He remained seated. I knelt before him. His eyes fell into mine, and he wore a faint smile

"What are you doing, Penelope?"

"I want to suck you."

"Suck my what?"

"Suck your cock," I said, my voice choking from arousal.

He opened his legs a little wider so that I could place myself between him and hold his big erection in my hand. Taking it by the base, I placed the creamy head on my lips. Its stickiness sat on my tongue. I channeled a delicious ice cream and licked away. I looked up and noticed that his eyes were closed and his lips had parted.

"Put it in your mouth. Suck it hard."

Being a novice, I followed his advice.

"Ah… that's nice. You've got a beautiful mouth."

I moved his wide shaft in and out. His length was way too long to fit, and I started to gag. He removed it from my mouth.

Helping me up off my knees, he took me into his arms and walked me to his bed, where he gently lowered me. He parted my thighs and lowered his face between my legs.

He licked and sucked at my clit, making my toes clench. As I arched my back, I nearly swallowed his tongue with my pussy. Cream trickled down my inner thigh, and as he entered me with his tongue, fireworks went off.

Turning me over, he entered me in one hungry thrust, and going so deeply that I cried out. His mouth on my neck, he rasped, "Do you want me to stop?"

"No. I like it this way."

"Good, because I've been thinking of doing this all day. Your beautiful ass against my stomach."

I pushed aside the question of how he came to have so much spare time to think of my ass, even though hearing that made my vagina spasm violently as his thrusts deepened.

"I'm addicted to you," he said, sounding tortured as his cock entered again, the friction so intense that my moans deepened.

We were like animals surrendering to a primal form of lust. The only time I'd been in that pose was for yoga, and it had never felt that good. He'd positioned me on all fours, my tits bouncing up and down in his palms, his mouth biting into my neck as he impaled me. My lips parted as my sighs tangled with his tormented groans, which turned into growls the harder he thrust.

The pain of his driving hardness should have hurt, but it became addictive, and the more I surrendered, the more the heat intensified. Contractions became spasms until I succumbed to a hot gush of bliss that seemed to stretch beyond a climax.

Blake's panting gasps dampened my ear. "Oh... Penelope," spilled out of his groan. And then he released in a spasm as semen shot in so deep it felt like it would drown my brain.

He fell on his back and gasped for air.

Blake seemed out of it for quite some time. I wondered if he might have died. His eyes closed and his wet lips parted, like an animal who'd just feasted to the point of gluttony.

I remained inert as well. *So that's what hard-driving sex feels like.*

We turned to face each other.

He stroked my cheek. "You're beautiful."

"That was pretty full-on."

"You orgasmed, though. I felt you."

I nodded. *I sure did. Unimaginably so.*

"Did I hurt you?" he asked, studying my face.

"No... but it was dirtier than the last time."

He rose from the bed, and as he strode to the sideboard, his ass flexed with each step. Perfectly proportioned, his legs were athletic and long. I imagined him being a fast runner or a long jumper.

He headed to a bottle of Scotch. "Can I offer you a drink?"

"Only water," I said.

He poured me a glass from a crystal decanter and then poured himself a shot of whisky.

Setting the glass by my side, he joined me on the bed.

"You don't like it like that?"

I turned to look at him. "I do. But I also feel like a slut."

His brows squeezed tight. "Oh." His mind ticked away, searching for the right response. "That's not how I see you at all. You're sensuous and raw. You're very, very sexy."

I took a deep breath. "I hope I don't get hurt, that's all."

Blake remained quiet for a moment. "Let's enjoy each other, and see where it goes." He turned to face me. "You know more about me than any other woman I've ever been with."

I sensed that I'd affected him. Either that, or he was a great actor.

"Do you think I'm a slut?"

A subtle smile touched his lips, and I suddenly cringed at how childish I'd sounded.

"I think you're a voluptuous woman who's very fuckable and who I just want to get down and dirty with. It's a natural desire. I'd be bored otherwise."

"Really? You seem to like to talk about art. And we talk about all kinds of things."

"You're smart. That just makes me want to fuck you even more. I don't tolerate stupidity and ignorance in anyone, man or woman. And dumb women don't give me a hard-on."

I gnashed my teeth. "That's a compliment?"

"More than a compliment." He stroked my hair. "The moment I saw you, I knew I had to have you."

"Have me? You mean at that virgin-selling venue?"

"I definitely noticed you there. But it was at the exhibition. I saw you across the room."

"What did you look at first? My tits or my eyes?"

"Your hair."

"Huh?" I hadn't expected that.

"And your ass." He grinned. "You had your back turned to me."

I chuckled dryly. "It's hard to miss, I suppose."

"It's fucking sexy. And I love rubbing against it."

"I'm not into anal sex."

"I don't want to fuck you up the ass. I'm not into that. I like your cunt. It's hot and tight. A perfect fit." He kissed my neck. "You're perfect."

"You're coarser now that I know you."

He sniffed. "Intelligent multi-syllabic words are called for when discussing politics, art, or philosophy. Decorum and proper English is a must when talking to the elderly and in formal encounters. However, we are talking about sex." He cocked his head, which made me smile.

"Why did you pull out of my mouth? Wasn't I doing it properly? I've never had a dick in my mouth before."

He raised an eyebrow, and for some reason, my eyes landed on his cock which had started to thicken again. Blake loved talking about sex, which made two of us, judging by how inflamed I'd become.

"Because I didn't want to drown you in cum. Let's take that a little slower."

"But I come in your mouth," I said.

Blake's lips twitched into a smile. His fingers walked between my legs and parted them almost roughly.

"You're a banquet. Your flavor's exquisite." His eyebrow lifted. "I look forward to feeling your beautiful lips on my cock again. You're a natural, Penelope. It felt too nice. I wanted to come inside of you."

I looked down at his rising dick again. *Oh my...* The burn between my legs pulsed through me. *Didn't we just fuck?*

TWENTY-SEVEN

BLAKE

OPTING FOR SOMEWHERE discreet, I met Peter Barnes at my club.

"This is posh," he said, surveying the room.

I asked, "What would you like?"

He gazed at my glass. "Maybe a single malt. Since you're paying."

I turned toward the waiter, who came immediately. Since it was a Monday, the place was nearly empty, with just a couple of older gents in the corner—regulars—who were lost in conversation.

We sat at my usual table by the window. Ever since Dylan Fox had locked me in cupboards as a boy, I'd developed this manic need to see outside.

"Have you got a trace on the Serbian girl?"

He nodded. "She's back with Fox."

"They're prostituting her again?"

"I'm not sure. But probably." He gestured to the waiter, who set down his drink, which he took to with the thirst of an alcoholic.

"Bring us the bottle," I told the waiter.

I'd met men like Barnes before—freaks of nature, who would put in a hard day's work on a bottle of whisky.

"Do you know where she's staying?"

He nodded. "I've traced her to a flat in Brixton."

"Is she there alone?"

"Not sure. I've seen a few young women come and go. As I have older men." He raised an eyebrow.

"They're working from there, then." I changed the subject. "What have you got on that estate in Southwark?"

"It's filled with lowlifes. Supplies half of London with drugs."

I nodded. My veins froze when I thought of Penelope living there, and it bugged me that she'd kept it a secret from me.

"I need to know more about who a friend of mine lives with."

"I'll need a photo of your girlfriend."

I frowned. "I didn't mention she was that."

He smirked. "I know the signs. You stuttered a little. I could see it in your eyes."

His perceptiveness became him, considering he was a detective, but my body still tensed. I'd always managed to keep my heart hidden.

IF EVER THERE WAS a place to share with a creative friend, it was Bath. With Roman Britain etched all over its cobbled paths and honey-colored walls, that city captivated me.

As we sped along the freeway in my car, I noticed Penelope's fingers grip her seat.

"Am I going too fast?"

"A little." She turned to me wearing a tight smile. "But it's to be expected in James Bond's car. I'm half expecting a seat to eject and pistons to fire bullets." She giggled.

I smiled at her girlish silliness, which always made me lighter.

I turned off at the exit and slowed down as we crossed onto the one-lane road.

Penelope unwound the window. "Mm... country air."

"How long has it been since you left London?"

"I've never left. I haven't been anywhere."

I glanced at her, thinking of her life at that run-down hovel.

As we drove over an ancient cobbled bridge, Penelope effused, "How gorgeous. I love old bridges. Do you mind if I take a photo?"

I slowed down, stopped the car, and glanced at my watch.

"Are we running late?" she asked, holding her phone in camera position.

"It's fine. We've got an hour, and we're twenty minutes away."

She stepped out of the car. "I won't be long—I promise."

That rustic environment suited her. With her hair out, the sun streaked red highlights through her normally dark mane, which against my pillow looked black.

Her smile was wide, like that of a girl at a fairy theme park. She wore a voluminous skirt that on anyone else would have looked like someone's hand-me-down, but Penelope's natural flair and individuality made it work. As she walked, her tits bounced and my cock lengthened—a reminder of her on top with her tits in my face.

My sudden loss of control around Penelope startled me.

She slid back in. "Oh, it's so photogenic with all that clinging ivy."

I started the engine and took off. "This place is nothing but photogenic."

"I want to do a series on bridges with figures of men in suits and historical women in flowing gowns."

"You have a penchant for contradictions."

"Not always. You've only seen the triptych. My earlier works were mainly ethereal figures. I've never really grown out of fairy tales. They were my escape as a young girl and still are when I paint."

"What are you escaping from?" I asked.

She shrugged. "I've always used art as an escape, as an expression of my inner world while giving me a break from the real world."

"But isn't your inner world a mirror of the real world, given that that's all you've ever known?"

"That's the scientific interpretation. I believe the subconscious is filled with symbols and registers with the soul. There's a deep well of memories passed onto us."

"That's a very spiritual interpretation," I replied.

"Art is that for me, although I'm not religious in the conventional sense."

"You're free-spirited and openhearted—qualities that one needs to make great art."

She smiled sadly. "My lecturers are always on my back. I just like to enter a dreamworld and paint. My intellect is nowhere to be found."

"But once you step away from the artwork, the intellect gets involved, doesn't it?"

She nodded. "Of course. But I'm more inclined to react emotionally."

"You're just sensitive. Which is what makes you special." I squeezed her hand. "You don't like conceptual art?"

She scrunched her nose. "Not really. I just like to paint and draw. I went to art college to learn how to mix paints and to study technique. It's overly intellectual. They've threatened to fail me. So far, they haven't. I received a scholarship on the strength of my work, not because of this." She tapped her head.

"You're following the path of the masters, like Michelangelo and Raphael, who were apprentices. You're the most talented person I've ever met, Penelope."

A sad smile touched her lips. "Maybe if I was born in another time."

"Female artists were a rarity in Michelangelo's time. Artemisia Gentileschi, for example, had a hard time."

Her face lit up. "She's someone I've spent a whole semester reading about. I can't believe you know about her."

"I went to university, Penelope."

"Did you study art history?"

"I did one semester on the Renaissance. I've read a lot. And I've traveled to Italy. I have a keen interest in art."

"Is that why you like me?" she asked.

"One of the reasons." I paused to choose my words carefully. "When I discovered you created that enchanting triptych, my yearning to fuck you *rose* considerably."

Penelope laughed. "At least you're a cultured sex maniac."

I stared her in the eye. "I'm not a sex maniac, Penelope. I'm just insatiable around you."

A grin touched those lips that had wrapped themselves around my dick earlier so seductively. "I *am* wondering how many women you've fucked, though."

"I've lost count." I paused for a response, but she remained silent. "Jealousy can't be retrospective. I don't even look at other women." I stroked her warm, curvy thigh. "Let's just say that you're the only woman I've ever wanted to keep seeing."

"What makes me that special?"

"You're a very unique woman. I believe you'll do great things."

After a pause, I heard sniffles. Casting a side-glance, I noticed tears pouring down her cheeks.

I stopped the car.

"Why are we stopping?" Penelope asked.

I removed a tissue from under the console and passed it over to her. "Are you okay?"

"Thank you for believing in me." She looked at me with those big watery eyes.

I held her, like a close friend would. As someone who didn't normally hug, that was new for me.

Noticing her smudged eyeliner, I passed her another tissue. "Here. You might want to fix your makeup."

She pulled down the sunshade and looked into the mirror. "Oh. Shit. Look at me. I'm a mess."

"A beautiful mess."

She dabbed her eyes and then fell into my arms. Her lips were sweet and salty. I'd never been much into kissing, but with Penelope, my lips were sore because they couldn't stay away.

TWENTY-EIGHT

PENELOPE

THAT ANCIENT CITY HAD my creative juices flowing and other bodily fluids, too, thanks to Blake. I took endless photos, including some with Blake as the subject, looking devilishly handsome. It was the most relaxed I'd seen him. He was so patient as I positioned him in front of a jaw-dropping facade chiseled by the Romans. His hair was tousled, and he wore that sultry smirk so well. His eyes twinkled a breathtaking aquamarine after I'd asked him to remove his Mr. Cool shades, and my legs went to jelly.

After grabbing a quick coffee to go—we were running late thanks to my need to gawk at everything—we made a dash for Blake's meeting.

As we drove through the lush grounds of the estate, I sighed at its beauty. The gray-stone mansion was surrounded by a garden of flowers and manicured shrubs that seemed to glow in the sunlight.

After parking the car, we walked up a pebbled path and were met by a flirtatious realtor, who giggled like a child and fluttered her eyelashes shamelessly. Once we'd done our initial introduction, she largely ignored me.

I left them to discuss business and headed down the embankment. The colors were so vivid that when I blurred my eyes, the scenery resembled a Monet painting, especially with the shimmery stream at the bottom of the garden, trickling under an arched bridge.

Blake gestured for me to join them. Dressed in a tan sports jacket, he had sexy rich guy written all over his handsome figure. I could almost smell the hormones pinging off the pretty blonde, who seemed to hang on to his every word.

After she wiggled off, I asked, "Can we look inside without her tagging along?"

Blake grinned. "That's my intention. I'm not super keen on a salesperson at my heels, hyping up the property in my ear."

"Something tells me she'd babble about anything."

He chuckled. "Are you jealous?"

"Maybe."

He took my hand, which meant a lot to me.

I gushed at the heavily ornamented ceilings and the wall of windows that led one's eye to the garden. Persian rugs strewn about gave the place a warm vibe, and I sighed at the staircase, which snaked up to a stained glass window on the landing.

I left Blake and visited the main bedroom upstairs, where I stepped onto the balcony and breathed in the country air.

Blake returned to the bedroom. "Okay. I've seen enough. Let's go."

I almost ran to keep apace. "What's wrong, Blake?"

"We need to go."

"You don't like it out here?" I panted.

"I prefer London," he responded curtly.

"What's not to like? This place is gorgeous."

"I'll buy it and turn it into a hotel, giving Londoners a place to escape for a weekend."

"But it's beautiful. You're not going to gut it?"

"I have a design team who come in and fit it out with the mod cons people demand. I can't charge obscene fees otherwise."

He seemed so cold suddenly. "But you must keep that lovely balcony, the carved ceilings, and the staircase. They're works of art."

He nodded. "Those stay. The kitchen will be renovated and a few walls knocked out here and there."

"Here and there? It's perfect the way it is. Places like this need to be preserved."

"And it will, wherever possible." He placed his hand on my back and moved me along.

I studied him. "I'm sensing something."

"Penelope, too many questions. It's business. Now, let's have lunch, and then I must visit the Cotswolds."

I followed him silently to the car. His brusque tone hurt. It was difficult to believe this was the same man who earlier had asked me to wear a lacy teddy, only to tear it off with his teeth.

Then, there was the awkwardness of the night before. After a slow session of lovemaking followed by a more debauched session, he'd held me while our panting eased and then had gone to sleep elsewhere.

I lay there wide-awake. He'd warned me, and I'd accepted the deal, so I had no right to bicker.

In the middle of the night, blood-chilling cries had me scurrying out of bed. As I placed my ear to the door, I was riddled with indecision. He sounded tormented like he was in real pain, so I snuck into the room and found Blake writhing, his face contorted in agony. Although instinct screamed at me to wake him, I held back, which was wise, because the cries subsided, and within a breath he looked peaceful. Although I'd ached to climb in and hold him, as a mother would a suffering child, I had to creep out.

Blake's sudden dark mood brought that experience flooding back.

"Have I done something wrong?" I asked.

"No. It's just me. It was probably a bad idea bringing you here."

"What?" That issued out of my mouth like a missile.

"I have to visit someone. You can either come with me, and you can sightsee, or you can stay here. I'll pay for an afternoon spa session if you like." He turned to look at me, and his face softened.

"What's at the Cotswolds?"

"There's an old friend who I visit. She looks forward to it, so I can't not go."

"She?"

"She's not a young woman."

"Is she your mother or a family member?" I asked.

His brow contracted. "Milly's an old friend of the family."

I nodded. "I'd like to go with you. That's if you want me to." I paused to think. "Or maybe you'd prefer me to go back on the train to London."

He shook his head. "Of course not." He sighed. "I'd like you to come with me. Only, I'm not big on questions."

"Sure. I get it. We're fuck buddies."

"You're more than that."

He turned and gazed at me with that remote expression of his that hinted at someone in conflict with himself.

One hour later, after Blake decided he wanted me with him, we found ourselves in a picturesque village with rustic cafés and gift shops selling locally crafted products.

After lunch, Blake peered down at his watch.

"You'd best be off, I suppose," I said.

"Are you going to be okay?"

"I'll just head over to that charming pub over there by the duck pond. I'll have a glass of wine and do some sketching." I smiled, liking the sound of that.

He touched my hand and lingered. I sensed he wanted to say something, but I couldn't read him. "Would you like to come and meet Milly?"

I contracted my eyebrows. "Huh? I thought…"

"Come on. I'd like you to meet her. She's like a mother."

"Really? I'd love that. Only why the change of heart?"

"I can't say." He turned to look at me, holding my hand. "Around you, I don't know myself anymore."

Is that good or bad? I was too on edge to ask. I'd already had my fill of questions for one day.

Ten minutes later, we drove into a grand old mansion set in stunning gardens, where people stooped in frames tottered while others were pushed along in wheel chairs.

"Milly's very old?" I asked.

"She's ninety," Blake responded as he pulled into the car park.

He opened the door for me and helped me out, which I could have done quite easily myself, but I'd grown fond of his gentlemanly ways.

We walked up the path hand in hand. I felt like his girlfriend, even if I did wonder whether Blake was atoning for his earlier coldness.

The place resembled more a luxury hotel than a nursing home. I found my eyes drawn in all directions. The floor mosaic, for one, made me gasp with wonder, and the ceiling fresco made my neck ache.

"It's the original," said Blake.

"Really? From the eighteenth century?"

"Seventeenth, I believe," he said, making my desire for him rise again—not that it ever flagged, but I loved the fact that he knew little details like that.

MILLY WAS A SWEET OLD THING. Her face lit up when she saw me, and she looked like she would burst into tears after Blake introduced us.

"Oh, Blake, my boy. She's beautiful."

He went over and hugged her and whispered something.

I remained quiet. Considering how private Blake was, it seemed a privilege just being there.

Blake placed chocolates and magazines on a table.

She smiled sweetly, and pointed at a seat close to her. "Sit here, my lovely, and let me look at you."

I sat by the window with the million-dollar view of rolling hills and glowing green meadows.

"Blake, you didn't tell me about Penelope."

He answered with a faint smile, which was his way of remaining mysterious.

"Should I order tea?" she asked.

I shook my head. "We just had a few cups earlier. I'm fine, thank you."

"So tell me about yourself," she said.

"There's not much to say," I said, looking over at Blake, hoping he'd jump in with how he fell madly in love with me at first sight.

"So how did you meet Blake? And do make it romantic." She looked at me with a gentle smile. "I love romance."

"We met at an art exhibition. Penelope's a very fine artist." Blake's eyes brimmed with pride.

I smiled at him, bathing in his compliment as one would the sun on a fine warm day.

After a little small talk, which didn't give much away about Blake's past, we ended up playing cards and giggling over silly things.

Blake was so heartwarmingly caring around Milly that I wanted to cry and laugh at the same time.

That was when I really fell in love with him.

We'd had one very intense month together. There was so much we didn't know about each other still, and the thought of Blake learning about my life growing up made my heart shrink.

Will he still consider me a rising star?

But Blake didn't do relationships, I had to remind myself. For all I knew, he would tire of me soon.

Blake rose. "I'll be back in a minute." He turned to Milly. "Now, don't you start gossiping."

Her little giggle sounded like a child's. She was so sweet.

After Blake left, she said, "I can't tell you how lovely it is to see Blake with a girl. He's not like all the other boys. He's special. He's delicate, though." She turned almost disturbingly serious. "He was close to my beautiful boy." She drifted off into another dimension, which jarred me.

"Your son?"

She sighed. "Harry was my only child. When he died, my heart broke. I was never the same again."

"Oh. I'm sorry to hear that."

"There's that devil Dylan Fox. Watch him. He's evil. Don't let him go near Blake." She leaned forward and grabbed my hand. "Promise me you'll protect Blake."

My mouth opened, but nothing came out. A flood of questions choked a coherent sentence and kept it from flowing.

Is she telling me that Dylan Fox killed her son and might do the same to Blake?

The shock must have shown, because she added, "I'm sorry, love, to sound so bleak, but you're the only friend Blake's ever brought here. I need to know someone's looking out for my boy." She placed her finger before her mouth. "It's our secret."

Blake strode back in, and a smile instantly chased away my frown.

He sat down and said, "Do you feel like a walk?"

Milly replied, "No. Tell me all about how you met. Make it as romantic as possible. Exaggerate even."

I looked at Blake and smiled.

TWENTY-NINE

BLAKE

I LOUNGED BACK IN my favorite armchair at the club. There was something about that worn leather smell that conjured up images of powerful men making momentous decisions.

"I'm in love," said James.

I'd known James for a long time and he'd never uttered those words before. He'd admitted to being in lust, yes, but not in love.

"That's nice," I said.

He looked at me. "You're not going to ask with whom?"

"Lilly."

He smiled brightly. "We've been together every night this week."

"That's serious."

"I've asked her to the masked ball."

I thought of Penelope, who I'd invited to the ball. Looking stunned, she'd asked, "What will I wear?"

"A gown," I answered. Penelope's somewhat quirky approach to wardrobe, which I generally admired, came to mind, so I suggested a stylist.

Her face scrunched at that suggestion. "Can't I choose my own?"

I acquiesced. She had me agreeing to all kinds of things, even introducing her to Milly, which was out of character for me. But the joy on Milly's face had been worth it, despite Penelope's questions about Raven Abbey on our return.

I looked at James. "Have you seen where they live?"

"No. She doesn't want me to know. I imagine it's in a poor area. I don't care. She's so beautiful and nothing like all the others. Lilly appreciates the smaller things. I'm over self-entitled rich girls, even though the family is on my back to marry well." He raised an eyebrow.

"Marry? I don't think I've ever heard you utter that word without following it with a sneer."

He laughed. "I'm still not hooked on the idea. But I have to admit, Lilly's doing things to me that I'd never thought myself capable of."

I shared that with James. Penelope had taken possession. She'd brought out deep emotions that I'd never experienced before. I'd even agreed to therapy for my nightmares.

"There's an issue," he said. "Lilly is being stalked by that fucker who bought her."

My sources had connected the Russian to Dylan Fox.

"That's an ugly scene, as is the scum running it."

"Dylan Fox," said James. "That's right. You two go way back. I suppose that set up is legal. The oldest profession, as they say."

"They traffic underage girls," I said.

"Then it should be shut down." James shifted in his seat.

"Who told you about the Cherry Orchard?"

He took a while to answer me, which I thought odd. "Tommy told me about it. You remember Tommy? He's the comedian slash bad boy. An earl, no less. But he likes them young and with cherry intact." His eyebrows lifted. "But not that young."

I nodded.

"That Vlad the Impaler had better keep away from Lilly. She's terrorized by him," he added.

"I've got someone keeping an eye on things. That said, it would be prudent to hire a couple of bodyguards. Make sure you source them from a reputable firm." I thought of Tatiana and how she'd mysteriously disappeared from the shelter even with two men guarding her.

James nodded slowly. "Lilly's staying with me."

"That's radical."

"I'm crazy about her. She's so sweet. And she cooks delicious meals. That's a novelty. At home, we always had cooks or dined out, as one does." He grinned. "It's nice seeing her in the kitchen. It's a serious turn-on."

"You need to keep her safe. I'll talk to my man if you like."

"So, you're going all caped crusader?" he asked.

I sniffed. "Even if I wanted to, there aren't any telephone booths left for changing into tights."

He laughed. "You've got the footballer's thighs for it." He finished his drink and looked up at the waiter for a refill. "The ball, then. Next week. Are you taking Penelope?"

"I am."

"Well, well. The society girls will be gutted. Blake Sinclair taken."

I rolled my eyes and shook my head. "That sounds like I'm owned."

"You are somewhat." He smirked. "You get this look whenever Penelope's name is mentioned."

I pulled my head back. "How?"

"You seem happier in general. And your eyes twinkle."

"I didn't realize I was that transparent."

AFTER I LEFT JAMES, Patrick dropped me off at a café to meet Penelope, who insisted on making her own way there. Her stubborn independence played havoc with my need for control.

As it was, she arrived late. With her hair in plaits, she wore a purple velvet skirt over brown boots.

"Hey. I'm sorry," she panted. Her beautiful face had a healthy, rosy glow, reminding me of how she looked after an orgasm.

I pulled out the chair for her.

"I'll abstain from giving you a lecture on how selfish it is to make someone wait."

She leaned in and kissed my lips. "I'm sorry. I'll make up for it." She licked her finger and held it up.

"I'll hold you up to that."

She grinned.

"Have you eaten? Or do you just want coffee?" I glanced down at my watch.

"Are you in a hurry?" she asked.

"I have a few pressing matters to deal with and then…"

She tilted her head. "Then…?"

"I've got an appointment with a therapist." I tensed my shoulders. The thought of a stranger's interrogation twisted a nerve.

"Oh, that's fantastic news." She smiled sadly. "I know it's a difficult thing for you. Thank you."

I smiled faintly and cast my eyes down. Her caring tenderness was like sun in my eyes, even though her softness massaged my soul.

"Do you wish to order something?" I asked.

"Take-away coffee and maybe a sandwich. We're going somewhere, you said."

I beckoned the waiter over and let Penelope make her order. I didn't need anything except perhaps a Scotch, but because it was only two o'clock in the afternoon, I abstained.

We left the café and jumped into the Bentley.

I leaned forward toward Patrick. "Back to Duke Street, where we were earlier."

He nodded, and we drove off.

"Where are we going?" she asked, as my hand stroked her thigh.

"It's a surprise." I grinned.

THIRTY

PENELOPE

WHEN WE PARKED AT a terrace house overlooking the park, I wondered if we were visiting someone.

I waited for Patrick to open my door. He liked doing that. Even if it felt strange stepping out with a tall, burly fellow holding a door open in broad daylight, it always attracted attention.

Blake touched my skirt. "Is this new?"

"Uh-huh. I picked it up at Oxfam."

His brows knitted. "Why are you shopping there? Why don't you take the credit card I offered?"

"You don't like it?"

"It's nice. And you look, as always, unique and beautiful. But I can afford to buy you new clothes. Whatever you desire."

"But new things aren't always as unique as old things."

"That's the beauty of designer clothes—they're one-offs." He brushed my cheek, and his eyes impaled me.

My heart skipped a beat at the thought of making love just like we had the night before. Divinely heavy after shaking through multiple orgasms, I'd fallen into a deep sleep and hadn't even noticed Blake sneaking off.

I hated us sleeping apart. And knowing that he planned to visit a therapist filled me with hope. I only wished he'd open up to me.

I followed him through the filigree iron gate, and we came to a red door with a brass knocker.

Blake opened the door.

"Oh, you live here, too?" I asked.

Making room for me to pass, he remained quiet.

We walked down the hallway and entered a large sunny room with a bay window that overlooked the park. There was a sofa, a coffee table, and Tiffany lamps positioned on empty bookshelves. The mid-tone-blue walls with their white ornamented cornices were bare.

Blake crooked his finger for me to follow. We stepped into a kitchen overlooking a garden brimming with flowers and herbs.

I couldn't imagine why he'd brought me there.

Blake led me by the hand to a room surrounded by windows looking out at the garden.

"How lovely," I said.

"It's yours."

I frowned. "Huh? What do you mean?"

"The house is yours. I bought it for you," he declared, looking pleased.

"You can't be serious?"

He pointed. "This would make a great studio. There's even a sink for washing your paints. The light ..."

"I can't take this," I interrupted, gulping back disbelief, even though I had quickly grown in love with the place. How could I not? It was stunning. The garden. The park views. A studio to die for. "This must have cost you over a million pounds."

"I made that in a couple of days, Penelope." He cocked his beautiful head.

My jaw dropped at that admission. "I'd love to live here. I really would."

He took me into his arms, and I melted into his strong frame. "Then there's no problem."

"Maybe I could pay you rent." I thought about the cash in my account.

I wondered if I could move my mother to this house. But the thought of that sat uncomfortably in my gut. Renting her a flat somewhere close would be the best option so that I could look out for her.

"No rent. It's yours. Please." His chin touched his neck as he peered into my eyes. The sun hit his eyes, making them spellbindingly turquoise.

"Come upstairs."

I followed him up to the second floor and found a large bedroom with a little balcony that overlooked the park. It was so perfect that a tear splashed onto my cheek.

Blake smiled tenderly and held me. "You deserve it. Think of the great art you'll create. And I know where you live."

I pulled away. "What?"

"I know you live at that rundown estate."

"You've had me followed?"

"Not as such. Your friend Lilly's being stalked by a man who has some pretty nasty connections. She's being watched, and you've been spotted there. A little digging revealed that's where you live with your mother."

"A little digging? You know about my mother?" I sank down onto the bed and buried my head in my hands. Although it heartened me to learn that Lilly was being protected, I felt violated.

"A guy's been spotted going in and out. He looks shady."

"That's Frank." I let out a sigh. The knots started to unwind. Too raw to fight it, I surrendered.

Blake sat on the bed, holding my hand. "There's nothing to be ashamed of. My family life wasn't pretty."

I turned sharply to face him. "Tell me. It will make me feel better."

"It's a long shitty story. I'm not ready for that." His eyes wore a hint of fragility.

"You live such a privileged life. How the hell could I admit to coming from that slum?" I looked down at my feet.

"Don't judge a billionaire by his cover. Behind many a success story, there's a junkyard of seedy transactions and hidden scandals."

"Is that what happened to you?"

"Not as such." He opened his hands. "I meant that most people are ashamed of something. And the richer the person is, unless they've been under a rock, the more likely that they have a parent who's addicted to drugs and alcohol, has affairs, or conducts shady deals." He cast me an earnest half grin. "I would never judge you based on your family. I don't subscribe to that form of snobbery." He fixed his gaze on me. "I'm with you because of *you*, Penelope."

I took a deep breath. "My mom's a junkie. She's been shooting up heroin all my life." I couldn't look at him. His pity would have killed me.

Painful silence created distance between us. He lifted my face to meet his. It wasn't sympathy in his eyes but something more profound— recognition and understanding, as though he'd been there himself.

"That's not your fault. You don't have to wear the shame of your mother's habit."

A lump had settled in my throat. I couldn't talk.

"Will you accept my offer of rehab for your mother? Or I should ask, would she accept it?"

I shook my head in disbelief. "We've been seeing each other barely a month, and you buy me a house. And now you're offering to pay for my mom's rehab. Blake…"

His lips drew a tight line. "This is small change." He pointed to the walls. "As is paying for your mother's rehab."

"I don't know what to say." I crumbled with emotion. Tears streamed down my face.

By radiating a calm, nonjudgmental manner, Blake managed to soothe me.

"You'll have to tell me about your life growing up, Blake. It seems hardly fair that you know all about mine."

"I don't know about your father."

"Nor do I." My dryness reflected my lack of emotion on that subject.

He studied me. A line deepened between his dark eyebrows. "I take it you don't know who your father was?"

I shook my head.

"Sometimes that's not a bad thing," he murmured as if to himself.

"Why would you say that?"

"This is a big topic. The father topic. Let's leave that for some other time. And I have a therapy session starting." He glanced down at his gold watch. "I need to go. You can stay, if you like, and think of how you'd like to furnish it."

"No. I'll catch a ride with you. I'm meeting Lilly. We have some shopping to do. Our rich boyfriends have invited us to a ball." I smiled brightly for the first time since stepping into that house, which I'd accepted with open arms, having fallen in love with it.

He placed his arm around my shoulders and drew me in tight. "Something red and not too low in the cleavage area."

"Huh?" I turned to look at him with a glint of mischief. "I thought I might go for the whole slut look. You know, high split, low neckline, no panties." I lifted my eyebrow.

He pinned me gently against the wall and kissed me. His hand went under my skirt, and his fingers traveled up to my panties. "That makes me want to fuck you."

"So, you approve of that kind of dress?"

"No. Only for me. In the bedroom. A slut. Out in the world, you're the pinnacle of modesty and taste."

I unclasped myself from his arms and cast him a challenging smirk. "You're bossy."

"Mm... and you feel hot." His hands squeezed my ass. "I have to go." He looked at me with those bedroom eyes. "I could cancel."

Shaking my head, I said, "No. This is good. I want to sleep with you in my arms. I need that."

He removed a stray strand of hair from my face and kissed me tenderly. "I'd like that, too."

Following a session of indecent fondling in the back of his limousine, leaving me hot and swollen, Blake dropped me off to meet Lilly.

A mixture of excitement at the prospect of shopping for gowns and something deeper pushed me along. I felt in my bag, and the keys with an angel key ring fell into my hand.

Sheldon's sweet face lit up my phone. "Hey, Shelly."

"Penny, where have you been hiding? We've got a lecture on the neo-classical movement happening right now. Where are you?"

"Shit. I forgot all about it. I thought that was next week." I huffed. I loved that period of art. *How could I have forgotten?* "Okay. I'll jump in a cab. Thanks for reminding me. I'll see you."

"You've missed half of the lecture."

"Shit. Can I look over your notes?"

"Sure. If you can make out my silly doodles and the odd scribbled thoughts."

I laughed. "I'll see you later. We'll have dinner."

"Sure. I miss you, Penny. Mr. Rich and Powerful has kidnapped you."

"I'll see you later at Soho, around seven. I'm shopping for a gown. I'm off to the masquerade ball." A bubble of excitement entered my words.

"Oh… the Doge's Ball?"

"Uh-huh."

He screamed. "Oh my God. I want photos. Lots of them. That's the ball to attend before dying."

I laughed. "I need to find a designer gown and a mask."

"We'll study some images of the Venice festival tonight. I can't wait. I love masks."

"Me too." I smiled. "See you soon, sweetie."

I ran into the café and found Lilly looking pale, holding a glass of wine.

"I'm so sorry."

"Don't worry. I'm used to you. You're always late." She raised an eyebrow.

I ordered a coffee to go. "You're starting early." I pointed at her glass.

"Oh, Penny." Her voice trembled.

"Shit. What's happened?"

"He's stalking me again." She bit her lip.

"Crap. Has he approached you?"

She nodded. "He wants to see me. He was nice about it. I pleaded with him to leave me alone."

"What about James?"

"He knows. He's a little shaky about it too."

"Has this Alex threatened him?"

She shook her head. "No. But if he follows me to James's house, which is where I am most of the time, who knows what he might do."

The waiter delivered my coffee. I nodded thanks.

"Don't worry, Lil, we'll make sure nothing happens." I touched her hand and gave a reassuring smile. "Come on. Let's go shopping for the ball."

She finished her wine in one gulp. "I can't wait. I just wish fatso would go away."

Shopping soon proved to be more a trial than fun. We found ourselves dealing with apathetic shop assistants acting all superior. They saw us as lower-class girls wasting their time.

But then Lilly blurted that we needed something for the Doge Ball that our rich lovers had invited us to. After that, the salesgirl almost jumped out of her skin to help us. I was tempted to give her the finger, but the gowns were too gorgeous to ignore.

Lilly settled for a blue dress with a low neckline and a split up the thigh, while I went for one that had a scooping neckline, after Lilly encouraged me to show off my assets. I wondered if I should send Blake a photo but decided against it, since it would only feed his need for control.

The tulip-shaped dress cascaded in fine silk to my feet. Its vibrant red made me sigh.

"Oh, Penny, that's so you. It's gorgeous," crooned Lilly.

"The price tag ain't gorgeous at five thousand pounds."

"Don't worry about it. Hasn't Blake given you a limitless credit card?"

"I didn't take it."

The shop assistant, who was within earshot, mirrored Lilly's shock.

"Then you're crazy. He's loaded."

"He bought me a house."

Lilly's face scrunched. "You're fucking kidding me."

I nodded. "Uh-huh. In Paddington. A terrace. Two stories. A view of the park."

I turned to the assistant, who stood close by. "I'll take it."

When we walked out onto the street with parcels in hand, Lilly asked, "So is your mother moving in?"

"I'm going to rent her an apartment. Away from the estate."

"She won't want to move," said Lilly.

I shrugged. "Maybe not." I stopped walking. "But I've got to get on with my life. I can paint there. And it's within walking distance of college. And I'll finally get away from that slum we've called home all of our lives."

"Living with your rich, oversexed boyfriend?" She raised a brow.

"He won't live there. It's too soon. And he doesn't do relationships."

"From where I'm standing, it looks like a relationship."

That buoyed me. "I'll be a kept woman, I suppose." I stopped walking. "Do you think that's wrong?"

"No fucking way. I think it's brilliant. You're beautiful, talented, and a good person. Go, sister." She stood there with her hands on her hips.

I hugged her. "Thanks, Lil." I checked the time. "I promised to meet Shelly for dinner. Crap."

Lilly laughed. "I'm sure he's used to it." She hailed a cab. "Do you want to share a cab? I can drop you off at Soho."

We hailed a taxi, and ten minutes later I was at Sheldon's.

I let myself in and found him in the kitchen, eating pasta.

"I'm so sorry," I said.

"There's some in the pot for you, sweetie."

I went over and had a sniff. The delicious saucy aroma made my tummy rumble. "Yum."

"Have it all. I'm full."

"You're such a darling. Thanks."

After I finished a big plate of pasta, which had me guilting over calories, we headed to the internet to study masks.

"I like the stick mask," said Sheldon.

"Mm. I like the lacy black one."

He nodded. "Sexy." He brought up an image of Venice, where the Grand Canal had a parade of masked and caped characters.

"That is so surreal and seriously beautiful. I want to paint those figures."

"Many have," said Shelly, leaning on his elbows. "They're so enchanting. I'm in love. Let's go to Venice."

I smiled at his contagious enthusiasm.

"I think I'll settle for a black lace number. Simple but sexy. It will go with my new gown."

Sheldon looked over at my shopping bags, which I'd left on the armchair.

"Oh, do please show."

I sprang up and opened the box, lifting the red silk gown out of the tissue paper.

"Oh my…" He covered his mouth with his hand. "It's so Rita Hayworth. It's gorgeous."

I placed it in front of me.

"I'll want pictures, darling."

I giggled. "A black lace mask will work with that, don't you think?"

"Definitely. What are you doing with your hair?"

"A stacked bun, I think."

"That will work. You've got a lovely long neck."

Falling onto the couch, I looked up at him and tears welled up.

"What's wrong, Penny?"

"He bought me a house."

"Huh?" His brow pinched. "Fuck. That's serious. Has he asked you to marry him?"

I shook my head and sniffled. "I wouldn't anyhow. It's too soon, and he's got a few issues."

"Mm… don't they all, darling."

Sheldon poured me a glass of wine. "So, what are the issues?"

"He can't sleep with me."

"But you're having sex, aren't you?" he asked. "Oh, please tell me he's really gay."

I laughed. "No. He's seriously straight. I meant we sleep separately."

His mouth stretched into a grimace. "Ouch. I know how that feels, only my lover leaves the house in the middle of the night. I even suggested he wear a balaclava." He giggled but then went straight-faced again. "Is he having nightmares?"

I nodded. "He's worried he may hurt me. He thrashes about."

"Off to a shrink for him."

"I made him promise me that he'd work on it."

"And is he?"

"He actually had his first therapy session today."

Just then my phone buzzed, and we both jumped. I looked down at the screen. It was Blake. "Talk of the devil."

A shiver ran down my spine at the synchronicity. It wasn't the only time that had happened. Often when I spoke of him, or even thought of him, he'd call.

"You're in sync. A sign of true love," said Sheldon.

I smiled and all the concern of Blake's issues faded away. All I felt was a burning need to have his hands all over me.

The message read: *Where are you?*

I replied: *At Sheldon's house.*

Can we meet? Tonight?

I looked up at Sheldon.

"He wants to see you?" he asked.

I nodded.

"Let me guess—this is every night so far?"

I nodded again, taking a deep breath. My body was dying to be crushed by Blake's strong manly body. I was just as addicted as he was.

THIRTY-ONE

BLAKE

PENELOPE PERFORMED A SLOW pirouette. The red gown floated in the air and cascaded against her curvy figure like a dream. Her almond-shaped eyes smiled, encased in a black lace mask.

"You look beautiful." I took her into my arms. "It's an exquisite gown. A little low-cut." My finger traced her milky soft cleavage, which prickled against my palm, and traveled to her spiked nipples.

My cock jerked against my fitted tux pants as I pressed against her.

She giggled. "Blake, we probably should go. And it took me ages to dress."

I ran my hand up her leg to her stockings and above to the naked thigh. "I look forward to seeing you in your garter later on." I pinched her ass and finished with a visit to her wet cunt. "Penelope."

A smile touched her beautiful pout. "Yes."

"You're deliciously wet."

"That's because of the way you're touching me, and seeing you in that tux isn't helping."

I laughed. It was the lightest I'd been all day.

The day hadn't started so well, though. I'd had a meeting with Peter Barnes, who informed me that Tatiana was indeed working for Dylan again, just as we'd suspected.

"What would have motivated that?" I asked him.

He shook his head. "Maybe it's all she knows."

"But she seemed determined to start afresh."

"Some of the girls haven't known anything else. Maybe the shelter, with its bare essentials, put her off. I imagine the girls are lavished with gifts and eat well in return for their services." His eyebrows rose.

"If I'm to take Fox down, I need her to testify."

Barnes studied me. "You know that's close to impossible, don't you? Some of his clients are very powerful men. All with a predilection for young flesh."

"Pedophiles, you mean?"

He nodded mechanically. "There's an island owned by a reclusive billionaire, somewhere off Spain. Called Lolita."

I sniffed. "How original."

He smiled at my sarcasm. "I'm afraid this ring's impenetrable. It would take a very brave individual to bring them down."

"Keep digging anyway." I pulled out an envelope filled with cash. "Here."

He stuffed it in his pocket without counting it. "Thanks. I'll see what more I can find out."

PATRICK OPENED THE CAR door for Penelope, and she slipped in gracefully. I joined her, and sat close.

The night was clear and balmy. I stroked her long neck, and reached into my lapel for a small box.

"Here." I handed it to her. "Something to go with that lovely gown."

She looked down at the box and then at me, frowning. "Haven't you already given me everything?"

"I'm rich. Open the box." I pointed at it.

She lifted the velvet ribbon with a teardrop diamond pendant attached. "It's stunning. I love the simplicity of the choker. It's so Victorian and feminine."

"Yes, it's very sexy. I'm not into fussy jewelry." I took the diamond choker from her. "Here, let me tie it on."

She turned around, and I knotted the velvet ribbon, placing a finger inside to make sure it wasn't too tight. She turned around and smiled shyly. Her vulnerability touched me as I looked from her neck to her big limpid eyes.

I held her. "You're an exquisite creature."

She pulled away and looked at me. "Is it a diamond?"

"I wouldn't buy a fake."

"It must have cost you a fortune."

"Money is there for beauty. That's my motto in life. Take it and enjoy. Only don't wear it when visiting your mother."

Her eyes darkened. "I'll give it back to you after the ball, if you like."

I lifted my hands. "Please don't take offense. I was referring to the people that hang around that place."

"Thanks to your generosity, I can use the money from the paintings to rent her an apartment away from there."

"I can help if you like."

A sad smile touched her painted lips. "Blake, you've already done so much."

I placed my arm around her waist and breathed in her fragrant soft hair.

The grounds were lit in purples and reds projecting onto the overtly ornamental Baroque palace.

"It looks like a big wedding cake," said Penelope as I helped her out of the car.

"If one goes for eating bricks," I replied dryly.

Penelope giggled while adjusting her mask. "How's that?"

"Striking," I answered, removing the leather mask from my lapel.

"Yours is so simple," said Penelope, sounding disappointed.

"I'm not into ostentation." I held her hand, and we entered the grounds guarded by men in livery.

The chandeliers dazzled, and the regal ballroom was filled with the usual lords, ladies, and offspring. As a nod to the Venice festival, the ball, as always, showcased Baroque music.

"It's so old world," said Penelope, taking a glass of champagne from a tray.

"A bit stuffy. But an attractive building."

She glanced up at the fresco of a bacchanalian romp. "Oh my, that's gorgeous."

"Penny!" came a voice from behind.

We turned, and there stood Lilly, holding James's hand.

James came up to me. "Blake, old man. Look at you." He turned and acknowledged Penelope. "And look at you. You're both going to win the Gorgeous-Couple-of-the-Night award, I think. You're sure to make front cover of *Hello*."

I smiled at Lilly. "Blue's your color."

She said, "Thanks" and then directed her attention to Penelope, touching the diamond at her throat. "This is gorgeous, Penny."

Penelope glanced over at me, smiling widely. Her excitement brought a smile to my face.

"Back in a minute. Off to the girl's room," she said.

I indulged in Penelope's effortless beauty as she glided off, arm in arm with Lilly. She had the admiration of the males she passed. Penelope's natural elegance confirmed my belief that grace was innate and not something one could learn or only possess with money.

We had our own admirers, too, with the usual cohort of wealthy daughters ogling us. I wasn't fooled by those expensive gowns and rounded vowels. Those girls showed no qualms about getting down and dirty with any rich stranger who took their fancy.

"Oh, if it isn't Blake Sinclair," I heard over my shoulder as a waft of Chanel No. 5 drifted my way.

I turned and recognized a woman from the last ball, who'd taken me into the Dark Room for a little dirty playtime. Her name had slipped my memory. Leaning in, she whispered, "I'm still waiting for you to return the favor."

"I'm with someone." My cool response hopefully said it all.

Her mouth turned down, and her eyes cooled as she floated off.

James smirked. "Ghosts of past dalliances all over the place."

"Why are we here again?" I asked.

"Because it's tradition. And let's face it—just seeing our girls dressed up makes it worthwhile." He lifted his glass. "And they always serve top champagne. And let's not forget the Dark Room."

The Dark Room was a secret chamber for hedonists, a leftover tradition from the days of rakes. The more conservative guests had no idea of its existence. Only those keen on debauchery knew of its location, which was somewhere in the bowels of that castle.

"Not tonight. I'm not parading my girl in that den of wolves."

James laughed. "What, not even a threesome?" He lifted a brow.

"I'm not as kinky as you."

"Says Mr. Voyeur."

"I haven't done that for a while."

"Penelope's really gotten to you," said James.

"Does Lilly know of your penchant for threesomes?"

He nodded sheepishly. "She doesn't mind the idea of being tongued by a girl. She just doesn't want me to fuck the other girl. I can live with that. Lilly's enough for me."

"So why do you need to watch her with another girl?"

"There's something tantalizingly erotic watching two girls at it." James's brow arched.

That came as no surprise. The guy was more sordid than I could ever be. "I'm a vanilla man myself."

"To each his own. And as long as everyone's having fun. There's Emma over there. She's rather partial to bit of cunt sucking." James nodded subtly toward a woman dressed in a man's suit.

"You're licentious and wanton," I said, thinking of the previous ball. when I'd entered the Dark Room and had two girls perform lewd acts on my cock.

As that murky little image played out in my mind, Penelope glided toward me, and my heart warmed. The pull she had on me worried me. I wondered if I shouldn't seek another appointment with the therapist to discuss my addiction to Penelope. The first appointment had gone poorly, unsurprisingly. I'd ended up leaving with a script for sleeping pills, after my reluctance to apprise the therapist of my soap-operatic past.

I held out my hand to Penelope. "Let's go into the ballroom."

"Yes. Lets." She smiled, brimming with excitement.

The music suited the florid surroundings, as the waltzing guests swirled around. Most of the younger women wore fitted gowns revealing as much flesh as possible.

"I think I'm wearing the most fabric," said Penelope.

I noticed men's heads turning toward her. "You're dazzling. Mystery tantalizes."

Accentuated by the lace mask, her eyes had a teasing smile. "Then that explains my attraction to you, Blake, because you're the very personification of mystery."

"Let's keep it that way. You might tire of me otherwise."

She studied me closely. "You don't like the person you're hiding?"

I paused to think. "That's a big question and probably best suited to midnight after a few Scotches."

She took my hand. "One day, you'll tell my about your family, I hope."

"It's not that interesting."

"I disagree. It's sounds fascinating. I prefer that to someone who's had a boring life, when every Sunday's scones and jam."

"I'm rather partial to scones and jam." I grinned.

Penelope smiled and, to my relief, abstained from further questions.

"Come. Let's dance."

"Waltz?" Her pretty lips twisted.

"Just let me lead. I'm dying to feel you against me."

THIRTY-TWO

PENELOPE

BEING SWIRLED AROUND felt like a dream. I'd never heard classical music played live. Lifted by the ethereal music, I glided along as though my feet floated in the air.

Blake held onto me steadily. When I managed to leave his magnetic blue eyes, I observed those around us. The older guests painted dramatic figures in white masks, capes, and three-cornered hats, in what looked like a macabre version of Disneyland.

The younger women, whose eyes were on Blake for most of the time, wore their red-carpet glamor effortlessly as they sashayed about, well-practiced at working the room.

Dressed in a black tuxedo that looked as though it had been sewn onto him, Blake looked like that sophisticated class of man one saw in Hollywood movies. His combed-back dark hair revealed a face that bore so many shades of handsome that I couldn't stop looking at him. His sultry eyes gleamed back at mine, hijacking reality.

"I have to sit down. These shoes are killing me," I said.

Blake led me to a silk-covered chair. "I'll go and get us another drink." He looked around and then back at me. "Will you be okay here for a moment?"

"Of course. I'll do my best to fight off the suitors." I giggled.

Blake returned a faint smile. "I won't be long."

He strode off, leaving in his wake an audience of salivating women. Blake's animal magnetism was on fine display with that tall and upright bearing, which, although dignified, radiated the promise of something wild and untamed. Or maybe that was just my oversexed mind?

Lilly came over and plonked herself down. "There you are," she said, breathlessly.

"Have you been running?" I asked.

She shook her head with a smile. "No. James took me for a roam around. There's this Dark Room." She fanned her face. "Oh my God."

"What do you mean?"

She cupped her mouth. "It's more of an orgy room, I think."

"Really?" I recalled art history lessons about the wanton behavior of the upper classes as depicted in erotic Victorian art. I pictured masked guests with bare asses and women with their bodices ripped open, bosoms spilling out, and their stocking-clad legs apart. No detail spared.

"Apparently, it's a secret. There's a dungeon. And getting there is kind of creepy in that haunted-house way." She grimaced. "It was like something out of a movie. It even had a bookshelf that turned into a secret doorway."

My mouth gaped with wonder. "I'm dying to see it." I looked for Blake but couldn't spot him. "I'd better wait for Blake."

James handed Lilly a glass of champagne and whispered something in her ear. Lilly, who was already tipsy, giggled.

After they wandered off, I went looking for Blake. I spied him in conversation with a man, who pointed rather aggressively into his face.

Blake pushed him against the wall, and the other man sneered in return.

Having noticed me there, Blake turned his back to the creepy man and left him alone.

Rubbing his neck, Blake said, "I haven't managed to get that drink."

"Who was that guy? That didn't look friendly. Is something the matter?"

"Forget about him. Come." He led me away.

As questions mounted, Blake managed to distract me by taking me on a tour of the fascinating castle and its endless chambers.

Designed in different themes, each room boasted a luxury of detail, from tapestries depicting historical events, to walls painted in rich colors and fringed with scrolled gold leaf. There was plenty to see, not least the fireplaces the size of small rooms, which were flanked by statues of goddesses.

With phone in hand, I photographed as much as I could. The detailed cornices of angels and griffins were my primary focus.

Blake, who had a fine eye for detail, enjoyed pointing out subtle elements. All that earlier cloak-and-dagger shit had vanished, and we sauntered from room to room as one would in a gallery. I loved discussing art with Blake. He was so attentive, informed, and deeply involved.

We finally settled in a room I chose for its fine fresco of Narcissus gazing into a pond. Reclining on a chaise lounge, I said, "Lilly mentioned a Dark Room in a dungeon."

Standing by the fireplace, Blake's face darkened. "That room's not for you."

"And it's okay for you?"

He shook his head. "No. It's a secret chamber for deviants to get their rocks off."

"An orgy, you mean?"

"Penelope, let's just enjoy being here and leave the dirty bits out."

"Even later?" I raised a brow.

He came to me and lowered himself close. His hand slid over my naked arm. "No."

"Who was that guy?"

"A nasty, rotten piece of work, who I once knew."

"From Raven Abbey?" I asked.

He nodded mechanically.

"I'd love to know about your life there," I said.

"It's not a pretty story. Not for here and now."

"But I will want to know."

His gaze went beyond my eyes piercing my soul. "I'm all for the present. The past doesn't interest me."

"But why this shroud of mystery?"

"A shroud of mystery? You should write poetry, Penelope." He ran his hand over my arm again. "This past month with you has changed me. I'm not sure who I am anymore."

"That doesn't sound good, does it?" I asked, wishing he'd remove his mask, my eyes flitting between his eyes and that mouth that my lips hankered after.

"My past is dirty. And you're a pure soul, Penelope."

I sat up, turning to face him square on. "Hey. I don't even know who my father was. For all I know, he was a junkie or a pimp or a dealer. My mother can't remember." An ironic laugh grated my throat. "She probably can't even remember having me."

Blake removed his mask. A sheen of pity darkened his eyes.

"Once, I found her slouched on the couch with a needle stuck in her vein. I couldn't tell if she was dead or alive." My voice trembled.

"I want to help," said Blake.

I removed my mask to wipe my eyes. The room and its splendor, which earlier had warmed my spirit now reminded me of the stark contrast between Blake and me.

"So now that you know all about my crappy past, surely yours can't be worse. I feel naked, while you hide yourself in those expensive designer suits."

"Penelope, it's not a competition on who's had the most fucked-up life, because if it were, I'd win hands down." He combed back his hair, and boy, I craved him more. The darker he became, the more my body seethed with desire.

"That wasn't what I meant. I know it's not a fucking competition. Hell, Blake. Don't you get it?" I stood up. "I need some air."

He followed me out. Frustration with Blake's inability to let me in fueled me along. I couldn't stop thinking of that man who'd cornered Blake. His rigid, unsettling body language pestered me like a thorn digging into my skin.

THIRTY-THREE

BLAKE

I'D BEEN ATTENDING THE masked ball at Annerley Castle for eight years, and I'd never seen Dylan Fox there before. Even with the passing of time, those beady, perpetually sniggering eyes still made my skin crawl.

Penelope was right: one couldn't escape one's past. The fact that her mother was a junkie hadn't changed the way I felt for Penelope. In many ways, Penelope's shame kept my shame company. And the more naked her soul, the more attached I became.

I followed Penelope out, and seeing her clutching her arms, I removed my jacket and placed it over her shoulders.

"Penelope, let's do this some other time. You'll be the first to know."

She turned around, and her eyes looked so large under the moonlight that I knew I couldn't hide anything from her. "The first to know about your past?" Her lips parted. "Is this real?"

I took her into my arms and drew energy from her heartbeat against my ribcage. "It's real for me."

"And it's real for me. I'm in love with you, Blake." Her trembling voice echoed through my body.

An aching pause followed. I'd never uttered that foreign word to anyone. Ever. And no one, not even my mother, had ever said that word to me. I couldn't hold that against her though—my mother was that riddled with emotional pain—her heart was probably buried in ice.

Penelope left my arms and stared up at me.

Expectation pierced the air.

If aching for her was love, then I loved her, all right. I grappled with that, wondering if it was my cock, my heart, or even my soul that ached for her.

Maybe all three.

"Have I frightened you?" she asked.

I shook my head and held her close. I kissed her tenderly. Her lips, cool from the night air, tasted like pure honey. It was a new flavor. Normally, her lips were musky like her cunt after I'd ravaged her.

"Why don't we go inside?" I asked with the brightest smile I'd worn all night. For some reason, I felt light. I'd almost forgotten about Dylan Fox.

Penelope agreed and took my hand. "Can you at least call me Penny?"

I turned to look at her. "I love the way 'Penelope' dances on my tongue. But Penny it is." I brushed her cheek.

She smiled gently.

"I wonder what happened to Lilly and James?"

"Knowing James, they're in the Dark Room."

"Is he sleazy?"

I chose my words carefully. "James likes experimenting. But he's honest and a good person, I believe. He wouldn't force her to do something she didn't want to do."

"Lilly's impressionable. I hope he's not into orgies," she said.

"They're both grown-ups, Penny."

We were just about to enter the ball when she said, "I think I prefer Penelope." She stopped walking. "But only from you."

"Good. I prefer it too."

We shared a smile, and spying a passing waiter, I grabbed two glasses of champagne.

As bubbles chased away the bitterness of seeing Dylan Fox earlier, he entered my space again. Before I could even process his ugly presence, a girl came over and hugged me.

"Oh, Blake. It's you. Why didn't you call me like you promised?"

I stared at the young girl, who looked familiar. She held a stick mask, which she removed from her face. I instantly recognized Tatiana from the photos Barnes had shown me.

Maintaining a cool facade, I replied, "I don't know you."

"Yes, you do. We met at the Cherry Orchard. Three years ago."

I looked at Dylan Fox, who'd just taken photos of Tatiana embracing me with his phone.

Penelope, meanwhile, stood by and watched. Her attention flitted from me to the young girl, who I knew was only seventeen. "Aren't you going to introduce me?" she asked.

"I don't know this girl."

I took Penelope's hand gently and led her away.

"Ah, ah... not so quickly, Sinclair." Dylan looked Penelope up and down, wearing a sleazy smirk. "You're very pretty."

"Fuck off, Dylan." I clenched my fists.

"We have to talk. Call me tomorrow." He handed me a card. "This is not going away. Tatiana and you. Three years ago." He arched an eyebrow.

I looked at Penelope. "We have to leave. Now."

Her brow crumpled. "Who's that young girl? Is that right... you were with her at the Cherry Orchard three years ago?"

"No. It's fucking bullshit."

"What's going on?" Penelope demanded.

"Let's get out of here."

"He mentioned the Cherry Orchard. You were there that night. Are you into buying virgins? Underage ones?"

"I'm not, Penelope. I'm being set up."

I held onto her. I wasn't going to let her run, even though I felt her body tighten against mine as she followed along.

PENELOPE SAT IN THE armchair in my bedroom, watching me pace about liked a trapped tiger. "I've never met that girl."

I told Penelope all about Barnes and how I'd been approached to protect Tatiana from Fox. "Fox is setting me up," I concluded.

"So you keep saying. What's his connection to you?"

"We grew up together. He tried to kill Sir William, his father, and I ended up saving the man. Twice. Dylan's father left me everything and wrote Dylan out of the will. There were court hearings. It was a fucking circus. But Sir William had an ironclad clause, making the will uncontestable. He had evidence that Dylan had tried to murder him."

"But how?"

"The cook said it was poisonous mushrooms. He'd seen Dylan sneaking into the kitchen."

"Then why didn't he stop Sir William from eating them?"

"Because Dylan strangled the cook."

Penelope grimaced. "I take it the cook survived."

I nodded. I was the one who felt the breath under his nose.

"You mentioned Dylan tried to kill his father twice."

"The second time was opportunistic, given that Sir William was choking on a chicken bone. Luckily, I'd entered the room when I did. I found him frothing at the mouth while his son watched on."

"How was he saved from eating the mushrooms?" Penelope asked.

"The cook revived in time to warn me. And just as Sir William held the fork to his mouth, I burst in to warn him."

"Where was your mother in all of this?"

"She was his personal maid. They were very close."

"In *that* way?"

"Probably." I took a deep breath.

"Didn't that concern you? I mean, where was your father?"

"In jail for killing someone in a drunken brawl." I exhaled tightly. "It didn't worry me knowing that my mother was close to Sir William because for one, my father was a sadistic brute, and for two, Lady Catherine, Dylan's mother, had been having an affair with the gardener for years."

Penelope shook her head. "My God. It was a soap opera in there."

I sniffed. "That it was."

"So this Dylan couldn't contest the will, and he's now trying to get his money by other means, is that right?"

I nodded. "I hadn't seen him for years until that night at the Cherry Orchard."

"You told me you went there out of curiosity after James invited you."

A cold feeling gnawed my gut. I stared at Penelope. "That's right." I stopped pacing. "I need you to do something for me."

She looked up at me.

"I need you to hang low. He's affiliated with nasty people. If something happened to you, I'd fucking kill him."

Her face scrunched in fear. "Oh. Please don't talk like that. You're scaring me."

I knelt down at her feet. "I've never used that *love* word before because..." I let out a slow breath. "I don't know how to." I paused. One minute felt like ten.

There was no pity, only compassion that I detected in Penelope's teary eyes. I kissed her hand and held onto it. "I need you in my life."

"I'm not going anywhere, Blake. I'm not hiding. I want to be with you."

I lifted her in my arms and took her to bed. My dick was hard as steel. This time it wasn't solely due to her heart-melting beauty, but also because of her belief in me and my shedding of a skin.

THIRTY-FOUR

PENELOPE

LILLY LOOKED AT ME all wide-eyed and rosy-cheeked. "You wouldn't believe what we got up to."

Going on Blake's account of the Dark Room, I braced myself for some filth. "Tell me."

"I looked for you. You left early."

I sighed. It had been an intense night. We didn't end up sleeping much. Blake made slow, achingly tender love to me, and then he stayed with me as I held him close. He tried to move into the other room, but I wouldn't let him. It resulted in him feasting on me so slowly and completely that I left my body, as I moaned through one orgasm after another. His cock was red-raw and greedy.

"We did. There was this guy there. Dylan Fox. He's evil and connected to the Cherry Orchard."

"I met him."

"You did?" I asked.

"He spoke to James at the ball."

"Oh." For some reason that struck me as odd, given Blake's closeness to James.

"So tell me about the Dark Room."

"A woman went down on me, and James watched."

I studied her face for signs of regret or even shame, but she seemed rather relaxed. "Were you coerced into it?"

"Did James force me, you mean?"

I nodded.

"No. I was buzzing from a party drug."

I squirmed at that image. "You let others fuck you?"

She shook her head.

Although my mind filled with questions, I had to leave Lilly for a life-drawing class. It was my last week of college, and I'd fallen behind on two written assignments. I'd become too preoccupied with Blake and his life at Raven Abbey. Add to that what Milly had revealed, and I understood why he would often retreat into himself.

I headed for the spare easel. The model was Rubenesque, which suited me. I loved working with curves and found women easier to draw. Luckily for me, I was to be marked on that session of drawings.

"There you are," said Sheldon.

I clipped the paper to the board. "Hey, Shelly."

"I haven't seen you for so long. I miss you."

"I know. You'll have to come over to my new house," I said.

"You do realize that you're living close to my parents?"

I shook my head. "I know. It's crazy. The neighbors look at me as though I'm a freak. Initially, they thought I was a squatter."

"I can imagine." He sniffed. "Snobby assholes. I'll have to come over just before drag night and rub myself up against the lamp post in front of their house."

I laughed. I'd seen Sheldon before a drag night—something he did for a little fun and to frock up. "I'm sure the rich and mighty have seen it all before. The masked ball had its fair share of deviants."

"I'm dying to hear about it."

"All in good time, my friend. I'd better get cracking." I pointed to the model. "She's gorgeous."

"Yes, nice and curvy." He smiled. "Let's have a drink after class. Yes?"

I nodded distractedly. There was something I needed to tell Blake.

THIRTY-FIVE

BLAKE

SMALL PRINT SWAM AROUND as I peered down at the contract, and the muddle of heritage layers and council stipulations failed to sink in.

I peered up at my screen. My chest tensed as I opened the photos sent to me anonymously. I didn't need to be Einstein to guess the sender. There were images of me holding Tatiana at the ball, obscuring my face. The sapphire ring, which I never removed, gave me away. That ring had belonged to Sir William, who on his deathbed had slipped it off his finger and placed it in my hand, making me promise I'd wear it in his memory.

Ironically, that ring was now evidence against me, as no doubt Fox was aware. The seedier images included half-naked shots of me. One of the women I'd bought for sex must have taken them.

I'd been set up. *Pure and fucking simple.*

They were masterfully devised shots of me lying on my side, revealing a scar from when I'd slipped on a rock as a child. Tatiana sat up, naked, and by my side. She looked so hair-raisingly young with that flat chest that my gut knotted.

I looked up. Peter Barnes stood at my door.

"Come in." I pointed to the chair.

When he was seated, I asked, "How did you hear about Tatiana?"

"One of the guards who works for Fox. We were in the army together. He's a little ruffled by what's going on in there. He's seen the young girls." He paused. "He's got a family to support and Fox pays his security well."

"So why's he turning on his boss?"

"Because Tatiana came to him with some sob story that she wanted out and needed protection. That's how I met her. She seemed pretty fucking genuine. Crying and desperate to make a new life for herself, promising to testify against Fox."

"I'm being blackmailed." I studied him for a moment. Barnes had come recommended by a fellow card player, who'd hired him to spy on his cheating wife.

He held up his hands. "Hey. I'm not in on this. I've got a daughter. That scene makes me fucking sick."

He might have been in one bar brawl too many, but intuition told me I could trust him.

"Do you mind if I look at the images?" he asked.

I handed over the folder. "Here."

He studied the six shots.

"They're vague. There's none with your face except for this one." He pointed to a photo of me in the foyer of the Cherry Orchard.

"The scar on my back and the ring," I said.

"The scar could have been photoshopped. The ring too."

I hadn't thought of that. "They photoshopped her in my fucking bed." I headed to the bottle of whisky, poured two glasses and then passed one to Barnes.

"If she testifies, you're in trouble. Judges take the word of the supposed victim in this type of case."

A tight breath left my chest. "Which they're threatening to do."

"What does he want?" he asked.

Good fucking question. "My empire."

He whistled. "That's a lot of money."

I peered down at the images that had turned my day upside down. It had already started uncomfortably enough. Penelope, after pleading with me to sleep in her bed, reported how I'd squeezed the life out of her during one of my nightmares. The fear in her eyes made me want to run, only I didn't have damp caves in the middle of the blustery moors to hide in.

"I've seen worse. These could be contested." He drained his glass in one well-practiced gulp. "This one, however"—he pointed to the shot of me at the Cherry Orchard— "demonstrates that you're into buying young girls by the mere fact of your presence."

"But he's incriminating himself, isn't he? That suggests he's dealing in underage girls." I opened my hands.

"He's a silent partner," he reminded me. "I've got an ex-Eastern European mafia contact. He might know something about that scene. His son goes to school with my daughter of all things." He sniffed. "It's kind of strange how one meets people these days. And with the lack of proper jobs, desperation leads people to take jobs they'd prefer not to, if you get my meaning."

I nodded slowly. "Discretion only. I don't want my name mentioned."

"No. Of course." He rose and then paused. "How did you hear about the Cherry Orchard in the first place? Given that it's an invite-only, dark-alleyway joint."

"I'm about to call him right now," I said, feeling the heat at the back of my neck. I smelled a rat.

"I'll have to grab the name of your contact at some point." He lifted his hand and left.

My phone buzzed. I peered down at an image of Penelope in that beautiful red gown that I'd snapped the night of the ball. I picked up. "Hey, beautiful."

"Blake, I have to race to a lecture, but I thought you should know. I met Lilly for breakfast, and during a conversation about the ball, she told me that she'd met Dylan Fox through James. Apparently, they seemed rather friendly."

I squeezed the life out of my phone. "I have to go. Tonight?"

"Sure. Are things okay?"

"We'll talk later." I ended the call. Abrupt as it was, I had no control over my actions. The word *betrayal* hit my brain with such a heavy thud that my head ached.

I pressed on James's number. It went to voicemail. I kept it brief. "We need to talk."

THIRTY-SIX

PENELOPE

BLAKE PACED ABOUT RUBBING his head, leaving it a sexy mess of hair. His mouth glistened from his brushing tongue, which for one twisted moment had my body reacting with greedy need. I was amazed that a man as dark and haunted as Blake could send my hormones into overdrive. And my desire only intensified as he paced about in my new living room, pausing every now and then to stare out the window, lost in thought.

"He's not returning your calls?" I asked.

He shook his head.

"I can call Lilly if you like."

Blake had only given me fragments—something about James having betrayed him and that Dylan Fox wished to destroy him. Just enough to worry me.

He looked at me. "No. Don't involve her."

"Something happened earlier," I said in a thin voice. "When I visited my mother, Jimmy, one of the local guys…"

"One of the dealers that loiters about, you mean?"

I bristled at his biting tone. "He's not a bad person. Desperation does that to people, you know?"

He attempted a weak smile. "That's the second time I've heard that today." Blake took my hand. "I interrupted. You were saying?"

"Jimmy told me that the Russian had come looking for Lilly. Brent confronted him and it broke out into a punch-up. The Russian came off second best."

"Who's Brent?"

"That's Lilly's brother. He's very protective, especially since she's been staying with James. Maybe now for a good reason."

"I hope you're looking for a new place for your mother. I've got an open checkbook, Penelope. I don't want you going back there."

"You've given me so much, and I'm really grateful. At times, I still find it difficult to process. But you can't tell me what to do, and I'm about to fail my degree." Tears blinded me. For the first time ever, I'd received a fail mark on one of my assignments due to missing extended deadlines.

"Oh?" His brow crinkled. "But you're a brilliant artist, Penelope. You're unique. You stand out from the crowd."

My face was saturated as I sniffled and blew my nose in the most unladylike fashion. I'd reverted to Penny from the estate, and not that cool art student with the rich boyfriend.

"I've scored high on my practical, but my written work sucks. It always has. But I managed to bumble through it with the help of Sheldon and, believe it or not, my mother."

"Your mother?" Blake's frown was understandable. I'd also been shocked at my mother's innate intelligence when she put her mind to helping me.

"She's really good at English. Even junked out, she would help me express my ideas on paper."

This retelling of one of our rare but finer moments together made me bawl like a baby.

Blake took me into his arms, which was the first time we'd held each other since he'd arrived with a dark shadow in tow.

My eyes seemed to have a burst a pipe as tears poured out. It had been an edgy day, starting in the morning, when Blake crushed me while we slept, and then ending with me learning that my degree hung on a thread. The thought of repeating another semester froze my veins.

"Take me to her," said Blake.

I frowned. "What?"

"I want to meet your mother."

"You do?" My tears dried, and my heart banged against my ribcage. *Am I ready for that?*

"Please. It will help me."

"How?" I froze on the spot.

"I just want to meet her."

"Look, Blake, don't worry about it. I'll spend the next few days focusing, and I'll finish that essay."

"What's the subject?" Although his change of subject was jarring, I welcomed it.

"How the Pre-Raphaelites informed the neo-classical movement."

"I've got an idea," he said, brightening.

"About the Pre-Raphaelites?"

He laughed, which was rare for him but beautiful. "No, although I do love the collection at the Tate. You enjoyed our little trip to Bath."

"I did. I've even started sketching my new bridge series." I smiled as he took my hand.

"Why don't we go there for a couple of days? While you're working on your paper, I can arrange renovations for my new spa."

My spirit came alive. "I'd love that."

"I actually got a distinction for English, so if I can help in anyway..." Blake's gentle smile gave him that rare boyish look that I loved.

"Oh, that would be super." I fell into his arms, and our lips met for a soft, tender kiss that quickly developed into one of need and hunger. I pulled away and smirked. "So, you're not just a pretty face?"

Blake wore a half grin that dimpled his cheek and made me want to eat him.

He squeezed my ass and then fondled my breasts. A sliver of electricity gusted through me. The more intense Blake's life was the harder his cock became.

His fingers moved inside my panties and tickled my clit.

"And you're very creamy," he rasped, waltzing me to the sofa. My body relaxed entirely, not only because his ravishing tongue promised to send me over the edge but also because my mother hadn't been mentioned again.

THIRTY-SEVEN

BLAKE

I'D SUGGESTED INVITING HER mother out, but Penelope shook her head, telling me her mother never left her flat. She'd rung ahead, and when she closed the call, she looked at me and said, "I don't really want to do this."

"What did your mother say?"

"She asked if I had any cash." Penelope looked up at me and bit a nail. "That's normal for her. Let's not go. It won't be pretty."

"I want to meet her. I'm not going to judge her. But will she mind me seeing her? That's more the point."

"My mother's self-respect went out the window years ago. In fact, you know, I don't think she's got any. That sounds awful, I know. But..." She shrugged.

I stroked her cheek. "Hey, it's all good. I just want to meet her."

She took a deep breath. "Okay, then. But I warned you."

THE CRUMBLING ESTATE WAS predictably squalid. Penelope greeted a skinny guy wearing loose, low-slung sweatpants. His fancy trainers seemed incongruous on that skinny drug-riddled frame. He scratched his arms and almost looked shy around Penelope, which was cute but still harrowing. I hated her being there, let alone sharing a laugh with a drug dealer.

They'd grown up together, she assured me as we walked along the cracked pavement.

Graffiti was splattered across the walls, not in any artful fashion but in that angry *I hate the world* way.

Penelope insisted on going first. Seeing how shaky and affected she was, I held her hand.

People yelling over blaring TVs and loud thumping rap music filtered through as we moved past the endless doors in that crowded estate.

I examined large cracks around the entrance, and as we stood at the threshold of Penelope's childhood home, I wondered if it was even structurally safe. The place needed to be condemned.

"Have you got a key?" I asked.

She shook her head. "No. The door's always open."

"Really?"

She smiled. "There's nothing to steal. Only Oxfam hand-me-downs."

I frowned.

"Hey. No pity or judgment, remember?"

I took her hand and squeezed it gently.

She opened the door and called out, "Mom."

Beneath the blaring TV, a voice said, "Hello, darling."

Penelope stepped into the haze, gesturing for me to enter a room that had smoked a million cigarettes.

I stood before her mother, who slouched on the sofa, watching telly. "Hi, I'm Blake, Penelope's boyfriend."

Penelope's face turned sharply to mine, a sparkle of surprise in her eyes.

How else can I describe myself? "A rich lover who's so addicted to your daughter he needs to see her, taste her, fuck her every night?"

Penelope's mother lifted her slouched spine, appearing more like a frail sixty-year-old than someone in her mid-forties. "Oh." She studied me and then gave me her hand, which was small, cold, and shaky.

Her green eyes reflected back a life of sadness and bad choices. I struggled to look at her, because she didn't even try to hide behind a screen of pleasantries.

"I'm Sandy." Her uncertain stare flitted between Penelope and me. "Please sit." She pointed to a chair buried in clothes.

Penelope quickly removed them and then headed to the untidy kitchen, where the bench tops were scattered with used packaging.

She opened the fridge. "There's beer but no food, again."

"I'm okay, Penny. Please don't make a fuss." Sandy cast me a tight smile.

She had the guarded expression of a person so broken that she wasn't going to let anyone in. I recognized it because my mother had often put up that same wall. But instead of drugs, she drank, mostly with Sir William, who also loved to drink. I'd often find them sharing a bottle, and laughing at ridiculously childish things.

"Is there anything you need?" I asked, reaching for my cellphone.

She studied me. "I could use some smokes. And there's my script."

Penelope removed the prescription from her mother's hand. "This is for your methadone?"

Sandy nodded and scratched her arms. "Yes, love." She smiled at me meekly.

It was so sad. I understood the hopelessness of it all. I could see that this woman didn't want to wake up. Hell stood at her doorstep, and she'd buried herself in drugs to ward it off.

"How about food?" I looked over at Penelope, who nodded, biting a nail. "I can arrange for Patrick to pick up that script if you like. And buy some food."

Penelope shook her head. "No. She's had her quota." She looked at her mother. "How about a pizza?"

Sandy nodded with resignation. I could see the disappointment etched on her face at the lost opportunity to feed her desperate habit. "One with pineapple and ham."

Penelope removed a sticker from the fridge and took out her phone. "Do you feel like some pizza?" she asked me.

"No, I'm good," I replied. "But if you want to stay and eat, I'm okay with that."

Penelope read me like a book, and I hated myself for being so transparent. "I'm not hungry." She looked at her mother. "We just popped in to see how you are, and Blake ..."

I interjected, "I asked Penelope to introduce us."

Probably due to being stoned, Sandy seemed more relaxed than the two of us. "It's nice of you to drop in, love. Don't fuss about." She winced at the noise Penelope made as she tossed out bottles and cleaned the kitchen.

I rose from the chair and entered the kitchen.

"Don't come in here," said Penelope. "It's disgusting."

"I removed my jacket. I can help."

Her eyes grew wide and teary again. Having me witness the squalor that was once her life was understandably difficult for her. Even if my body hadn't been so addicted to hers and I hadn't fallen under the spell of her beauty, knowing Penelope as one human knew another, I would have done everything in my power to help her flourish and succeed.

"No, please don't," she implored.

"I'll order a cleaner for tomorrow. I'll request they come every week." I removed the decrepit dishcloth from her hand.

She gulped back emotion staring at her feet. I lifted her chin. I wanted to tell her it was okay, that I understood, and that I'd lived in a similar hovel before moving to Raven Abbey.

Penelope lowered the volume on the TV, telling her mother, "Just for a minute while I order that pizza."

Sandy nodded before staring blankly at the screen again. I'd almost become invisible, which was fine. Questions were never my thing.

After Penny finished the call, she lowered herself down on the couch and sat next to her mother. "We aren't going to stay. I've ordered the pizza. Blake wanted to meet you. We're together. I want to find you a flat, somewhere nice, away from here. What do you think?"

"No. I'm staying here. This is my life. My friends are here. The only time I'm leaving is in a bag."

A deep, frustrated breath shot out from Penelope. "That will be soon if you keep this up."

"Don't talk so loudly, love." She attempted a smile. "This is my life. You've got yourself a nice boyfriend, and I'm happy. Really happy that my beautiful girl's making a good life for herself."

"But we could pay for rehab and move you into a nice flat. Frank could even visit."

"No," she insisted. "I like it here. And no rehab. I'm happy."

I interjected, "If there's anything you need..."

She stared up at me. "Some cash would be good." Her frailty vanished with those words, and suddenly, she'd become an opportunist. Pure survival mode.

"Mom!" Penelope rose and stood before her with her hands on her hips as though their roles had changed, which I sensed had happened a long time ago. I wondered if Penelope had even had a childhood.

"Right, then," Penelope said. "I'll order food and have it delivered. The cupboards and fridge will be filled every week. I'll hire a cleaner. But I'm not handing over cash. You'll only shoot it up."

Now I understood why Penelope wore fear in her face at the mention of drama, and why at times, instead of the youthful nonchalance befitting a twenty-three-year-old, her face wore the world-weary expression of someone double her age.

I'd buried the stench of my past so deep that I'd forgotten what it smelled like until then.

THIRTY-EIGHT

PENELOPE

IT HAD BEEN A ROUGH night. Visiting my mother with Blake had brought up all kinds of emotions—namely, guilt and helplessness.

How the hell am I going to save her?

Blake handed me a stiff drink, which I really needed. His eyes touched mine, and a gentle caress followed. I released a tight breath.

"Do you think I should be doing more?"

He studied me. "For your mother?"

"Yes. Do you think I should force her into rehab?"

"She'd have to be willing, and from what I observed, she's not."

"True." I visualized a couple of men taking her screaming into a car and me watching on twisted with despair. "If I don't force her, I'll be forever haunted, knowing that I could've done more. But if I do, then it will have to be heavy-handed." I laid my face in my hands.

Blake sat next to me on the bed and placed his arm around me as a brother would. I needed it that way—not as that hungry lover but as an understanding soul. He'd become both, which had one side of my spirit soaring while the other shriveled.

"You're not acting irresponsibly. The fact that you're concerned for her well-being speaks volumes."

Tears poured down my face. "I've never cried so much, Blake. You must think I'm a weak, helpless child."

He stretched over for the tissues and handed me a few. "It's okay. You're a sensitive woman, even if you seem stronger than me at times." His eyes shone with sincerity.

"How could that be? I'm a dribbling mess," I said.

"At least you're willing to look life squarely in the face. There's an honesty about who you are."

"And you aren't?"

He took a deep breath. "There are many skeletons I left behind. One day I'll open that cupboard, but for now, I'll just continue to shed a skin. Thanks to you."

"Thanks to me?"

"I feel lighter around you, Penelope. Although the background noise is getting louder."

"Dylan Fox?"

He nodded grimly and finished his drink in one gulp. He rose. "Let's not do this now. Let's just try to help your mom. I'm sure we can find a way."

I smiled sadly. "Thanks."

"Hey. It's me that should be thanking you."

"Why's that?"

"For having the courage to invite me into who you really are." He held up the decanter, poured some more into a glass, and took a sip. I could see that the night had affected him as deeply as it had me.

Blake strolled over to his jacket and removed his cell. "I'm waiting to hear from James."

"Anything?" I asked as he scrolled down his messages.

He shook his head. "Let's forget all about it for now."

I removed my cardigan. The room as always was very warm, so I headed for the French doors to the balcony.

"No. Don't open them, just take off your clothes." His commanding tone had returned. Instead of repelling me, it aroused me.

"I just need to taste you." His lips touched my neck, which sent ripples through me.

I smelled his arousal mingled with that fine cologne, which traveled straight to my sex. His fingers undid my bra clasp, and my breasts fell heavily onto his hands.

"I need to look at you." His voice was strained with longing.

A deep ache overwhelmed me. I removed my clothes, while Blake, the voyeur, sat back and watched, his legs slightly apart to allow room for his growing erection.

"Maybe I should learn a few moves. You know, like a stripper," I said with a nervous giggle. I preferred being in the dark without his eyes all over my chubby bits.

"No. I hate that sleazy shit."

I stood before him, naked except for my panties. "And this isn't?"

"It's very different. We're lovers." He stared at me with that aroused look he got whenever I was naked. He made me feel like I was the most desirable woman in the world. "Remove the panties, and go over to the table."

His authoritative rasp tickled my pussy.

"Bend over."

I laid my naked chest over the cool mahogany wood, my ass in the air, and my sex swollen.

My heart beat wildly, as he stood close and unzipped his pants. He rubbed his hard cock against my ass. His finger slid inside of me, making my walls spasm.

"Your tight cunt is nice and wet. You feel very nice." His staggered breath choked his words.

He fluttered over my clit with excruciating softness that sent anticipation of an orgasm rushing through me. His hard dick sat against my slit.

"You're beautiful," he murmured, inching the wet head of his cock inside of me.

He pushed in gently. The stretching ache made me moan. I parted my thighs wide to take him whole. He removed it slowly and then re-entered with a hard thrust that made me cry out.

His mouth landed on my neck and bit me gently, his palms taking my breasts as his pounding intensified.

Flexing my pelvis, I pushed my ass against him, encouraging him as we moved together, his pelvis fast and agile each time his large cock threatened to rip me in half. Pain had never felt so bone-meltingly good. His breath grew thick and ragged, his mouth on my neck moist and hot.

Smothering my breasts, his hands moved with that greedy hunger of lust.

In and out, the ravishing friction set off uncontrollable spasms. My moans increased.

His growls vibrated through me as a hot release poured out of him, and his gasp "I love you" penetrated through me.

Tears filled my eyes—pleasure, pain, and something indescribably profound.

He lay over me for a moment, having lost himself completely, as had I, while taking his weight on his strong, sinewy arms.

Basking in the afterglow of an orgasm that tingled from my toes, almost blasting me away, I turned around and looked at the mess of a man before me. I laughed.

His serious expression ironed out slightly, and a tiny smile touched his lips.

"What?"

"Nothing. That was so intense and amazing."

His eyes remained dark and serious. "You're mine, Penelope."

I didn't even flinch at that statement of ownership. He could have me. Totally. "As long as you're mine," I said with a sigh.

I fell into those deep-blue pools of complexity. One side of his mouth lifted, which I supposed was as good as a *yes*.

"Are you hungry?" he asked.

Although his swift change of mood jolted me out of our romantic bubble, I responded with an emphatic, "Yes. I'm starving."

He left for the bathroom and returned with a towel, which he handed to me. "How about if I get Maria to whip up some pasta?"

"Yum. Maria's a legend."

"That she is. Italian food's always been one of my weaknesses," he said, zipping up his pants.

"One of your weaknesses?" I lifted an eyebrow.

"Well." He grinned as he came toward me and brushed back my hair. "Girls with long dark hair and big brown eyes and…" His hands fondled my breasts.

"You're insatiable." I giggled.

"You're my weakness, Penelope."

"That may not be a good thing."

"Enough deep stuff for one night. Huh?" He tilted his handsome head and made me smile. "I'll go and see what Maria's been cooking."

"Great." I tightened the tie of his cozy bathrobe.

Just as he was about to leave, Blake paused. "There's something you could do for me, if you don't mind."

"What's that?"

"Call Lilly and find out what's happened to James."

"You want me to be your spy?"

"I need to find him. He's not returning my calls, which is very unlike him."

I nodded pensively. "Sure. I'll see what I can find out."

When I finally got through to Lilly, she told me that James was fine and even described their most recent sexual escapade. It was another girl-on-girl encounter, but this time, she said, "He got in on the action."

I cringed at how normal she made that seem, and steered the conversation away from her sexual escapades. "Tell me about James and Dylan Fox at the masked ball."

"Not much to say, only that they seemed chummy. Why?"

It sickened me hearing that James was chummy with Blake's enemy. I ignored her question. "Did you hang close? I mean, did you hear what they talked about?"

"I didn't hear anything. But come to think of it, James was kind of upset afterward."

"That Dylan Fox is a really bad guy."

"It was just that one time at the ball. He had an icky vibe about him, I have to admit. Creepy eyes."

I recalled how my bones had chilled from his creepy and undressing stare.

AFTER TWO DAYS OF hard work, I'd completed my essays. Inspired by Blake's unwavering belief in me, I put my head down and voilà, I finished.

Blake left me alone to work, while he met with designers for his new spa, which I couldn't wait to visit. I even found some time to sketch by the charming pond at the bottom of the hotel where we stayed.

Blake had missed his calling as an editor. He made excellent suggestions and pointed out repetitions, ambiguities, and grammatical errors. I kept shaking my head, and he'd respond with a questioning frown. The man just didn't accept compliments. He didn't have a vain bone in that beautiful body.

On the downside, my sheet clawing while Blake slept had darkened an otherwise perfect weekend. He'd warned me. His writhing and gut-wrenching cries not only kept me awake but turned me into a quivering wreck as well.

By morning, instead of making love, Blake sat at the end of the bed, shirtless, with his head in his hands. Looking raw, he looked up at me with those apologetic big blue eyes.

I wanted him more. His vulnerability brought him closer, even if he hated himself for it.

"Blake, you need help," I murmured gently, trying to bring him back. But he'd retreated into a solitary wilderness. His silence wedged a gap between us.

When we drove back home, I broached the subject of his violent nightmare with careful pauses. His hand reached out to mine, and without turning to look at me, keeping his eyes on the road, he murmured, "I'll continue to seek help."

"That means everything to me." I chose my words carefully, for it felt like a breakthrough of sorts. "I know you guard your privacy. But perhaps if you open up, it will help. You know I'm here for you, don't you? You can tell me anything."

"The truth will make you run."

"Blake, you've seen how I've lived all my life. It's far from pretty." I took a breath. "I've even witnessed a murder."

Blake turned sharply. "Really?"

I nodded solemnly. "One doesn't live twenty-three years at that estate without seeing something evil. I'm telling you this because I'm stronger than you might think."

"Oh, there's no question about that. I sensed that from the beginning. You're stronger than me."

"Not physically." I reached out and stroked his muscular arm.

His beautiful mouth lifted at one end. It was the sunniest he'd been all morning.

He took a deep breath. "I should have brought my sleeping tablets."

"I don't want you to take those just to sleep with me," I said.

"Then what do you want?"

His frustrated tone made me wince. "Normal, I suppose."

"Then you're with the wrong man. I don't do normal."

I bit my lip. A storm of emotion churned away.

Sulking, I turned my face to the window and stared at the streak of blurry green landscape. My eyes burned with tears.

"Penelope, I think you know how much you mean to me."

I sniffled and removed a tissue from my bag. "I guess we're fuck buddies."

"I hate that term. It's crass. We're not mindless teenagers. It's more than that. *You're* more than that. I just didn't expect this to happen."

"What to happen? Say it."

"*You* to happen."

"You make it sound as though I'm a disease."

"You're not." His voice had a frustrated edge. "You've given me more pleasure in the past couple of months than any woman I've ever known. And it's not just the sex. I like talking to you. You're incredibly smart, brighter than most. And your art, your creativity, your drive... you're one very special girl."

Special girl? I wanted to be the love of his life. I wanted to hear that he couldn't live without me.

"What's wrong, Penny?"

I turned to face him. "You called me Penny."

A little smile touched his lips. "That's what you wanted."

Short, sweet, and evasive as always. That was Blake. Not *short* of course, as he was tall and broad and so fucking beautiful, I wanted to devour him. And the darker he got, the sexier he became. Only, I wasn't sure my nervous system could cope.

We arrived at my new house—the house that bound us together.

He leaned in and kissed me gently on the lips. "I have an important meeting, but I'll drop in later. Okay?"

A cold feeling swept through me. Separation anxiety. I had it bad after two days together not just fucking but watching a little telly, talking about art, and working on my projects together as well. I'd loved every minute. Even if the nightmares soured things a little, those tender moments of closeness had meant everything to me.

"Are you okay?" he asked.

I shrugged. "I'm scared because I've fallen hard for you." I opened the car door and hurried out to avoid another stretch of silence.

I went to the door, and just as I was turning the key, I turned and noticed Blake watching me from the car. Our eyes met, and his face softened into a gentle smile. It was Blake's way of telling me that things would be okay and that we'd find a way.

I lightened. My clutching core released, and I blew him a kiss. His smile widened. It worked. We were good. For now.

LOST IN A DAYDREAM, I was sitting in my sunny living room overlooking the park when my phone buzzed. Blake's handsome face, trying to smile looked directly at me. His sultry stare seared into me with the same look as when he was inside of me.

"Hey," I said.

"Penelope. I'm afraid I can't come over later. I'm off to the Cotswolds. Milly's dying." His voice had a slight tremor.

"Oh. I'm sorry."

"I'm not sure when I'll be back. I want to stay with her. I'll call you."

"Sure. Please take care," I murmured.

"Bye."

And that was it. No "I love you." It was probably too much to expect and selfish of me to think about that. Milly meant the world to Blake. She was like family. In any case, I'd only heard him utter those words once, while he was in the throes of an orgasm.

I rose from the sofa. I had to stop thinking about Blake. There were things to do. When I wasn't in my studio, which was most of my spare time, I liked the kitchen to potter around in—I loved how it overlooked the garden. And I needed to organize rehab for my mother. I'd decided we'd drag her there screaming if necessary. I had to try something, or else I'd end up drowning in guilt for not doing enough.

I picked up my phone and pressed on Sheldon's animated face. "Hey."

"Hey, Penny."

"What are you doing now?"

"I'm in my studio, looking for any excuse not to work." He laughed.

"Why don't you come over to my new house? I baked some cupcakes, and there's a bottle of prosecco in my fridge."

"How can I refuse." He giggled. "I'm dying to see your new little house."

"It's not so little."

"That's right—a double-story terrace. Woo-hoo. We are stepping up."

"I can't wait for you to see it." I smiled. His contagious excitement bubbled through me.

"I'll jump in a cab now. Text me the address."

"Will do. Can't wait."

The cupcakes I'd baked sat prettily on the bench. I'd made them for Blake as a surprise, knowing his fondness for freshly baked cakes—a weakness he'd admitted to along with mentioning my tits and pussy. He had to, of course, make his love of sweets erotic. I didn't mind. Blake could keep whispering dirty little nothings all he wanted as long as he kept wanting me.

A pang of pathos touched me. I knew how much Milly meant to him. Leaning on my elbows, I contemplated his relationship with that sweet old soul, when the door knocker sounded.

I answered the door and found Sheldon standing there. "Hey, Penny."

I stepped out of the way, and he entered. "My God, overlooking the park." He whistled. "He didn't skimp, did he?"

I released a deep breath. "Blake's pretty generous."

"He really likes you." He stretched out his arm. "Show the way."

We entered the sunny living room. "It's a little bare. I haven't had time to shop."

Sheldon turned in a circle. "It's so sunny, and a gorgeous bay window—how delightful. You'll have to have a party."

"Maybe when, and if, I graduate."

"'If?' You'll be okay. You submitted your essays. You'll pass. You're brilliant."

I tilted my head. "You're so supportive. Let's go into the kitchen, and I'll open the prosecco."

"I like the sound of that. And there's that delicious smell of baking in the air. Yum."

When we entered the kitchen, I stood by as Sheldon looked out the window.

"The garden's gorgeous."

"Isn't it? I love being here. And wait till you see this." I led him into my studio.

When he saw the large space boasting the type of natural light an artist pined for, he squealed with approval, drawing an excited giggle from me.

"Oh my God, Penny." He went over to the bench, where my studies were scattered.

"These look great," he said, studying the pencil sketches.

"I've started working on one already." I pointed at my easel.

He stepped in front, and my heart beat with anticipation. Apart from Blake, no one had seen it.

"Oh my." His eyes switched between me and the painting. "This is amazing. Let me guess—the masked man is Blake? And you're the one in the ball gown?"

I nodded.

"You're carrying a briefcase," he said, studying it.

"In the next painting, that briefcase flies open," I said.

"Pandora's box?"

"Am I that predictable?" I didn't hide my disappointment. A little mystique went a long way.

"I just know you and your work. And I love that idea. The story of a mysterious billionaire and a young innocent soul whose life is also complex."

"You got it in one." I took hold of his hand. "That's why I love you. You get me."

"And I miss you," he said, hugging me. "I've become so unproductive. I liked having all of this around me. You motivated me."

"You can come here and work whenever you like. There's room for another easel and plenty of bench space."

"I might take you up on that. I don't work alone well. Too many years at art college, I think." He giggled.

"Come and have a drink."

I poured us a glass of bubbly, and we sat at the kitchen table, in the middle of which a plate of cupcakes smiled back at us.

The rest of the afternoon, we drank, laughed and then watched a movie together. It was like always, only this time, instead of me being at Sheldon's house, he was at mine. I saw him out at ten o'clock after he got a booty call from the love of his life, the cop.

When I settled back, I replied to a message Blake had sent me earlier.

He'd written: *I'll probably be here all night. Speak in the morning.*

Not even an *X* for a kiss. He was dealing with the impending death of someone close, I reminded myself.

I replied: *Feel free to call me at any hour if you need to talk. Love, Penny XXX.*

THIRTY-NINE

BLAKE

MILLY OPENED HER EYES. Her cool hand touched mine before she drifted off again. I asked if she was in pain, and she shook her head. She seemed peaceful.

Her quivering finger pointed to the drawer.

I pulled it open and found her journal.

"It's all there." She struggled to speak.

All there? My heart froze. *What will I find?*

I leaned in and whispered, "You've been like a mother to me. I'll always cherish your memory."

A tear slid down her pale cheek. "I've always tried to protect you... I'm sorry. I should have owned up to it ...too scared you'd hate me." She heaved. Breathless, she paused. "Just remember, I'll always protect you..."

Those were her last words.

Milly's paranormal inference shouldn't have surprised me. She'd always believed in ghosts.

I leaned in and kissed her withered cheek. Her last breath touched my face. One tear escaped my eyes. Just one. I wanted to cry more, but the tears remained frozen, close to my heart. The words "owned up to" kept ringing in my ears.

DRIVING INTO THE NIGHT, I wasn't ready for London. I needed a room alone, a bottle of whisky, and nothing but silence. No pulsating lights or the rib-punching noise of a bustling city.

I found a hotel through an app and booked it. It was only ten minutes up the road and somewhat shabby.

As I parked the car, people staggered into the hotel, obviously soaked in booze. It was that kind of place. Opulence would have been inappropriate and disrespectful to Milly. I needed to mourn somewhere real.

The room was clean, and that suited me. In any case, something told me I might not get much sleep.

I could count on one hand how often I'd cried. A knot of guilt twisted at the lack of tears I'd shed for my mother. It was when I'd found Harry hanging from our childhood tree that my spirit spewed out despair. Seeing my friend dangling from the tree that we'd climbed had broken me.

I poured a generous serving of whisky. It wasn't the time for moderation, and when it came to liquor, I had, according to Milly, the liver of an Irishman. I smiled at the memory of her and lifted my glass in a salute to the moon. "To you, Milly."

I returned to the journal that lay on the bed. Grabbing the lamp, I placed it over the page. In order to acquaint myself with her cursive writing, I read slowly.

Dear Blake, read this first. The rest is just the ramblings of a dotty woman.

When Harry died, tears poured out of me like blood from a torn artery. I wanted to scream the house down. Instead, I ran into the wood and yelled at God, telling him I no longer believed in him. How could I? Considering the evil-doing of men who preached his word. Harry's death came one week to the day after I killed that rotten priest.

I stopped reading. My heart palpitated wildly. *Milly killed Reverend Michael? But how? Didn't I kill him?*

Memories flooded back. I thought about that sickening crack of the skull followed by a deafening echo as the blood-stained candlestick crashed to the ground.

Pacing, I gulped down my drink, reliving that ugly moment that had been festering in my soul and haunting me all this time.

Frame by frame, I replayed that fatal encounter.

As he grabbed me one time too many, I seized a candlestick. For a fat man, he was strong. Just as he unzipped my pants, I cracked the brass stick over his skull.

The ground vibrated at my feet from his heavy thud. I didn't even look. I just dropped the weapon and ran.

An hour later, I returned to the scene. The candlestick had disappeared, and the place had become a crime scene. I trembled at the thought of prison. I was only fourteen.

Lucky for me, nothing had happened because the weapon was never found.

I continued reading the journal.

I entered the chapel and discovered that horrible priest moaning on the ground, his skull cracked and bleeding.

"Did you try to touch Harry?" I demanded.

"Please help me," he whimpered.

I stood over him. "Tell me the truth, or else I'll leave you to bleed to death."

"I love Harry," he moaned, his eyes pathetic and lost, pleading for mercy.

Possessed by anger so fierce that the very devil shot through my veins, I picked up the bloodied candlestick and knocked the evil bastard dead.
No other mother would lose her son again.
I hid in the forest, crying like a madwoman.
When I returned to the church, the candlestick had gone. My heart was in my mouth. The police had yet to arrive.

I tried to imagine what might have happened to the incriminating weapon. My fingerprints and Milly's were stamped all over it. Taking a deep breath to still my nerves, I returned to the page.

One week later, Harry hung himself. And it was my fault. The police had spoken to him, and then my son disappeared. I should have owned up to it. But I was too weak. In the end, as you know, they closed the case.
When Sir William told me one day that you'd saved his life, I knew I had to act, even though your mother had sworn me to secrecy.
Mary was like a younger sister to me. We both had had husbands who bashed us. She was pregnant with you the same time that I carried Harry.
She was a very beautiful woman, so it didn't surprise me that Sir William had taken a fancy to her. Your mother told me that she'd been Sir William's lover for many years, even while living with that savage man, who you thought was your father.
I couldn't judge either Sir William or your mother harshly. They'd both married badly. Sir William was a handsome man with black hair and deep-blue eyes. I never understood why Lady Catherine ended up in the arms of Gareth Wolf, that scruffy gardener.
Sir William wanted to marry your mother, but imagine the scandal, given that her husband was in prison.

One day, she confessed that you were Sir William's son. I should have guessed. You both had the same eyes.

The blood drained from my face. *Sir William, my father?* My father was the refined, elegant man who I'd admired for all those years, not that brute languishing in prison.

I opened the window and yelled. It burst out of me like an exorcism. My heart thundered. But it wasn't enough. Blood raged through me, so I grabbed the pillow, smothered my face in it, and cried my guts out.

Relief, frustration—an overflow of colliding emotions spewed out of me onto that pillow. After I got that out of my system, I filled a glass with whisky and drank it with the thirst of a man possessed.

Taking a deep, steadying breath, I picked up the journal and continued reading.

I managed to convince Mary to tell Sir William that you were his son. That was the same day that Lady Catherine, who'd been drinking heavily, told Dylan, in front of me and one other, that his father was Gareth Wolf.

It was then that I decided to collect a strand of your hair and Dylan's for concrete proof. Mainly for legal reasons so that you would inherit what was rightfully yours.

Sir William cried. He kept asking your mother why she'd waited so long. On his own admission, they were tears of relief. He'd always seen good in you and evil in Dylan.

On his deathbed, Sir William told Mary he'd changed his will. The DNA test and a testimony by the cook sat with the solicitor. Should Dylan have contested the will, he would have incriminated himself.

As for Lady Catherine, Sir William left her enough to keep her from spitting vitriol.

Your mother came to me the day before her disappearance, making me promise to watch over you. She was only forty, and I told her that she'd be around for a long time. The look on her face contradicted that.

Sir William made me swear on his grave never to reveal that he was your father. I could only assume it was to protect you from Dylan.

Never one to go against my word, I obeyed. Sir William was a good and honest man. I couldn't have asked for a fairer boss.

But I couldn't have gone to my grave with such a burdened soul.

I can now rest in peace.

All I ask is that my ashes be scattered in the wood by Raven Abbey.

FORTY

PENELOPE

HE STOOD BEFORE MY bed like an apparition. I jumped. It was early morning and still dark outside.

"Sorry to startle you like this," he said.

"What are you doing here, Blake?" I asked, lifting myself up from the bed.

"I had to see you."

I turned on the lamp. He looked different. His large eyes were alert.

Sitting on the side of the bed, he said, "I let myself in. I have a key." His half smile was so sweet that I leaned forward and held him.

"Are you okay?"

"I'm a Fox."

"Huh?" I asked.

"I'm a Fox, and Dylan, that lowlife, is a mongrel. A nobody. Just a piece of dirt."

"Have you been drinking?"

He removed his shirt and dropped his pants. He stood before me like a Greek god. My eyes traveled down to his cock, which had gone steel hard as his fingers slid over my skin, leaving a trail of heat.

I moved over, and he joined me in bed. I parted my lips, ready to speak, when his mouth landed on mine. His plunging tongue swirled around mine. We hadn't seen each other for a day, but it seemed like longer.

My body melted in his arms. I knew something big had happened. In that gaze lay the pain of loss but also a sense of release. I could feel it in his body as he held me.

"What's happened?" I asked, pulling away to stare into his eyes.

"I want to feel you. I need to know that you're real."

Before I could speak, his lips burned onto mine. His body, hot and needy, rubbed against me, his cock hard and moist against my palm.

His finger slid inside me. "I need to fuck you."

I surrendered by opening my thighs wide. He sucked back a breath through his teeth while entering me, his beautiful face on mine, and his eyelids heavy. His mouth fell open, and a groan touched my face.

He turned me around. "I need you this way." His hands smothered my breasts, his lips on my neck biting gently.

He thrust harder than I was used to. Something had bitten him. Overflowing with desire, I opened up and released my muscles, welcoming his fiery entrance. His cock moved teasingly against my walls. The friction was intense.

Red and raw, his cock moved in and out. With each entry, he hit an erogenous spot. My eyes rolled to the back of my head, and I trembled through one spasm after another as toe-squeezing pleasure ravaged my senses.

His breath tickled my ear. "Come for me, Penny."

He must have possessed magical powers, because that breathy plea registered in the same spot as where his dick landed and I released a deluge. A primal groan echoed off the walls as he shot into me as though impregnating me with his soul.

In a strangled tone, he murmured, "You're mine."

I *was* his. No question about it. He could do what he wanted with me at that point. I'd grown so attached to him that our spirits were one.

We held each other, and he kissed me so tenderly that it seemed his trembling lips were crying. Or maybe that was me.

As I held onto him, Blake fell asleep. He looked like a boy and was unexpectedly peaceful.

A few hours later, we woke in the same position, his head on my chest. No cries. He hadn't moved at all.

Something had changed.

He opened his eyes. Streaks of aquamarine shimmered before me, and I fell into them as I would the sea.

"Tell me you're not a dream," he said.

I shook my head slowly. "Why would you think that?"

"Because I have just had the best sleep I've ever had. It was me and you alone in a sunny, flourishing meadow."

"How's Milly?" I asked, studying him and wondering if he'd taken a trip or something.

"She passed. It was peaceful." Blake lifted himself up. "What time is it?"

"It's only ten."

"I'd better get moving. I left my car at some weirdo hotel. It's probably been stripped bare. I caught a cab." He smiled.

That was new too. He didn't smile like that ever.

I couldn't believe how buoyant he seemed, standing before me naked.

"Should we have a shower?" I asked.

He was about to say no, but I stood naked before him, and he took me into his arms. "I guess I need a little bit of breakfast." He wore a dark grin.

"You want to eat?" I asked, unsure if that was what he meant.

"Yeah. I sure do. I want to devour your cunt."

My pussy hissed in anticipation. I cocked my head. "You're being a little vulgar this morning."

He drew me tight and squeezed my ass. "Vulgarity in the morning leads to one thing only."

"And that is…?" I asked smiling.

"Pleasure. Unadulterated and dirty. The best kind."

I giggled. "Blake Sinclair, you're a sex maniac."

"I'll own that. But only with you." He looked at me, and intensity removed that rare smile.

"Blake, why aren't you sad?" I asked.

"I am sad. But for the first time in my life, I'm also free."

I furrowed my brow.

"Enough talk. I'm thirsty." His eyebrow arched.

I was thirsty too. My palate salivated at the thought of swallowing him whole.

A FEW DAYS HAD PASSED, and it had been such a blissful period for both of us. He slept in my arms every night, as quiet as a baby.

Blake mentioned the journal and then handed it to me. "Here, it's all there."

"You're entrusting me with this?" I asked.

He shrugged. "You're in my life, Penny."

Blake had taken to calling me that, and we'd entered a new phase in our relationship.

"I've still got a few issues to deal with, though."

"Have you spoken to James?" I asked.

"No. I've been too busy organizing Milly's funeral. She asked that her ashes be scattered at Raven Abbey in the forest, where her son's ashes were released. Would you like to come?"

I grew as excited as a child would be at the suggestion of visiting Disneyland. "I would love to—very much. I've never visited the moors." My mood flipped from that of joy to curiosity. "What happened to the candlestick?"

He took a deep breath. "I don't know." His eyes reverted to a darker shade of blue.

FORTY-ONE

BLAKE

"WHY HAVE YOU BEEN avoiding me, James?" I nodded at the waiter, who set down our drinks.

To get James to meet me, I'd virtually blackmailed him by threatening to tell his parents about Lilly.

"I've been caught up in a few things."

"How do you know Dylan Fox?"

James toyed with his glass. "From a few years back. He used to host these island parties."

"Island parties? By that you mean, sex parties?" I asked.

That little mischievous sparkle was missing. I'd never encountered James looking so serious. "Yep." He looked down at his hands.

"Did you lure me to the Cherry Orchard for a specific reason?"

"Why would you think that?"

"Oh, come on, James. No more games. I'm being set up by Fox, and you're right in the middle of it. You were spotted looking all chummy with Fox at the ball. It's pretty easy to join the dots."

He took a deep breath. "What's he got on you?"

"Some doctored images of me with a disturbingly underage Serbian girl named Tatiana."

"Tatiana?" He looked surprised.

"You know her?" I asked.

He moved his shoulders as though to release tension.

I leaned forward. "Just fucking tell me."

His hesitation tested my patience. James knew what I was capable of. I'd had my share of punch-ups at college, often protecting him from those belittling initiations that wealthy boys overdosing on testosterone inflicted.

"I fucked her."

"Tatiana?"

"But not when she was underage," he said. "Only about a year ago."

"What, at the ripe old age of sixteen?" I didn't hide my sarcasm.

His chest deflated. "He's blackmailing me. I had to lead you to him. It was either your head or mine. Sorry, old man."

"Don't give me that fucking 'old man' shit. I want the whole fucking story. What's he got on you?" I gulped down the whisky and lifted my chin to waiter.

When he arrived, I said, "Leave the bottle."

"Of course, sir. More ice?"

I shook my head. Once he was out of earshot, I leaned over and said, "I'm waiting."

I topped up his empty glass.

"The island parties involved virgins, some of whom were underage."

I frowned at him. "Shit."

He lifted his hands in defense. "Hey. I had no idea. She told me she was eighteen. And she fucking looked it."

I took a deep breath. "How old?"

He bit his lip. "Fifteen."

"You're fucking kidding. And now he's got that on you. But wouldn't that incriminate him for organizing those grubby events?"

"No. He's under radar. He's a sly prick."

"He's got proof of you with a minor, and he's blackmailing you to get at me. Anything else?"

He shook his head. "It was just to invite you to the Cherry Orchard."

"Which is where photos of me were taken." I sighed. "Who's his front?"

"No idea. I just went along to the island. Rupert invited me during a card session. He just told me that there would be some young, sexy girls. Not underage, though. I even asked that. They were kind of borderline. You know, that spectrum of thirteen to twenty."

"Fuck. Thirteen?" I shook my head in disgust. "You didn't, did you?"

"No fucking way. I was with Cristina, a Russian girl."

I sipped solemnly, contemplating the shitshow before me.

"Did you fuck Tatiana?" he asked.

"No way. I like my women to look like fucking women."

Knowing that about James, I wasn't sure how our friendship could survive. My stomach churned from disgust.

"Yeah. You've always had a thing for mature, chubby women."

"At least they're not emaciated and bordering on being fucking underage."

"Hey. Steady, Blake. That's bollocks. I was in the dark."

He took a deep breath. "What does he want?"

"Money. What else?"

"Much?" he asked.

"About four billion."

He whistled. "Fuck. He's aiming high."

"He thinks it's his blood right. What he's about to learn, however, is that his father, Sir William Fox, was actually my father and that he's the spawn of his mother's affair with the gardener."

James mouth parted. "Holy shit. I always sensed you were from good stock."

I cocked my head. "I don't subscribe to that elitist nonsense."

He grinned. "I take it you plan to see him face-to-face."

I nodded. "It won't be the first time I've knocked his teeth out."

"You can be a warrior when you want to. That's for sure. But hey, you don't want to go to jail over this."

"I don't plan to."

"I'm pretty unsettled with those images out there," said James. "What about a professional..." He looked about. "A hit?"

"Not my thing."

"Look, I'm really sorry to drag you into this."

I sat back. "Are you still with Lilly?"

"She's at my house. That creepy, fat Russian's still stalking her."

"You probably need to deal with him, then."

"Do you think that something might happen to Lilly?" he asked.

"You're the one that's been fraternizing with that lot." I raised a brow.

"I had my hand forced. I was young and stupid. I fucked up. I hope you and I are okay."

I had a flashback to our days in college. James had been there for me, when the gentry ostracized me for not being one of them.

I stood up. "I must go."

He looked up at me with a sheepish smile. "I hope we're good."

That wasn't going to be easy, knowing how I held onto things. And betrayal was at the top of my bad list.

"Can't say." I left it at that.

FORTY-TWO

PENELOPE

THE EMAIL ARRIVED WITH my results. My hand shook as I pressed the key down. I'd worked around the clock to get those final assignments in.

My eyes ran down the form, collecting the word *pass* along the way with distinction and ninety-eight percent for drawing. My art history essay also gained me a distinction. A cascade of joy rippled through me. I leapt off the seat and cried out, "I passed."

It was morning, and breakfast was coming. Now that Blake had miraculously been cured of his nightmares, he'd tangled around me like a snake all night.

He strolled back in from the bathroom and kissed me. "That's marvelous. I knew you would. You'll look sexy in a cap and gown."

I scrunched my nose. "I'll look silly."

"No, you won't. You could wear a sack, and you'd still be a sex kitten." He played with a strand of my hair. "Breakfast's on its way. I have to do something in my office for a moment. Do you mind? I won't be long."

"No, of course."

"Give me fifteen minutes. Breakfast should be ready by then. Okay?" He kissed me sweetly on the lips.

"All good." I smiled, indulging in his elegant stride.

Life was great for me, except that I'd tried to move my mother somewhere nice and clean, but she'd refused to budge. As Blake put it, my mother was married to her habit. I hated hearing that. It sounded like a cop-out to me. In spite of that, I was at a loss about how to change things. I could have called family services, but they would have taken her by force. The thought of that sent a cold shiver down my spine.

Around fifteen minutes later, Pierce knocked at the door.

"Come in."

He was like a sweet uncle. "Good morning, Penelope. I'm not sure where you want your breakfast?"

"Oh, just leave it there, thanks. I'll go and tell Blake."

"I can if you like," he said.

"No. I will. Thanks, Pierce. It smells marvelous."

"That's Maria for you. She's made us all a little chubbier with her amazing cooking."

I giggled, thinking of Blake, who wasn't chubby. He was just broad and muscular in that knee-weakening masculine way.

Pierce left the food on the table, and I headed to Blake's office which was more like a small library. I entered the room, and loved how the sun filtered through the colored-glass windows, infusing the space with a moody, warm glow.

My eyes settled on his desk, where I noticed an open folder with photos. I stretched my neck to look at them.

The image showed Blake on his side, his back to the camera. I recognized the scar. A very young girl, lying up on her side, faced him, wearing a flirtatious smile.

My heart sank to my feet. I ran out of his study. Blake was coming down the hallway. The blood drained from his face. He must have guessed what I'd seen.

"Penny!"

I ran into his bedroom, grabbed my shoes and jacket and ran out onto the pavement.

Blake followed me out and held me. "Where are you going? Let me explain."

I shrugged out of his arms. "Don't touch me. She's a fucking child."

A pair walked past and turned.

"Not here, Penny. Come inside. Let's talk about this." He grabbed my hand. "I've been set up."

I yanked my hand away. "I feel sick. She looked really fucking young. And what about all those young girls at that club where I first saw you?" My eyes pooled with tears. Having been on a high, the fall was steep, crashing me down to the gutter.

A cab happened to come by, and I hailed it.

Barefoot, Blake watched on helplessly, his hair uncombed and looking like we'd been fucking hard all morning. Which, of course, we had.

Was it just sex disguised as love?

That thought bounced around in my frantic mind, which switched between that image of the young girl on her side and Blake pleading innocence.

I arrived at Sheldon's. That was the only place I could think of going to. Being at my new home didn't feel right, and I just couldn't stomach the thought of the estate.

"Sweetie," said Sheldon at the door. "What's happened? Your exam results weren't good?"

"I did really well," I said flatly.

"But that's brilliant, isn't it?" He let me pass.

I followed him into the kitchen. "Sorry for barging in like this."

"No. It's good. Roger's just left." He smiled sweetly. His policeman boyfriend had finally owned up to their relationship, and I couldn't have been happier for him.

I hugged him. "You look so well."

"Mm... that's what a little morning rough and tumble will do for one's day." He giggled, but then his face became serious again. "I'm sorry to be so upbeat when you're clearly not. What's happened?"

I grabbed a glass of water and gulped it down, hoping to dilute the bitter taste of anguish. "I've left Blake."

His eyebrows contracted. "Why?"

"It just happened. We were so good, in such a great place. He was sleeping with me. No nightmares. I was—or should say am—in love with him." I buried my face in my hands, and sobs gave way to a deluge of tears. Just hearing myself say that had finally broken me.

Sheldon passed me a box of tissues. "You found him cheating?"

I blew my nose. "I discovered an image of him in bed with a girl that looked very underage."

Sheldon grimaced. "Really?"

I nodded.

"Let's have a coffee and think this through."

"Thanks Shelly for being here."

He hugged me, and tears erupted again.

I blew my nose. "He said he was being set up."

Sheldon lifted the espresso from the stove. "Then he might be. You don't know for sure."

"I felt like fainting. It was disgusting seeing that young girl..."

"He's very rich and powerful. It's feasible that somebody might have set him up." Sheldon poured coffee into two cups.

I picked up a cup and sipped. "But they were in bed together," I reiterated. Each time I uttered those ugly words, it didn't get easier.

"What about Photoshop?" asked Sheldon.

"That thought did cross my mind, and Blake mentioned it, but I don't know what to believe."

"Has he been calling?"

My phone was off. I turned it on out of curiosity, and sure enough, there were some messages but only one from Blake.

I listened to his first.

"Penny, I've been set up by Dylan Fox. You saw how he threatened me at the ball. That was photoshopped. I'll do everything to prove it."

"It's from him?"

I nodded glumly, staring down at a mysterious number. I listened to the message.

"This is Detective Constable Stephens. I'm calling about your mother. It's urgent that you call."

My hand shook.

"What's wrong, Penny? You look pale."

"I've got to make this call."

I pressed on his number, and he picked up straightaway. "Detective Stephens."

"Um... yes, this is Penelope Green. You left me a message about my mother, Sandra Green."

"Yes, I'm afraid I've got some bad news."

My legs started to tremble. I fell into the chair and took a deep breath.

"Your mother died from an overdose a few hours ago."

"An overdose?"

"Yes, heroin, I believe. Can you come into the station now?"

"Yes." Tears splashed over my lips. "Um, can you text me the address, please?" My throat thickened with sobs. I could barely speak.

"I'm sending it now."

"Thanks," I said.

I closed the call and stared wide-eyed into space. My mind was empty for once, as though neurons had been ripped out. All that remained was raw emotion drowning my senses.

Sheldon stood before me and opened his arms. I fell into them and bawled my eyes out. I must have cried more in that one hour than in my entire life.

"My mom's dead. She OD'd. I have to go to the police station."

"Oh my God. I'm sorry, Penny." He stepped back as I grabbed my bag. "Do you want me to come with you? I really would like to be there for you, love."

I shook my head. "Thanks, but no. It's okay. I've been kind of expecting this to happen." I blew out a breath. "It doesn't make it any less painful, though."

As I left Sheldon at the door, he said, "If there's anything I can do, I'm here. Call me."

I returned a sad smile.

FORTY-THREE

BLAKE

I AGREED TO MEET Fox at a private club where the well-heeled rubbed shoulders with shady characters.

"Looking handsome as always," he said.

"I haven't got all day. I've got a funeral to attend."

"Oh, that's right, your girl's mother died from a heroin overdose."

I contracted my brow. "How the fuck do you know that?"

"Oh, I know everything about pretty Penelope."

I lurched toward him. "If you go near her…"

His smirk stretched into a smile. "We've already tried that."

"What?" As I eyeballed him, James's suggestion to remove this ugly asshole became increasingly tempting.

"The junk dealers at that squalor she calls home gave my two guys a going over. One of my men's fucking spleen ruptured. She's got a few close buddies at that scummy joint."

"When?" My head went into a spin. I'd tried calling Penelope, but she wouldn't pick up. I'd left countless messages and was about to visit her at the estate when I heard the news of her mother's death. I thought it best to give her space.

"Yesterday." He leaned back. "I figured we might need some leverage."

"You go near her again, and I'll crush you with my bare hands."

"Oh, it's love. How sweet," he sang. "You're weak like that, aren't you? I remember how googly-eyed you were over Rebecca with the tits that bounced about in her low-cut tops. I fucked her too, just before you did." He leaned back, looking pleased with himself. "How does it feel to know that your dick swam in my spunk?"

I grabbed him by the collar, and my head landed close to his smarmy brow. It took all my willpower not to knock his teeth out.

All I could think of was Penelope's safety. I couldn't understand why she was at the estate. Her mother's funeral was being held that afternoon. Regardless of her refusal to see me, I planned to attend. We'd been through a lot together, and she knew more about me than anyone else. But over and above everything, Penelope had become a part of me.

I had to win her back, even if it meant losing everything.

A security guard came toward us, and as I released Fox's collar, it suddenly occurred to me to press record on my cell. I should have done that earlier, but I was too consumed with thoughts of Penelope to think clearly.

"I've got to make a call. Give me a minute," I said.

He took his phone out. "I haven't got all day."

After finding the record function on my phone, I placed it in my top pocket. Although sly as a snake, Dylan was also stupid in a lot of ways, a flaw that I'd always taken advantage of.

I sat down and sipped whisky. "This is the deal—Tatiana tells Penelope that I never touched her."

"That's going to cost your fortune. Fortune that belongs to me by birthright."

"It doesn't belong to you, Fox, and I know that for a fact. DNA results, sitting at the solicitor's, prove that you are no more Sir William's son than Harry was."

His smirk flattened, and an evil glint transformed him into the devil that he really was. "I don't give a fuck. You owe me."

Now, for most people, hearing that their father wasn't who they'd thought he was should have rattled them, or at the least, shocked them. Fox, however, remained stone-cold sober. No emotion. Textbook psychopath.

"I want the files as proof that you photoshopped that image."

"I didn't. One of my tech whiz kids did." He wore a self-satisfied grin. "I have a few of those. My girls aren't just pretty faces with tight pussies, you know."

"You fucking disgust me."

He laughed. As always, Fox took delight in my repulsion. I recalled his laughter at my tears when, as a boy, he'd used my dog for target practice.

"That overactive dick of yours made it easy for me, given your use of prostitutes. It wasn't easy getting that shot. Most of them were unpredictably loyal and refused. But then there was Mariah."

I flinched. Mariah was the last person I would have expected to betray me. I reflected on our last few sessions. She'd grown attached, and I'd stopped returning her calls. Perhaps this was her revenge.

"So Mariah took the shot, and this whiz kid made it look as though I was in bed with Tatiana. Bravo."

"Yeah. I thought so. And it was your good buddy James that we have to thank for all of this. Because those shots going into the club are nicely incriminating."

I pointed my finger in his face. "The underage girls lead back to you, Fox."

"That club's not in my name." He smirked.

I exhaled a breath. "So what next?"

"I want my inheritance."

I cocked my head. "I think you can stop calling it that now, don't you?"

"I don't give a damn as to whether I'm a Fox or a..."

"Or a Wolf." Now it was my turn to smirk. "How apt. Gareth Wolf, the gardener your mom was bonking, was your dad. I always thought you were fucking common."

He shrugged. "Unlike you, I'm not a fucking snob. I couldn't give a shit where I sprouted from." His beady eyes wore a smarmy grin.

"You'll hear from my lawyer."

He nodded. "Good."

"If you go anywhere near Penelope, your balls will be the first thing to come off."

"You get your solicitor onto this. You were ignoring my messages. We had to do something to gain your attention." He arched his ugly eyebrow.

FORTY-FOUR

PENELOPE

MY NERVES WERE SO raw I hadn't slept. After that encounter at the estate with those thugs, I decided to stay with Sheldon. I should have all along, but I needed to go back to where my life began to wallow and howl. I couldn't stop blaming myself for not being there to care for her. If I hadn't been indulging in Blake, I would have been there to call for help. And if Jimmy and Brent hadn't kicked the living daylights out of those heavies who'd tried to force me into their van, I wouldn't have been there to arrange my mother's funeral.

The chill in my body had not yet thawed. *Talk about stars misaligning*. It had been one hell of a crappy week.

I stepped into the local hall. Given my mother's staunch atheism, it would have seemed hypocritical to have a service in a church. Instead, Frank and I decided to hold it at the local hall, the same place where as kids we'd attended lessons or whatever community services were offered in a bid to give us a break from our miserable lives. For me, it was art. I'd learned how to paint in that little hall, which changed my life.

Sheldon held one of my hands and Lilly the other. Brent sat by her side.

Tears poured out of me as though an artery to my soul had burst.

"Oh, Penny. I'm so sorry." Lilly's tears became mine, and it all started again. My throat was so thick I couldn't talk.

I looked up at Brent. "Thanks for yesterday."

"Hey. It's cool. You can always count on me." I cast him a sad smile of gratitude.

Sheldon whispered, "Blake's here."

My legs trembled. I was too frightened to look. My eyes were blurred from weeping. I was a train wreck.

It had been a week since I'd run out of his home.

I loved him so much it hurt. That bone-chilling image hadn't diluted the intense passion I felt for him. Knowing what I now knew, ours was a dark descent into desire—a feast of fucking. *But it's more than that*, my soul whimpered.

He stood so close that a dizzying haze engulfed me. Sensing his breath on my neck, I leaned against Sheldon, who whispered, "I've got you."

"Penelope." Blake's deep voice penetrated through me.

I turned, and his sky-blue eyes fell into mine. Suddenly, we were alone. He looked tired and beautiful, and I just wanted to forgive him. *But who is he?*

"Thanks for coming." I kept it brief.

Normally clean-shaven, Blake had stubble around his jaw, accentuating his sensual lips. I tore my eyes away from him and looked down at my knotted fingers to maintain composure.

"Penelope."

Gazing up at him, I struggled to fight back more tears.

He took my hand. "I'm really sorry about your mother."

I looked away. "Thanks."

"After the service, will you give me a moment, please?"

Tears dripped down my cheeks. I must have looked a wreck as I glanced up at him. Drowning in his eyes, I surrendered with a nod before returning to my seat.

During the service, people spoke of my mother's kindness and how she'd helped the local kids with their reading and writing. My heart expanded, knowing that her life hadn't been a complete waste.

There was no end to my tears, and I sagged, weighed down by a heavy heart.

After the service, I witnessed Blake handing Jimmy a check. I took a deep breath and joined them.

"Hey, man, this is unnecessary. Penny's one of us. I mean, she's the good one." He turned and, acknowledging my presence, nodded. "Hey, I'm sorry about Sandy. She was a good woman."

"Thanks for coming, Jimmy." I nodded to the other guys, who'd gathered around him. The dealers. The so-called bad guys.

"Hey, we didn't supply her. Ever. You know that, don't you? She was like our mom."

"Yeah. I know, Jimmy." I looked down at the check in his hand. "Take it. He can afford it."

"But fuck. One hundred thousand? Shit." His face contorted in shock.

I almost smiled.

"Go somewhere. Start afresh. Stop dealing," I said.

He looked at Blake. "I can't take this, man."

"Please." He nodded. "It's yours. The other guy…"

"Brent," I corrected. "That's Lilly's brother."

"I gave him a check too. Take it." Blake tapped Jimmy on the arm. It was a strange pairing, and my heart went out to Blake. He seemed so soft. I wanted to fall into his arms and kiss him.

"Penelope." He looked deep into my eyes. "Can you please give me a moment alone?"

I followed him behind the hall. Over the road, at my old playground, I saw kids kicking a soccer ball around, full of energy and laughing like any child. I wondered if their moms or dads were junkies or alcoholics or sad, weak creatures that society had forgotten about.

"Blake, that was incredibly generous of you."

"It's small change. I would've given everything to save you. I'd go poor tomorrow if need be."

"You'd lose everything for me?" I asked.

"I might be about to."

My face pinched. "You can't give into blackmail on my behalf."

His face lit up slightly. "You believe that those photos were doctored?"

"How did they get that image of you on your side?"

"One of the women I was with must have taken it." He cleared his throat. "Before I met you, I used to hire professionals for my needs." He paused, looking contrite. "You know my views on relationships and ..."

"Then what was I?" I interrupted, refusing to overanalyze the fact he'd used prostitutes for sex. *Would I prefer a bevy of bitter exes following us around?*

"You were—I mean you *are*..." He took a deep breath.

For someone normally eloquent, Blake couldn't articulate his feelings. Just as I was about to push for more, Sheldon and Lilly found us.

"Hey," I said. "I'm coming."

"Take your time," said Lilly, acknowledging Blake. "We just thought we'd head over to the Lion for a few drinks."

I nodded and looked over at Sheldon. "Are you going too?"

"Yeah. Of course." He whispered, "With all those butch bad boys, I wouldn't miss it for the world."

Sheldon's cheekiness made me giggle, and boy, did I need some light relief. I kissed him. "Thanks."

"For what, sweetie?"

"For making me laugh."

He hugged me. "We'll see you there." He pointed at our local pub, a sticky-carpeted run-down place that was older than the estate. If the walls could talk, they'd reveal enough book-worthy material to fill crime shelves.

"Sure. Won't be long." I smiled. My spirit inflated. I had my friends and a history. Clean or dirty, it didn't matter. I'd finally unshackled myself from shame.

Studying his cell, Blake remained a few steps away.

I joined him. "You were saying?"

"Can we do this somewhere else?" he asked, shifting his weight.

"No. It's either here or nowhere. You need to get used to who I am. I am this." I pointed to the gray concrete surrounds.

"You're a sophisticated, creative, and beautiful woman."

"That's what you want me to be. But scratch the surface, and these people are the only people I've ever known. Except for Sheldon, that is."

"Penelope, even if you remained here at the estate, I'd still love you." He stopped at *that* word. I think he surprised himself because he looked down at his feet and took a breath.

Then he looked up again, and our eyes locked. Mine welled up with tears again. That artery of anguish hadn't healed. A thick lump in my throat blocked any coherent response.

He showed me his cell and pressed a button. "Penelope, please listen to this."

Muffled voices sounded. He placed the phone close to my ear. I listened as the two men discussed the photos. When Fox admitted to doctoring the image, Blake looked at me.

I removed the phone. "I believe you. I believed you before."

"Then why push me away?"

Good question. "Because one minute, I'm a struggling artist trying to manage a drug-addicted mother, and the next, I'm living amongst posh people in a posh suburb and letting a billionaire with a mysterious past fuck my brains out."

His brow wrinkled. "You make it sound sordid."

"But it's all about sex, isn't it?"

He held out his hand. "Your friends are waiting. Let's go and have a drink."

"You want to go the Red Lion? No one speaks proper in there."

"I'm not a snob, Penny. You forget, I'm from Yorkshire." He spoke in a northern accent, and accustomed to his well-educated voice, I chuckled.

"Come on, then," I said, allowing his hand to remain. It seared into mine. "You didn't answer my question. But I can wait." I wore a faint smile, and his eyes softened heartwarmingly.

FORTY-FIVE

BLAKE

"DO YOU COME TO this place very often?" I asked, stepping out of the dingy bar.

"Blake, don't do that."

"Do what?" I asked.

"Try to control me."

I lifted my hands. "Hey, it was only a question."

Noticing that Patrick had the car ready, I took Penelope's hand, and we headed over.

Seeing her slide onto that leather seat was such a simple pleasure, but profound nevertheless. My spirit lifted, especially after she glanced up at me with a faint smile.

As we drove away from the bar, my breathing returned to normal. The lingering stink of the run-down bar was a cogent reminder of how wealth had weakened me, because the stench of poverty seemed more pungent than it used to be.

The ride back to Mayfair was quiet. Our bodies were close together, and my hand was in hers. If it weren't for the ache between my legs, I would have described it as sweet, almost innocent. But as I glanced down at Penelope's nipples tightening against her blouse, my longing for her was far from that.

When Patrick pulled up at the curb, I jumped out and opened the door for her.

"Are you hungry?" I asked as we stepped into the hallway. I thought of the French fries at the pub that I could barely look at, let alone eat.

Following me into the living room, she nodded with a gentle smile.

"Make yourself at home. I'll be back in a minute." I kissed her tenderly. The warm softness of her lips sent a bolt of desire through me. I wanted to devour them right there, with my cock buried deep inside of her, but delayed gratification was something I'd learned to master when young and alone.

After I returned from the kitchen, I found Penelope curled up on the sofa, asleep. She looked so beautiful and peaceful I didn't have the heart to disturb her, so instead, I placed a blanket over her.

Just as the food arrived, Penelope woke. Sitting up and combing back her hair, she yawned. "Did I crash out?"

"You did. Only for an hour."

"I haven't slept much this week." She rubbed her eyes.

"Neither have I."

We shared a sympathetic smile.

"Come have something to eat, and then we can sleep," I suggested.

"Sleep?"

I returned her grin. "Whatever you desire."

After we'd eaten the delicious meal in comfortable silence, I asked, "What would you like to do now?"

"I'd love a shower," she said, stretching.

"I'll run it for you. I could use one myself." I suddenly felt formal with her, as though we hadn't been mindlessly fucking for months.

"From memory, it's big enough for both of us." Her arched eyebrow made me smile.

I headed into the bathroom and turned on the faucets. I removed my clothes, and my eyes remained on Penelope as she removed her black skirt and blouse.

I took her into my arms and walked her under the cascade of water. We held each other as pleasant warmth splashed over us. I squirted some body wash on my hand and massaged her back.

"Oh, that's so nice," she purred.

I slid my fingers along her indented waist to her peach-shaped ass and massaged it. Then I leaned in close, my body pressing onto hers, and kissed her neck. Her moans sent a bolt of hunger to my cock. I caressed her clit, which winced at my touch.

I turned her around, and our lips crushed together. Just kissing her electrified me. Her lips caressed mine as my tongue entered her deeply and urgently.

"I need to taste you." I stared into her heavy-lidded eyes, which mimicked my own. I was so aroused I could hardly breathe, my heart pumping desire down to my engorged dick.

She widened her legs in response.

I got down on my knees and licked my way up her thigh, arriving at her inflamed clit. I twirled my tongue and sucked back her juices as if it were a delicious treat until she cried out and came all over my lips. I entered her with my finger, which made her tremble. She was so wet and ready to be fucked. I groaned.

Standing up, I turned her around and rubbed my dick against her round ass, my hands all over her plump, firm breasts. She arched her back, her ass gyrating against my belly, enticing my cock.

The intensity of the pleasure shivered through me, as though I'd been starved and had taken my first bite of a delicious banquet.

I moved my palms against her spiky nipples. "You're so fucking tight. Do you want me to fuck you hard?"

"Please."

Her sighs registered straight to my dick. I bit into her neck to stymie the growls that rumbled through me. The snug fit and sheer pleasure of being inside her was so excruciatingly intense that I wanted to blow straight away.

I continued grinding my pelvis against her perfect butt until her muscles spasmed and tightened around my cock. Trembling in my arms, Penelope cried out, her convulsing pussy squeezing me so tight that it only took one more thrust, and I came so intensely it felt as though I'd poured everything into her.

No woman had ever made me orgasm so violently.

After my breath returned, I murmured, "I need you in my life, Penny."

"I like being in your life." She turned to face me.

I pushed her hair away from her face and kissed her tenderly. It was a kiss of love, our lips fusing our souls.

"Will you marry me?" Although I never expected to utter those words, they arrived with little effort or thought.

She stepped out of the shower and into the warmed towel I held open for her.

Penelope's silence left me suspended.

Grabbing a towel, I dried my hair. "Too much? Too soon?"

She shook her head. Her eyes pooled with tears. "I don't know what to say. We've only known each other for a few months."

"I love you." I held her. "This has been the worst week of my life. And that's saying something." I paused for her to respond but she looked at me expectantly. "I missed not having you close to talk to and to hold. It wasn't just my dick missing you."

Her limpid, moist eyes met mine, and a sad smile touched her lips.

"Why didn't you ring me after those thugs tried to abduct you?"

"I wanted to. But I was trying to hate you. Those photos really gutted me."

"You do believe me, don't you? I'm not into young girls. If anything, I go for mature women."

She turned dark. "Mm... prostitutes."

"I can't change my past." I brushed back my wet hair with my fingers. "I'm *not* into young girls. The mere thought of it disgusts me."

"Why were you at the Cherry Orchard?"

"James was blackmailed into drawing me there."

"But you went."

Good point. "It was out of curiosity. I had no idea that half the girls were that fucking young."

"Did you go in and watch them?"

I nodded. "Only because I wanted to see you. If you'd been there, I would have bought you, no question about it."

She grimaced. "That was never going to happen." She made a mock smile. "Did you watch any of the girls spread their legs? Even Lilly?"

"No. I didn't go that far. Lilly would know that."

She followed me into the bedroom. "Why is James being blackmailed?"

Taking a deep breath, I repeated James's story. Her eyes rolled with disgust when I told her about the sex parties on the island and the underage girls. I couldn't blame her. Even in the retelling, I was repulsed.

I poured a shot of whisky and held up the bottle.

Penelope shook her head. "Just water, thanks."

I passed her a glass of water. "Let's go to bed."

I undid her towel and held her close, breathing her in. Her soft warmth melted my heart.

"I've missed this more than I could've imagined," I said quietly, almost to myself.

"The sex, you mean?" Penelope looked up at me.

"No. I mean. Yes. I find it hard not to touch you and"—I was about to say "fuck" but opted instead for a term I'd never used before—"make love to you. But it's more than that."

We lay down, and I held her in my arms. All the dramas unfolding around me faded away. Her head rested on my shoulder as I stroked her gently. She turned to look at me, and my lips met hers. It was tender kiss, soft and profound, filled with emotion. I tasted her tears.

"Are you okay?"

"I just can't believe I'm here with you and that this is all real."

"It's real, all right." I stroked her hair. "I really missed this."

"What? Fucking me?"

"We're not fucking right now." I looked at her. "I meant, just holding you. It surprises me."

"How so?"

I exhaled. "I'm normally claustrophobic. I used to hate being hugged."

"That just makes you uptight."

"Yep. Guilty as charged." I sniffed. "I don't have to put on an act around you."

"Why would you anyway? Have you looked in the mirror lately?"

"I try to avoid them. In any case, that's just superficial crap. It's what's in here." I tapped my head.

"So, you only like me for my brain?" she asked with a teasing smile.

I fell into her seductive dark eyes and grinned. I pointed to her face. "You're also pretty easy on the eyes."

I stroked her breasts and palmed her cherrylike nipples. "I'd be lying if I didn't admit to getting hard watching the bounce of your beautiful tits when you walk." My fingers continued down to her pussy. "And you have a very sexy pussy."

"I don't like cats. I prefer dogs." She cocked her gorgeous head, and I laughed.

I parted her folds, and my finger entered her creamy pussy. "You're mine. No one has ever been here. I want it to remain that way. I want this tight little cunt for myself."

She let out a sigh as I continued to rub her clit. "You're dirty. You know that?"

"Mm... nothing wrong with being dirty around someone you love, is there?"

She bit her lip and shook her head, her eyes watery and her cheeks flushed. "No. I like dirty too. And..." She stroked my throbbing cock. "I love your big dick inside of me."

She rubbed herself against me provocatively.

She turned, but I held her there.

"No. I want to see your eyes when you come."

Her sweet smile was so seductive that my dick was engorged to the point of eruption. One week without sex with Penelope seemed a lifetime. I was clearly addicted.

She spread her legs wide and allowed me on top. Her nails dug into my arms as my dick slid in. Although she was tight, she was lubricated from my earlier orgasm.

Her pelvis grinding against mine and the heat and intensity of feeling her threatened to take me over the edge. I fondled her breasts as our groins gyrated in perfect rhythm, her tightness engorging my hungry cock.

My lips ate hers as we found our rhythm, I felt her little cunt tighten around my dick, and moaning sweetly in my ear, she shuddered in my hands while, at the same time, I climaxed.

"I love you" was the last thing I remembered saying before succumbing to a satisfyingly deep, nightmare-free sleep.

FORTY-SIX

PENELOPE

RAVEN ABBEY LOOKED LIKE something out of *Grimm's Fairy Tales*. I almost expected a scarf to float out of the turret's window. It certainly was an artist's playground, and I couldn't wait to create some sketches.

I was so taken with the facade, climbing up the stairs to what was now a hotel, that I tripped, and Blake caught me in those strong arms of his.

"You lived here?" I asked, my mouth wide. The grand entrance with the double staircase that spiraled to the first floor captivated me.

Blake nodded.

"Hello, Mr. Sinclair," said the woman at the desk.

"Morning, Claire. This is Penelope, my girlfriend. Just taking her for a tour."

"Welcome," she said in a broad Irish accent.

"There's a fresh batch of scones being served." She gave me a bright smile.

Blake looked at me, and I nodded keenly. The country air had stimulated my appetite.

We broke our journey by staying at Nottingham, which was like stepping back in time. I gasped in wonder as we wandered through the forest, imagining Robin Hood in a tree, about to pounce. We even stayed at a castle that was now a hotel. I was convinced there were ghosts, given the creaking doors and howling wind, but it made for an entertaining experience, although I couldn't have done it alone.

Blake's tanned features had a healthy, warm glow. He looked different. In London, he wore cosmopolitan sexiness with ease, but in the country, the light made his eyes bluer, and he looked ruggedly handsome amidst nature.

The visit was primarily to scatter Milly's ashes, and after my emotionally challenging fortnight, the countryside was just what I needed. I was touched that Blake, a normally private person, wished to show me his birthplace.

There was no question—I did want to marry him. After that heart-wrenching break, I couldn't imagine my life without Blake. I just needed to know that it wasn't only lust, given that he couldn't take his hands off me. I loved having them all over me. Our deep sexual connection was torrid and addictive.

But can we do forever?

We sat in a big sunny room converted into a restaurant. Butter melted all over the freshly baked scones. I added some raspberry jam and whipped cream, and after taking a bite, I sang, "Yum."

Blake wiped his lips and nodded. "Mm... they're terrific all right." He smiled wickedly. "Even the simple act of eating scones and jam is erotic around you." He pointed at my cleavage.

I looked down and saw that some jam had slid down my front. "Ah... damn." I grabbed a napkin to wipe it.

He shook his head. "No. Don't. Leave it, and I'll lick it off. With pleasure. In fact, this jam is so damn delicious I can imagine it spread all over you."

I giggled and heated up at the same time. But I ended up cleaning it up anyway after noticing an elderly couple entering the room.

"This was once the ballroom," said Blake, pointing up at the chandeliers.

I was in awe of the stained glass windows. "It's overwhelmingly beautiful. I can't believe you lived here. Did you play in this room too?"

He smiled sweetly. Blake wore the type of smile advertising agencies would have sold a kidney for. When I first met him, his lips had rarely curled.

"Why are you looking at me like that?" he asked.

"It's just nice to see you relaxed. I don't think I've ever seen you like that before."

He reverted back to his natural earnestness. "I've had an eventful, life-changing three months, Penny." His hand landed over mine.

"As have I," I returned. "I'm so grateful to be here, especially after hearing about it. But I only see magic here."

"There's magic because you're here. It's a form of alchemy. We have an effect on places. You bring light and beauty even to that run-down estate where you were born."

It was another Blake-making-me-melt moment. I unstuck my legs from the chair. "That's profound and very complimentary."

The sun poured in for the first time. Although the morning had been gray, suddenly, at that very moment, a burst of warm light settled on us like an aura binding our spirits. Blake's eyes smiled in acknowledgement of it.

After I polished off my third scone, I said, "Since you moved here as a young boy, how was it that your mother and Sir William..." I sought a delicate choice of words.

"My mother worked at Raven Abbey all my life. We moved here after that asshole she married went to prison. Clearly, my mother and Sir William..." He paused.

"Your father, you mean," I interjected.

"Yes." He rubbed his neck. "That still sounds strange, even if it's elevating knowing that I share DNA with such a great man."

"Then Sir William and your mother formed a relationship before you were born."

"So it would seem," he said with slight hesitancy.

I reached over and touched his hand. "I hope you're not judging your mother for cheating on her savage wife-beating husband."

He shook his head. "No. I forgave her a long time ago. I just didn't know that I was the result of it."

"Thank God." I smiled. "I couldn't imagine a world without you."

A sad smile touched his lips and turned his eyes a tender turquoise shade. "And I couldn't imagine my life without you."

We touched hands and remained lost in each other's gazes.

Snapping out of that brief moment of enchantment, Blake glanced down at his watch. "I just realized I'm running behind. I need to go to Leeds to visit the solicitor."

"Then can I stay here until you return? I'd love to draw."

"Of course." He touched my hand. "I'll let him know." He removed his cellphone from his jacket. "Let's head up to the room."

After Blake made his call, we climbed the serpentine staircase to the room that had once been Sir William's. A sigh of wonder left my chest. The huge room with large windows overlooking a thick wood seemed to go on forever.

Crimson walls were framed in gold-leaf detail, drawing my attention to the gilded neoclassical art. Since that was one of my favorite periods, I ogled at the languid goddesses poised by arches and in forests.

"Oh my God. I don't think I'll ever leave this room. It's so delightfully feminine. Were the paintings Sir William's?" I asked, noticing that the original works were screwed into the wall.

He nodded. "Although I was advised to place them in a vault, I couldn't do that."

"How noble. I hate the idea of beauty hidden away from the world."

A faint smile touched his lips. "I share that view. In any case, most people are vetted, and we have their details, so if they tried to steal a painting, we'd find them."

Blake smiled again. I sensed that this journey back to his former home had had a significant impact on him due to Sir William being his biological father.

He pushed me onto the bed gently and ravished my mouth. "I've been dying to do that all morning."

I giggled. "How long's it been? Three hours?" I thought how we'd fucked like teenagers, making the floorboards creak, at the castle. Blake had grumbled something about how, when it came to places to fuck, only modern buildings delivered discretion. He possessed surprising modesty for a man with such an overactive libido.

His mouth ate at mine, and his hand slipped under my skirt and into my panties.

"You're very wet, Penny."

"Must have been the yummy scones and the paintings."

He unzipped his pants and lowered his briefs. His big hard cock sprang forth. "I thought it might have been my animal charms."

"That too." I touched his cock, recalling how I'd gagged after I'd sucked on it that morning.

He placed his head between my legs. I never tired of that tongue, and Blake went down on me more often than I blew him. I thought I wasn't doing it properly. I'd even asked him, to which he replied that his dick loved my cushiony lips but desired my tight cunt even more.

It was raw, unbridled lust, and as his tongue whipped up another sheet-gripping orgasm a torrent of pleasure gushed through me.

His hands slid over my body as though on a voyage of discovery, soft and tender, and then he parted my legs almost roughly, which I liked too.

"I thought you had an appointment," I said breathlessly.

"That can wait." He entered me in one thrust that made my eyes roll to the back of my head.

His deep penetration hit spots that made my pussy convulse from the scorch of sensation. He rolled me on top of him, and as I moved up and down, his eyes were on mine, love written in them.

Blake's cum-stained lips parted. His heavy breath expressed the aching arousal I felt grinding over his hard cock, and I opened like a flower as the buildup moved toward what promised to be another convulsive climax.

My drenched nipples ached from endless sucking, and my breasts were smothered by his constant fondling.

Blake's eyes were hooded, and he became lost in his own erotic bubble. His chest collapsed, and a raging release erupted through me, clutching his cock and drowning it in a torrent.

His head fell back, and a gasp turned into a groan as he emptied himself into me.

I fell into his arms. Our breathing was rapid and in tandem as we gradually made our way back.

"You're an exquisitely sensuous creature," he whispered.

AFTER BLAKE LEFT FOR his meeting, I went for a walk in the forest.

A pretty bird with blue wings had me sighing with wonder. It really did feel as though I'd stepped into a fairy tale. Golden gossamer sunbeams filtered through the trees as though sent from heaven.

The forest had hints of the supernatural, as though I could step into a beam of light and be whisked away to another time. I wished I could, even though I would miss Blake.

Infiltrated by these strange but pretty thoughts, I ambled along the avenue of glistening soft green leaves. Taking a deep breath of fresh air, I lifted my head up to the giant trees and found the sky smiling back at me.

At the end of a path snaking from the wood, I spied a cute picture-perfect cottage. Bathed in sun, the garden exploded in an array of colors.

I headed over to take a photo, expecting to see a witch. It didn't give me a bad vibe, though. If anything, I'd been transported to another time, when technology was only a word and not a way of life.

Stooped over, gathering herbs, a woman with long dark hair noticed me and smiled. "Hello there."

"Hello. I was just admiring your lovely cottage. I hope you don't mind me looking."

"Not at all. It's such a nice day to be out and about. Are you a tourist?"

I nodded. "That I am. From London. I'm staying at Raven Abbey."

"Oh, how nice. I'm just collecting some chamomile."

I looked over the picket fence. "This garden is so perfect. The colors are amazing."

"Many come by and take photographs. I imagine there are a few postcards getting around." She chuckled.

"It's wonderfully photogenic, and your garden's a delight."

"Thank you. It's a labor of love."

"My name's Penelope."

"I'm Marion," she said, smiling sweetly.

"I envy you living out here in this wonderland."

"It's not an easy life. I have to work at it. I grow most of my food, and I have some animals at the back."

"That's so admirable, though."

She smiled again.

"Well, I'd best be getting back."

"Nice meeting you, Penelope."

"And you."

I watched her as she went back into her home.

I ARRIVED TO FIND Blake asleep. He looked so peaceful that I couldn't disturb him. I held up the bottle of whisky. For some reason, I felt like a hit.

"It's a bit early for that." I heard from behind.

I turned to see Blake with his hands behind his neck, smiling and looking relaxed.

"Did you go for a walk in the forest as planned?" He rose from the bed. "I might as well join you." He lifted the crystal decanter and poured himself a shot.

"I did. I met someone who lives in a cottage outside the wood."

"Right. A man?" His frown nearly made me chuckle.

"No. A woman."

"That cottage belonged to Gareth Wolf. But he's no longer alive."

"Her name's Marion. She grows her own food and has animals. She was lovely."

"Marion?" Blake studied me. "What did she look like?"

"She had dark eyes and hair and a scar on the side of her face. Very pretty, though."

The frown on his face deepened. "What side?"

"Huh? The scar?" I asked, feeling a tightening knot in my tummy from Blake's sudden intensity.

Gulping down a shot of whisky, he nodded.

"On the left side."

An aching gap of time fell between us.

"I'm going there now," he said at last.

The breath that I'd been holding escaped. "Why? Do you know her?"

He didn't seem to hear me. I followed Blake and half expected him to stop me, but he seemed lost in a trance as I scurried along behind him.

FORTY-SEVEN

BLAKE

WE SHOULD HAVE BEEN scattering Milly's ashes at twilight as she'd requested. Instead, I almost ran along. I knew that forest path so well I could have moved through it with a blindfold on and still found the cottage that now housed my undead mother.

It had to be her. The scar gave it away. It was from her fucking savage husband after he'd held a knife to her throat before slashing her face in one of his drunken jealous rages. Hiding under the table as a six-year-old, I watched on, shivering through a cold sweat. That experience, which felt like fingernails digging into a wound, flashed before me.

But why fake her own death?

It was assumed she'd fallen into the river. They'd even sent in divers. Now I understood why her body had never been found.

I slowed down just as we reached the edge of the wood. At my shoulder, Penelope stood. Her panting blended with the hum of scurrying birds.

She clutched her arms. "Why are we going to the cottage? Do you know her?"

"I think she's my mother." I took a deep, steadying breath and held out my hand. "Come."

"What makes you think that?"

"Your description and the scar on her face."

"But that's kind of vague, isn't it? I thought your mother's name was Mary."

"*Marion* is close enough, wouldn't you say?" I said.

Her small, soft hand clasped mine, and suddenly, the tension dissolved. I could face anything with her by my side. Her reassuring half smile had a calming influence.

"I hope she doesn't mind us bursting in like this."

"It's only six o'clock, Penny."

As we moved along the path, memories of playing by the cottage flooded back. I opened the squeaky gate, and my tread became hesitant. With each step, my pulse accelerated.

"Perhaps you should go first," I said.

Penelope knocked tentatively while I waited there. A bead of sweat slid between my shoulder blades. A part of me hoped it wasn't her. Because the thought of her abandoning me was unbearable.

It took some time before we heard footsteps.

When she opened the door, I hid to the side.

"Oh, Penelope, how nice to see you so soon."

It was her. I recognized the voice. I walked like an invalid to the door.

When she caught sight of me, my mother placed her hand over her mouth. "Oh my God. Blake."

She leaned against the wall as if she might faint.

As I helped my mother onto a chair, Penelope ran into the kitchen and brought back a glass of water.

The glass trembled in my mother's hand while she sipped.

Although her eyes were drowning in tears, I recognized suffering and guilt.

A lump blocked the words forming in my throat. I fought with all my might to remain strong. I glanced over at Penelope. She bit her lip, and a tear slid down her cheek.

I lowered myself down to a seat facing my mother and waited for her to settle. Penelope reached for a box of tissues and handed them to my mother.

She wiped her nose, and a sob escaped her as she attempted to speak. She cleared her throat. "I'm sorry, Blake. I had to go away."

"But you haven't left. And what about the staff? Haven't they seen you?" I paused for a breath. "As you probably know, I retained them when I converted Raven Abbey into a hotel."

"Only one knows about me, and that's Rebecca. She lives in Leeds with Ben. You remember Ben, Alistair's boy?"

I nodded. Questions rammed at me like a raging bull.

"I'm sorry I haven't offered you anything," she said in that soothing tone that once calmed me.

Penelope rose. "I can arrange it if you like."

My mother smiled at her. "So, you're both together?"

I nodded.

"Oh, I'm so pleased. I enjoyed our little time today." Her sad smile made the lump grow in my throat.

I wanted to hold her. Hug her. But I needed to hear why she'd left me without a word.

"I think this calls for something stronger than tea," she said, rising. She stopped and stroked my cheek. "You're exactly like him."

"Like who?"

"Sir William. Did Milly tell you?"

I nodded. "Did Milly know you were alive?"

"No." She lifted a bottle. "Sherry, whisky? I have some beer in the fridge."

"A whisky would be good," I replied. She looked over at Penelope, who shook her head.

My mother poured two generous shots and passed me a glass.

I took some time to gather my thoughts, sipping. "Why?" I finally asked.

My mother looked down at her glass. "To hide from that horrible beast that I married."

"He's still alive?" I asked.

She shrugged. "I'm not sure. But I can't risk it. I received letters from prison. I never told you at the time, because I didn't wish to alarm you. You had your own demons."

"You know about that?"

"About the priest, you mean?" she asked.

I nodded.

She let out a deep breath. "I only learned about it the day before Milly struck that blow. I had no idea. I'd been a bad mother." She sighed. "Out of touch. Even Milly confessed to not suspecting anything until she got it out of Harry, who told her that the sick bastard priest had touched you too. Knowing that you worked in the chapel in the mornings, I went there."

"You weren't a bad mother. But running away without telling me—that's hard to accept." I stared her in the eye. "Did Milly tell you she finished the priest off?"

She appeared haunted. "I watched it happening."

My brows met. "By that, you mean you saw me?"

She nodded.

"You hid in the chapel?"

"It's a dark place, darling. Even during the day."

She continued, "I didn't expect Milly to run in. She didn't see you leave. She thought Harry had struck that first blow." My mother paused for a breath. "After you struck him, I struggled with whether to call an ambulance or pick up that candlestick and finish him off. But my legs froze. And then Milly arrived, and she had the courage to do what I couldn't. I'm glad she did. He was evil. Too many boys. It all came out after that. Many locals opened up about their sons, some of whom took their lives, like poor Harry." She sighed mournfully. "The local police investigated but closed the case after the weapon wasn't found. I think they realized there were too many suspects. And it had already had a heavy impact on the community. I'm sorry for not protecting you. If I'd known..." Tears poured down her face.

A lump settled in my chest as I took my mother's hand to comfort her. I took a deep breath. "Did you remove the candlestick?"

She nodded, pointing at the mantelpiece.

There it stood, like a trophy, gleaming and glaringly obvious.

"You can't have that here. What if they find it?"

"Nobody comes here, my love. Only tourists and lovely strangers, like Penelope."

"And from what I heard you had a casual chat. What if the next person is a man or someone with malicious intent? You're out here alone."

She chuckled. "Oh, Blake, you always had an overactive imagination. I can protect myself. In any case, I have the candlestick."

Her dark humor failed to allay my sudden paranoia. "I'm not sure, I feel comfortable seeing it there."

"It's a testimony to whoever's up there." She pointed to the sky. My mother had always been religious, although not necessarily in the Christian sense.

"Why didn't you tell me? I've missed you for all these years. The pain of not knowing what happened to you has never left me."

Penelope sat close and held my hand.

"My sweet boy. He threatened to come for me. I was terrified. After William died, I had little choice."

"But I would've protected you. You could have lived with me." I took a breath to still my emotions. "Milly recently passed away. That's why I'm here—to scatter her ashes in the wood close to Harry's."

A sad smile touched her face. "You've always been a good boy."

For a moment, I forgot that I was a thirty-year-old man. I wanted her to cradle me. I'd become that young child who once craved her warmth and protection.

"Had I gone to London Jack would've followed me. And then he'd have created problems for you." Her voice cracked again. "I should've intervened sooner."

Her change of subject jolted me back to my abuse by that depraved priest.

"How do you know that Jack's still alive?"

"I don't. But I can't risk it, son." Her distraught features brought back the awful abuse my mother had suffered while living with that man. I finally understood why she'd gone into hiding.

I persisted nevertheless. "I could've protected you."

"Darling, I knew that if you remained here, caring for me, you would've become the lord of the manor. Look at you now. You're a sophisticated man of the world. And turning Raven Abbey into a tourist destination has brought so much wealth into the community. It was a sacrifice I'd make again."

"But how have you managed to lay low? It's such a small place. Everyone knows everyone."

"I keep to myself. I grow my own food. I have a goat, chickens, and a cow. Online shopping is also pretty useful." She smiled at Penelope. "I've always been a sucker for a pretty dress."

"Aren't you lonely?" I asked.

"No. I have my garden. Books. Memories. And now I have you. You will visit again?" Her imploring smile melted my heart.

"I'd like you to come back with us. I have a very big house in London."

"I knew you'd do great things. Milly was right to arrange that DNA test. William was always close to you. He loved you even before he discovered that you were his own flesh and blood. He told me that before dying. He didn't like Dylan and was relieved to learn that Dylan was Gareth's son." She stared wistfully into the distance. "He was the love of my life, Blake. I hope you don't think poorly of me."

"You gave me life, Mother."

We hugged, and that lump in my throat thickened.

FORTY-EIGHT

PENELOPE

WE ENDED UP STAYING for tea. The stories of Blake growing up at Raven Abbey warmed me. It was nice to hear about the good times.

Mary insisted we stay the night, but Blake explained that we needed to be in the city by morning. Given the whirlwind events of that day, I'd forgotten I had my graduation ceremony to attend. Putting aside Blake's dark history at Raven Abbey, I found myself enchanted by that Gothic estate.

Mary saw us to the door, wearing a wide smile. Her heart seemed to spill over.

Blake appealed to his mother again. "Why don't you to come and live with me in London?"

"Darling, just come and visit as often as you can. And stay next time. There's a guest room. It's even got a double bed." Turning to me, she said, "It's been so nice meeting you. I'm elated that my boy's with such a lovely girl."

I hugged her.

"Now, you be careful getting back. There are some hidden burrows and bogs." Mary pointed at the dark, misty wood.

"I can use my cell for light," said Blake. "Speaking of which, why haven't you got one?"

"I disappeared." She grinned.

"Not anymore," said Blake. "I'll send you a phone. That way we can communicate. I need to know you're okay." He held her hand. "Yes?"

She nodded with a smile. "Please come back soon."

We waved a final goodbye and headed for the wood.

Treading lightly on the uneven ground, I admitted, "If you weren't here, I'd never attempt this."

He stopped walking and turned to face me. The moon was full, which only added to the magic of the misty surrounds. Its pearly beams lighting our path also helped.

I couldn't get the story of the priest out of my mind. "Blake."

He turned to look at me.

"Um… did the priest…?" I sought a delicate way to ask that horrible question. His face darkened, and I swallowed tightly.

"He didn't go all the way."

"I'm sorry to ask. It's just that…"

"He only touched my dick." His matter-of-fact tone contradicted the gravity of the subject.

"How old were you?"

"Twelve."

"Did it just happen once?"

He shook his head.

"Is that the reason for your nightmares?"

Blake rubbed his neck. "That, and me assuming I'd murdered him. Life with my stepfather wasn't exactly fun either." He sighed. "I've got enough material here"—he tapped his head— "to keep a shrink going for years."

"You can talk to me about anything, I want you to know." I gave his hand a gentle squeeze. "I'm sorry to have asked. I just needed to know."

His brow pinched. "Does that tarnish me?"

Gulping, I shook my head.

"It's left an indelible stain."

I took his hand again. "Please, don't think like that. You were just a victim of a disgustingly depraved beast."

"I should've stopped him sooner."

"How often?" I asked. My stomach grew tighter with each question. I felt like an interrogator.

"Only four times."

"And did he...?"

"He played with my dick." His voice cracked.

"I would've killed him. If anyone hurt you, I wouldn't think twice."

A faint smile touched his face. The intensity of the moment slowly vanished, which helped me breathe evenly at last.

"I'm sorry to have asked," I said again.

"You're the only living person I could trust to tell, apart from my mother."

"Does Dylan Fox know?"

He shrugged. "It's possible. The walls always had eyes and ears here."

I fell into his arms, and we held each other as the moon illuminated her magic over us. It was more a healing embrace of acknowledgement—for me, having finally found a way into this closed man, and for Blake, I intuited, the relief of having unburdened his soul.

Blake held out his hand. "Come on. Let's put that behind us, shall we?"

Taking his hand, I smiled.

My spirit warmed knowing that, with each step, our bond had deepened. "This is so insanely picturesque, especially with the moon illuminating the trees. Am I dreaming?"

"No, darling. It's very real." He turned to look at me. "Have you decided yet?"

"On what?"

Blake stopped walking. "You've forgotten already?"

"No, of course not." I paused. "Why do we need to do this so soon?"

His face became sullen again. "Let's go." He took my hand.

We'd only taken a step when I stopped. "I love you, Blake."

His eyes impaled me, penetrating to my core. Could I live with a man whose brooding presence made me shiver one minute and then ache from desire the next?

"And I love you. I found my mother, and now, after losing Milly, I'm not alone."

"Is that why you want to marry me? Because you fear loneliness?" I asked, uncertain where to park my emotions. A part of me needed to hear that Blake couldn't live without me, while the other craved independence and wanted me to succeed by my own means.

He drew me close. "No. I don't have a problem being alone. I just can't imagine my life without you." His words breathed a warm, moist stain onto my neck—a reminder of his dirty little utterances when he was deep inside of me. "I'm a very private man. I've given you so much of myself that it weakens me."

I stared into his eyes. "How has that made you weak? It's courageous to let a person in."

"You've witnessed my vulnerabilities. I'm not the strong heroic type that a beautiful woman like you deserves."

"That's bullshit, Blake. I don't need someone flying through a window, brandishing a weapon to save me."

His lips curled, and the lines on his brow smoothed. "You've been watching too many sword-fighting movies, I think."

I smiled sadly. "I like the fact that you're complicated. I'm touched that you've entrusted me with your painful secrets. I know how difficult that must feel." I paused for a response, but his eyes just burned into mine. "In many ways, we're very similar, considering my not-so-pretty life growing up."

He took my hand. "We're kindred spirits, Penny. With you by my side, I can conquer the world."

"Is that what you want to do?" I asked.

"No. It's a figure of speech." He led me along. "Come on. Let's get back. I'm hungry."

"But we've eaten," I challenged.

He cocked his head and grinned. I wanted to eat him there and then.

An owl's hoot aroused in me the magic of the forest at midnight.

In the distance, a gentle breeze swayed silhouetted trees as they performed an arboreal ballet. Coated in a diaphanous veil of mist, the scene was set for a glorious Gothic tale. A howling wolf was all that was missing.

I crushed Blake's palm. "I'm so glad you're here, though. I'd be too chicken to do this alone." The sound of rustling made me jump.

"Don't worry. It's only a creature." Blake pointed at a rabbit. "I used to come here often at night."

"Really?"

He played with a strand of my hair and nodded. "You're a natural fit in here. I can see you in a flowing gown."

"Now who's going all classic movies?"

He laughed. "More *Grimm's Fairy Tales*, I think."

Another owl hooted, which made me smile. "That's so magical."

"I also love them. As a teenager, I had a Harry Potter moment and tried to train one as a pet."

"Really? I love hearing stories about your life growing up here."

He sniffed. "They're nicer in the telling."

"What was your pet owl's name?" I asked.

"He wasn't domesticated. He'd perch on the tree outside my bedroom window. I named him Orson. Orson Owl."

I giggled. "That's sweet."

The freshness of the night awakened my face. A large bird flew just over my head, startling me into Blake's strong hold.

"That was only a raven."

"It was so large."

"They are. Amazing creatures. They're everywhere here."

"Hence the title," I said.

"They used to frighten Milly and many of the women around here. They're all very superstitious, and heavily into folklore."

"Witchcraft, you mean?"

He nodded. "Siobhan, one of the maids, practiced. My mother would go to her for advice. She read the tarot. I never believed in any of it myself."

"But this is the setting. The ambience is ripe with druidic history."

"It is. I think having you here makes me appreciate it more."

We stood on the grounds of the estate. The lunar-illuminated graystone edifice painted a grim picture. I almost expected to find vampires and maidens in transparent robes floating about with teeth marks on their milky necks.

I pointed to the turret, which the moon had flooded with mystery. With that dreamy atmosphere storming my senses, I experienced a creative orgasm. I fidgeted for my cellphone.

"That's an image that I hated and loved as a boy."

"It's one that's going into my sketchbook," I said, aiming the phone toward it. "It will probably be a bit hazy, but wow, even better."

Blake smiled. "Thanks."

"For what?" I frowned.

"For being you."

FORTY-NINE

BLAKE

PENELOPE SAT UP IN the four-poster bed, her thick dark hair free and her full breasts spilling out of a red silk negligee. I brushed my lips with my tongue, as my heart pumped blood-hot desire to my dick.

I removed my clothes and walked toward the bed, dropping them along the way. Penelope lifted the cover for me, and I slid up close.

Moving over slippery silk, I rubbed her erect nipples and stared into her softened dark eyes. Our lips touched, burning and melding together. It was a kiss of love as much as passion, which soon turned into a blaze of need as her curves danced against my body.

I lowered the thin strap of her gown and caressed her breasts, trailing kisses over her milky soft skin. I sucked her nipples until they were so erect that my cock went to steel.

My addicted body rubbed against hers. We hadn't made love since the morning, and the desire to be buried deep inside of her had taken control.

I parted her curvy thighs and placed my head between them, licking her clit until her sweet, juicy orgasm spurted over my tongue.

Rolling her over, I lifted her nightie. She went to remove it, but I stopped her. I loved the red silk dripping over her curves.

Her tits fell into my hands, and I positioned myself behind her. As I slid into her slick cunt, the fit was so tight and resistant that I sucked back a slow breath between my clenched teeth.

It was slow and deep, making pleasure shiver through every pore of my body.

Her muscles contracted tightly. Her moans deepened the harder I penetrated. Her ass danced on my belly as her wet pussy sucked my dick impatiently, imploring me to thrust harder.

I pulled back her hair gently and bit her neck. "Come for me, Penny."

The friction was so intense, with her pussy swallowing my cock whole, that my eyes watered.

Blood rushed through me, and color exploded before my eyes, overcome by a mind-shattering climax. At the same time, Penelope moaned loudly as her creamy pussy convulsed around my dick.

We fell into each other's arms, breathing heavily.

Stroking her soft hair, I felt complete and content. "I love you, Penny."

THE ROOM WAS AWASH in black. As I sat there, admiration flushed through me. Penelope was the first person I'd seen who looked sexy donning a robe and cap.

She stood at the podium and received a certificate. Her shy smile brought a big one to my face, helping me to forget all about Dylan Fox.

One hour later, we found ourselves at a high-spirited graduates' party in a cavernous, grungy warehouse.

When James turned up with Lilly, Penelope ran up and hugged her.

It was a little awkward for me at first. I hadn't forgiven James. But after a few drinks, I loosened up a little.

He drew me away from the thumping techno throb. "I've been doing some digging on Dylan Fox."

I glanced over at Penelope, dancing with Lilly and Sheldon, and suggested, "Let's go outside, where I can hear you."

We stepped out into the back alleyway, and James reached into his pocket for a soft pack of cigarettes.

"You've taken them up again?" I asked.

"I need something." He grinned tightly.

The easygoing guy I'd always known was tense and kept looking over his shoulder. His eyes were slightly baggy, and he looked pale.

"That bad, eh?"

"He's got a few of us dangling along," he said.

"What do you mean?"

"Fox is not just blackmailing me. There's even a prince in the mix."

I jerked my head back. "Shit. From the pedophile-island affair you mean?"

He nodded. "Teenage girls are irresistible amongst that lot."

"And you, it would seem," I replied dryly.

"I swear, I thought she was seventeen. That's what she told me." He looked at me so earnestly that I didn't recognize him. Drama changed people. I knew that well enough.

"Other than dragging me into this web of deceit, what else has he got you doing?"

"Nothing. But..." He held up his finger. "I've stumbled on something that could help. A cop, who Fox had on his payroll before the guy turned religious, has been knocked off. He was just about to talk."

"How do you know this?"

"Because I've got my own private detective sniffing about. He's come up with some CCTV footage showing a car running him down. The driver involved is one of Fox's minions."

"That's useful evidence," I said.

"We either get the bastard jailed or have him..." He ran his finger along his neck.

"That won't be me," I shot back.

"There's something else." He looked around before continuing. "There's an investigative journalist. She's got a couple of key witnesses from those island hookups. I think you should speak to her."

"Do you have her number?"

He handed me a scrap of paper. Wearing a contrite smile, he said, "Look, I'm really sorry. He had me over a fucking barrel."

"I wouldn't have seen Penelope if I hadn't visited the Cherry Orchard. That said, betrayal never sits well."

"I'll make it up to you, old man. Promise."

I nodded reflectively. I wasn't sure if we could ever get back to how things were.

When we returned to the pulsating warehouse, Penelope asked if we could leave. Noisy, crowded rooms had never been my thing. I was glad to be leaving.

Lilly came up and wished us a good night. By the way James held onto her, I could see that she wasn't one of his passing fancies. He wore a protective, besotted vibe I recognized.

As we made our way to the Bentley, where Patrick awaited us, I sensed the presence of someone following. I turned, and two bearlike males overshadowed us.

"Go to the car," I whispered.

Penelope looked at me with wide-eyed apprehension.

"Just go," I said.

She hurried to the car, where I spied Patrick stepping onto the pavement.

I faced the men. "What do you want?"

The bigger of the two threw a punch, which I managed to block with my forearm. At the same time, the other lunged at me, and I crunched my knee into his balls. The one who had stumbled back from my punch reached into his pocket, and with perfect timing, Patrick entered the fray, brandishing a gun.

I kicked the thug to the ground and stood on his hand while Patrick had the other man in a headlock. It all happened in a matter of seconds.

I moved my foot onto the fat man's gut. "Are you just trying to rob me? Or are you connected to Fox?"

He struggled to speak. "He's sent us to remind you."

"Give him this message: if he wants to talk to me, he knows where I am. He doesn't need to send fat thickheads. Got that?"

Patrick asked, "Should I call the cops?"

I shook my head. "I just want to get home."

Pointing his gun at the pair, Patrick waited until they disappeared before he got back into the car. That was one of the many advantages of having a driver who'd fought for the Special Forces. In addition to his unwavering loyalty, Patrick had the strength of six men.

As we drove past them, I turned and noticed the pair shuffling off, looking the worse for wear.

Penelope handed me a tissue. "Are you okay?"

Her glassy-eyed fear broke my heart. I took her hand and nodded reassuringly. "I'm fine."

She shook her head. "I've seen plenty of fights. But hell, where did you learn to fight like that?"

I almost laughed, more out of nervous tension than humor. "Where I come from, kids did that for a pastime. We didn't have coloring books or video games to entertain us."

Her lips turned up at one end before tightening again. "Was that just a random attack?"

"Yep. Random," I lied.

For someone running a crime syndicate, Dylan Fox hadn't chosen his minions well. Apart from that recording, I now held another trump card. The thugs who'd attempted Penelope's abduction had become mine to manipulate. All it took was a little cash and witnesses promising to testify against them. I shook my head in disbelief at Dylan's stupidity, which shouldn't have surprised me. Even as a young boy, he'd been brainless and sadistic.

FIFTY

PENELOPE

TWO SECURITY GUARDS LOITERED by my house, looking very conspicuous. Blake had arranged it. He'd also insisted that Patrick drive me everywhere, mumbling something about keeping me safe, which fed my paranoia.

Blake sent me a quick message that he had a pressing deadline. I hadn't seen him for a whole day and night, which wasn't long, but given how inseparable we'd become, I still felt it. I'd become accustomed to sharing my bed with him. I missed his hungry mouth crushing mine, and his hot needy body pressed against me, touching me in a way that opened me wide as his big dick ravished me.

That proposal of marriage hung in the air. I wondered if I could spend my life with such a man, who could go from being hot and passionate, to icy and remote within a breath.

Yet, my body, heart, and soul belonged to him.

All these thoughts followed me along as I made my way to his house. I thought that if Blake could pop in whenever he liked, then so could I.

I lifted the brass knocker tentatively. Pierce answered, and although normally jovial, he seemed a little taken aback.

"Hey, Pierce." I used my jolliest voice.

He hesitantly led me through.

I heard a female voice and looked at Pierce, who returned an apologetic smile, which only served to incriminate Blake and knot my gut.

I headed toward the voices, which came from his office, and knocked on the door. Being ajar, it opened.

A very attractive woman with a notepad sat opposite him. Blake had his legs stretched out, denoting a casual, intimate discussion. He turned toward me, and the color in his face drained away. "Penny."

I bit my lip. "I thought I'd drop in." I looked over at the blond woman with the long legs and fitted blouse showing her curves. I felt faint. "Am I interrupting something?"

"This is Amelia." Blake looked at her and said, "And this is Penelope."

Not his girlfriend? Just Penelope. Mm...

My fingernails impaled my sweaty palms.

"I see you're occupied. I just thought I'd drop in to say hi." My eyes wandered over to Amelia, who remained blank faced.

I turned and walked out. Blake followed me into the living room.

"Hey." He took my hand. "It's not what you think."

"Really? You looked pretty chummy. Why do I get this feeling I'm intruding?"

"Because you are." His matter-of-fact tone felt like a slap in the face.

"Well, then, fuck you." I stormed out.

He followed me to the door. "Penny, don't be like this."

A flicker of vulnerability coated his eyes, wielding some kind of talismanic power over my heart. The best I could do was throw daggers at those gorgeous blue eyes. I wanted him to be ugly, not beautiful, especially with that woman being in his office.

Burning jealousy raged through me. I ran off, bludgeoning myself with the gut-wrenching question: *Did he taste her with the same hunger dripping from his lips?*

I ended up at Sheldon's house. He opened the door. "Hey, Penny."

"I hope I'm not barging in on anything."

"No. Roger's gone to work." He smiled. "Let's have a coffee."

I sat up at the kitchen island, cupping my chin. "I think I just behaved like a baby."

Sheldon passed me a cup of coffee. "What happened?"

"I found Blake at home in his office talking with a beautiful busty blonde, and now I'm spitting blood."

A slow smile grew on his face. In the retelling, I sounded ridiculously melodramatic.

"Did he explain?"

I shook my head. "He just told me he was in the middle of something."

"He's mad about you. At the party, last weekend, he spent the whole night either with his arm around your waist or watching you dance."

I smiled sadly, reflecting on the nicer moments from our night out. "It got very dark and seedy after that."

"Oh... that sounds yummy."

I shook my head. "Not like that. I mean literally. These two guys attacked Blake, and he went wild."

Sheldon's eyes widened. "Really. That's so alpha."

"Trust me, it's sexier in the telling. At the time, it was terrifying." I puffed out a breath. It had been one hell of a week.

"He knew them?"

"I think so. He has this childhood connection who's blackmailing him. He's really evil and after Blake's fortune."

My cell vibrated in my bag. I looked up at Sheldon apologetically. "I might see who that is."

"I think you should, sweetie."

It was Blake.

I picked up and walked into the other room.

"Penny. At last. I've been trying to call you."

"I only left your house an hour ago," I said.

"Can we meet. ASAP. Please."

His tension came through the phone as I gripped my cell. "Okay."

"At your place. In an hour?"

The tough side of me that didn't take crap screamed that I should get an explanation. My emotions, on the other hand, had me capitulating with a wimpy "Okay."

After I closed call, I looked at Sheldon apologetically.

"Let me guess. Blake?"

"Am I being too forgiving?" I asked.

"You haven't heard his excuse yet. For all you know, she could be a KGB spy."

I laughed. "You're worse than me."

"That's why we're artists," he said with a giggle.

I hugged him. "Thanks for being here for me. I have to go."

"I miss having you around." His mouth turned down.

"There's just so much going on." I shook my head. "I'm not even myself anymore."

"Hey. It's a new chapter. It sounds pretty exciting. Do what you're great at. Make art."

"I have so many sketches from our time away at Raven Abbey. It was Gothic in the true sense of the word."

"Yum. You must take me there."

"I will, one day soon. Promise." I hugged him and left.

THE SAME TWO BULKY men sat in a car parked near my home. If they were trying to fit into the scenery, it wasn't working. If anything, it resembled a scene in a movie, only I couldn't turn it off.

When I entered my house, I found Blake sitting on the couch, his legs crossed, and his arm stretched over the back of the settee. If only I could have edited that earlier encounter in his office, I would have pounced on him. Wearing a cream cashmere pullover, he looked like he should have been on the cover of *Vogue*. His tongue ran over those lips, and all

I wanted to do was sit on his lap and let him fondle my breasts, with his hard cock buried deep inside me.

"You're not using Patrick to drive you around," he said.

I plonked my bag down. "I know this is technically your home, but I feel a little invaded with you letting yourself in like this. You wouldn't let me do that in your house." I tilted my head.

"Although this *is* your home, it's also our home."

"Who was she?"

"Please sit down, Penny." He tapped the cushion by his side on the sofa.

I sat with space between us.

"Amelia's a journalist. She's staying at my house."

I glowered at him. "Why?" Before he could answer, I added, "And you didn't think to tell me?"

He bit his lip and frowned. "I'm sorry. I should've. But I didn't want to speak over the phone."

"Hello, I'm around the corner."

He touched my arm, and I pulled it away roughly.

"Don't try to charm me, mister."

His lips twitched into a faint smile.

"Why is she staying at your house?" I persisted.

"She's onto a story that needs to come out. When it does, it will free me from Fox's clutches."

"Why does she have to stay with you?" I was more interested in the domestic detail than the cloak-and-dagger stuff.

"Because it's dangerous for her to be anywhere else."

"She's beautiful." Fighting back tears, I hated how weak I'd become.

"She's not my type. And... I'm with you." He stroked my cheek. "I'm very loyal. I don't cheat."

"But you're a sex addict."

He studied me with those piercing blue eyes. "I was. They weren't you. You're my first-ever girlfriend." He paused. "And I want to spend my life with you."

I wanted to hold him so badly, but I held my ground. "Why have you stayed away and not contacted me?"

"I don't want to talk about what's happening with Amelia over the phone. I've been up all night. She's got enough material to have Fox locked up for life. We just have to find a way to publish it."

"But why didn't you come here and tell me? I hadn't heard from you, which isn't normal for us."

He rubbed his neck. "I'm sorry. I got caught up with Barnes, my PI, and then Amelia turned up and showed me everything she's obtained on Fox, and it became an all-night affair."

"All-night affair? Did she sleep with you?"

"How can you think that?"

"You looked really cozy together." I sulked. Petulance had taken an ugly grip on my spirit.

He stroked my hair. "I love you."

I looked up. His eyes shimmered with an intense sincerity that was impossible to fake.

I took a deep breath. "I still don't understand why she needs to stay there."

"Because it's the safest place. This story is huge, involving very powerful men. Security guards at a hotel somewhere just won't do it. I'm talking very powerful men." His eyebrow lifted.

"You could have come over and alerted me. You owed me that, at least."

"You're right. I fucked up." His turquoise eyes shone with contrition. "I'm new to this boyfriend thing. Will you forgive me?"

I allowed his warm hand to remain on mine.

"What's her interest in this case?" I asked.

"Her younger sister was trafficked onto the island and, at the age of fourteen, forced to have sex with parties of men. She committed suicide last year and left a note filled with names and details. Amelia, who's a journalist, has spent the past year gathering sources and information. She's discovered that Fox is trading under a different name and that the island's owned by a lord he fraternizes with."

Despite Blake's explanation, which more than exonerated him, I still read Amelia as a threat, which left me with a streak of guilt for being so pettishly selfish. "But why can't she stay somewhere else? She's so fucking good-looking."

Blake caressed my cheek. "She's not a patch on you."

His lips fused onto mine. The heat from his body made mine melt. His hands slipped under my blouse and unclasped my bra.

"I need you naked," he said.

How could I refuse? My desire for his devouring hands and body overpowered any niggling jealousy.

I lifted my blouse over my head, and his eyes traveled to my naked chest.

I peeled off my jeans. His eyes left a trail of promises down my body. He removed his trousers, and that bulge pushing against his briefs sent a swelling ache of anticipation between my legs.

"I need to taste you." His voice was heavy with want.

I rubbed his cock, which grew rock-hard, dwarfing my hand.

His breath roughened as he parted my thighs wide, his eyes smoldering as they traveled from my face to my pussy. He placed his head between my legs, licking me so softly that I winced. The pleasure gripped my muscles, aching arousal swept me away. He entered me with his finger as I surrendered, gasping, in a toe-curling release.

He stood up and wiped his lips. I rolled over. I needed hard sex. I loved the way Blake felt when he was driven by lust.

The first deep thrust caused my eyes to roll to the back of my head.

"I need to *really* fuck you." His words were strangled by desire.

I arched my back and gyrated my ass against his belly as he penetrated.

As he moved in and out, his heavy breath moistened my ear, and I saw stars. It was raw, primal addictive sex.

My eyelids fluttered, and my legs trembled. As the burning swell of his impaling dick hit nerve spots, I succumbed to a powerful orgasm that stretched time as intensely as his dick stretched me. Blake's deep groan filled the room as though he'd given me everything of himself.

Embracing, we basked in the afterglow of blissful surrender.

Blake whispered, "I love you, Penny."

"I love you, too, Blake."

FIFTY-ONE

BLAKE

AMELIA'S ARTICLE WAS WELL written and highly controversial and therefore potentially litigious. "That's rather detailed," I said, leaning back on my chair in my study.

She nodded pensively.

I noticed she wasn't herself. "Is there something the matter?"

"I think I'm being followed," she replied.

I sat up. "You were followed here?"

She shook her head. "I lost them. It was after I left my apartment that I noticed something, so I chose another route."

"Have you spoken to anyone?"

"I interviewed someone connected to Lord Preston, who, being a sworn enemy, seemed eager to expose the lord."

"Maybe he's a plant," I said.

"Perhaps. This is big."

"How far are you from finishing the story?"

"I'm waiting on a statement from one of my key witnesses, who was lured to the island on the pretense of a modeling job."

"Is she being protected?" I asked.

"She's in New York."

"Then let me suggest that you don't communicate through email or phone."

"We're using courier."

I nodded. "Where's the courier delivering it?"

"My work. At the community paper."

"I'll arrange a car and driver for you. You'll have to remain here until the article's published."

She studied me. "Your girlfriend won't mind?"

"She understands."

At least, I hope she does.

Amelia had already been staying in my guest room for a week.

I glanced at my watch. "I have to go. Is there anything you need?"

She shook her head. "No, I'm good. It should be all over in a day or two at the most."

"Send me a text if you need anything. I know it feels as though you're penned in, but it needs to be that way."

"I understand. And hey, thanks." She smiled. "If it wasn't for your kind support, I probably wouldn't have gotten this far."

I collected my jacket. A Beretta weighed down the inside pocket. I hated guns, but since the arrival of Fox and after that little tussle with his heavies, I'd decided it was best to carry it. The classic pistol belonged to Sir William, who'd waxed lyrical on its sleek Italian design. I didn't see the beauty myself. Firearms had brought nothing but grief to humankind.

THE DARK BAR WAS a perfect meeting place for someone like Fox, in that, just like a vampire, I imagined daylight being his enemy.

"I almost thought you weren't coming," he said, clicking to the barman. "Another pint."

"I'll have one too," I said.

He waited for the beer to be delivered and then said, "So what do I owe the pleasure of this meeting? I'm still waiting for what's mine."

"You'll be waiting for a while still."

His smarmy expression ironed out. "Look, Sinclair. This is no longer a game. I've got something of yours."

"So you keep saying. Those heavies the other night were a classy touch."

"Your fighting skills have improved since I knocked you around and made you cry like a girl."

I clenched my fists. "You've got a selective memory, Dylan. The last time, it was me who had an imprint of your crooked teeth on my knuckles."

He smirked back at me.

"I know about that pedophile island. And I know about the cop who you had killed. There's CCTV footage sitting somewhere safe, should something happen to me." I paused to study his cold eyes for a reaction. Unsurprisingly, his face remained blank. "Now that wasn't too bright, was it?" I cocked my head.

"And I know where your pretty artist girl lives. I have instructed a couple of my men, horny little devils that they are, to take her and fuck her senseless and get her to work."

That gusted cold fear over my spirit. "Along with all the other girls you traffic?"

I thought about Penelope, whose trenchant independence could make her vulnerable. I had to get her out of London.

The next week would be crucial. This cancer—not just for me but for the safety of underage girls as well—had to be removed.

"Two billion, and it all ends here."

"Oh, so you've lowered your price," I said.

"I'd hate to see a man with such delicate tastes go without."

"Stop your heavies. Don't threaten my girlfriend, or else you'll get nothing." I had to dangle a carrot before him despite my intention of delivering zero.

"I've brought something of yours along today," he said.

Just as I was about to speak, a figure stepped into the light, his heavily scarred face decrepit and cold eyes bone-chilling.

My brows squeezed. "What are you doing here?"

Fox laughed. "Now, that's not a nice way to greet your father."

"He's not my fucking father. Sir William was my father."

The vile monster, who I'd once considered my father, sniggered. "You're my fucking son. I fed you."

"You fed me nightmares. You attacked my mother. And you're no fucking father of mine." I stood up.

"Not so quickly," he said, taking me by the arm. "You owe me."

"I owe you nothing." I shoved him off me.

"I know you killed that fucking priest. The rumors were all over the village. You weren't convicted out of plain fucking luck. I know the cop that whitewashed that case. His retirement fund's almost run out. It wouldn't take much to make him talk."

"I had nothing to do with that priest."

His thin lips twisted into an evil grin I recognized well. "You scrub up well. You were always a good-looking boy. Did the lord of Raven Abbey touch you up too?"

Cartilage crunched under my fist. Incited by hatred and revenge for what that bastard did to my mother, I enjoyed it. That punch felt good.

I went to hit him again when chilling steel pricked my neck. I pulled out my pistol and placed my foot over my evil stepfather, who was on the ground, his nose bloodied. Satisfied that he wasn't going anywhere, I turned and directed the pistol at Fox's chest.

He dropped the knife.

I spat, "Get out of my fucking life."

FIFTY-TWO

PENELOPE

AS WE DROVE UP the driveway to Raven Abbey, I turned to look at Blake. "I hope you stay long enough to visit your mother. She'll be sad if you don't."

He looked tired. "All in good time. She understands. I speak to her every day. I have some important business to attend to in the city." He held my hand. "It's got to be this way for now. A bodyguard's here to protect you. You must take him with you—just until the article's released, and Fox is locked up." He smiled. "I'll stay tonight, though."

He jumped out, opened the boot, and removed my luggage.

Although a week at Raven Abbey meant that I could sketch to my heart's content, I still grappled with withdrawal anxiety.

When we entered Sir William's former room, it almost felt as though I'd arrived home, in a weird way. That beautiful penthouse suite, with its classical accents, bathed me in delight. But that was with Blake around, kissing every inch of my skin and making love to me as though we were alone in some sensual paradise.

Reality bit hard when Blake introduced me to my bodyguard, who had the adjoining room. Blake had even made me promise not to reveal my whereabouts to Sheldon or Lilly. I pretended I was off to Scotland, which nearly fell apart when Sheldon begged to come along. He had a thing for men in kilts, he'd admitted with a giggle. If only I felt as blithe as that. I found myself suddenly missing those days when I studied shadows for creative reasons, and not out of paranoia.

Blake looked down at his phone. I've got to take this.

"Amelia," he said into his cellphone, walking to the end of the very large room, where I couldn't hear him.

My jealousy levels were at fever pitch. She was still staying in his guest room. And the fact that he'd be returning to London made my stomach twist in knots.

After finishing the call, he suggested, "Let's go and have something to eat. The dining room's lovely at this hour."

Sulking, I stared down at my feet.

"You said you wished to see the stained glass windows in the afternoon." He didn't seem to notice that my emotions were about to explode.

I rose and followed him out, glum and refusing to capitulate to that sexy smile. If anything, I wanted to scream. Silently, I entered the dining room, that, had I been upbeat, I would have gushed over.

When we were seated, Blake touched my hand. "I'm sorry to drag you into my dirty world."

"Mm..." I stared down at my fingers.

He touched my hand. "Penny. There's only you. You're the only woman I want. Remember that."

"But why does she have to stay at your house? Can't she stay at a hotel with a legion of your men watching over her?"

His lips twitched with amusement. "A legion of my men? You make me sound like Caesar."

I grinned.

He looked into my eyes. "Amelia has a boyfriend. He's staying there too."

I frowned in disbelief. "Really? But isn't that dangerous?"

He let out a deep breath. "Yeah. I'm not wrapped in the idea. But at least this way, it allays your fears. This article is vital."

I relaxed all of a sudden.

"I'm not sure having you stay here was the greatest idea, though," he said, looking around.

Although Blake had suggested Bath or even Scotland, I'd begged to return to Raven Abbey.

"This Dylan Fox doesn't strike me as too bright, and anyhow, I have my own heavy shadowing me. I love it here. And at least I can visit your mother."

He nodded distractedly. "Sure. But promise me you won't go anywhere without him."

Blake's intensity made my heart pump, but this time it wasn't from the thought of sex.

I WAVED BLAKE GOODBYE as he drove off in his James Bond car. Mr. Cool and Sexy. Even in the car with his shades on, he looked good enough to devour. He'd certainly made a meal of me. My legs were still weak from the torrid session the night before. He'd asked—no, commanded me—to strip and lie on the bed and masturbate. His debauched desires inflamed me. He drank everything I had to offer. The more drama there was in Blake's life, the greedier he became for my body, it seemed.

I walked back up to my opulent room, fell onto the bed, and slept.

It was afternoon when I woke to a raven crowing noisily outside my window. The creature's beady eyes stared into mine as though trying to tell me something.

After I dressed, I headed downstairs, where I found my security guard sitting in wait reading his phone screen.

He peered up and nodded. His neck was as thick as his head, and he was a giant. We were sure to make an odd pair.

"So how's this going to work?" I asked as he followed me out onto the vast grounds.

"I'll stay in the background in order to give you space and privacy."

"Your name?"

"Tony." His cool, seemingly impenetrable expression relaxed into a warm smile.

"I thought I might go for a wander. The village, I'm told, is a mile away. Is that too long a walk?" I asked, noticing his shiny black SUV parked in the distance.

"I could use the exercise," he said.

"Okay then. Off we go. And hey, you don't have to walk behind me."

"That's okay, ma'am. It's my job. I'm meant to remain in the background."

I shrugged. "Come on, then."

FIFTY-THREE

BLAKE

MARIA GLANCED OVER AT me and then at Amelia, and although she normally kept her opinions to herself, which I appreciated, she drew me away and whispered, "What happened to Penelope?"

"Amelia's a journalist. She's not replacing Penelope," I said.

"I like Penelope very much. She's good for you. She's made you a man."

I frowned. "Right." I thought about that and had to ask, "What was I before?"

"You were a mess, *caro mio*. A beautiful man with a head full of worries."

I smiled meekly. "She's made me happy. But I was always a man." I raised a brow.

She twirled her hand and smiled.

We sat at the table and ate silently. Amelia looked up every now and then, and smiled shyly. That night was to be the last night of her stay.

Penelope had skyped me earlier and played with her nipples at my request. She needed to see how hot I was for her, to keep her jealousy at bay. Had our situation been reversed, I wouldn't have handled it well. As it was, I'd even hired the most unattractive security guard from the team to watch over her.

"Is the editor lined up for tonight?" I asked.

She nodded. "He's aware that I'm sending the article. As you can imagine, after he read my outline, he's keen, and a little worried."

"But you haven't revealed any of the participants' names, have you? Only the name Gareth Lion." It didn't take long for me to connect Dylan Fox to that pseudonym.

"True. But the fact that the article states that some very powerful men were involved will cause a rumbling."

I nodded, thinking of the stir among the upper classes.

Justice needed to be served, regardless of the criminal's station in life. And Dylan should have been jailed a long time ago. If Sir William had pressed charges, as he should have, perhaps this could have been avoided. For me, at least.

After dinner, Amelia sat in my study with her laptop. I watched her press Send.

Looking up at me, she smiled. "There. It's done. Now I can return to my life."

I scribbled a check for fifty thousand pounds. "Here."

She stared at it and then me. "I can't take this. I was only doing my job. In any case, the *Guardian*'s paying for this story."

"Not much, though. Good journalists are an endangered species. Let's just say I'm investing in quality journalism. In fact, give that back."

She handed it over, almost looking disappointed. Her wince as I tore it up didn't go unnoticed.

I scribbled a new check for two hundred thousand pounds, knowing that it would make a huge difference to her life. I admired her work ethic. She was intelligent, tenacious, and hardworking, deserving of a break.

"I won't hear any protests. It's yours. All your years of hard work. You've earned it."

The piece of paper trembled in her hand. Her green eyes widened. "But this is exorbitant."

I changed the subject. "What now?"

She took a steadying breath. "They'll publish the story, and by afternoon, it will go viral. Everyone will be seeking information on Gareth Lion. And I'm certain more girls will testify."

THE FOLLOWING DAY, as Amelia had predicted, the story dominated the airwaves. Even the morning show on television, which Maria normally had on in the kitchen, ran it. I went in to grab a banana when it came on. The story described a private island where unsuspecting young females were plied with alcohol and drugs and cajoled into sex and in some cases, raped. Most of the girls were underage.

Maria handed me a cup of coffee. She did the sign of the cross. "*Dio mio,* how evil."

I returned a solemn nod and then left to meet James, who I'd planned to catch up with at our club, which was a five-minute walk from my home.

Although it was a little early for my first drink, I agreed on a fiery hit as he sat before me, pale and biting a nail.

"I'm fucked. I thought they'd keep me out of it."

I held up my hands. "It wasn't me."

He released a deep breath of resignation. "I suppose it wasn't going to end well."

"But from what you've said, there are bigger fish to fry. I can't imagine they'll charge everyone involved."

He sniffed. "Yeah, well, that would wipe out half of the upper classes."

"That many?" I asked, shocked that so many men had a thing for young girls.

"For an intelligent, experienced man of the world, Blake, you are surprisingly out of touch with the habits of the rich."

I shrugged. "Yeah. Well... it's fucking immoral. In the true sense of the word."

He lifted his hands in defense. "She told me she was seventeen." His tone was rougher and more serious than I'd ever recalled. Always the easygoing one, James had never allowed anything to ruffle him, which I'd put down to a privileged upbringing. Now that he'd been thrown into the pits, the dirty game of life had knocked reality into him, forcing him to grow up and take some responsibility.

FIFTY-FOUR

PENELOPE

AFTER ONE WEEK INTO my stay, I'd filled an entire sketch pad with Raven Abbey's facade.

It was late afternoon, and Blake had called, suggesting that I visit his mother. He'd spoken to her, and she was looking forward to my visit and even hoped I would stay the night, which appealed to me.

Tony, my bodyguard, showed me pictures of his young daughter. I could see that he missed her madly, and I asked him if he'd like to return earlier than he'd planned.

He shook his head. "I need the work. And Blake Sinclair pays really well. I just wanted to show you a picture of Carly."

I smiled. "She's lovely." I headed toward the dirt path. "So, are you ready for a walk in the forest?"

He nodded. "I've lost a bit of weight with all this exercise. It's better than standing around looking threatening."

I laughed along with him, having grown to like him.

We made our way into the thick wood, and although it was afternoon, the forest was bathed in shadows. I stood in a rare beam of sunlight and lifted my face. A robin in a tall oak greeted me.

I heard a rustle behind me and assumed it was Tony, who always insisted on walking a few steps back to protect me.

Leaning against a tree, I took a break. After a few moments, I heard scuffling, which I assumed was the sound of creatures scurrying about.

But then I heard men's voices. I walked out of the scrub and saw Tony on the ground, clutching his stomach. Blood puddled around him. He'd been stabbed.

When I ran to him, he shook his head. "Run" exited silently from his mouth. Just as I was searching for my phone, a man came toward me.

In the space of a breath, I started running as fast as I could, stumbling along the way until I found a thick piece of scrub to hide in.

I'd only just settled, after having my skin scratched and bitten, when my phone buzzed. He came into view, headed toward me.

My heart raced, and I could barely breathe. Luckily, it wasn't too far to the cottage.

I bolted like lightning. He was a big heavy man who struggled to keep up. I kept running until I arrived at the cottage. I pushed the gate open and knocked on the door, nearly banging it down.

Mary came to the door. Her smile faded when her eyes traveled over my shoulder. My pursuer was there at the doorstep.

"What do you want?" she asked him.

"You've come back from the grave. And to think I mourned your passing, you bitch."

As Mary's eyes widened, telling me to run, he grabbed my arm and shoved me into the cottage.

"What are you doing here, Jack?" asked Mary.

"I've come to visit my dear wife."

"How did you know I was here?"

"A little fairy told me." He looked over at me.

"Leave her be," implored Mary. "This is between you and me."

My heart was in my mouth—I could hardly speak. "I didn't know he was there. He killed Tony, my guard."

Mary turned to Jack. "Do you want to go to prison again?"

My cell sounded. As I removed it from my pocket, Jack snatched it from me and took the call. "Oh, it's my billionaire son, who refuses to acknowledge his dear old dad." His face contorted into a malicious grin.

"I'm just visiting your lovely mother, and your girlfriend's even here. Mary's come back to life it seems."

I tried to escape, but even while holding the phone, he managed to lock the door and push me to the ground. His big foot rested on my back.

Lying there with my cheek pressed against the cold hard floor, I couldn't see Mary, and I prayed that she'd escaped.

"I want cash. Plenty of it," he barked into the phone. "I'm sending my account details. I want ten million. If it's not there by today, there'll be no happily ever after for you."

As Jack listened to Blake, I writhed like a rattlesnake to free myself. But his foot pressed heavily onto my spine.

He closed the call and then tied my legs and wrists with curtain cords. Then he picked me up roughly, pushed me into the bathroom, and locked the door from the outside.

I heard scuffling and Mary screaming.

I was trying to free my wrists, using my teeth, when the door burst open. He was a big ugly brute more than six feet tall, with evil sneering eyes.

I'd forgotten to breathe, and my heart pounded madly.

He dragged me out and pushed me onto a chair. Holding some tape, he wrapped it tightly around my wrists, the chair, and my body before taping over my mouth.

While he was securing my body onto the chair, Mary scrambled into the kitchen. Suddenly, she appeared with a knife. It all happened so quickly. She went to lunge at him, but he grabbed her wrist, and I felt the clang of the knife hitting the floor in my ankles. My heart shriveled at the lost opportunity.

"You were never that bright." Pushing her into a chair, he yelled, "Sit."

As he taped up her hands and feet, I tried to wiggle free, but I was bound up too tightly.

My phone buzzed again. I wished I could answer it. He went over to it, picked it up, and listened.

He responded, "I will text an email. Send me proof of that transaction."

I couldn't believe that monster even had an email account, let alone lived in the real world. He ended the call and looked at me. "You've obviously left your mark on Blake." His greasy eyes looked up and down my body, which was covered in cold sweat. My nerves were so frazzled that I was close to wetting my pants.

Such was his strength that he lifted Mary's chair effortlessly and carried it to the bedroom.

At least I didn't have to watch, which was a small mercy, although her cries were like razor blades digging into my flesh.

Using my body to push the chair along, I was focusing on the knife on the floor when someone burst through the door.

It was Tony. He'd somehow managed to bandage his wound with his shirt. He looked at me, and I cocked my head toward the bedroom, where the monster's grunts could be heard.

Holding a pistol, he placed a finger in front of his mouth for me to remain quiet.

That was easy enough to do. I just wished I could seal my ears from poor Mary's screams mingling with that monster's groans.

All went quiet just for one second, and then a gunshot echoed through my ribcage. And another.

Mary ran out. With her ripped dress hanging off her, she grabbed scissors and cut me free.

Clutching his belly, Tony came out and fell to his knees.

"Is he dead?" Mary asked, holding her mouth.

He nodded and then fell unconscious to the floor.

Mary fumbled at her phone. Sobs muddied her words as she gave directions for an ambulance.

FIFTY-FIVE

BLAKE

I DROPPED EVERYTHING AND flew to Raven Abbey in a helicopter before jumping into the gardener's SUV and driving like fury down the dirt track to the cottage.

When I arrived, I found the two women I loved huddled tightly together and shaking. I held them both.

After a few strong hits of whisky, my mother was restored. Penelope was another matter.

I held her trembling hand, caressing it. I couldn't stop apologizing for placing her in such peril.

"You weren't to know he'd come here," she replied.

As placating as her soft tone was, it didn't ease my crippling guilt. I should have predicted Jack's return.

My phone buzzed, and I took the call. At the other end, my security guard's wife relayed the comforting news that Tony was doing fine. The wound hadn't ruptured a vital organ. I released a deep sigh of relief and thanked her for the good news. She wouldn't hear my heartfelt apologies, telling me that he was only doing his job.

I replied, "Your husband's a hero. I won't forget this." I closed the call and looked at Penelope. "Tony's okay."

"Oh, that's great." She sighed. "If it weren't for him..." She shook her head. "He crawled through that door on his knees. I don't know how he managed it."

"He was in the Special Forces. They're trained to withstand all kinds of traumas." I paused to collect my thoughts. "I'll pay off their mortgage and give them some cash."

"That's so kind of you, darling. He deserves it," said my mother.

"Are you sure you're okay? Should I call a doctor?"

She shook her head decisively. "I'm tough enough. I've been through it before. And to be honest, I'm relieved." She smiled tightly. "He's gone. That's all that counts. And now I can show my face to the world again."

Just hearing her say that removed a heavy weight from my shoulders. I, too, felt a little lighter. Jack Blackburn was a nasty fiend. He wouldn't be missed by anyone.

"I hate the idea of you hidden away here alone. We want you in our life." I stared at Penelope, who nodded with a sympathetic smile.

IN THE COMING DAYS, the media went into overdrive. More victims from the private-island sex parties had come out. The name Gareth Lion was mentioned everywhere, leading me to the conclusion that Dylan Fox would soon be exposed.

Penelope sat up in the bed, wearing a permanent frown. "I can't help but feel that had I not visited your mother…"

"He would've bludgeoned the information out of some poor local if it wasn't you."

She winced.

"I'm sorry." I smiled sympathetically. "I shouldn't talk about him."

"It's helping. I need to know that I'm not responsible for what happened. He was such a savage." She held her arms.

I nodded gravely. "At least now my mother's free of him."

"I can understand why she went into hiding."

I undid my robe and joined her in bed. Penelope's body was so soft, warm, and fragrant that my mind filled with the promise of bliss as I pushed the ugly memory of Jack Blackburn away.

Our lips touched. Her mouth trembled. It felt chaste, honest, and uncertain. My tongue gently parted her soft lips and coiled around her tongue, raising my temperature. The heat of passion took over.

My hand slid under her silky nightie, where her heavy breasts jiggled provocatively in my hands. Blood drained from my brain and engorged my cock.

I sucked her ripe nipples—which tasted like cherries—and teased them with my teeth. Her warm silky thighs puckered under my roaming hands. I reached her cunt, and her need to be touched drenched my finger.

"Penelope," I rasped.

"Blake," she returned with a sigh as she opened her legs wider. I buried my head under the covers and found her inflamed and hot. She tasted different. She was always arousing, but there was a new flavor that probably had something to do with anxiety. I ravished her until she poured everything out, and the bitter musky flavor turned sweet and creamy.

I entered her with my finger. "You feel exquisite. I'm dying to be inside of you," I whispered.

Placing the head of my cock between her folds, I penetrated her in one hungry thrust.

Her lips parted and a moan issued forth.

"I want you on top." Holding her, I swung her around.

Her hair was out and wild. Her tits bounced up and down. Her supple pelvis thrusted like a dancer possessed, taking all of me, until I couldn't hold my release any further. Her lips parted, releasing a tormented sigh, which was followed by my own jaw-clenching growl.

The climb to the summit had been excruciatingly mind-blowing. Had I died after that release I would have left with a smile. But I needed more of her. I'd become greedy. The more we fucked, the more I craved Penelope.

"I love you," I gasped, pouring out everything I had, which was more than just sperm.

FIFTY-SIX

PENELOPE

WE WERE BACK AT Mayfair, and after pouring himself another shot of whisky, Blake said, "I hate how I've dragged you into this ugly world of mine."

"I'm stronger than you think." I took a sip of my G&T. "I lost count of the times I found my mother unconscious, my heart in my mouth while I searched for a pulse."

Pity touched his eyes. "Oh, Penny. That's awful."

"I'm not looking for sympathy. I just need you to know that I'm fine. I'm more worried about you."

He slumped into a brocaded armchair and stretched out his long legs. "If you're well, I'm well." His smile splashed some much-needed warmth over me. "For a while there, I thought you'd leave me. I wouldn't have blamed you. Only…" He took a breath.

"Only?"

"It would have broken me." His mouth lifted at one end, as though he was admitting to weakness.

"I'm not going anywhere, Mr. Sinclair," I said, trying to make light of an intense moment. Then I grew serious. "I'm too deeply involved with you." I sat on his lap and placed my arm around him. A sad smile made his handsome face beautiful. I wanted to stroke him as a mother would, only I felt his hardness under my thigh, and he reverted to being that sexy, hot-blooded male I'd become greedy for.

"We have no control over our family," I said.

"No. The only control we have over our past is to hide from it."

"Or keep it secretly locked away." I was referring to his sexual history—a subject Blake evaded.

"There's only ever been you, Penny. Remember that." His eyes softened, and the makings of a smile touched his lips. Lifting me up, he carried me over to the bed.

"I need to see you naked. Take off your top, and play with your tits for me."

Smirking, I tilted my head. "Are we going to get dirty?"

He unzipped his trousers and dropped them. His strong athletic legs and that large bulge tenting from briefs aroused a burning swell of desire.

"Yes." He lowered his briefs.

I unclasped my bra, and his eyes hooded. I played with my breasts, giggling. It still felt a little awkward, but it aroused me nevertheless, especially when Blake touched his inflamed penis.

"Is this working?" I asked.

"You have no idea how hot you are. Remove your panties, and open your legs for me."

His bossy tone and heavy breathing registered straight to my pussy.

"Keep touching yourself," he said.

I did as I was told and stroked my throbbing clit.

He licked his lips. "Fuck yourself with your finger. Slowly."

While he fondled my breasts, I entered myself. An aching burn sizzled through me as he sucked my nipples. I released my muscles, and a warm, toe-curling wave flooded me.

"Your face looks beautiful when you come," he murmured.

I took his hard, veiny dick in my hand and licked my lips. I lowered myself and placed the wet head in my mouth, moving my lips slowly up and down his shaft. He groaned as my tongue flicked over his creamy head.

"I'm going to come pretty quickly," he warned, breathing heavily.

I increased the speed and pressure of my mouth. His long dick made me gag, but I persisted, moving his steel-hard shaft in and out while holding onto the thick base.

I caressed his hardened balls, and semen spurted onto my tongue.

"Penny," he gasped.

I continued. I wanted to swallow everything he had. He normally pulled out so he could fuck me, but I wanted to take him over the finish line.

Hot semen gushed to the back of my throat. Blake's head dropped back, and he groaned.

I wiped my lips, and he joined me on the bed.

His heart pounded against my chest. "Where did you learn to do that?"

"I learned from the best," I replied.

His eyebrows gathered. "Careful. I'm possessive."

"About my past?" I looked at him. "You're my first, silly. You know that. But if I'd been blowing guys, you wouldn't have a right to judge, would you?"

He grimaced as though I'd hit him. "That's what makes you so special, Penny. You've only ever been with me. You're mine."

"Then tell me about your little adventures."

He separated from my hold, rose, and headed to the bottle of whisky. That perfect ass, which I loved to clutch onto, flexed as he moved with the grace of a tiger.

"Must we go there?"

"I'm just curious. What happened to your ex-girlfriends? Did you break their hearts? Did you lick them to the point of madness, like you do me?"

He gulped back a shot, and a deep frown grew. "I went out with a few women at college, but when it all got too heavy, I walked away. Penelope, I've never had what we have with any woman. Ever. Know that. This is our little bit of heaven." He took a breath. "Your taste is exquisite. Your eyes, your curves, your talent, and your brain add up to one perfect woman. A woman I want to spend my life with."

His penetrating gaze impregnated my soul. My eyes pooled with tears. It wasn't just those compliments that made my heart sing, but the way his eyes turned that breathtaking shade of blue whenever he was being sincere.

"I'd love that," I answered finally, my throat thick with emotion.

He tilted his head, as he often did when questioning me. "You'd love what, Penny?"

"I'd love us to be together." My eyes fell into his gaze. "Forever."

"Then you'll marry me?" His frown faded away.

"Only..."

He opened his hands. "What?"

"If I'm to spend my life with you, I need to know about your past. It will eat away at me otherwise."

FIFTY-SEVEN

BLAKE

MY FUCKED-UP SEXUAL history was anything but pretty. *How can I tell Penelope that I attended orgies where I fucked myself raw?* I pictured the ugly, sordid little scenes of debauchery that at the time I'd invested my broken soul in.

While some used drugs as escape, I'd once used sex.

I never thought in my wildest dreams that I'd fall in love, let alone hear myself uttering the words, "Will you marry me?"

It all flashed before me like some low-budget porn movie, only I was the one ramming it in and not some male with a big dick and enough front to fuck for a living.

"Must we do this?" I sighed, watching her cover herself up. "I was enjoying looking at you."

She shook her head. "If we're to be together, I'd like to know something about your sexual history."

"Suffice it to say, I fucked around." I pulled a contrite smile. "I wasn't looking for a girlfriend. I'd sworn off ever marrying. But that's changed because of you."

After a gaping pause, she asked, "Do you want children?"

"I don't like the idea of sharing you."

"What about if I want a child or two?"

"We could always adopt, I suppose," I said, tentatively, given that I wasn't very fond of that idea either.

"What?" Her face burned with indignation as though I'd suggested eating a cat. "Does the idea of me having your child turn you off?"

I chose my response carefully. "No. But the world's overpopulated, Penny. We don't even recognize parts of the country. It's dry and orange, where it should be green and lush."

She nodded pensively. "So it's for political reasons that you don't want children?"

I puffed out a breath. "To be honest, I've never really given it much thought."

Her face contorted. "But you have sperm. You're happy to spray it around…" Penelope paused, and the growing smile on my face dragged her in for a chuckle. Unfortunately, she reverted to earnestness again. "You know what I mean."

"Darling, this is the twenty-first century. We have contraception. We have choices."

"Choices? Like terminations?"

"That's a woman's choice, and she's got a right to make that call. Penny, I love you." I held out my hands, hoping that the interrogation would end there.

A gentle smile touched her lips. "And I love you, Blake. But I'm going to want to have a child one day."

It was only natural that someone as caring as Penelope would want to give birth. It was pure idealism thinking that I could marry this unique and beautiful woman and keep her to myself.

"Then maybe we can come to an arrangement," I said.

"Meaning?"

"Just give me a few years. We can travel. Enjoy the world. I mean you're about to turn twenty-four, Penny. There is time."

Her frown faded, and she moved close and hugged me. "Thank you."

"So is that a yes?" I asked.

She drew out of my arms. "Only after you tell me how many girlfriends you've had."

My spirit deflated. "Why are you doing this to me? I'm fucking exhausted."

She smiled sympathetically. "Okay. You're off the hook for now. But I will want to know."

Penelope removed her shirt, and I joined her on the bed. My dick sprang to action as my hands felt her warmth again. "Can we get a little dirty?"

Wearing a cheeky grin, she replied, "Why naturally."

THE FOLLOWING DAY, I turned on the internet and found images of Fox plastered everywhere. He'd been outed much to my relief.

My phone buzzed. "James."

"They've caught him. A few names are missing, though. I think they're all going to be shitting themselves," he said.

"What about the royal? Has he been exposed?"

"I don't know. I've just heard whispers. Rumors. He wasn't present that one time I visited the island."

"That will now hopefully end there." I sighed. "I could use a break from drama. It's been one hell of a month. One hell of year, really. And one hell of a life."

"Are we going to get philosophical? If so, we need to meet at the club," he said.

"Sure. Why not? I'm half an hour away, if you like."

"I'll see you there. The hair of the dog." He chuckled. "I hit it hard last night."

"Tell me something new."

He laughed.

I set my cell down and cast my attention to the sketch pad that Penelope had left behind. Wavering at first, I wondered if she'd mind me looking. I flicked the cover over anyhow. Although the darkly contorted faces made me wince, her considerable talent astounded me.

I turned the page and found studies of me. She'd never asked me to pose, but I'd seen her doodling away on occasions, peering up at me and smiling, then lowering her head again. My remote expression had a bite of darkness. The mirror had never shown me that face before. Nevertheless, her drawing was disturbingly accurate, because she'd captured me. I recognized my soul in that veiled stare. I'm not sure what disturbed me the most—that I'd been so transparent or that Penelope saw me that way.

After calling my mother to see how she was, I grabbed my jacket and headed to the club. I hadn't been there for a while. And after this visit, it would be sometime again because I had a surprise in store for Penelope: I'd booked us a trip to Italy.

The waiter nodded. "Mr. Sinclair."

I returned the greeting and headed over to James at our little corner table by the window.

"Ah... there you are." He saluted, back to his cheery self. He waited for me to be seated. "A single malt?"

"Sure."

"You're looking well, Blake."

"I feel good. I've asked Penelope to marry me."

His eyebrows merged. "Now that I wasn't expecting. What happened to your staunch bachelor forever ambition?"

"I'm no longer that man. And"— I splayed my hands— "I'm happy."

"How long's it been?"

"Six months."

"That's not that long, you know. Why not cohabit and see how that goes?"

"We're already doing that. We've become inseparable. And what's more, I like it, as I do the thought of marrying her. It feels natural. It feels right."

"What have you done with that hardened cynic, Blake Sinclair?"

I laughed. "I have to pinch myself sometimes. She's even talked me into having children."

His hissed grimace made me chuckle. "Speaking of which…"

James's mood suddenly changed.

"Don't tell me Lilly's expecting?"

He nodded solemnly.

"You're not happy about it?" I asked.

"It's too soon. I'm not sure what to do." He exhaled.

"I can imagine."

"Also, my parents don't approve of Lilly." He pulled a mock smile. "Rather predictable, really. They think she's too common."

"But you don't feel that way, do you?"

"Lilly's not cultured or educated like some in my circle. But she's funny, sharp-witted, and brighter than me most of the time. She thinks Kierkegaard is something out of Ikea." He chuckled. "But she always beats me at chess and backgammon." He sniffed.

"Then she's bright," I said.

"Yeah. And to be honest, I'm not looking for a girl I can sit and talk politics or philosophy with. That's why I've got you." He touched my arm.

"It was a bit touch and go there for a minute," I admitted.

"I hope you've forgiven me. You have, haven't you?"

"I'm still wary. But I haven't forgotten your support at college. You didn't judge me like the others. You were a constant friend. I only hope there are no more surprises." I raised an eyebrow.

"No. That's about as bad as I've been. Illegally speaking." His mouth turned up at one end. "I swear, I didn't know her age. I puked when I found out."

"Let's leave it behind us, shall we?"

He smiled. "That calls for another drink, I think."

He clicked for the waiter.

"Leave the bottle," he instructed.

James poured me out a large measure.

"Steady. It's only five o'clock," I said.

"Are you moderating your habits?"

"I probably need to. It's been a big year." I lifted a brow. "So, back to Lilly."

He nodded grimly. "I'm really super attracted. When we broke up that time, I pined for her. And she's living with me. I mean, I've never done that before."

I thought about this. "She's your partner, James. She's living with you. Any moment, she'll have connubial rights."

"Don't I know it." He took a solemn sip before adding, "It's not the money. It's just that I'm not ready for fatherhood. And after a baby's born, a woman's body..." He opened his hands. "You know what I mean?"

I sipped my whisky in contemplation. "I read somewhere that love changes us. And to be honest, the sex I had before Penelope was ordinary at best. Sex with strangers didn't give me that much pleasure in the end."

He nodded wistfully. "Lilly and I have amazing chemistry. I haven't had that before."

"Well then, you're in love," I declared.

"Maybe. To be honest, if she wasn't pregnant, I'd be really happy to keep things as they are. It's nice coming home and smelling a roast cooking. Lilly's a great cook. And she bakes." He shook his head in disbelief. "Homemade bread. The other day, she whipped up a Black Forest cake. Hell. Now, that takes some skill. And I nearly ate the whole lot in one go." He smiled.

"That sounds like domestic harmony to me."

"Yep. It's nice." He looked down at his drink. "I just don't want to be a dad. Not yet, at least. Maybe never." He looked up at me with a guilty smile. "I've even suggested..."

"An abortion?"

"Yep. I know, it's bad of me..." He exhaled slowly. "Shit. Shit. Shit. What am I going to do?"

Just as I was about to answer him, my cell vibrated. I removed it from my pocket. I'd been sent a news bulletin. I clicked on the link. "Dylan Fox a.k.a Gareth Lion has been killed."

I looked up at James.

"You look pale. What is it?" asked James.

"It's Fox. He's been run over and killed. Outside the Cherry Orchard, apparently." My mind went into overdrive. "He was the only one with the list of names."

"It's pretty obvious it's a hit. Too many big names involved."

I exhaled a deep breath, nodding in agreement.

FIFTY-EIGHT

PENELOPE

I'D JUST PUT MY FINISHING touches to a new series. I hadn't stopped working, which was normal for me. I would have remained in my studio all day and night if I could.

The dramatic Gothic façade and history-soaked walls of Raven Abbey had invaded my imagination. They were pure gold for someone as hooked on surrealism as I was.

Tilting my head to and fro, I studied the panels together. My technique had improved in that I'd sketched so much that the architectural detail came naturally. Almost like magic.

A knock came at the door. When I opened it, I expected to see Sheldon, who normally popped in for a coffee in the mornings, but instead found Lilly clutching her arms.

"Come in. You look cold," I said.

She stepped into the hallway. "I raced out without grabbing a cardigan."

"Go into the kitchen, and I'll grab you something to wear."

I returned with a cardigan and passed it to her. "Here. This should fit."

She put it on and rubbed her arms. "Thanks. That's better." Looking up at me, her big blue eyes were bloodshot and teary.

"Are you okay, love? Can I make you a coffee or a tea?" I asked softly.

"Tea would be nice," she said, biting a fingernail.

I poured hot water into two cups with teabags.

"It's so nice here. And sunny," she said, smiling sadly.

"Lilly, what's the matter?" I passed her a cup.

She took a sip and then looked up at me, her eyes pooling with tears. "I'm pregnant."

I sat down. "Oh no. I thought you were on the pill."

"I must've forgotten to take it." She sighed. "I'm going to have to move back home."

"Back home with Brent?"

"Yeah."

"I'm sure he'll be cool about it," I said, thinking of Brent and how protective he was of Lilly.

"He's got a girlfriend living there now. Remember I told you about Jade?"

I nodded. So much had happened that I'd almost forgotten the happy news that lovely Brent had finally met a girl.

"Come and live with me," I suggested.

The memory of Blake just that same morning ripping off my panties and fucking me over the kitchen table entered my thoughts, sending a swelling ache through me.

Sex would just have to return to the bedroom. And my loud moans and screaming orgasms would have to be muted for a while. A small price to pay to help a friend in need.

"But would Blake mind?" she asked.

"It's my house. He bought it for me, and I'm sure he won't mind. In any case, I stay at his house most of the time. I just come here and work. He does stay here occasionally. But it's all good."

"I'll be in the way, then." A tear slid down her cheek.

"No, you won't. It's a really big house, and there's a guest room." I sat next to her and placed my arm around her shoulder. "Tell me what happened with James."

"We argued. He doesn't want to be a father. And when he suggested a termination, I ran away. I can't do that." She broke into sobs.

Holding Lilly's hand to comfort her, I jumped when my phone buzzed. It was Blake. "I need to take this. Sorry." I walked out into the living room. "Hey."

"Penny. I need you to come down to the police station and make a statement."

"Huh?"

"Fox is dead. And I'm a suspect."

"Holy shit." *Not another drama*, I thought. I didn't know how much more I could take. And poor Blake.

"I need an alibi," he said.

"Yes, of course. I mean... were we..."

"It happened last night in the early hours. He was run down by a car. Just near the Cherry Orchard. There's no CCTV, and I was with you in bed."

"Of course. I'll be there ASAP. Text me the details. Are you okay?"

"I'm fine. I have to go. I'll see you soon. Okay?"

"Yes." I closed the call. A few seconds later, a text came through with the details.

I headed back into the kitchen. Blood had drained from my face.

"What's happened?" asked Lilly.

"I have to go to the police station. Fox has been murdered, and Blake's a suspect."

"Shit. He wouldn't have done it, though. Would he have?" she asked.

"No. It was early morning. A car ran him down."

"Maybe it was an accident," said Lilly.

"Outside the Cherry Orchard?"

She winced at the mention of that place. "He's a monster, according to James. He had something over James, too, I believe."

I rose. "Look, I have to go. But hey, stay here. Make yourself at home. Eat something. I'll get you a key when I return. Okay?"

She hugged me. "Thanks, sweetie. You're the best."

I SAT IN THE COLD, sterile room, explaining where I'd spent the previous night, which was simple enough since I'd spent the night with Blake.

"We fell asleep together. That's what I remember."

The detective studied me. The gap of silence was so excruciatingly wide that it felt like a drill chiseling into my head.

Rising from his seat, he started to pace. "Have you ever met Dylan Fox?"

"Yes. Once. At a ball."

"I believe they grew up together, and that Blake was bequeathed the estate that belonged to Fox's father. We also found information about Blake Sinclair on Fox's computer. I believe Fox was blackmailing him." He waited for a comment, but I remained quiet, my muscles gripping onto the chair. "Your boyfriend had motive."

I shrugged. "I don't involve myself in Blake's personal affairs."

"But you're a couple. He described you as his fiancée. His significant other."

That's nice.

I finally relaxed. "We talk about other things. And Blake's not someone who talks a great deal about himself."

"Mm... I've noticed," he said quietly. "Okay." He closed his notebook. "Let's leave it there."

I found Blake peering down at his phone. He looked up. Those eyes looked so blue and lost that I wanted to jump on his lap and console him.

"Hey." He rose and took my hand. "Are you okay?"

I nodded.

"Come on. Let's get out of here."

FIFTY-NINE

BLAKE

I STOPPED WALKING AND took Penelope's hand. Public displays of anything, let alone affection, fitted me as awkwardly as a pair of high heels. So I surprised myself when I took her into my arms and held her.

Our relationship, despite my greedy addiction for her body, had become much more than just sexual. I loved having her around reading a book, doodling or watching telly.

Her poise brought me indescribable pleasure. Having her close comforted and calmed my spirit. I'd been living in a cage before. It was strange— I had thought that a relationship would imprison me, but in fact, it had freed me.

Penelope removed herself from my arms and looked up at me. She seemed so tiny without heels.

"Did they ask some challenging questions?" I asked.

"Not really. Just the standard 'where were you' question."

I studied her for signs of stress. "I hope you can forgive me for dragging you into yet another ugly scene. I imagine there aren't any more to come." I smiled.

I'd been probed and interrogated for two hours. In the end, I had nothing to give them other than the truth. I reminded the detective that Fox had made a lot of enemies, powerful people who had much more to lose than me. The fact that I wasn't embroiled in the pedophile-island scandal had helped.

After twenty-three years of having that bastard in my shadow, a protracted ordeal by anyone's standards, I felt lighter as we moved along the path.

Penelope stopped walking. "Just answer me honestly. Were you responsible?"

Even though I understood her need to ask, the fact that she thought me capable of murder stung. "I was with you all night."

"You could have hired someone," she argued. The coolness in her tone was like vinegar to a wound.

"Look at me, Penelope," I said. She turned and gazed up at me. "Why would I wait until now?" I opened out my hands. "If anything, I had more reason to strike after that abduction attempt on you." I paused to read her reaction. "I wouldn't do anything to jeopardize what we have."

I wiped away the tear that touched her cheek and kissed her tenderly in broad daylight, surrounded by a rush of people oblivious to our struggle, which instead of breaking us, had brought us closer together.

"I believe you." A sigh of resignation followed. "To be honest, I would have forgiven you anyway, as bad as that sounds. He was evil." She smiled sadly. "I do worry about Lilly, though."

"Why? Because of James?" I asked, relieved to have the conversation veer away from me.

"They're no longer together. She's staying with me. I hope you don't mind."

"It's your house, darling. You can let anyone stay, as long as it's not another man, of course."

She wore an impish grin. "I'm too sore, so even if I wanted to, which of course I don't, I couldn't let another man fuck me."

That worried me. "Am I that rough?"

"This morning in the shower…" She tilted her head.

"I thought you liked it."

"Yeah. It was nice." Her soft voice made my dick lengthen.

"I'm wearing jeans." There was a lot to be said for loose-fitting pants.

"I like you in jeans." Her hand landed in my pocket and squeezed my ass. "So you see, Mr. Insatiable, I don't have anything left for another man." Her smile faded. "I don't want another man. It's the last thing I'd ever do."

"I trust you. It's just the way men look at you—like that dick that just passed. His eyes were all over your tits."

"I can't help that, Blake."

"No, you can't, you sexy temptress." I drew her close.

That made her giggle, and we headed off for coffee and cake in an attempt to remove that dank, dark police station from our minds.

THE FOLLOWING DAY, I arrived at Penelope's and, recalling Lilly now lived there, knocked on the door.

Lilly answered and stepped out, allowing me pass.

"I hope you don't mind me staying. I'll try not get in the way."

Following her down the long hallway, I replied, "It's all good. It's a big house."

"Penny's painting." She appeared so sad that I felt a pang of sympathy and, at the same time, anger at James for not doing the right thing by her.

"How are you?" I asked.

"Yeah. I'm good. I'm looking for a small shop. I'm going to set up my own beauty salon."

"If there's anything I can do to help..."

"Oh, that's so nice. I'm good, though. My brother can help with handyman stuff, like shelving and painting."

"I'm glad to hear."

She shrugged and touched her belly. "I'll have another little mouth to feed, so I've got to think ahead. And there's no way I'm going back to living at our old flat."

"You've got Penelope looking out for you. And if you want any advice on business, feel free to ask."

She smiled meekly in return.

I stepped into Penelope's studio, which had that typical turpentine-and-linseed-oil smell in the air.

Dressed in a white shirt splattered in paint, with her hair in a bun, Penelope stood before a canvas and squinted. She hadn't heard me enter, and when she looked up, she jumped.

"Hey. Sorry to startle you," I said, joining her.

I kissed her on the cheek. My attention went to the canvas, and my eyes nearly popped out of my head. She'd painted me.

"Do you like it?" she asked. "I painted it from a few sketches I've made."

I stepped back and studied the work. Wearing a dark jacket and a black turtleneck, I appeared downcast. She'd captured that mood well and created an impressive picture-perfect likeness. Penelope described it as "brooding and introspective." And that it was. By my side, and in the background, a woman with long black hair, wearing a red gown with a train, ascended stairs toward a Gothic arch.

"I take it that's you?" I pointed to the girl in the painting.

"It's an idealistic version of me." Her eyebrow arched. "Her ass is smaller."

I didn't laugh because I was so absorbed in the painting and how well it had been rendered. "It's stunning. Very Gothic."

"Yeah. In other words, old-fashioned." She smiled as her eyes flicked from me to the large canvas.

"If I wasn't the subject, I'd buy it. It's masterful, darling." I placed my arm around her waist. "Your talent leaves me breathless." I leaned in and kissed her warm, soft neck. "As do your curves. I would have preferred her more voluptuous. She looks like a maiden. Young and innocent."

"That's exactly what she is. Climbing or soaring to womanhood, scaling the heights of passion and romance."

"It's beautiful. Like you."

"Why don't you like yourself in it?" she asked, looking a little dejected.

I shrugged. "I look very serious."

"You look sexy, as always. Give me a mysterious, serious man any day."

I grinned. "I'm not always like that. As you know."

"No. You're a lot lighter than when we first met. That's for sure."

"You sound disappointed," I said.

"Far from it. It's just, some days it feels like I'm in a dream and I'll wake up and revert to that frightened girl whose mother spent most of her time slumped on the sofa."

"I'm here for you. Always."

We stared into each other's eyes, acknowledging our deep connection.

SIXTY

PENELOPE

THERE WERE PEOPLE everywhere, crowding around the entrance of the Palazzo Vecchio, while my neck hurt from gazing up at the famous David. It was only a copy but so well captured that I sighed with disbelief.

I was in Florence. And it wasn't a dream.

Looking devilishly handsome, Blake strode toward me with that cosmopolitan, sexy man-of-the-world strut, and as always, women ogled him.

"Hey, Mr. Good-Looking," I said.

He passed me a bottle of water that he'd queued up in a long line for.

"Thanks," I said.

"This place is packed." He shook his head as another busload of tourists poured out.

"Yes, I'm afraid we're forty years too late," I said. I didn't mind, however. Crowds had never bothered me.

"More like three hundred years," he said dryly.

I giggled, and he smiled back.

"Verona or Venice?" he asked.

"Both?" I asked.

"I'll book tickets for the Verona Arena."

"And that is…?"

"It's an ancient amphitheater famous for open-air opera. They're staging *La Bohème*. One of my favorites. Would you like to go? It's tomorrow night. There'll be a full moon."

I fell into his blue eyes, which sang in the afternoon light. Blake fitted in naturally with Florence's infinite beauty.

I shook my head in wonder. "What can I say but yes? I've never been to the opera. What will I wear?"

He stood up and took my hand. "Let's go shopping, shall we?"

I floated along, my arm linked with Blake's, as women glanced at me with envy. They wanted to be me. Now that was a first for a girl who'd spent most of her life subsisting on crumbs.

I studied my ring finger, where a huge spellbinding diamond-encircled ruby collected the sunlight.

The first day we arrived in Florence, Blake had taken me to an antique jewelry shop and bought me a pair of ruby drop earrings. Then he asked to see an antique ring. The owner told us it had belonged to a princess. He drew circles with his hands as he narrated the fairy tale of that ring. Blake cast me a side-glance with that subtle smirk of his. The dealer might have been spinning a story, but I enjoyed every second of it. It was pure theater.

Watching Blake slide the ring onto my finger, the dealer's face lit up with joy. I thought he was going to kiss me. Scrolled with diamonds, the ring housed a large ruby, which changed to purplish red in the light, making my heart skip a beat.

"Do you like it?" asked Blake.

"I love it. But it's ridiculously extravagant."

"Beauty's never extravagant. And it looks perfect on you. Only, try not to drop paint on it." He tilted his head so adorably that I wanted to slap him.

"I can't have this, Blake," I protested.

He ignored my pleas and turned to the man, whose face had been rejuvenated by the promise of a big sale. "Do you take this?" Blake presented a gold card.

"*Si, signore*," he sang.

I stared down at my magical engagement ring, instantly adopting it as my amulet. Every time I looked at it, elation danced in my veins.

It had been a beautiful week, floating around Florence as though I was in a movie.

Blake read Dante's *Inferno*, which he informed me was his second reading, having studied it at university. But reading it in Florence, which was the home of the writer, felt so real and authentic, it added magic to a book that he greatly admired.

My eyes were too addicted to the sights, and to my very handsome fiancé, to focus on reading. *Who would have thought a man balancing a book on his thighs could be so arousing?*

I knew what was under that book. I'd devoured it for breakfast as he had devoured me. How intoxicating it had been making love in that historic penthouse with arched windows overlooking the Ponte Vecchio, the Arno, and the rolling hills beyond.

As we walked along the strip of shops, Blake said, "We could go to Milan for the dress if you like."

"But the opera's tomorrow night."

He smiled. "That's why private jets were invented."

I shook my head in disbelief. He wasn't kidding. We'd flown to Italy in his private jet. I hadn't even known he owned one.

A green gown caught my eye. "That's nice. And as much as I'd love to visit Milan, I'm happy to stay one more night here. I'm in love with this place."

He kissed me gently on the lips. "So am I. And it looks better with you in it."

My heart melted. "What a nice thing to say."

The shopkeeper gushed and gesticulated. I'd apparently chosen an original designer gown, the price tag of which made my jaw drop. Blake insisted I try it on.

I stepped out of the dressing room, and the shopkeeper's eyes lit up. The fit was perfect. The green silk cascaded down to a small train.

Blake nodded. "It was made for you."

My cleavage pouted more than I thought suitable for a classy event, but Blake disagreed, and without further discussion, he paid for it. The shopkeeper seemed to dance behind the counter.

As we were leaving, Blake said, "Promise me one thing."

"And what's that?" I recognized that devilish glint in his eyes and expected something salacious.

"Don't wear anything under that gown."

He drew me close, and I felt his thick arousal against my thigh.

"Siesta?" he whispered, leaving a hot stain on my neck.

I nodded. "I could do with a lie down."

VERONA WAS THE LAND of lovers, I soon discovered. Wafting along in my green gown, I imagined being an Italian actress in a '60s movie. My earlier fear of being overdressed was completely unfounded. Women had arrived in death-defying heels, slinking along in a rainbow of designer gowns. The contrast was striking as they settled around the historic carved-stone arena.

We sat down, and once again, my neck strained. I couldn't stop staring at the dreamlike ambience. Everything seemed so surreal, especially with that large magical moon hovering above us.

The audience applauded when the soprano stepped out, and then there was respectful silence. Her voice seemed to bounce off the stars. I'd never understood opera's allure until that moment. Mesmerized and emotionally gripped, I fell under its spell.

Blake's eyes had that sheen of emotion too. I imagined that even the most stoic person would have struggled to remain unmoved.

By the last act, I'd become liquid. Blake's hand slid under my gown, which had a slit. Although it was not visible when I walked, due to the voluminous cascade of fabric, the design proved ideal for horny boyfriends with a penchant for a little public fondling.

While the soprano sang her heart out to her lover, Blake's fingers meandered up my thigh. We were flanked by patrons, and the danger of being caught played havoc with my arousal. But they were so riveted by the soprano's heartfelt aria that just as she reached her high note, so did I.

"One to tell the grandchildren," Blake said as we left.

I stopped walking. "What, that you fingered me at the opera? Or that we watched *La Bohème* in Verona?"

"That's sublimely coarse." He laughed. "Come. There's something else I'd like you to see."

SIXTY-ONE

BLAKE

WE FINALLY ARRIVED IN front of the famous balcony. The bronze statue of Julietta positioned in front gave it away. Under the moonlight, there was something magical about the fictional home of Juliet. And just as I'd hoped, there were only a handful of visitors, mainly staggering along after a long day of soaking in the charms of that ancient city. It was nothing like the daytime, when people came in droves to see the famous balcony. That was why I chose midnight for our visit.

Spotting the bronze statue, Penelope wandered over to study it. "This is the Juliet from Shakespeare," she said, smiling innocently.

I glanced over at a man I'd arranged to meet us there. "One minute. There's someone I need to talk to."

Her puzzled frown made me grin.

"This is Massimo." I introduced the actor to Penelope, who nodded. "And this is my wife-to-be, Penelope."

Massimo held out his hand. "*Ciao. Tanto piacere.*"

Penelope was about to take his hand when he leaned in and kissed her on both cheeks.

"I'd better explain," I said, smiling at Penelope's mystified frown.

"Massimo's here to marry us."

"Oh?" A line grew between her brows. "But don't we need a celebrant and licenses?"

"We do. This is more a declaration of my love for you." I caressed her cheek. "We can make it official when we return home."

"But I don't have a ring for you."

I removed a box from my pocket with two golden wedding bands.

I passed one to her. "You hold onto that one."

She stared at it as though it were a piece of magic. A little sparkle shone off it, and she looked up at me in wonder, making me smile.

"Am I putting you on the spot?" I asked. "Would you like to do this?"

Her eyes glistened with tears. "Of course. Yes. Please."

Massimo's reciting of an Italian love poem made it seem even more magical. His mellifluous words kissed the air and our spirits.

When he finished, he took us through our vows.

Penelope looked up at me, her eyes wide and teary.

I placed the ring on her shaky finger, and she did the same on mine. We kissed, while Massimo used my phone to take a photo of us by the statue.

We smiled at each other.

It felt good. No, it felt brilliant. Nothing else mattered anymore. Just us.

"Come. Let's buy you a drink," I suggested to the actor.

He nodded with a big smile. "I know a nice little place, not far. Fresh pizza all night."

I looked at Penelope, who returned an enthusiastic nod, saying, "Yum."

After spending an hour with Massimo, listening to his stories of living in Verona as an actor in the opera, we saluted him.

The night was perfect—still and warm. It was as though someone had made it so just for us. And it was very special.

We remained outside sitting at a table, drinking champagne.

"It's so romantic, what you did." Penelope's eyes sparkled. "Am I really your wife?"

"Oh, you are. You're mine."

"And you're my husband. That means you're mine."

We clinked glasses. Peering down at the gold ring on my finger, I liked how it felt.

I called over the waiter and asked in Italian, "Have you got any fresh cake?"

He tipped his head as if I'd asked if he was a woman or something crazy like that. He crooked his finger. "*Viene.*"

I looked at Penelope. "Back in a minute."

The waiter showed me a glass encasement of cakes. "Which would you like?"

I pointed to the chocolate cake. "Two pieces."

He nodded approvingly and kissed his fingers.

When I rejoined her, Penelope said, "Your Italian's so good. And it suits you. Can you make love to me in Italian?"

I laughed. "I'm not sure if I can translate smut into Italian."

"Like, 'I love your tight wet cunt and I want to fuck your tits.'"

"Why, Mrs. Sinclair, you're being rather ribald and prurient."

Her squealed giggle was so contagious that I joined her.

"Prurient? Ribald? You're showing off, dear husband."

"Not at all. It's all there in the Queen's English."

The waiter brought our cakes and placed them down.

Penelope licked her lips. "I'm going to waddle back to England at this rate."

"I like a big ass," I said, taking a forkful of cake. Flavored with liqueur, rich chocolate, and nuts, it was delicious.

She scowled. "Is it that big?"

"No. It's perfect."

We ate in silence, making little sounds of pleasure, almost akin to sex.

She wiped her mouth. "That was something else."

"Wasn't it? One can't have a wedding without champagne and cake."

"Well called." She smiled wistfully. "Well called on everything. This has been so beautiful."

"I'm in awe of your beauty." I touched her hand. "I knew straightaway."

"What do you mean?"

"After I saw you at the Cherry Orchard, I couldn't get you out of my mind. And then at the gallery, when you turned, I knew I'd never be the same again."

"You make it seem so dramatic, as though I've changed you."

"You have." I stared at her. "For the better. I'm not that man anymore. When I look back, I hated that person I paraded as."

"I didn't. I mean, I thought you were a little stuck-up, but I saw compassion too. I sensed it was a form of protection." Her eyes shone. "I hope I can keep you excited."

"Oh, I think you'll do just fine." My grin smoothed out. "It's not always about sex, anyway. It's companionship. I feel like you're my best friend. I no longer have to hide. For someone who guards his privacy, that's big."

"You're also insatiable."

"Is that a problem?" I asked, raising an eyebrow.

"If having multiple orgasms every day is a problem, then I think I can manage somehow." She giggled.

I leaned in and lowered my voice. "Your pussy is very sexy. And responsive in a way that..."

"What way?"

"I like how you taste."

"Is that why you wanted to marry me?" she asked.

I nearly laughed at that preposterous notion. "It's not just sex. But you're an exciting woman to fuck... to make love to... and to just hang out with."

Her smile grew wide. "Nice." She paused to think. "In any case, I'm crazy about your penis."

My grin widened. "Good. Then we're on the same page. Mutual genital admiration."

Her squealed laugh at three in the morning in that ancient city had a special magic about it.

EPILOGUE

TWO YEARS AND NINE MONTHS LATER...

MAX TUGGED AT MY skirt, pointing at the peacock before charging after it. I giggled, watching my son run with wild abandon.

It was my birthday, and the weather couldn't have been sunnier. Blake had insisted on a weekend bash at Bath. We'd moved there when I got pregnant, and I instantly fell in love with the place. I couldn't have been happier. It was a big step for Blake, the city slicker, to take, even though he still commuted to London regularly, having kept Mayfair.

I'd gifted my house to Lilly, who'd opened up her own very successful beauty salon up the road. Rich clients came from everywhere. Her nail designs, which involved a myriad of swirly colors, had become legendary. And when it came to applying makeup and facials, no one came close.

Sheldon stood by the table of canapés with his husband, Roger. Yes, they'd married. I was his best woman at what had turned out to be a very strange but fun affair. There were Sheldon's posh family and friends mixing with Roger's police colleagues and family who, although awkward at first, had soon relaxed and turned it into one hell of a party.

Mary, my mother-in-law, and her new partner, Elliot, chatted with Sheldon and Roger. She lived with us in Bath. It was such a huge estate with so many living quarters, I'd lost count. That made big bashes, like the one we hosted that day, fun and accommodating. I loved the idea of having all the people I loved staying with us.

Blake walked toward me, bouncing Juliet in his arms. It had taken him five minutes to get used to the fact that I was pregnant. I'd conceived in Italy, and nine months later, not just one baby but two exited my belly. I had to have a caesarean.

I cried when I saw Blake, the man who'd sworn off fatherhood, holding a baby in each arm. Those little bundles of joy cradled in his biceps. That guarded cynic that I'd fallen hard for was unrecognizable. I could never have hoped for a more caring and devoted man to have children with.

"Hey, gorgeous." Blake smiled at me. He put Juliet down, and she clung to his leg. She adored her father.

"Elliot was just telling me that he's building a mud-brick folly at the back of his home."

"That sounds nice and rustic," I said. "He's nice. Your mom looks really happy."

He nodded with a sparkle in those blue eyes with accents of the sky. "She is. He's a good man."

"James looks a little glum over there, though."

"Doesn't he? He's still broken over Lilly."

"Oh well. It's for the better. She's in love. And to someone he introduced her to." I grimaced, recalling the dramatics of that past year.

After a sojourn in LA to hang low while the scandal of the depraved island affair played out in the media, James returned home, hoping to rekindle his relationship with Lilly. All the while, he'd continue to send money for their daughter. Although that had helped raise my estimation of him slightly, I was relieved that Lilly had turned her back on him.

It was late afternoon, and James seemed a little over the limit as he strutted unevenly toward us. "Hey, you two," he said with a big cheesy smile. "This is a marvelous place you've got here." He regarded Blake. "I miss you at the club, though."

"I'll be at Mayfair next week. We can catch up then. Like the good old days."

James looked at me and then Blake. "It's not exactly like the good old days, though. You're hitched. A father of not just one but two children. And all in three years." He shook his head. "My God."

Blake gave me a subtle wink. "Time sweeps us along, and we can either grab a branch and pull ourselves out or keep rolling down the rapids."

"And I've been rolling down the rapids, right?"

"You've always been adventurous, James," said Blake, his tone neutral and devoid of judgment.

James let out a deep sigh. "Yeah. And look where it's got me."

"How was LA?" I asked.

"Predictable," he said, sounding tired.

"How?" I asked.

He paused to think. "It's wild." He sniffed. "Exciting at times. But it's impossible to get a decent cup of tea."

We had to laugh at that time-honored English obsession with tea.

"But apart from that, it was sex, drugs, and rock'n'roll. No, let me rephrase that—sex, drugs, and techno." He chuckled.

"I look forward to hearing about it," said Blake.

"Not too much to tell. It all just blurs into one big endless party. Everyone ends up indistinguishable. And to be honest, I probably would have extracted more joy from reading Proust than hanging out at another *anything goes* weekender in Malibu."

Blake laughed. "Well, I'll be. Proust? James, we'll make a deep man out of you yet."

Instead of smiling, James looked at me and Blake seriously. He'd changed. His eyes kept flitting over to Lilly, who giggled raucously with Sheldon while Jasmine, her pretty three-year-old daughter, skipped about with Max.

"She's so beautiful," he said almost to himself.

"Lilly or Jasmine?" I asked.

"Both," he said.

I felt so sorry for him suddenly.

A motorbike roared in the distance, stirring me out of my thoughts.

"Nice Harley-Davidson," said Blake, staring at the gleaming motorcycle with high handlebars.

It was Lilly's new boyfriend, Reggie, arriving in style. He possessed that bad-boy swagger that Lilly loved, only he was anything but that. The filthy-rich son of a lord, and a billionaire in his own right, Reggie was a tattoo artist. He was passionate about the art form, and his heavily tattooed arms proved it. Besotted with Lilly, he was sweet with Jasmine and loved kids. With a clownish life-of-the-party personality, he possessed a big voice and a head full of crude jokes but was always respectful when that was called for.

Wearing a sunny smile, he strutted toward Lilly with a soccer ball under his arm.

"Here comes David Beckham," muttered James sarcastically.

"Are you going to be okay?" asked Blake.

I loved the way he cared for those around him. And although James didn't really, in my book, warrant that kind of sympathy, I loved my husband for his empathy and understanding. As Blake had said, everyone was entitled to one or two fuck ups, as long as they redeemed themselves, and there was no harm done to children or animals.

Noticing Lilly and Reggie heading our way, James snuck off, probably to the bottle of whisky in the study—a place where Blake went to read and be alone. I needed that, too, but I headed to my very large studio at the back of the property to paint.

"Hey, pretty girl," I said, looking at Lilly, who really had blossomed into a beautiful woman. Her blond locks waved down her back, and those big blue eyes danced with glee.

She placed her arm around my waist and drew me close, as a loving sister would.

I nodded at Reggie. "Welcome."

"Thanks for inviting me. It's a grand old place." He bounced the soccer ball, and the children came running.

"Thought I'd kick a ball around. You don't mind? You're not worried about the grounds or anything?"

I shook my head decisively. "Why would I be?"

He shrugged. "Just that my family get a bit uppity when we play cricket or soccer on their well-manicured lawns." He used an exaggerated upper-class accent, making us giggle.

Max bent down and tried to pick up the ball. "Come on, little man. I'll show you how to bend it."

Reggie dribbled the soccer ball along, and the children chased him.

"He's great around kids," I said.

Lilly watched on with a big sunny smile. "I'm so fucking blessed to have met him. He's gorgeous."

She fanned her face. "And so giving. And he's devoted to Jazzie."

"I was hoping Brent would come," I said.

"He had to work. He said he'll try to pop in tomorrow."

"I'd like that. He's part of the family. I hope he knows that."

"Oh, you know my brother. He's not a fan of the snobby upper classes."

"But we're not that, you and I."

"No. We're not. But look at us."

"Yes... look at us." I beamed.

We both stared at each other smiling and hugged.

Yes, life had delivered in the most surprising way.

Out of waste and neglect, beautiful—sometimes even astoundingly unique—flowers bloom.

And to think it all had started out of desperation at a place called the Cherry Orchard.

THE END

Printed in Great Britain
by Amazon